# ROUND THE SOFA.

BY THE AUTHOR OF
"Mary Barton," "Life of Charlotte Brontë," &c. &c.

TWO VOLUMES.

VOL. I.

LONDON:
SAMPSON LOW, SON & CO., 47 LUDGATE HILL.
1859.

LONDON: PRINTED BY WILLIAM CLOWES AND SONS, STAMFORD STREET.

## PREFACE.

MOST of these Stories have already appeared in Household Words: one, however, has never been published in England, and another has obtained only a limited circulation.

## ROUND THE SOFA.

LONG ago I was placed by my parents under the medical treatment of a certain Mr. Dawson, a surgeon in Edinburgh, who had obtained a reputation for the cure of a particular class of diseases. I was sent with my governess into lodgings near his house, in the Old Town. I was to combine lessons from the excellent Edinburgh masters, with the medicines and exercises needed for my indisposition. It was at first rather dreary to leave my brothers and sisters, and to give up our merry out-of-doors life with our country home, for dull lodgings, with only poor grave Miss Duncan for a companion; and to exchange our romps in the garden and rambles through the fields for stiff walks in the streets, the decorum of which obliged me to tie my bonnet-strings neatly, and put on my shawl with some regard to straightness.

The evenings were the worst. It was autumn, and of course they daily grew longer: they were long enough, I am sure, when we first settled down in those gray and drab lodgings. For, you must know, my father and mother were not rich, and there were a great many of us, and the medical expenses to be incurred by my being placed under Mr. Dawson's care were expected to be considerable ; therefore, one great point in our search after lodgings was economy. My father, who was too true a gentleman to feel false shame, had named this necessity for cheapness to Mr. Dawson; and in return, Mr. Dawson had told him of those at No. 6 Cromer Street, in which we were finally settled. The house belonged to an old man, at one time a tutor to young men preparing for the University, in which capacity he had become known to Mr. Dawson. But his pupils had dropped off; and when we went to lodge with him, I imagine that his principal support was derived from a few occasional lessons which he gave, and from letting the rooms that we took, a drawing-room opening into a bed-room, out of which a smaller chamber led. His daughter was his housekeeper: a son, whom we never saw, was supposed to be leading the same life that his father had done before him, only we never saw or heard of any pupils; and there was one hard-working, honest

" BOUND THE SOFA."

little Scottish maiden, square, stumpy, neat, and plain, who might have been any age from eighteen to forty.

Looking back on the household now, there was perhaps much to admire in their quiet endurance of decent poverty; but at this time, their poverty grated against many of my tastes, for I could not recognize the fact, that in a town the simple graces of fresh flowers, clean white muslin curtains, pretty bright chintzes, all cost money, which is saved by the adoption of dust-coloured moreen, and mud-coloured carpets. There was not a penny spent on mere elegance in that room; yet there was everything considered necessary to comfort: but after all, such mere pretences of comfort! a hard, slippery, black horse-hair sofa, which was no place of rest; an old piano, serving as a sideboard ; a grate, narrowed by an inner supplement, till it hardly held a handful of the small coal which could scarcely ever be stirred up into a genial blaze. But there were two evils worse than even this coldness and bareness of the rooms : one was that we were provided with a latch-key, which allowed us to open the front door whenever we came home from a walk, and go upstairs without meeting any face of welcome, or hearing the sound of a human voice in the apparently deserted house Mr. Mackenzie piqued himself on the noiselessness of his establishment; and

ROUND THE SOFA.

the other, which might almost seem to neutralize the first, was the danger we were always exposed to on going out, of the old man sly, miserly, and intelligent  popping out upon us from his room, close to the left hand of the door, with some civility which we learnt to distrust as a mere pretext for extorting more money, yet which it was difficult to refuse: such as the offer of any books out of his library, a great temptation, for we could see into the shelf-lined room; but just as we were on the point of yielding, there was a hint of the " consideration " to be expected for the loan of books of so much higher a class than any to be obtained at the circulating library, which made us suddenly draw back. Another time he came out of his den to offer us written cards, to distribute among our acquaintance, on which he undertook to teach the very things I was to learn; but I would rather have been the most ignorant woman that ever lived than tried to learn anything from that old fox in breeches. When we had declined all his proposals, he went apparently into dudgeon. Once when we had forgotten our latch-key we rang in vain for many times at the door, seeing our landlord standing all the time at the window to the right, looking out of it in an absent and philosophical state of mind, from which no signs and gestures of ours could arouse him.

The women of the household were far better, and more really respectable, though even on them poverty had laid her heavy left hand, instead of her blessing right. Miss Mackenzie kept us as short in our food as she decently could we paid so much a week for our board, be it observed; and if one day we had less appetite than another, our meals were docked to the smaller standard, until Miss Duncan ventured to remonstrate. The sturdy maid-of- all-work was scrupulously honest, but looked discontented, and scarcely vouchsafed us thanks, when on leaving we gave her what Mrs. Dawson had told us would be considered handsome in most lodgings. I do not believe Phenice ever received wages from the Mackenzies.

But that dear Mrs. Dawson! The mention of her comes into my mind like the bright sunshine into our dingy little drawing-room came on those days ; as a sweet scent of violets greets the sorrowful passer among the woodlands.

Mrs. Dawson was not Mr. Dawson's wife, for he was a bachelor. She was his crippled sister, an old maid, who had, what she called, taken her brevet rank.

After we had been about a fortnight in Edinburgh, Mr. Dawson said, in a sort of half-doubtful manner to Miss Duncan

" My sister bids me say, that every Monday evening a few friends come in to sit round her sofa for an hour or so,—some before going to gayer parties and that if you and Miss Greatorex would like a little change, she would only be too glad to see you. Any time from seven to eight to-night; and I must add my injunctions, both for her sake, and for that of my little patient's, here, that you leave at nine o'clock. After all, I do not know if you will care to come; but Margaret bade me ask you;" and he glanced up suspiciously and sharply at us. If either of us had felt the slightest reluctance, however well disguised by manner, to accept this invitation, I am sure he would have at once detected our feelings, and withdrawn it; so jealous and chary was he of anything pertaining to the appreciation of this beloved sister.

But if it had been to spend an evening at a dentist's, I believe I should have welcomed the invitation, so weary was I of the monotony of the nights in our lodgings ; and as for Miss Duncan, an invitation to tea was of itself a pure and unmixed honour, and one to be accepted with all becoming form and gratitude : so Mr. Dawson's sharp glances over his spectacles failed to detect anything but the truest pleasure, and he went on.

"You'll find it very dull, I dare say. Only a few old fogies like myself, and one or two good sweet young women : I never know who'll come. Margaret is obliged to lie in a darkened room,—only half-lighted I mean, because her eyes are weak, oh, it will be very stupid, I dare say: don't thank me till you've been once and tried it, and then, if you like it, your best thanks will be to come again every Monday, from half-past seven to nine, you know. Good-bye, good-bye."

Hitherto I had never been out to a party of grownup people; and no court ball to a London young lady could seem more redolent of honour and pleasure than this Monday evening to me.

Dressed out in new stiff book-muslin, made up to my throat, a frock which had seemed to me and my sisters the height of earthly grandeur and finery Alice, our old nurse, had been making it at home, in contemplation of the possibility of such an event during my stay in Edinburgh, but which had then appeared to me a robe too lovely and angelic to be ever worn short of heaven I went with Miss Duncan to Mr. Dawson's at the appointed time. We entered through one small lofty room, perhaps I ought to call it an antechamber, for the house was old-fashioned, and stately and grand, the large square drawing-room, into the centre .of which Mrs. Dawson's sofa was drawn. Behind her a little was placed a table with a great cluster candlestick upon it, bearing seven or eight wax-lights; and that was all the light in the room, which looked to me very vast and indistinct after our pinched-up apartment at the Mackenzie's. Mrs. Dawson must have been sixty ; and yet her face looked very soft and smooth and child-like. Her hair was quite gray: it would have looked white but for the snowiness of her cap, and satin ribbon. She was wrapped in a kind of dressing-gown of French grey merino: the furniture of the room was deep rose-colour, and white and gold,—the paper which covered the walls was Indian, beginning low down with a profusion of tropical leaves and birds and insects, and gradually diminishing in richness of detail till at the top it ended in the most delicate tendrils and most filmy insects.

Mr. Dawson had acquired much riches in his DTO-fession, and his house gave one this impression. In the corners of the rooms were great jars of Eastern china, filled with flower-leaves and spices; and in the middle of all this was placed the sofa, on which poor Mrs. Margaret Dawson passed whole days, and months, and years, without the power of moving by herself. By-and-by Mrs. Dawson's maid brought in tea and macaroons for us, and a little cup of milk and water and a biscuit for her. Then the door opened. We had come very early, and in came Edinburgh pro-fessors, Edinburgh beauties, and celebrities, all on their way to some other gayer and later party, but coming first to see Mrs. Dawson, and tell her their Ion-mots, or their interests, or their plans. By each learned man, by each lovely girl, she was treated as a dear friend, who knew something more about their own individual selves, independent of their reputation and general society-character, than any one else.

It was very brilliant and very dazzling, and gave enough to think about and wonder about for many days. Monday after Monday we went, stationary, silent; what could we find to say to any one but Mrs. Margaret herself? Winter passed, summer was coming, still I was ailing, and weary of my life; but still Mr. Dawson gave hopes of my ultimate recovery. My father and mother came and went; but they could not stay long, they had so many claims upon them. Mrs. Margaret Dawson had become my dear friend, although, perhaps, I had never exchanged as many words with her as I had with Miss Mackenzie, but then with Mrs. Dawson every word was a pearl or a diamond.

People began to drop off from Edinburgh, only a few were left, and I am not sure if our Monday evenings were not all the pleasanter.

There was Mr. Sperano, the Italian exile, banished even from France, where he had long resided, and now

teaching Italian with meek diligence in the northern city; there was Mr. Preston, the Westmoreland squire, or, as he preferred to be called, statesman, whose wife had come to Edinburgh for the education of their numerous family, and who, whenever her husband had come over on one of his occasional visits, was only too glad to accompany him to Mrs. Dawson's Monday evenings, he and the invalid lady having been friends from long ago. These and ourselves kept steady visitors, and enjoyed ourselves all the more for having the more of Mrs. Dawson's society.

One evening I had brought the little stool close to her sofa, and was caressing her thin white hand, when the thought came into my head and out I spoke it.

" Tell me, dear Mrs. Dawson," said I, " how long you have been in Edinburgh; you do not speak Scotch, and Mr. Dawson says he is not Scotch."

" No, I am Lancashire Liverpool-born," said she, smiling. " Don't you hear it in my broad tongue ?"

" I hear something different to other people, but I like it because it is just you; is that Lancashire ?"

" I dare say it is; for, though I am sure Lady Ludlow took pains enough to correct me in my younger days, I never could get rightly over the accent."

" Lady Ludlow," said I, " what had she to do with you ? I heard you talking about her to Lady Made-

line Stuart the first evening I ever came here; you and she seemed so fond of Lady Ludlow ; who is she ? '

" She is dead, my child; dead long ago."

I felt sorry I had spoken about her, Mrs. Dawson looked so grave and sad. I suppose she perceived my sorrow, for she went on and said,

" My dear, I like to talk and to think of Lady Ludlow : she was my true, kind friend and benefactress for many years; ask me what you like about her, and do not think you give me pain."

I grew bold at this.

" Will you tell me all about her then, please Mrs. Dawson?"

"Nay," said she, smiling, "that would be too long a story. Here are Signer Sperano, and Miss Duncan, and Mr. and Mrs. Preston are coming to-night, Mr. Preston told me; how would they like to hear an old-world story which, after all, would be no story at all, neither beginning, nor middle, nor end, only a bundle of recollections."

" If you speak of me, madame," said Signer Sperano, " I can only say you do me one great honour by recounting in my presence anything about any person that has ever interested you."

Miss Duncan tried to say something of the same kind. In the middle of her confused speech, Mr. and

Mrs. Preston came in. I sprang up; I went to meet them.

"Oh," said I, "Mrs. Dawson is just going to tell us all about Lady Ludlow, and a great deal more, only she is afraid it won't interest anybody : do say you would like to hear it!"

Mrs. Dawson smiled at me, and in reply to their urgency she promised to tell us all about Lady Ludlow, on condition that each one of us should, after she had ended, narrate something interesting, which we had either heard, or which had fallen within our own experience. We all promised willingly, and then gathered round her sofa to hear what she could tell us about my Lady Ludlow.

MY LADY LUDLOW,
CHAPTER I.

I AM an old woman now, and things are very different to what they were in my youth. Then we, who travelled, travelled in coaches, carrying six inside, and making a two days' journey out of what people now go over in a couple of hours with a whizz and a flash, and a screaming whistle, enough to deafen one. Then letters came in but three times a week: indeed, in some places in Scotland where I have stayed when I was a girl, the post came in but once a month ;but letters were letters then ; and we made great prizes of them, and read them and studied them like books. Now the post comes rattling in twice a day, bringing short jerky notes, some without beginning or end, but just a little sharp sentence, which well-bred folks would think too abrupt to be spoken. Well, well! they may all be improvements,I dare say they are; but you will never meet with a Lady Ludlow in these days.

I will try and tell you about her. It is no story : it has, as I said, neither beginning, middle, nor end.

My father was a poor clergyman with a large family. My mother was always said to have good blood in her veins; and when she wanted to maintain her position with the people she was thrown among,principally rich democratic manufacturers, all for liberty and the French Revolution,she would put on a pair of ruffles, trimmed with real old English point, very much darned to be sure,but which could not be bought new for love or money, as the art of making it was lost years before. These ruffles showed, as she said, that her ancestors had been Somebodies, when the grandfathers of the rich folk, who now looked down upon her, had been Nobodies,if, indeed, they had any grandfathers at all. I don't know whether any one out of our own family ever noticed these ruffles,but we were all taught as children to feel rather proud when my mother put them on, and to hold up our heads as became the descendants of the lady who had first possessed the lace. Not but what my dear father often told us that pride was a great sin; we were never allowed to be proud of anything but my mother's ruffles: and she was so innocently happy when she put them on,often, poor dear creature, to a very worn and thread-bare gown,that I still think, even after all my experience of life, they were a blessing to the family. You will think that I am wandering away from my Lady Ludlow. Not at all. The Lady who had owned the lace, Ursula Han-bury, was a common ancestress of both my mother and my Lady Ludlow. And so it fell out, that when my poor father died, and my mother was sorely pressed to know what to do with her nine children, and looked far and wide for signs of willingness to help, Lady Ludlow sent her a letter, proffering aid and assistance. I see that letter now: a large sheet of thick yellow paper, with a straight broad margin left on the left-hand side of the delicate Italian writing,writing which contained far more in the same space of paper than all the sloping, or masculine hand-writings of the present day. It was sealed with a coat of arms,a lozenge,for Lady Ludlow was a widow. My mother made us notice the motto, " Foy et Loy," and told us where to look for the quarterings of the Hanbury arms before she opened the letter. Indeed, I think she was rather afraid of what the contents might be; for, as I have said, in her anxious love for her fatherless children, she had written to many people upon whom, to tell truly, she had but little claim; and their cold, hard answers had many a time made her cry, when she thought none of us were

looking. I do not even know if she had ever seen Lady Ludlow: all I knew of her was that she was a very grand lady, whose grandmother had been half-sister to my mother's great-grandmother; but of her character and circumstances I had heard nothing, and I doubt if my mother was acquainted with them.

I looked over my mother's shoulder to read the letter; it began, "Dear Cousin Margaret Dawson," and I think I felt hopeful from the moment I saw those words. She went on to say,—stay, I think I can remember the very words:

DEAR COUSIN MARGARET DAWSON, I have been ' much grieved to hear of the loss you have sustained in ' the death of so good a husband, and so excellent a clergyman as I have always heard that my late cousin ' Richard was esteemed to be.'

" There !" said my mother, laying her finger on the passage, " read that aloud to the little ones. Let them hear how their father's good report travelled far and wide, and how well he is spoken of by one whom he never saw. COUSIN Eichard, how prettily her ladyship writes! Go on, Margaret!" She wiped her eyes as she spoke: and laid her finger on her lips, to still my little sister, Cecily, who, not understanding anything about the important letter, was beginning to talk and make a noise.

You say you are left with nine children. I too f should have had nine, if mine had all lived. I have none left but Rudolph, the present Lord Ludlow. He is married, and lives, for the most part, in London. 1 But I entertain six young gentlewomen at my house at

Connington, who are to me as daughters—save that, ' perhaps, I restrict them in certain indulgences in dress ' and diet that might be befitting in young ladies of a higher rank, and of more probable wealth. These 4 young persons—all of condition, though out of means are my constant companions, and I strive to do my ' duty as a Christian lady towards them. One of these young gentlewomen died (at her own home, whither she had gone upon a visit) last May. Will you do me the favour to allow your eldest daughter to supply her ' place in my household ? She is, as I make out, about sixteen years of age. She will find companions here ' who are but a little older than herself. I dress my young friends myself, and make each of them a small "allowance for pocket-money. They have but few opportunities for matrimony, as Connington is far re-' moved from any town. The clergyman is a deaf old widower ; my agent is married; and as for the neigh-' bouring farmers, they are, of course, below the notice ' of the young gentlewomen under my protection. Still, ' if any young woman wishes to marry, and has con-

' ducted herself to my satisfaction, I give her a wedding 1 dinner, her clothes, and her house-linen. And such as e remain with me to my death, will find a small com petency provided for them in my will. I reserve to ' myself the option of paying their travelling expenses, disliking gadding women, on the one hand ; on the 1 other, not wishing by too long absence from the family ' home to weaken natural ties.

' If my proposal pleases you and your daughter or rather, if it pleases you, for I trust your daughter has ' been too well brought up to have a will in opposition to yours let me know, dear cousin Margaret Dawson, and I will make arrangements for meeting the young gentlewoman at Cavistock, which is the nearest point to which the coach will bring her. My mother dropped the letter, and sat silent.

"I shall not know what to do without you, Margaret."

A moment before, like a young untried girl as I was, I had been pleased at the notion of seeing a new place, and leading a new life. But now, my mother's look of sorrow, and the children's cry of remonstrance: " Mother; I won't go," I said.

"Nay! but you had better," replied she, shaking her head. " Lady Ludlow has much power. She can help your brothers. It will not do to slight her ofler."

So we accepted it, after much consultation. We were rewarded, or so we thought, for, afterwards, when I came to know Lady Ludlow, I saw that she would have done her duty by us, as helpless relations, however we might have rejected her kindness, by a presentation to Christ's Hospital for one of my brothers.

And this was how I came to know my Lady Ludlow.

I remember well the afternoon of my arrival at Han-bury Court. Her ladyship had sent to meet me at the nearest post-town at which the mail-coach stopped. There was an old groom inquiring for me, the ostler said, if my name was Dawson—from Hanbury Court, he believed. I felt it rather formidable; and first began to understand what was meant by going among strangers, when I lost sight of the guard to whom my mother had intrusted me. I was perched up in a high gig with a hood to it, such as in those days was called a chair, and my companion was driving deliberately through the most pastoral country I had ever yet seen. By-and-by we ascended a long hill, and the man got out and walked at the horse's head. I should have liked to walk, too, very much indeed; but I did not know how far I might do it; and, in fact, I dared not speak to ask to be helped down the deep steps of the gig. We were at last at the top, on a long, breezy, sweeping, unenclosed piece of ground, called, as I afterwards learnt a Chase. The groom stopped, breathed, patted his horse, and then mounted again to my side.

" Are we near Hanbury Court ?" I asked.

" Near! Why, Miss! we've a matter of ten mile yet to go."

Once launched into conversation, we went on pretty glibly. I fancy he had been afraid of beginning to speak to me, just as I was to him ; but he got over his shyness with me sooner than I did mine with him. I let him choose the subjects of conversation, although very often I could not understand the points of interest in them: for instance, he talked for more than a quarter of an hour of a famous race which a certain dog-fox had given him, above thirty years before; and spoke of all the covers and turns just as if I knew them as well as he did; and all the time I was wondering what kind of an animal a dog-fox might be.

After we left the Chase, the road grew worse. No one in these days, who has not seen the byroads of fifty years ago, can imagine what they were. We had to quarter, as Randal called it, nearly all the way along the deep-rutted, miry lanes; and the tremendous jolts I occasionally met with made my seat in the gig so unsteady that I could not look about me at all, I was so much occupied in holding on. The road was too

muddy for me to walk without dirtying myself more than T liked to do, just before my first sight of my Lady Ludlow. But by-and-by, when we came to the fields in which the lane ended, I begged Randal to help me down, as I saw that I could pick my steps among the pasture grass without making myself unfit to be seen ; and Randal, out of pity for his steaming horse, wearied with the hard struggle through the mud, thanked me kindly, and helped me down with a springing jump.

The pastures fell gradually down to the lower land, shut in on either side by rows of high elms, as if there had been a wide grand avenue here in former times. Down the grassy gorge we went, seeing the sunset sky at the end of the shadowed descent. Suddenly we came to a long flight of steps.

" If you'll run down there, Miss, I'll go round and meet you, and then you'd better mount again, for my lady will like to see you drive up to the house."

" Are we near the house ?" said I, suddenly checked by the idea.

" Down there, Miss," replied he, pointing with his whip to certain stacks of twisted chimneys rising out of a group of trees, in deep shadow against the crimson light, and which lay just beyond a great square lawn at the base of the steep slope of a hundred yards, on the edge of which we stood.

I went down the steps quietly enough. I met Randal and the gig at the bottom ; and, falling into a side road to the left, we drove sedately round, through the gateway, and into the great court in front of the house.

The road by which we had come lay right at the back.

Hanbury Court is a vast red-brick house at least, it is cased in part with red bricks; and the gate-house and walls about the place are of brick,with stone facings at every corner, and door, and window, such as you see at Hampton Court At the back are the gables, and arched doorways, and stone mullions, which show (so Lady Ludlow used to tell us) that it was once a priory. There was a prior's parlour, I know only we called it Mrs. Medlicott's room; and there was a tithe-barn as big as a church, and rows of fish-ponds, all got ready for the monks' fasting-days in old time. But all this I did not see till afterwards. I hardly noticed, this first night, the great Virginian Creeper (said to have been the first planted in England by one of my lady's ancestors) that half-covered the front of the house. As I had been unwilling to leave the guard of the coach, so did I now feel unwilling to leave Randal, a known friend of three hours. But there was no help for it; in I must go ; past the grand-looking old gentleman holding the door open for me, on into the great hall on the right hand, into which the sun's last rays were sending in glorious red light,the gentleman was now walking before me, up a step on to the dais, as I afterwards learned that it was called,then again to the left, through a series of sitting-rooms, opening one out of another, and all of them looking into a stately garden, glowing, even in the twilight, with the bloom of flowers. We went up four steps out of the last of these rooms, and then my guide lifted up a heavy silk curtain, and I was in the presence of my Lady Ludlow.

She was very small of stature, and very upright She wore a great lace cap, nearly half her own height, I should think,that went round her head (caps which tied under the chin, and which we called " mobs," came in later, and my lady held them in great contempt, saying people might as well come down in their nightcaps). In front of my lady's cap was a great bow of white satin ribbon; and a broad band of the same ribbon was tied tight round her head, and served to keep the cap straight. She had a fine Indian muslin shawl folded over her shoulders and across her chest, and an apron of the same ; a black silk mode gown, made with short sleeves and ruffles, and with the tail thereof pulled through the pocket-hole, so as to shorten it to a useful length: beneath it she wore, as I could plainly see, a quilted lavender satin petticoat. Her hair was snowy white, but I hardly saw it, it was so covered with her cap: her skin, even at her age, was waxen in texture and tint; her eyes were large and dark blue, and must have been her great beauty when she was young, for there was nothing particular, as far as I can remember, either in mouth or nose. She had a great gold-headed stick by her chair ; but I think it was more as a mark of state and dignity than for use ; for she had as light and brisk a step when she chose as any girl of fifteen, and, in her private early walk of meditation in the mornings, would go as swiftly from garden alley to garden alley as any one of us.

She was standing up when I went in. I dropped my curtsy at the door, which my mother had always taught me as a part of good manners, and went up instinctively to my lady. She did not put out her hand, but raised herself a little on tiptoe, and kissed me on both cheeks.

" You are cold, my child. You shall have a dish of tea with me." She rang a little hand-bell on the table by her, and her waiting-maid came in from a small anteroom; and, as if all had been prepared, and was awaiting my arrival, brought with her a small china-service with tea ready made, and a plate of delicately-cut bread-and-butter, every morsel of which I could have eaten, and been none the better for it, so hungry was I after my long ride. The waiting-maid took off my cloak, and I sat down, sorely alarmed at the silence, the hushed foot-falls of the subdued maiden over the thick carpet, and the soft voice and clear pronunciation of my Lady Ludlow. My teaspoon fell against my cup with a sharp noise, that seemed so out of place and season that I blushed deeply. My lady caught my eye with hers, both keen and sweet were those dark-blue eyes of her ladyship's:

" Your hands are very cold, my dear; take off those gloves " (I wore thick serviceable doeskin, and had been too shy to take them off unbidden), "and let me try and warm them the evenings are very chilly." And she held my great red hands in hers, soft, warm, white, ring-laden. Looking at last a little wistfully into my face, she said" Poor child! And you're the eldest of nine! I had a daughter who would have been just your age ; but I cannot fancy her the eldest of nine." Then came a pause of silence; and then she rang her bell, and desired her waiting-maid, Adams, to show me to my room.

It was so small that I think it must have been a cell. The walls were whitewashed stone ; the bed was of

white dimity. There was a small piece of red stair-carpet on each side of the bed, and two chairs. In a closet adjoining were my washstand and toilet-table. There was a text of Scripture painted on the wall right opposite to my bed ; and below hung a print, common enough in those days, of King George and Queen Charlotte, with all their numerous children, down to the little Princess Amelia in a go-cart. On each side hung a small portrait, also engraved: on the left, it was Louis the Sixteenth, on the other, Marie-Antoinette. On the chimney-piece there was a tinder-box and a Prayer-book. I do not remember anything else in the room. Indeed, in those days people did not dream of writing-tables, and inkstands, and portfolios, and easy chairs, and what not. We were taught to go into our bedrooms for the purposes of dressing, and sleeping, and praying.Presently I was summoned to supper. I followed the young lady who had been sent to call me, down the wide shallow stairs, into the great hall, through which I had first passed on my way to my Lady Ludlow's room. There were four other young gentlewomen, all standing, and all silent, who curtsied to me when I first came in. They were dressed in a kind of uniform : muslin caps bound round their heads with blue ribbons, plain muslin handkerchiefs, lawn

aprons, and drab-coloured stuff gowns. They were all gathered together at a little distance from the table, on which were placed a couple of cold chickens, a salad, and a fruit-tart. On the dais there was a smaller round table, on which stood a silver jug filled with milk, and a small roll. Near that was set a carved chair, with a countess's coronet surmounting the back of it. I thought that some one might have spoken to me ; but they were shy, and I was shy ; or else there was some other reason; but, indeed, almost the minute after I had come into the hall by the door at the lower end, her ladyship entered by the door opening upon the dais; whereupon we all curtsied very low; I, because I saw the others do it. She stood, and looked at us for a moment.

" Young gentlewomen," said she, " make Margaret Dawson welcome among you;" and they treated me with the kind politeness due to a stranger, but still without any talking beyond what was required for the purposes of the meal. After it was over, and grace was said by one of our party, my lady rang her handbell, and the servants came in and cleared away the supper things: then they brought in a portable reading-desk, which was placed on the dais, and, the whole household trooping in, my lady called to one of my companions to come up and read the Psalms and Lessons for the day. I remember thinking how afraid I should have heen had I been in her place. There were no prayers. My lady thought it schismatic to have any prayers excepting those in the Prayer-book ; and would as soon have preached a sermon herself in the parish church, as have allowed any one not a deacon at the least to read prayers in a private dwelling-house. I am not sure that even then she would have approved of his reading them in an unconsecrated place.

She had been maid of honour to Queen Charlotte : a Hanbury of that old stock that flourished in the days of the Plantagenets, and heiress of all the land that remained to the family, of the great estates which had once stretched into four separate counties. Han-bury Court was hers by right. She had married Lord Ludlow, and had lived for many years at his various seats, and away from her ancestral home. She had lost all her children but one, and most of them had died at these houses of Lord Ludlow's ; and, I dare say, that gave my lady a distaste to the places, and a longing to come back to Hanbury Court, where she had been so happy as a girl. I imagine her girlhood had been the happiest time of her life; for, now I think of it, most of her opinions, when I knew her in later life, were singular enough then, but had been

universally prevalent fifty years before. For instance, while I lived at Hanbury Court, the cry for education was beginning to come up : Mr. Raikes had set up his Sunday Schools ; and some clergymen were all for teaching writing and arithmetic, as well as reading. My lady would have none of this; it was levelling and revolutionary, she said. When a young woman came to be hired, my lady would have her in, and see if she liked her looks and her dress, and question her about her family. Her ladyship laid great stress upon this latter point, saying that a girl who did not warm up when any interest or curiosity was expressed about her mother, or the " baby " (if there was one), was not likely to make a good servant. Then she would make her put out her feet, to see if they were well and neatly shod. Then she would bid her say the Lord's Prayer and the Creed. Then she inquired if she could write. If she could, and she had liked all that had gone before, her face sank—it was a great disappointment, for it was an all but inviolable rule with her never to engage a servant who could write. But I have known her ladyship break through it, although in both cases in which she did so she put the girl's principles to a further and unusual test in asking her to repeat the Ten Commandments. One pert young woman and yet I was sorry for her too, only she afterwards married a rich draper in Shrewsbury who had got through her trials pretty tolerably, considering she could write, spoilt all, by saying glibly, at the end of the last Commandment, " An't please your ladyship, I can cast accounts."

"Go away, wench," said my lady in a hurry, "You're only fit for trade; you will not suit me for a servant." The girl went away crestfallen: in a minute, however, my lady sent me after her to see that she had something to eat before leaving the house; and, indeed, she sent for her once again, but it was only to give her a Bible, and to bid her beware of French principles, which had led the French to cut off their king's and queen's heads.

The poor, blubbering girl said, " Indeed, my lady, I wouldn't hurt a fly, much less a king, and I cannot abide the French, nor frogs neither, for that matter."

But my lady was inexorable, and took a girl who could neither read nor write, to make up for her alarm about the progress of education towards addition and subtraction; and, afterwards, when the clergyman who was at Hanbury parish when I came there, had died, and the bishop had appointed another, and a younger man, in his stead, this was one of the points on which he and my lady did not agree. While good old deaf

Mr. Mountford lived, it was my lady's custom, when indisposed for a sermon, to stand up at the door of her large square pew, just opposite to the reading-desk, and to say (at that part of the morning service where it is decreed that, in quires and places where they sing, here followeth the Anthem): " Mr. Mountford, I will not trouble you for a discourse this morning." And we all knelt down to the Litany with great satisfaction; for Mr. Mountford, though he could not hear, had always his eyes open about this part of the service, for any of my lady's movements. But the new clergyman, Mr. Gray, was of a different stamp. He was very zealous in all his parish work; and my lady, who was just as good as she could be to the poor, was often crying him up as a godsend to the parish, and he never could send amiss to the Court when he wanted broth, or wine, or jelly, or sago for a sick person. But he needs must take up the new hobby of education; and I could see that this put my lady sadly about one Sunday, when she suspected, I know not how, that there was something to be said in his sermon about a Sunday-school which he was planning. She stood up, as she had not done since Mr. Mountford's death, two years and better before this time, and said,

"Mr. Gray, I will not trouble you for a discourse this morning."

MY LADY LUDLOW.

But her voice was not well-assured and steady ; and we knelt down with more of curiosity than satisfaction in our minds. Mr. Gray preached a very rousing sermon, on the necessity of establishing a Sabbath-school in the village. My lady shut her eyes, and seemed to go to sleep; but I don't believe she lost a word of it, though she said nothing about it that I heard until the next Saturday, when two of us, as was the custom, were riding out with her in her carriage, and we went to see a poor bed-ridden woman, who lived some miles away at the other end of the estate and of the parish : and as we came out of the cottage we met Mr. Gray walking up to it, in a great heat, and looking very tired. My lady beckoned him to her, and told him she should wait and take him home with her, adding that she wondered to see him there, so far from his home, for that it was beyond a Sabbath-day's journey, and, from what she had gathered from his sermon the last Sunday, he was all for Judaism against Christianity. He looked as if he did not understand what she meant; but the truth was that, besides the way in which he had spoken up for schools and schooling, he had kept calling Sunday the Sabbath: and, as her ladyship said, "the Sabbath is the Sabbath, and that's one thing it is Saturday ; and if I keep it, I'm a Jew, which I'm not. And Sunday is Sunday ; and

that's another thing; and if I keep it, I'm a Christian, which I humbly trust I am."

But when Mr. Gray got an inkling of her meaning in talking about a Sabbath-day's journey, he only took notice of a part of it: he smiled and bowed, and said no one knew better than her ladyship what were the duties that abrogated all inferior laws regarding the Sabbath; and that he must go in and read to old Betty Brown, so that he would not detain her ladyship.

" But I shall wait for you, Mr. Gray," said she. " Or I will take a drive round by Oakfield, and be back in an hour's time." For, you see, she would not have him feel hurried or troubled with a thought that he was keeping her waiting, while he ought to be comforting and praying with old Betty.

" A very pretty young man, my dears," said she, as we drove away. " But I shall have my pew glazed all the same."

We did not know what she meant at the time; but the next Sunday but one we did. She had the curtains all round the grand old Hanbury family seat taken down, and, instead of them, there was glass up to the height of six or seven feet. We entered by a door, with a window in it that drew up or down just like what you see in carriages. This window was generally

down, and then we could hear perfectly; but if Mr. Gray used the word " Sabbath," or spoke in favour of schooling and education, my lady stepped out of her corner, and drew up the window with a decided clang and clash.

I must tell you something more about Mr. Gray. The presentation to the living of Hanbury was vested in two trustees, of whom Lady Ludlow was one : Lord Ludlow had 'exercised this right in the appointment of Mr. Mountford, who had won his lordship's favour by his excellent horsemanship. Nor was Mr. Mountford a bad clergyman, as clergymen went in those days. He did not drink, though he liked good eating as much as any one. And if any poor person was ill, and he heard of it, he would send them plates from his own dinner of what he himself liked best; sometimes of dishes which were almost as bad as poison to sick people. He meant kindly to everybody except dissenters, whom Lady Ludlow and he united in trying to drive out of the parish; and among dissenters he particularly abhorred Methodists—some one said, because John Wesley had objected to his hunting. But that must have been long ago, for when I knew him he was far too stout and too heavy to hunt; besides, the bishop of the diocese disapproved of hunting, and had intimated his disapprobation to the

clergy. For my own part, I think a good run would not have come amiss, even in a moral point of view, to Mr. Mountford. He ate so much, and took so little exercise, that we young women often heard of his being in terrible passions with his servants, and the sexton and clerk. But they none of them minded him much, for he soon came to himself, and was sure to make them some present or other—some said in proportion to his anger; so that the sexton, who was a bit of a wag (as all sextons are, I think), said that the vicar's saying, "the Devil take you," was worth a shilling any day, whereas " the Deuce" was a shabby sixpenny speech, only fit for a curate.

There was a. great deal of good in Mr. Mountford, too. He could not bear to see pain, or sorrow, or misery of any kind; and, if it came under his notice, he was never easy till he had relieved it, for the time, at any rate. But he was afraid of being made uncomfortable ; so, if he possibly could, he would avoid seeing any one who was ill or unhappy; and he did not thank any one for telling him about them.

" What would your ladyship have me to do ?" he once said to my Lady Ludlow, when she wished him to go and see a poor man who had broken his leg. " I cannot piece the leg as the doctor can ; I cannot nurse him as well as his wife does; I may talk to him, but

he no more understands me than I do the language of the alchemists. My coming puts him out; he stiffens himself into an uncomfortable posture, out of respect to the cloth, and dare not take the comfort of kicking, and swearing, and scolding his wife, while I am there. I hear him, with my figurative ears, my lady, heave a sigh of relief when my back is turned, and the sermon that he thinks I ought to have kept for the pulpit, and have delivered to his neighbours (whose case, as he fancies, it would just have fitted, as it seemed to him to be addressed to the sinful), is all ended, and done for the day. I judge others as myself; I do to them as I would be done to. That's Christianity, at any rate. I should hate—saving your ladyship's presence to have my Lord Ludlow coming and seeing me, if I were ill. 'Twould be a great honour, no doubt; but I should have to put on a clean nightcap for the occasion ; and sham patience, in order to be polite, and not weary his lordship with my complaints. I should be twice as thankful to him if he would send me game, or a good fat haunch, to bring me up to that pitch of health and strength one ought to be in, to appreciate the honour of a visit from a nobleman. So I shall send Jerry Butler a good dinner every day till he is strong again; and spare the poor old fellow my presence and advice." My lady would be puzzled by this, and by many

other of Mr. Mountford's speeches. But he had been appointed by my lord, and she could not question her dead husband's wisdom; and she knew that the dinners were always sent, and often a guinea or two to help to pay the doctor's bills; and Mr. Mountford was true blue, as we call it, to the back-bone; hated the dissenters and the French; and could hardly drink a dish of tea without giving out the toast of " Church and King, and down with the Rump." Moreover, he had once had the honour of preaching before the King and Queen, and two of the Princesses, at Weymouth; and the King had applauded his sermon audibly with, —" Very good ; very good ;" and that was a seal put upon his merit in my lady's eyes.

Besides, in the long winter Sunday evenings, he would come up to the Court, and read a sermon to us girls, and play a game of picquet with my lady afterwards ; which served to shorten the tedium of the time. My lady would, on those occasions, invite him to sup with her on the dais; but as her meal was invariably bread and milk only, Mr. Mountford preferred sitting down amongst us, and made a joke about its being wicked and heterodox to eat meagre on Sunday, a festival of the Church. We smiled at this joke just as much the twentieth time we heard it as we did at the first; for we knew it was coming, because he always coughed a little nervously before he made a joke, for fear my lady should not approve: and neither she nor he seemed to remember that he had ever hit upon the idea before.

Mr. Mountford died quite suddenly at last. We were all very sorry to lose him. He left some of his property (for he had a private estate) to the poor of the parish, to furnish them with an annual Christmas dinner of roast-beef and plum-pudding, for which he wrote out a very good receipt in the codicil to his will.

Moreover, he desired his executors to see that the vault, in which the vicars of Hanbury were interred, was well aired, before his coffin was taken in ; for, all his life long, he had had a dread of damp, and latterly he kept his rooms to such a pitch of warmth that some thought it hastened his end.

Then the other trustee, as I have said, presented the living to Mr. Gray, Fellow of Lincoln College, Oxford. It was quite natural for us all, as belonging in some sort to the Hanbury family, to disapprove of the other trustee's choice. But when some ill-natured person circulated the report that Mr. Gray was a Moravian Methodist, I remember my lady said, " She could not believe anything so bad, without a great deal of evidence."

## CHAPTER II.

BEFORE I tell you about Mr. Gray, I think I ought to make you understand something more of what we did all day long at Hanbury Court. There were five of us at the time of which I am speaking, all young women of good descent, and allied (however distantly) to people of rank. When we were not with my lady, Mrs. Medlicott looked after us; a gentle little woman, who had been companion to my lady for many years, and was indeed, I have been told, some kind of relation to her. Mrs. Medlicott's parents had lived in Germany, and the consequence was, she spoke English with a very foreign accent. Another consequence was, that she excelled in all manner of needlework, such as is not known even by name in these days. She could darn either lace, table-linen, India muslin, or stockings, so that no one could tell where the hole or rent had been. Though a good Protestant, and never missing Guy Faux' day at church, she was as skilful at fine work as any nun in a Papist convent. She would take a piece

of French cambric, and by drawing out some threads, and working in others, it became delicate lace in a very few hours. She did the same by Hollands cloth, and made coarse strong lace, with which all my lady's napkins and table-linen were trimmed. We worked under her during a great part of the day, either in the still-room, or at our sewing in a chamber that opened out of the great hall. My lady despised every kind of work that would now be called Fancy-work. She considered that the use of coloured threads or worsted was only fit to amuse children ; but that grown women ought not to be taken with mere blues and reds, but to restrict their pleasure in sewing to making small and delicate stitches. She would speak of the old tapestry in the hall as the work of her ancestresses, who lived before the Reformation, and were consequently unacquainted with pure and simple tastes in work, as well as in religion. Nor would my lady sanction the fashion of the day, which, at the beginning of this century, made all the fine ladies take to making shoes. She said that such work was a consequence of the French Revolution, which had done much to annihilate all distinctions of rank and class, and hence it was, that she saw young ladies of birth and breeding handling lasts, and awls, and dirty cobblers'-wax, like shoemakers' daughters.

Very frequently one of us would be summoned to my lady to read aloud to her, as she sat in her small withdrawing-room, some improving book. It was generally Mr. Addison's "Spectator;" but one year I remember, we had to read "Sturm's Reflections," translated from a German book Mrs. Medlicott recommended. Mr. Sturm told us what to think about for every day in the year; and very dull it was. But I believe Queen Charlotte had liked the book very much, and the thought of her royal approbation kept my lady awake during the reading. "Mrs. Chapone's Letters" and M Dr. Gregory's Advice to Young Ladies " composed the rest of our library for week-day reading. I, for one, was glad to leave my fine sewing, and even my reading aloud, (though this last did keep me with my dear lady,) to go to the still-room and potter about among the preserves and the medicated waters. There was no doctor for many miles round, and with Mrs. Medlicott to direct us, and Dr. Buchan to go by for recipes, we sent out many a bottle of physic, which, I dare say, was as good as what comes out of the druggist's shop. At any rate, I do not think we did much harm; for if any of our physics tasted stronger than usual, Mrs. Medlicott would bid us let it down with cochineal and water, to make all safe, as she said. So our bottles of medicine had very little real physic in them at last; but we

were careful in putting labels on them, which looked very mysterious to those who could not read, and helped the medicine to do its work. I have sent off many a bottle of salt and water coloured red; and whenever we had nothing else to do in the still-room, Mrs. Medlicott would set us to making bread-pills by way of practice, and, as far as I can say, they were very efficacious, as before we gave out a box Mrs. Medlicott always told the patient what symptoms to expect; and I hardly ever inquired without hearing that they had produced their effect. There was one old man, who took six pills a-night, of any kind we liked to give him, to make him sleep ; and if, by any chance, his daughter had forgotten to let us know that he was out of his medicine, he was so restless and miserable that, as he said, he thought he was like to die. I think ours was what would be called homoeopathic practice now-a-days. Then we learnt to make all the cakes and dishes of the season in the still-room. We had plum-porridge and mince-pies at Christmas, fritters and pancakes on Shrove Tuesday, furmenty on Mothering Sunday, violet-cakes in Passion Week, tansy-pudding on Easter Sunday, three-cornered cakes on Trinity Sunday, and so on through the year: all made from good old Church receipts, handed down from one of my lady's earliest Protestant ancestresses. Every one of us passed

a portion of the day with Lady Ludlow ; and now and then we rode out with her in her coach-and-four. She did not like to go out with a pair of horses, considering this rather beneath her rank ; and, indeed, four horses were very often needed to pull her heavy coach through the stiff mud. But it was rather a cumbersome equipage through the narrow Warwickshire lanes; and I used often to think it was well that countesses were not plentiful, or else we might have met another lady of quality in another coach-and-four where there would have been no possibility of turning, or passing each other, and very little chance of backing. Once when the idea of this danger of meeting another countess in a narrow deep-rutted lane w r as very prominent in my mind, I ventured to ask Mrs. Medlicott what would have to be done on such an occasion ; and she told me that " de latest creation must back, for sure," which puzzled me a good deal at the time, although I understand it now. I began to find out the use of the " Peerage," a book which had seemed to me rather dull before; but, as I was always a coward in a coach, I made myself well acquainted with the dates of creation of our three Warwickshire earls, and was happy to find that Earl Ludlow ranked second, the oldest earl being a hunting widower, and not likely to drive out in a carriage.

All this time I have wandered from Mr. Gray. Of course, we first saw him in church when he read himself in. He was very red-faced, the kind of redness which goes with light hair, and a blushing complexion; he looked slight and short, and his bright light frizzy hair had hardly a dash of powder in it. I remember my lady making this observation, and sighing over it; for, though since the famine in seventeen hundred arid ninety-nine and eighteen hundred, there had been a tax on hair-powder, yet it was reckoned very revolu~ tionary and Jacobin not to wear a good deal of it. My lady hardly liked the opinions of any man who wore his own hair; but this she would say was rather a prejudice : only in her youth none but the mob had gone wigless, and she could not get over the association of wigs with birth and breeding ; a man's own hair with that class of people who had formed the rioters in seventeen hundred and eighty, when Lord George Gordon had been one of the bugbears of my lady's life. Her husband and his brothers, she told us, had been put into breeches, and had their heads shaved on their seventh birthday, each of them ; a handsome little wig of the newest fashion forming the old Lady Ludlow's invariable birthday present to her sons as they each arrived at that age ; and afterwards, to the day of their death, they never saw their own hair. To

  be without powder, as some underbred people were talking of being now, was in fact to insult the proprieties of life, by being undressed. It was English sans-culottism. But Mr. Gray did wear a little powder, enough to save him in my lady's good opinion ; but not enough to make her approve of him decidedly.

  The next time I saw him was in the great hall. Mary Mason and I were going to drive out with my lady in her coach, and when we went down-stairs with our best hats and cloaks on, we found Mr. Gray awaiting my lady's coming. I believe he had paid his respects to her before, but we had never seen him ; and he had declined her invitation to spend Sunday evening at the Court (as Mr. Mountford used to do pretty regularly,—and play a game of picquet too—), which, Mrs. Medlicott told us, had caused my lady to be not over well pleased with him.

  He blushed redder than ever at the sight of us, as we entered the hall, and dropped him our curtsies. He coughed two or three times, as if he would have liked to speak to us, if he could but have found something to say; and every time he coughed, he became hotter-looking than ever. I am ashamed to say, we were nearly laughing at him; half because we, too, were so shy that we understood what his awkwardness meant.

  My lady came in, with her quick active step—she always walked quickly when she did not bethink herself of her cane,as if she were sorry to have kept us waiting,and, as she entered, she gave us all round one of those graceful sweeping curtsies, of which I think the art must have died out with her,it implied so much courtesy ;this time it said, as well as words could do, " I am sorry to have kept you all waiting, forgive me."

  She went up to the mantelpiece, near which Mr. Gray had been standing until her entrance, and curtsying afresh to him, and pretty deeply this time, because of his cloth, and her being hostess, and he, a new guest. She asked him if he would not prefer speaking to her in her own private parlour, and looked as though she would have conducted him there. But he burst out with his errand, of which he was full even to choking, and which sent the glistening tears into his large blue eyes, which stood farther and farther out with his excitement.

  " My lady, I want to speak to you, and to persuade you to exert your kind interest, with Mr. Lathom— Justice Lathom of Hathaway Manor"

  " Harry Lathom ?" inquired my lady, as Mr. Gray stopped to take the breath he had lost in his hurry,—" I did not know he was in the commission."

  " He is only just appointed ; he took the oaths not a month ago,more's the pity I"

  "I do not understand why you should regret it. The Lathoras have held Hathaway since Edward the First, and Mr. Lathom bears a good character, although his temper is hasty "

"My lady! he has committed Job Gregson for stealing—a fault of which he is as innocent as I—and all the evidence goes to prove it, now that the case is brought before the Bench; only the Squires hang so together that they can't be brought to see justice, and are all for sending Job to gaol, out of compliment to Mr. Lathom, saying it is his first committal, and it won't be civil to tell him there is no evidence against his man. For God's sake, my lady, speak to the gentlemen; they will attend to you, while they only tell me to mind my own business."

Now my lady was always inclined to stand by her order, and the Lathoms of Hathaway Court were cousins to the Hanburys. Besides, it was rather a point of honour in those days to encourage a young magistrate, by passing a pretty sharp sentence on his first committals; and Job Gregson was the father of a girl who had been lately turned away from her place as scullery-maid for sauciness to Mrs. Adams, her ladyship's own maid; and Mr. Gray had not said a word of the reasons why he believed the man innocent, for he was in such a hurry, I believe he would have had my lady drive off to the Henley Court-house then and there; so there seemed a good deal against the man, and nothing but Mr. Gray's bare word for him; and my lady drew herself a little up, and said :

"Mr. Gray ! I do not see what reason either you or I nave to interfere. Mr. Harry Lathom is a sensible kind of young man, well capable of ascertaining the truth without our help"

"But more evidence has come out since," broke in Mr. Gray.

My lady went a little stiifer, and spoke a little more coldly:

"I suppose this additional evidence is before the justices; men of good family, and of honour and credit, well known in the county. They naturally feel that the opinion of one of themselves must have more weight than the words of a man like Job Gregson, who bears a very indifferent character, has been strongly suspected of poaching, coming from no one knows where, squatting on Hareman's Common which, by the way, is extra-parochial, I believe; consequently you, as a clergyman, are not responsible for what goes on there; and, although impolitic, there might be some truth in what the magistrates said, in advising you to mind your own business," said her ladyship, smiling,—"and they might he tempted to bid me mind mine, if I interfered, Mr. Gray; might they not ?"

He looked extremely uncomfortable; half angry. Once or twice he began to speak, but checked himself, as if his words would not have been wise or prudent. At last he said:

"It may seem presumptuous in me, a stranger of only a few weeks' standing—to set up my judgment as to men's character against that of residents" Lady Ludlow gave a little bow of acquiescence, which was, I think, involuntary on her part, and which I don't think he perceived, "but 1 am convinced that the man is innocent of this offence,—and besides, the justices themselves allege this ridiculous custom of paying a compliment to a newly-appointed magistrate as their only reason."

That unlucky word "ridiculous!" It undid all the good his modest beginning had done him with my lady. I knew, as well as words could have told me, that she was affronted at the expression being used by a man inferior in rank to those whose actions he applied it to, and, truly, it was a great want of tact, considering to whom he was speaking.

Lady Ludlow spoke very gently and slowly; she always did so when she was annoyed; it was a certain sign, the meaning of which we had all learnt.

"I think, Mr. Gray, we will drop the subject It is one on which we are not likely to agree."

Mr. Gray's ruddy colour grew purple, and then faded away, and his face became pale. I think both my lady and he had forgotten our presence; and we were beginning to feel too awkward to wish to remind them of it. And yet we could not help watching and listening with the greatest interest.

Mr. Gray drew himself up to his full height, with an unconscious feeling of dignity. Little as was his stature, and awkward and embarrassed as he had been only a few minutes before, I remember thinking he looked almost as grand as my lady when he spoke.

" Your ladyship must remember that it may be my duty to speak to my parishioners on many subjects on which they do not agree with me. I am not at liberty to be silent, because they differ in opinion from me."

Lady Ludlow's great blue eyes dilated with surprise, and—I do think—anger, at being thus spoken to. I am not sure whether it was very wise in Mr. Gray. He himself looked afraid of the consequences, but as if he was determined to bear them without flinching. For a minute there was silence. Then my lady replied :

" Mr. Gray, I respect your plain speaking, although

I may wonder whether a young man of your age and position has any right to assume that he is a better judge than one with the experience which I have naturally gained at my time of life, and in the station I hold."

" If I, madam, as the clergyman of this parish, am not to shrink from telling what I believe to be the truth to the poor and lowly, no more am I to hold my peace in the presence of the rich and titled." Mr. Gray's face showed that he was in that state of excitement which in a child would have ended in a good fit of crying. He looked as if he had nerved himself up to doing and saying things, which he disliked above everything, and which nothing short of serious duty could have compelled him to do and say. And at such times every minute circumstance which could add to pain comes vividly before one. I saw that he became aware of our presence, and that it added to his discomfiture.

My lady flushed up. " Are you aware, sir," asked she, " that you have gone far astray from the original subject of conversation? But as you talk of your parish, allow me to remind you that Hareman's Common is beyond the bounds, and that you are really not responsible for the characters and lives of the squatters on that unlucky piece of ground."

" Madam, I see I have only done harm in speaking to you about the affair at all. I beg your pardon, and take my leave."

He bowed, and looked very sad. Lady Ludlow caught the expression of his face.

" Good morning!" she cried, in rather a louder and quicker way than that in which she had been speaking. "Remember, Job Gregson is a notorious poacher and evildoer, and you really are not responsible for what goes on at Hareman's Common."

He was near the hall-door, and said something half to himself, which we heard (being nearer to him), but my lady did not; although she saw that he spoke. " What did he say ?" she asked, in a somewhat hurried manner, as soon as the door was closed" I did not hear." We looked at each other, and then I spoke :

" He said, my lady, that ' God help him ! he was responsible for all the evil he did not strive to overcome.' "

My lady turned sharp round away from us, and Mary Mason said afterwards she thought her ladyship was much vexed with both of us, for having been present, and with me for having repeated what Mr. Gray had said. But it was not our fault that we were in the hall, and when my lady asked what Mr. Gray had said, I thought it right to tell her.

In a few minutes she bade us accompany her in her ride in the coach.

Lady Ludlow always sat forwards by herself, and we girls backwards. Somehow this was a rule, which we never thought of questioning. It was true that riding backwards made some of us feel very uncomfortable and faint; and to remedy this my lady always drove with both windows open, which occasionally gave her the rheumatism; but we always went on in the old way. This day she did not pay any great attention to the road by which we were going, and Coachman took his own way. We were very silent, as my lady did not speak, and looked very serious. Or else, in general, she made these rides very pleasant (to those who were not qualmish, with riding backwards), by talking to us in a very agreeable manner, and telling us of the different things which had happened to her at various places,—at Paris and Versailles, where she had been in her youth,—at Windsor and Kew and Wey-mouth, where she had been with the Queen, when maid-of-honour—and so on. But this day she did not talk at all. All at once she put her head out of the window.

" John Footman," said she, " where are we ? Surely this is Hareman's Common."

" Yes, an't please my lady," said John Footman, and waited for further speech or orders. My lady thought awhile, and then said she would have the steps put down and get out.

As soon as she was gone, we looked at each other, and then without a word began to gaze after her. We saw her pick her dainty way, in the little high-heeled shoes she always wore (because they had been in fashion in her youth), among the yellow pools of stagnant water that had gathered in the clayey soil. John Footman followed, stately, after; afraid too, for all his stateliness, of splashing his pure white stockings. Suddenly my lady turned round, and said something to him, and he returned to the carriage with a half-pleased, half-puzzled air.

My lady went on to a cluster of rude mud houses at the higher end of the Common ; cottages built, as they were occasionally at that day, of wattles and clay, and thatched with sods. As far as we could make out from dumb show, Lady Ludlow saw enough of the interiors of these places to make her hesitate before entering, or even speaking to any of the children who were playing about in the puddles. After a pause, she disappeared into one of the cottages. It seemed to us a long time before she came out; but I dare say it was not more than eight or ten minutes. She came back with her head hanging down, as if to choose her way, but we saw it was more in thought and bewilderment than for any such purpose.

She had not made up her mind where we should drive to when she got into the carriage again. John Footman stood, bare-headed, waiting for orders.

" To Hathaway. My dears, if you are tired, or if you have anything to do for Mrs. Medlicott, I can drop you at Barford Corner, and it is but a quarter of an hour's brisk walk home ?"

But luckily we could safely say that Mrs. Medlicott did not want us; and as we had whispered to each other, as we sat alone in the coach, that surely my lady must have gone to Job Gregson's, we were far too anxious to know the end of it all to say that we were tired. So we all set off to Hathaway. Mr. Harry Lathom was a bachelor squire, thirty or thirty-five years of age, more at home in the field than in the drawing-room, and with sporting men than with ladies.

My lady did not alight, of course; it was Mr. Lathom's place to wait upon her, and she bade the butler, who had a smack of the gamekeeper in him, very unlike our own powdered venerable fine gentleman at Hanbury,—tell his master, with her compliments, that she wished to speak to him. You may think how pleased we were to find that we should hear all that was said; though, I think, afterwards we were half sorry when we saw how our presence confused the squire, who would have found it bad enough to answer my lady's questions, even without two eager girls for audience.

" Pray, Mr. Lathom," began my lady, something abruptly for her, but she was very full of her subject, " what is this I hear about Job Gregson ?"

Mr. Lathom looked annoyed and vexed, but dared not show it in his words

"I gave out a warrant against him, my lady, for theft, that is all You are doubtless aware of his character; a man who sets nets and springes in long cover, and fishes wherever he takes a fancy. It is but a short step from poaching to thieving."

"That is quite true," replied Lady Ludlow (who had a horror of poaching for this very reason): " but I imagine you do not send a man to gaol on account of his bad character."

" Rogues and vagabonds," said Mr. Lathom. " A man may be sent to prison for being a vagabond; for no specific act, but for his general mode of life."

He had the better of her ladyship for one moment; but then she answered,

" But in this case, the charge on which you committed him was theft; now his wife tells me he can prove he was some miles distant from Holmwood, where the robbery took place, all that afternoon; she says you had the evidence before you."

Mr. Lathom here interrupted my lady, by saying, in a somewhat sulky manner,—

"No such evidence was brought before me when I gave the warrant. I am not answerable for the other magistrates' decision, when they had more evidence before them. It was they who committed him to gaol. I am not responsible for that."

My lady did not often show signs of impatience; but we knew she was feeling irritated by the little perpetual tapping of her high-heeled shoe against the bottom of the carriage. About the same time we, sitting backwards, caught a glimpse of Mr. Gray through the open door, standing in the shadow of the hall. Doubtless Lady Ludlow's arrival had interrupted a conversation between Mr. Lathom and Mr. Gray. The latter must have heard every word of what she was saying ; but of this she was not aware, and caught at Mr. Lathom's disclaimer of responsibility with pretty much the same argument which she had heard (through our repetition) that Mr. Gray had used not two hours before.

" And do you mean to say, Mr. Lathom, that you don't consider yourself responsible for all injustice or wrong-doing that you might have prevented, and have not ? Nay, in this case the first germ of injustice was your own mistake. I wish you had been with me a little while ago, and seen the misery in that poor fellow's cottage." She spoke lower, and Mr. Gray drew near, in a sort of involuntary manner; as if to hear all she was saying. We saw him, and doubtless Mr. Lathom heard his footstep, and knew who it was that was listening behind him, and approving of every word that was said. He grew yet more sullen in manner; but still my lady was my lady, and he dared not speak out before her, as he would have done to Mr. Gray. Lady Ludlow, however, caught the look of stubbornness in his face, and it roused her as I had never seen her roused.

" I am sure you will not refuse, sir, to accept my bail. I offer to bail the fellow out, and to be responsible for his appearance at the sessions. What say you to that, Mr. Lathom ?"

" The offence of theft is not bailable, my lady."

" Not in ordinary cases, I dare say. But I imagine this is an extraordinay case. The man is sent to prison out of compliment to you, and against all evidence, as far as I can learn. He will have to rot in gaol for two months, and his wife and children to starve. I, Lady Ludlow, offer to bail him out, and pledge myself for his appearance at next quarter-sessions."

" It is against the law, my lady."

" Bah ! Bah ! Bah! Who makes laws ? Such as I, in the House of Lords—such as you, in the House of Commons. We, who make the laws in St. Stephen's, may break the mere forms of them, when we have right on our sides, on our own land, and amongst our own people."

" The lord-lieutenant may take away my commission, if he heard of it."

"And a very good thing for the county, Harry Lathom; and for you too, if he did,—if you don't go on more wisely than you have begun. A pretty set you and your brother magistrates are to administer justice through the land! I always said a good despotism was the best form of government; and I am twice as much in favour of it now I see what a quorum is ! My dears !"

suddenly turning round to us, " if it would not tire you to walk home, I would beg Mr. Lathorn to take a seat in my coach, and we would drive to Henley Gaol, and have the poor man out at once."

" A walk over the fields at this time of day is hardly fitting for young ladies to take alone," said Mr. Lathom, anxious no doubt to escape from his tete-a-tete drive with my lady, and possibly not quite prepared to go to the illegal length of prompt measures, which she had in contemplation.

But Mr. Gray now stepped forward, too anxious for the release of the prisoner to allow any obstacle to intervene which he could do away with. To see Lady Ludlow's face when she first perceived whom she had

had for auditor and spectator of her interview with Mr. Lathom, was as good as a play. She had been doing and saying the very things she had been so much annoyed at Mr. Gray's saying and proposing only an hour or two ago. She had been setting down Mr. Lathom pretty smartly, in the presence of the very man to whom she had spoken of that gentleman as so sensible, and of such a standing in the county, that it was presumption to question his doings. But before Mr. Gray had finished his offer of escorting us back to Hanbury Court, my lady had recovered herself. There was neither surprise nor displeasure in her manner, as she answered:

" I thank you, Mr. Gray. I was not aware that you were here, but I think I can understand on what errand you came. And seeing you here, recalls me to a duty I owe Mr. Lathom. Mr. Lathom, I have spoken to you pretty plainly,—forgetting, until I saw Mr. Gray, that only this very afternoon I differed from him on this very question; taking completely, at that time, the same view of the whole subject which you have done; thinking that the county would be well rid of such a man as Job Gregson, whether he had committed this theft or not. Mr. Gray and I did not part quite friends," she continued, bowing towards him; "but it so happened that I saw Job Gregson's wife and home,I felt that Mr. Gray had been right and I had been wrong, so, with the famous inconsistency of my sex, I came hither to scold you," smiling towards Mr. Lathom, who looked half-sulky yet, and did not relax a bit of his gravity at her smile, " for holding the same opinions that I had done an hour before. Mr. Gray," (again bowing towards him) " these young ladies will be very much obliged to you for your escort, and so shall I. Mr. Lathom, may I beg of you to accompany me to Henley ?"

Mr. Gray bowed very low, and went very red ; Mr. Lathom said something which we none of us heard, but which was, I think, some remonstrance against the course he was, as it were, compelled to take. Lady Ludlow, however, took no notice of his murmur, but sat in an attitude of polite expectancy; and as we turned off on our walk, I saw Mr. Lathom getting into the coach with the air of a whipped hound. I must say, considering my lady's feeling, I did not envy him his ride,—though, I believe, he was quite in the right as to the object of the ride being illegal.

Our walk home was very dull. We had no fears; and would far rather have been without the awkward, blushing young man, into which Mr. Gray had sunk. At every stile he hesitated,—sometimes he half got over it, thinking that he could assist us better in that

way; then he would turn back unwilling to go before ladies. He had no ease of manner, as my lady once said of him, though on any occasion of duty, he had an immense deal of dignity.

MY LADY LUDLOW.
CHAPTER III.

As far as I can remember, it was very soon after this that I first began to have the pain in my hip, which has ended in making me a cripple for life. I hardly recollect more than one walk after our return under Mr. Gray's escort from Mr. Lathom's. Indeed, at the time, I was not without suspicions (which I never named) that the beginning of all the mischief was a great jump I had taken from the top of one of the stiles on that very occasion.

Well, it is a long while ago, and God disposes of us all, and I am not going to tire you out with telling you how I thought and felt, and how, when I saw what my life was to be, I could hardly bring myself to be patient, but rather wished to die at once. You can every one of you think for yourselves what becoming all at once useless and unable to move, and by-and-by growing hopeless of cure, and feeling that one must be a burden to some one all one's life long, would be to an active, wilful, strong girl of seventeen, anxious to

get on in the world, so as, if possible, to help her brothers and sisters. So I shall only say, that one among the blessings which arose out of what seemed at the time a great, black sorrow was, that Lady Ludlow for many years took me, as it were, into her own especial charge ; and now, as I lie still and alone in my old age, it is such a pleasure to think of her !

Mrs. Medlicott was great as a nurse, and I am sure I can never be grateful enough to her memory for all her kindness. But she was puzzled to know how to manage me in other ways. I used to have long, hard fits of crying; and, thinking that I ought to go home and yet what could they do with me there?and a hundred and fifty other anxious thoughts, some of which I could tell to Mrs. Medlicott, and others I could not. Her way of comforting me was hurrying away for some kind of tempting or strengthening food—a basin of melted calves'-foot jelly was, I am sure she thought, a cure for every woe.

" There! take it, dear, take it!" she would say; " and don't go on fretting for what can't be helped."

But, I think, she got puzzled at length at the non-efficacy of good things to eat; and one day, after I had limped down to see the doctor, in Mrs. Medlicott's sitting room—a room lined with cupboards, containing preserves and dainties of all kinds, which she perpetually

made, and never touched herself—when I was returning to my bed-room to cry away the afternoon, under pretence of 'arranging my clothes, John Footman brought me a message from my lady (with whom the doctor had been having a conversation) to bid me go to her in that private sitting-room at the end of the suite of apartments, about which I spoke in describing the day of my first arrival at Hanbury. I had hardly been in it since; as, when we read to my lady, she generally sat in the small withdrawing-room out of which this private room of hers opened. I suppose great people do not require what we smaller people value so much,—I mean privacy. I do not think that there was a room which my lady occupied that had not two doors, and some of them had three or four. Then my lady had always Adams waiting upon her in her bed-chamber; and it was Mrs. Medlicott's duty to sit within call, as it were, in a sort of anteroom that led out of my lady's own sitting-room, on the opposite side to the drawing-room door. To fancy the house, you must take a great square, and halve it by a line; at one end of this line was the hall-door, or public-entrance ; at the opposite the private entrance from a terrace, which was terminated at one end by a sort of postern door in an old gray stone wall, beyond which lay the farm buildings and offices; so that people could

come in this way to ray lady on business, while, if she were going into the garden from her own room, she had nothing to do but to pass through Mrs. Medlicott's apartment, out into the lesser hall, and then turning to the right as she passed on to the terrace, she could go down the flight of broad, shallow steps at the corner of the house into the lovely garden, with stretching, sweeping lawns, and gay flower-beds, and beautiful, bossy laurels, and other blooming or massy shrubs, with full-grown beeches, or larches feathering down to the ground a little farther off. The whole was set in a frame, as it were, by the more distant woodlands. The house had been modernized in the days of Queen Anne, I think; but the money had fallen short that was requisite to carry out all the improvements, so it was only the suite of withdrawing-rooms and the terrace-rooms, as far as the private entrance, that had the new, long, high windows put in, and these were old enough by this time to be draped with roses, and honeysuckles and pyracanthus, winter and summer long.

Well, to go back to that day when I limped into my lady's sitting-room, trying hard to look as if I had not been crying, and not to walk as if I was in much pain. I do not know whether my lady saw how near my tears were to my eyes, but she told me she had sent for me, because she wanted some help in arranging the

drawers of her bureau, and asked me—just as if it was a favour I was to do her—if I could sit down in the easy chair near the window—(all quietly arranged before I came in, with a footstool, and a table quite near)—and assist her. You will wonder, perhaps, why I was not bidden to sit or lie on the sofa; but (although I found one there a morning or two afterwards, when I came down) the fact was, that there was none in the room at this time. I have even fancied that the easy-chair was brought in on purpose for me , for it was not the chair in which I remembered my lady sitting the first time I saw her. That chair was very much carved and gilded, with a countess' coronet at the top. I tried it one day, some time afterwards, when my lady was out of the room, and I had a fancy for seeing how I could move about, and very uncomfortable it was. Now my chair (as I learnt to call it, and to think it) was soft and luxurious, and seemed somehow to give one's body rest just in that part where one most needed it.

I was not at my ease that first day, nor indeed for many days afterwards, notwithstanding my chair was so comfortable. Yet I forgot my sad pain in silently wondering over the meaning of many of the things we turned out of those curious old drawers. I was puzzled to know why some were kept at all; a scrap of writing may-be, with only half-a-dozen common-place words written on it, or a bit of broken riding-whip, and here and there a stone, of which I thought I could have picked up twenty just as good in the first walk I took. But it seems that was just my ignorance ; for my lady told me they were pieces of valuable marble, used to make the floors of the great Roman emperors' palaces long ago; and that when she had been a girl, and made the grand tour long ago, her cousin, Sir Horace Mann, the Ambassador or Envoy at Florence, had told her to be sure to go into the fields inside the walls of ancient Rome, when the farmers were preparing the ground for the onion-sowing, and had to make the soil fine, and pick up what bits of marble she could find. She had done so, and meant to have had them made into a table ; but somehow, that plan fell through, and there they were with all the dirt out of the onion-field upon them; but once when I thought of cleaning them with soap and water, at any rate, she bade me not to do so, for it was Roman dirt earth, I think, she called it but it was dirt all the same.

Then, in this bureau, were many other things, the value of which I could understand locks of hair carefully ticketed, which my lady looked at very sadly ; and lockets and bracelets with miniatures in them, very small pictures to what they make now-a-days, and call miniatures; some of them had even to be looked at through a microscope before you could see the individual expression of the faces, or how beautifully they were painted. I don't think that looking at these made my lady seem so melancholy, as the seeing and touching of the hair did. But, to be sure, the hair was, as it were, a part of some beloved body which she might never touch and caress again, but which lay beneath the turf, all faded and disfigured, except perhaps the very hair, from which the lock she held had been dissevered; whereas the pictures were but pictures after all—likenesses, but not the very things themselves. This is only my own conjecture, mind. My lady rarely spoke out her feelings. For, to begin with, she was of rank: and I have heard her say that people of rank do not talk about their feelings except to their equals, and even to them they conceal them, except upon rare occasions. Secondly, and this is my own reflection, she was an only child and an heiress ; and as such was more apt to think than to talk, as all well-brought-up heiresses must be, I think. Thirdly, she had long been a widow, without any companion of her own age with whom it would have been natural for her to refer to old associations, past pleasures, or mutual sorrows. Mrs. Medlicott came nearest to her as a companion of this sort; and her ladyship talked more

to Mrs. Medlicott, in a kind of familiar way, than she did to all the rest of the household put together. But Mrs. Medlicott was silent by nature, and did not reply at any great length. Adams, indeed, was the only one who spoke much to Lady Ludlow.

After we had worked away about an hour at the bureau, her ladyship said we had done enough for one day ; and as the time was come for her afternoon ride, she left me, with a volume of engravings from Mr. Hogarth's pictures on one side of me (I don't like to write down the names of them, though my lady thought nothing of it, I am sure), and upon a stand her great prayer-book open at the evening-psalms for the day, on the other. But as soon as she was gone, I troubled myself little with either, but amused myself with looking round the room at my leisure. The side on which the fire-place stood, was all panelled,—part of the old ornaments of the house, for there was an Indian paper with birds and beasts, and insects on it, on all the other sides. There were coats of arms, of the various families with whom the Hanburys had intermarried, all over these panels, and up and down the ceiling as well. There was very little looking-glass in the room, though one of the great drawing-rooms was called the " Mirror Room," because it was lined with glass, which my lady's great-grandfather had brought from Venice when he was ambas-

sador there. There were china jars of all shapes and sizes round and about the room, and some china monsters, or idols, of which I could never bear the sight, they were so ugly, though I think my lady valued them more than all. There was a thick carpet on the middle of the floor, which was made of small pieces of rare wood fitted into a pattern; the doors were opposite to each other, and were composed of two heavy tall wings, and opened in the middle, moving on brass grooves inserted into the floor—they would not have opened over a carpet. There were two windows reaching up nearly to the ceiling, but very narrow, and with deep window-seats in the thickness of the wall. The room was full of scent, partly from the flowers outside, and partly from the great jars of pot-pourri inside. The choice of odours was what my lady piqued herself upon, saying nothing showed birth like a keen susceptibility of smell. We never named musk in her presence, her antipathy to it was so well understood through the household : her opinion on the subject was believed to be, that no scent derived from an animal could ever be of a sufficiently pure nature to give pleasure to any person of good family, where, of course, the delicate perception of the senses had been cultivated for generations. She would instance the way in which sportsmen preserve the breed of dogs who have shown

keen scent; and how such gifts descend for generations amongst animals, who cannot be supposed to have anything of ancestral pride, or hereditary fancies about them. Musk, then, was never mentioned at Hanbury Court. No more were bergamot or southern-wood, although vegetable in their nature. She considered these two latter as betraying a vulgar taste in the person who chose to gather or wear them. She was sorry to notice sprigs of them in the button-hole of any young man in whom she took an interest, either because he was engaged to a servant of hers or otherwise, as he came out of church on a Sunday afternoon. She was afraid that he liked coarse pleasures; and I am not sure if she did not think that his preference for these coarse sweetnesses did not imply a probability that he would take to drinking. But she distinguished between vulgar and common. Violets, pinks, and sweetbriar were common enough; roses and mignonette, for those who had gardens, honeysuckle for those who walked along the bowery lanes; but wearing them betrayed no vulgarity of taste: the queen upon her throne might be glad to smell at a nosegay of these flowers. A beau-pot (as we called it) of pinks and roses freshly gathered was placed every morning that they were in bloom on my lady's own particular table. For lasting vegetable odours she preferred lavender and sweet-

woodroof to any extract whatever. Lavender reminded her of old customs, she said, and of homely cottage-gardens, and many a cottager made his offering to her of a bundle of lavender. Sweet woodroof, again, grew in wild, woodland places, where the soil was fine and the air delicate: the poor children used to go and gather it for her up in the woods on the higher lands ; and for this service she always rewarded them with bright new pennies, of which my lord, her son, used to send her down a bagful fresh from the Mint in-London every February.

Attar-of-roses, again, she disliked. She said it reminded her of the city and of merchants' wives, over-rich, over-heavy in its perfume. And lilies-of-the-valley somehow fell under the same condemnation. They were most graceful and elegant to look at (my lady was quite candid about this), flower, leaf, colour—everything was refined about them but the smell. That was too strong. But the great hereditary faculty on which my lady piqued herself, and with reason, for I never met with any other person who possessed it, was the power she had of perceiving the delicious odour arising from a bed of strawberries in the late autumn, when the leaves were all fading and dying. " Bacon's Essays " was one of the few books that lay about in my lady's room ; and if you took it up and opened it carelessly,

VOL. I. E

it was sure to fall apart at his " Essay on Gardens." " Listen," her ladyship would say, " to what that great philosopher and statesman says, * Next to that/—he is speaking of violets, my dear,— l is the musk-rose,'—of which you remember the great bush, at the corner of the south wall just by the Blue Drawing-room windows; that is the old musk-rose, Shakespeare's musk-rose, which is dying out through the kingdom now. But to return to my Lord Bacon: ' Then the strawberry . leaves, dying with a most excellent cordial smell/ Now the Hanburys can always smell this excellent cordial odour, and very delicious and refreshing it is. You see, in Lord Bacon's time, there had not been so many intermarriages between the court and the city as there have been since the needy days of his Majesty Charles the Second; and altogether in the time of Queen Elizabeth, the great, old families of England were a distinct race, just as a cart-horse is one creature, and very useful in its place, and Childers or Eclipse is another creature, though both are of the same species. So the old families have gifts and powers of a different and higher class to what the other orders have. My dear, remember that you try if you can smell the scent of dying strawberry-leaves in this next autumn. You have some of Ursula Hanbury's blood in you, and that gives you a chance."

But when October came, I sniffed and sniffed, and all to no purpose; and my lady—who had watched the little experiment rather anxiously—had to give me up as a hybrid. I was mortified, I confess, and thought that it was in some ostentation of her own powers that she ordered the gardener to plant a border of strawberries on that side the terrace that lay under her windows.

I have wandered away from time and place. I tell you all the remembrances I have of those years just as they come up, and I hope that, in my old age, I am not getting too like a certain Mrs. Nickleby, whose speeches were once read out aloud to me.

I came by degrees to be all day long in this room which I have been describing; sometimes sitting in the easy chair, doing some little piece of dainty work for my lady, or sometimes arranging flowers, or sorting letters according to their handwriting, so that she could arrange them afterwards, and destroy or keep, as she planned, looking ever onward to her death. Then, after the sofa was brought in, she would watch my face, and if she saw my colour change, she would bid me lie down and rest. And I used to try to walk upon the terrace every day for a short time : it hurt me very much, it is true, but the doctor had ordered it, and I knew her ladyship wished me to obey.

Before I had seen the background of a great lady's life, I had thought it all play and fine doings. But whatever other grand people are, my lady was never idle. For one thing, she had to superintend the agent for the large Hanbury estate. I believe it was mortgaged for a sum of money which had gone to improve the late lord's Scotch lands; but she was anxious to pay off this before her death, and so to leave her own inheritance free of incumbrance to her son, the present Earl; whom, I secretly think, she considered a greater person, as being the heir of the Hanburys (though through a female line), than as being my Lord Ludlow with half-a-dozen other minor titles.

With this wish of releasing her property from the mortgage, skilful care was much needed in the management of it: and as far as my lady could go, she took every pains. She had a great book, in which every page was ruled into three divisions; on the first column was written the date and the name of the tenant who addressed any letter on business to her ; on the second was briefly stated the subject of the letter, which generally contained a request of some kind. This request would be surrounded and enveloped in so many words, and often inserted amidst so many odd reasons and excuses, that Mr. Horner (the steward) would sometimes say it was like hunting through a bushel of chaff to find a

grain of wheat. Now, in the second column of this book, the grain of meaning was placed, clean and dry, before her ladyship every morning. She sometimes would ask to see the original letter; sometimes she simply answered the request by a " Yes," or a " No;" and often she would send for leases and papers, and examine them well, with Mr. Horner at her elbow, to see if such petitions, as to be allowed to plough up pasture fields, &c., were provided for in the terms of the original agreement. On every Thursday she made herself at liberty to see her tenants, from four to six in the afternoon. Mornings would have suited my lady better, as far as convenience went, and I believe the old custom had been to have these levees (as her ladyship used to call them) held before twelve. But, as she said to Mr. Horner, when he urged returning to the former hours, it spoilt a whole day for a farmer, if he had to dress himself in his best and leave his work in the forenoon (and my lady liked to see her tenants come in their Sunday-clothes; she would not say a word, may-be, but she would take her spectacles slowly out, and put them on with silent gravity, and look at a dirty or raggedly-dressed man so solemnly and earnestly, that his nerves must have been pretty strong if he did not wince, and resolve that, however poor he might be, soap and water, and needle and thread should be used

before he again appeared in her ladyship's anteroom). The outlying tenants had always a supper provided for them in the servants'-hall on Thursdays, to which, indeed, all comers were welcome to sit down. For my lady said, though there were not many hours left of a working-man's day when their business with her was ended, yet that they needed food and rest, and that she should be ashamed if they sought either at the Fighting Lion (called at this day the Hanbury Arms). They had as much beer as they could drink while they were eating; and when the food was cleared away, they had a cup a-piece of good ale, in which the oldest tenant present, standing up, gave Madam's health; and after that was drunk, they were expected to set off homewards; at any rate, no more liquor was given them. The tenants one and all called her " Madam;" for they recognised in her the married heiress of the Hanburys, not the widow of a Lord Ludlow, of whom they and their forefathers knew nothing; and against whose memory, indeed, there rankled a dim unspoken grudge, the cause of which was accurately known to the very few who understood the nature of a mortgage, and were therefore aware that Madam's money had been taken to enrich my lord's poor land in Scotland. I am sure—for you can understand I was behind the scenes, as it were, and had many an opportunity of seeing and hearing, as I lay or sat motionless in my lady's room, with the double doors open between it and the anteroom beyond, where Lady Ludlow saw her steward, and gave audience to her tenants,—I am certain, I say, that Mr. Homer was silently as much annoyed at the money that was swallowed up by this mortgage as any one; and, some time or other, he had probably spoken his mind out to my lady; for there was a sort of offended reference on her part, and respectful submission to blame on his, while every now and then there was an implied protest,—whenever the payments of the interest became due, or whenever my lady stinted herself of any personal expense, such as Mr. Homer thought was only decorous and becoming in the heiress of the Hanburys. Her carriages were old and cumbrous, wanting all the improvements which had been adopted by those of her rank throughout the county. Mr. Horner would fain have had the ordering of a new coach. The carriage-horses, too, were getting past their work; yet all the promising colts bred on the estate were sold for ready money; and so on. My lord, her son, was ambassador at some foreign place; and very proud we all were of his glory and dignity; but I fancy it cost money, and my lady would have lived on bread and water sooner than have called upon him to help her in paying off the mortgage, although he was the one who was to benefit by it in the end.

Mr. Homer was a very faithful steward, and very respectful to my lady; although, sometimes, I thought she was sharper to him than to any one else; perhaps because she knew that, although he never said anything, he disapproved of the Hanburys being made to pay for the Earl Ludlow's estates and state.

The late lord had been a sailor, and had been as extravagant in his habits as most sailors are, I am told,—for I never saw the sea; and yet he had a long sight to his own interests; but whatever he was, my lady loved him and his memory, with about as fond and proud a love as ever wife gave husband, I should think.

For a part of his life Mr. Horner, who was born on the Hanbury property, had been a clerk to an attorney in Birmingham; and these few years had given him a kind of worldly wisdom, which, though always exerted for her benefit, was antipathetic to her ladyship, who thought that some of her steward's maxims savoured of trade and commerce. I fancy that if it had been possible, she would have preferred a return to the primitive system, of living on the produce of the land, and exchanging the surplus for such articles as were needed, without the intervention of money.

But Mr. Horner was bitten with new-fangled notions, as she would say, though his new-fangled notions were what folk at the present day would think sadly behindhand; and some of Mr. Gray's ideas fell on Mr. Horner's mind like sparks on tow, though they started from two different points. Mr. Horner wanted to make every man useful and active in this world, and to direct as much activity and usefulness as possible to the improvement of the Hanbury estates, and the aggrandisement of the Hanbury family, and therefore he fell into the new cry for education.

Mr. Gray did not care much,—Mr. Horner thought not enough,—for this world, and where any man or family stood in their earthly position; but he would have every one prepared for the world to come, and capable of understanding and receiving certain doctrines, for which latter purpose, it stands to reason, he must have heard of these doctrines; and therefore Mr. Gray wanted education. The answer in the catechism that Mr. Horner was most fond of calling upon a child to repeat, was that to, " What is thy duty towards thy neighbour?" The answer Mr. Gray liked best to hear repeated with unction, was that to the question, " What is the inward and spiritual grace r" The reply to which Lady Ludlow bent her head the lowest, as we said our Catechism to her on Sundays, was to, " What is thy duty towards God ?" But neither Mr. Homer nor Mr. Gray had heard many answers to the Catechism as yet.

Up to this time there was no Sunday-school in Hanbury. Mr. Gray's desires were bounded by that object. Mr. Horner looked farther on : he hoped for a day-school at some future time, to train up intelligent labourers for working on the estate. My lady would hear of neither one nor the other : indeed, not the boldest man whom she ever saw would have dared to name the project of a day-school within her hearing.

So Mr. Horner contented himself with quietly teaching a sharp, clever lad to read and write, with a view to making use of him as a kind of foreman in process of time. He had his pick of the farm-lads for this purpose; and, as the brightest and sharpest, although by far the raggedest and dirtiest, singled out Job Gregson's son. But all this—as my lady never listened to gossip, or indeed, was spoken to unless she spoke first—was quite unknown to her, until the unlucky incident took place which I am going to relate.

## CHAPTER IV.

I THINK my lady was not aware of Mr. Homer's views on education (as making men into more useful members of society) or the practice to which he was putting his precepts in taking Harry Gregson as pupil and protege; if, indeed, she were aware of Harry's distinct existence at all, until the following unfortunate occasion. The anteroom, which was a kind of business-place for my lady to receive her steward and tenants in, was surrounded by shelves. I cannot call them book-shelves, though there were many books on them ; but the contents of the volumes were principally manuscript, and relating to details connected with the Hanbury property. There were also one or two dictionaries, gazetteers, works of reference on the management of property; all of a very old date (the dictionary was Bailey's, I remember; we had a great Johnson in my lady's room, but where lexicographers differed, she generally preferred Bailey).

In this antechamber a footman generally sat, awaiting orders from my lady; for she clung to the grand old customs, and despised any bells, except her own little hand-bell, as modern inventions; she would have her people always within summons of this silvery bell, or her scarce less silvery voice. This man had not the sinecure you might imagine. He had to reply to the private entrance; what we should call the back door in a smaller house. As none came to the front door but my lady, and those of the county whom she honoured by visiting, and her nearest acquaintance of this kind lived eight miles (of bad road) off, the majority of comers knocked at the nail-studded terrace-door ; not to have it opened (for open it stood, by my lady's orders, winter and summer, so that the snoto often drifted into the back-hall, and lay there in heaps when the weather was severe), but to summon some one to receive their message, or carry their request to be allowed to speak to my lady. I remember it was long before Mr. Gray could be made to understand that the great door was only opened on state occasions, and even to the last he would as soon come in by that as the terrace entrance. I had been received there on my first setting foot over my lady's threshold ; every stranger was led in by that way the first time they came; but after that (with the exceptions I have

named) they went round by the terrace, as it were by instinct. It was an assistance to this instinct to be aware that from time immemorial, the magnificent and fierce Hanbury wolf-hounds, which were extinct in every other part of the island, had been and still were kept chained in the front quadrangle, where they bayed through a great part of the day and night, and were always ready with their deep, savage growl at the sight of every person and thing, excepting the man who fed them, my lady's carriage-and-four, and my lady herself. It was pretty to see her small figure go up to the great, crouching brutes, thumping the flags with their heavy, wagging tails, and slobbering in an ecstacy of delight, at her light approach and soft caress. She had no fear of them; but she was a Hanbury born, and the tale went, that they and their kind knew all Hanburys instantly, and acknowledged their supremacy, ever since the ancestors of the breed had been brought from the East by the great Sir Urian Hanbury, who lay with his legs crossed on the altar-tomb in the church. Moreover, it was reported that, not fifty years before, one of these dogs had eaten up a child, which had inadvertently strayed within reach of its chain. So you may imagine how most people preferred the terrace-door. Mr. Gray did not seem to care for the dogs. It might be

absence of inind, for I have heard of his starting away from their sudden spring when he had unwittingly walked within reach of their chains; but it could hardly have been absence of mind, when one day he went right up to one of them, and patted him in the most friendly manner, the dog meanwhile looking pleased, and affably wagging his tail, just as if Mr. Gray had been a Hanbury. We were all very much puzzled by this, and to this day I have not been able to account for it.

But now let us go back to the terrace-door, and the footman sitting in the antechamber.

One morning we heard a parleying which rose to such a vehemence, and lasted for so long, that my lady had to ring her hand-bell twice before the footman heard it.

" What is the matter, John ?" asked she, when he entered.

" A little boy, my lady, who says he comes from Mr. Homer, and must see your ladyship. Impudent little lad!" (this last to himself.)

« What does he want ?"

" That's just what I have asked him, my lady, but he won't tell me, please your ladyship."

" It is, probably, some message from Mr. Homer," said Lady Ludlow, with just a shade of annoyance in

her manner ; for it was against all etiquette to send a message to her, and by such a messenger too !

" No ! please your ladyship, I asked him if he had any message, and he said no, he had none; but he must see your ladyship for all that."

" You had better show him in then, without more words," said her ladyship, quietly, but still, as I have said, rather annoyed,

As if in mockery of the humble visitor, the footman threw open both battants of the door, and in the opening their stood a lithe, wiry lad, with a thick head of hair, standing out in every direction, as if stirred by some electrical current, a short, brown face, red now from affright and excitement, wide, resolute mouth, and bright, deep-set eyes; which glanced keenly and rapidly round the room, as if taking in everything (and all was new and strange) to be thought and puzzled over at some future time. He knew enough of manners not to speak first to one above him in rank, or else he was afraid.

" What do you want with me ?" asked my lady; in so gentle a tone that it seemed to surprise and stun him.

" An't please your ladyship ?" said he, as if he had been deaf.

" You come from Mr. Homer's : why do you want to see me ?" again asked she, a little more loudly.

"An't please your ladyship, Mr. Horner was sent for all on a sudden to Warwick this morning.

His face began to work; but he felt it, and closed his lips into a resolute form.

"Well?"

" And he went off all on a sudden-like."

"Well?"

" And he left a note for your ladyship with me, your ladyship."

"Is that all? You might have given it to the footman."

" Please your ladyship, I've clean gone and lost it."

He never took his eyes off her face. If he had not kept his look fixed, he would have burst out crying.

"That was very careless," said my lady, gently. " But I am sure you are very sorry for it. You had better try and find it. It may have been of consequence."

" Please, Mum—please your ladyship—I can say it off by heart/'

" You! What do you mean ?" I was really afraid now. My lady's blue eyes absolutely gave out light, she was so much displeased, and, moreover, perplexed. The more reason he had for affright, the more his courage rose. He must have seen,—so sharp a lad must have perceived her displeasure, but he went on quickly and steadily.

"Mr. Homer, my lady, has taught me to read, write, and cast accounts, my lady: And he was in a hurry, and he folded his paper up, but he did not seal it; and I read it, my lady; and now, my lady, it seems like as if I had got it off by heart;" and he went on with a high pitched voice, saying out very loud what, I have no doubt, were the identical words of the letter, date, signature and all: it was merely something about a deed, which required my lady's signature.

When he had done, he stood almost as if he expected commendation for his accurate memory.

My lady's eyes contracted till the pupils were as needle-points; it was a way she had when much disturbed. She looked at me, and said,

" Margaret Dawson, what will this world come to ?'* And then she was silent.

The lad, beginning to perceive he had given deep offence, stood stock still—as if his brave will had brought him into this presence, and impelled him to confession, and the best amends he could make, but had now deserted him, or was extinct, and left his body motionless, until some one else with word or deed made him quit the room. My lady looked again at him, and saw the frowning, dumb-foundering terror at his misdeed, and the manner in which his confession had been received.

" My poor lad!" said she, the angry look leaving her face, " into whose hands have you fallen ?"

The boy's lips began to quiver.

" Don't you know what tree we read of in Genesis ? —No ! I hope you have not got to read so easily as that." A pause. " Who has taught you to read and write?"

"Please, my lady, I meant no harm, my lady." He was fairly blubbering, overcome by her evident feeling of dismay and regret, the soft repression of which was more frightening to him than any strong or violent words would have been.

" Who taught you, I ask ?"

"It were Mr. Horner's clerk who learned me, my lady."

" And did Mr, Homer know of it ?"

" Yes, my lady. And I am sure I thought for to please him."

" Well! perhaps you were not to blame for that. But I wonder at Mr. Horner. However, my boy, as you have got possession of edge-tools, you must have some rules how to use them. Did you never hear that you were not to open letters ?"

"Please, my lady, it were open. Mr. Homer forgot for to seal it, in his hurry to be off."

"But you must not read letters that are not intended for you. You must never try to read any letters that are not directed to you, even if they be open before you."

"Please, my lady, I thought it were good for practice, all as one as a book."

My lady looked bewildered as to what way she could farther explain to him the laws of honour as regarded letters.

" You would not listen, I am sure," said she, " to anything you were not intended to hear ?"

He hesitated for a moment, partly because he did not fully comprehend the question. My lady repeated it. The light of intelligence came into his eager eyes, and I could see that he was not certain if he could tell the truth.

"Please, my lady, I always hearken when I hear folk talking secrets; but I mean no harm."

My poor lady sighed: she was not prepared to begin a long way off in morals. Honour was, to her, second nature, and she had never tried to find out on what principle its laws were based. So, telling the lad that she wished to see Mr. Horner when he returned from Warwick, she dismissed him with a despondent look; he, meanwhile, right glad to be out of the awful gentleness of her presence.

" What is to be done ?" said she, half to herself and half to me. I could not answer, for I was puzzled myself.

" It was a right word," she continued, " that I used, when I called reading and writing 'edge-tools.' If our lower orders have these edge-tools given to them, we shall have the terrible scenes of the French Revolution acted over again in England. When I was a girl, one never heard of the rights of men, one only heard of the duties. Now, here was Mr. Gray, only last night, talking of the right every child had to instruction. I could hardly keep my patience with him, and at length we fairly came to words; and I told him I would have no such thing as a Sunday-school (or a Sabbath-school, as he calls it, just like a Jew) in my village."

" And what did he say, my lady ?" I asked ; for the struggle that seemed now to have come to a crisis, had been going on for some time in a quiet way.

" Why, he gave way to temper, and said he was bound to remember he was under the bishop's authority, not under mine; and implied that he should persevere in his designs, notwithstanding my expressed opinion."

" And your ladyship—" I half inquired.

" I could only rise and curtsy, and civilly dismiss him. When two persons have arrived at a certain point of expression on a subject, about which they differ as materially as I do from Mr. Gray, the wisest course, if they wish to remain friends, is to drop the conversation entirely and suddenly. It is one of the few cases where abruptness is desirable."

I was sorry for Mr. Gray. He had been to see me several times, and had helped me to bear my illness in a better spirit than I should have done without his good advice and prayers. And I had gathered, from little things he said, how much his heart was set upon this new scheme. I liked him so much, and I loved and respected my lady so well, that I could not bear them to be on the cool terms to which they were constantly getting. Yet I could do nothing but keep silence.

I suppose my lady understood something of what was passing in my mind; for, after a minute or two, she went on:—

" If Mr. Gray knew all I know,—if he had my experience, he would not be so ready to speak of setting up his new plans in opposition to my judgment. Indeed/' she continued, lashing herself up with her own recollections, " times are changed when the parson of a village comes to beard the liege lady in her own house. Why, in my grandfather's days, the parson was family chaplain too, and dined at the Hall every Sunday. He was helped last; and expected to have done first. I remember seeing him take up his plate and knife and fork, and say, with his mouth full all the time he was speaking : ' If you please, Sir Urian, and my Lady, I'll follow the beef into the housekeeper's room;' for, you see, unless he did so, he stood no chance of a second helping. A greedy man, that parson was, to be sure! I recollect his once eating up the whole of some little bird at dinner, and by way of diverting attention from his greediness, he told how he had heard that a rook soaked in vinegar and then dressed in a particular way, could not be distinguished from the bird he was then eating. I saw by the grim look of my grandfather's face that the parson's doing and saying displeased him ; and, child as I was, I had some notion what was coming, when, as I was riding out on my little, white pony, by my grandfather's side, the next Friday, he stopped one of the gamekeepers, and bade him shoot one of the oldest rooks he could find. I knew no more about it till Sunday, when a dish was set right before the parson, and Sir Urian said: ' Now, Parson Hemming, I have had a rook shot, and soaked in vinegar, and dressed as you described last Sunday. Fall to, man, and eat it with as good an appetite as you had last Sunday. Pick the bones clean, or by , no more Sunday dinners shall you eat at my table ! 7 I gave one look at poor Mr. Hemming's face, as he tried to swallow the first morsel, and make believe as though he thought it very good ; but I could not look again, for shame, although my grandfather laughed, and kept asking us all round if f .we knew what could have become of the parson's appetite."

" And did he finish it?" I asked. " O yes, my dear. What my grandfather said was to be done, was done always. He was a terrible man in his anger! But to think of the difference between Parson Hemming and Mr. Gray! or even of poor, dear Mr. Mountford and Mr. Gray. Mr. Mountford would never have withstood me as Mr. Gray did I"

" And your ladyship really thinks that it would not be right to have a Sunday-school?" I asked, feeling very timid as I put the question.

" Certainly not. As I told Mr. Gray, I consider a knowledge of the Creed, and of the Lord's Prayer, as essential to salvation; and that any child may have, whose parents bring it regularly to church. Then there are the Ten Commandments, which teach simple duties in the plainest language. Of course, if a lad is taught to read and write (as that unfortunate boy has been who was here this morning) his duties become complicated, and his temptations much greater, while, at the same time, he has no hereditary principles and honourable training to serve as safeguards. I might take up my old simile of the race-horse and cart-horse. I am distressed," continued she, with a break in her ideas, " about that boy. The whole thing reminds me so much of a story of what happened to a friend of mine—Clement de Crequy. Did I ever tell you about him?"

" No, your ladyship," I replied.

" Poor Clement! more than twenty years ago, Lord Ludlow and I spent a winter in Paris. He had many friends there; perhaps not very good or very wise men, but he was so kind that he liked every one, and every one liked him. We had an apartment, as they call it there, in the Rue de Lille; we had the first-floor of a grand hotel, with the basement for our servants. On the floor above us the owner of the house lived, a Marquise de Crequy, a widow. They tell me that the Crequy coat-of-arms is still emblazoned, after all these terrible years, on a shield above the arched porte-cochere, just as it was then, though the family is quite extinct. Madam de Crequy had only one son, Clement, who was just the same age as my Urian—you may see his portrait in the great hall—Urian's, I mean." I knew that Master Urian had been drowned at sea; and often had I looked at the presentment of his bonny hopeful face, in his sailor's dress, with right hand outstretched to a ship on the sea in the distance, as if he had just said, " Look at her! all her sails are set, and Fm just off." Poor Master Urian! he went down in this very ship not a year after the picture was taken ! But now I will go back to my lady's story. " I can see those two boys playing now," continued she, softly, shutting her eyes, as if the better to call up the vision, " as they used to do five-and-twenty years ago in those old-fashioned French gardens behind our hotel. Many a time have I watched them from my windows, It was, perhaps, a better play-place than an English garden would have been, for there were but few flower-beds, and no lawn at all to speak about; but instead, terraces and balustrades and vases and flights of stone steps more in the Italian style; and there were jets-d'eau, and little fountains that could be set playing by turning water-cocks that were hidden here and there. How Clement delighted in turning the water on to surprise Urian, and how gracefully he did the honours, as it were, to my dear, rough, sailor lad! Urian was as dark as a gypsy boy, and cared little for his appearance, and resisted all my efforts at setting oif his black eyes and tangled curls; but

Clement, without ever showing that he thought about himself and his dress, was always dainty and elegant, even though his clothes were sometimes but threadbare. He used to be dressed in a kind of hunter's green suit, open at the neck and half-way down the chest to beautiful old lace frills; his long golden curls fell behind just like a girl's, and his hair in front was cut over his straight dark eyebrows in a line almost as straight. Urian learnt more of a gentleman's carefulness and propriety of appearance from that lad in two months than he had done in years from all my lectures. I recollect one day, when the two boys were in full romp—and, my window being open, I could hear them perfectly—and Urian was daring Clement to some scrambling or climbing, which Clement refused to undertake, but in a hesitating way, as though he longed to do it if some reason had not stood in the way; and at times, Urian, who was hasty and thoughtless, poor fellow, told Clement that he was afraid. ' Fear!' said the French boy, drawing himself up; ' you do not know what you say. If you will be here at six tomorrow morning, when it is only just light, I will take that starling's nest on the top of yonder chimney/ ' But why not now, Clement ?' said Urian, putting his arm round Clement's neck. 'Why then, and not now, just when we are in the humour for it ?' ' Be-

cause we De Crequys are poor, and my mother cannot afford me another suit of clothes this year, and yonder stone carving is all jagged, and would tear my coat and breeches. Now, to-morrow morning I could go up with nothing on but an old shirt'

" ' But you would tear your legs ?'

"'My race do not care for pain/ said the boy, drawing himself from Urian's arm, and walking a few steps away, with a becoming pride and reserve; for he was hurt at being spoken to as if he were afraid, and annoyed at having to confess the true reason for declining the feat. But Urian was not to be thus baffled. He went up to Clement, and put his arm once more about his neck, and I could see the two lads as they walked down the terrace away from the hotel windows: first Urian spoke eagerly, looking with imploring fondness into Clement's face, which sought the ground, till at last the French boy spoke, and by-and-by his arm was round Urian too, and they paced backwards and forwards in deep talk, but gravely, as became men, rather than boys.

" All at once, from the little chapel at the corner of the large garden belonging to the Missions Etrangeres, I heard the tinkle of the little bell, announcing the elevation of the host.

Down on his knees went Clement, hands crossed, eyes bent down: while Urian stood looking on in respectful thought.

"What a friendship that might have been! I never dream of Urian without seeing Clement too, —Urian speaks to me, or does something, but Clement only flits round Urian, and never seems to see any one else!

" But I must not forget to tell you, that the next morning, before he was out of his room, a footman of Madam de Crequy's brought Urian the starling's nest.

" Well! we came back to England, and the boys were to correspond; and Madame de Crequy and I exchanged civilities; and Urian went to sea.

"After that, all seemed to drop away. I cannot tell you all However, to confine myself to the De Crequys. I had a letter from Clement; I knew he fet his friend's death deeply ; but I should never have learnt it from the letter he sent. It was formal, and seemed like chaff to my hungering heart. Poor fellow! I dare say he had found it hard to write. What could he—or any one—say to a mother who has lost her child ? The world does not think so, and, in general, one must conform to the customs of the world; but, judging from my own experience, I should say that reverent silence at such times is the tenderest balm.

Madame de Crequy wrote too. But I knew she could not feel my loss so much as Clement, and therefore her letter was not such a disappointmeut. She and I went on being civil and polite in the way of commissions, and occasionally introducing friends to each other, for a year or two, and then we ceased to have any intercourse. Then the terrible revolution came. No one who did not live at those times can imagine the daily expectation of news, the hourly terror of rumours affecting the fortunes and lives of those whom most of us had known as pleasant hosts, receiving us with peaceful welcome in their magnificent houses. Of course, there was sin enough and suffering enough behind the scenes ; but we English visitors to Paris had seen little or nothing of that, and I had sometimes thought, indeed, how even Death seemed loth to choose his victims out of that brilliant throng whom I had known. Madame de Crequy's one boy lived; while three out of my six were gone since we had met! I do not think all lots are equal, even now that I know the end of her hopes; but I do say, that whatever our individual lot is, it is our duty to accept it, without comparing it with that of others.

" The times were thick with gloom and terror. ' What next ?' was the question we asked of every one who brought us news from Paris. Where were these demons hidden when, so few years ago, we danced and feasted, and enjoyed the brilliant salons and the charming friendships of Paris ?

" One evening, I was sitting alone in Saint James' Square; my lord off at the club with Mr. Fox and others: he had left me, thinking that I should go to one of the many places to which I had been invited for that evening; but I had no heart to go anywhere, for it was poor Urian's birthday, and I had not even rung for lights, though the day was fast closing in, but was thinking over all his pretty ways, and on his warm affectionate nature, and how often I had been too hasty in speaking to him, for all I loved him so dearly ; and how I seemed to have neglected and dropped his dear friend Clement, who might even now be in need of help in that cruel, bloody Paris. I say I was thinking reproachfully of all this, and particularly of Clement de Crequy in connection with Urian, when Fenwick brought me a note, sealed with a coat-of-arms I knew well, though I could not remember at the moment where I had seen it. I puzzled over it, as one does sometimes, for a minute or more, before I opened the letter. In a moment 1 saw it was from Clement de Crequy. ' My mother is here,' he said: ' she is very ill, and I am bewildered in this strange country. May I entreat you to receive me for a few minutes ?' The bearer of the note was the woman of the house where they lodged. I had her brought up into the anteroom, and questioned her myself, while my carriage was being brought round. They had arrived in London a fortnight or so before : she had not known their quality, judging them (according to her kind) by their dress and their luggage; poor enough, no doubt. The lady had never left her bedroom since her arrival; the young man waited upon her, did everything for her, never left her, in fact; only she (the messenger) had promised to stay within call, as soon as she returned, while he went out somewhere. She could hardly understand him, he spoke English so badly. He had never spoken it, I dare say, since he had talked to my Urian.

## CHAPTER V.

" IN the hurry of the moment I scarce knew what I did. I bade the housekeeper put up every delicacy she had, in order to tempt the invalid, whom yet I hoped to bring back with me to our house. When the carriage was ready, I took the good woman with me to show us the exact way, which my coachman professed not to know; for, indeed, they were staying at but a poor kind of place at the back of Leicester Square, of which they had heard, as Clement told me afterwards, from one of the fishermen who \'7diad carried them across from the Dutch coast in their disguises as a Friesland peasant and his mother. They had some jewels of value concealed round their persons; but their ready money was all spent before I saw them, and Clement had been unwilling to leave his mother, even for the time necessary to ascertain the best mode of disposing of the diamonds. For, overcome with distress of mind and bodily fatigue, she had reached

London only to take to her bed in a sort of low, nervous fever, in which her chief and only idea seemed to be, that Clement was about to be taken from her to some prison or other; and if he were out of her sight, though but for a minute, she cried like a child, and could not be pacified or comforted. The landlady was a kind, good woman, and though she but half understood the case, she was truly sorry for them, as foreigners, and the mother sick in a strange land.

" I sent her forwards to request permission for my entrance. In a moment I saw Clement— a tall, elegant young man, in a curious dress of coarse cloth, standing at the open door of a room, and evidently— even before he accosted me—striving to soothe the terrors of his mother inside. I went towards him, and would have taken his hand, but he bent down and kissed mine.

" < May I come in, madame ?' I asked, looking at the poor sick lady, lying in the dark, dingy bed, her head propped up on coarse and dirty pillows, and gazing with affrighted eyes at all that was going on.

" ( Clement! Clement! come to me !' she cried ; and when he went to the bedside she turned on one side, and took his hand in both of hers, and began stroking it, and looking up in his face. I could scarce keep back my tears.

" He stood there quite still, except that from time to time he spoke to her in a low tone. At last I advanced into the room, so that I could talk to him, without renewing her alarm. I asked for the doctor's address; for I had heard that they had called in some one, at their landlady's recommendation: hut I could hardly understand Clement's broken English, and mispronunciation of our proper names, and was obliged to apply to the woman herself. I could not say much to Clement, for his attention was perpetually needed by his mother, who never seemed to perceive that I was there. But I told him not to fear, however long I might be away, for that I would return before night; and, bidding the woman take charge of all the heterogeneous things the housekeeper had put up, and leaving one of my men in the house, who could understand a few words of French, with directions that he was to hold himself at Madame de Crequy's orders until I sent or gave him fresh commands, I drove off to the doctor's. What I wanted was his permission to remove Madame de Crequy to my own house, and to learn how it best could be done; for I saw that every movement in the room, every sound, except Clement's voice, brought on a fresh access of trembling and nervous agitation.

"The doctor was, I should think, a clever man; but he had that kind of abrupt manner which people get who have much to do with the lower orders.

" I told him the story of his patient, the interest I had in her, and the wish I entertained of removing her to my own house.

" ' It can't be done said he. Any change will kill her.'

"' But it must be done,' I replied. ' And it shall not kill her.'

"  Then I have nothing more to say said he, turning away from the carriage-door, and making as though he would go back into the house.

" l Stop a moment. You must help me; and, if you do, you shall have reason to be glad, for I will give you fifty pounds down with pleasure. If you won't do it, another shall.'

" He looked at me, then (furtively) at the carriage, hesitated, and then said: ' You do not mind expense, apparently. I suppose you are a rich lady of quality. Such folks will not stick at such trifles as the life or death of a sick woman to get their own way. I suppose, I must e'en help you, for if I don't, another will.'

"I did not mind what he said, so that he would assist me. I was pretty sure that she was in a state to require opiates; and I had not forgotten Christopher Sly, you may be sure, so I told him what I had in my head. That in the dead of night,—the quiet time in the streets,—she should be carried in a hospital litter, softly and warmly covered over, from the Leicester Square lodging-house to rooms that I would have in perfect readiness for her. As I planned, so it was done. I let Clement know, by a note, of my design. I had all prepared at home, and we walked about my house as though shod with velvet, while the porter watched at the open door. At last, through the darkness, I saw the lanterns carried by my men, who were leading the little procession. The litter looked like a hearse; on one side walked the doctor, on the other Clement: they came softly and swiftly along. I could not try any farther experiment; we dared not change her clothes; she was laid in the bed in the landlady's coarse night-gear, and covered over warmly, and left in the shaded, scented room, with a nurse and the doctor watching by her, while I led Clement to the dressing-room adjoining, in which I had had a bed placed for him. Farther than that he would not go; and there I had refreshments brought. Meanwhile, he had shown his gratitude by every possible action (for we none of us dared to speak) : he had kneeled at my feet, and kissed my hand, and left it wet with his tears. He had thrown up his arms to Heaven, and prayed earnestly, as I could see by the movement of his lips. I allowed him to relieve himself by these dumb expressions, if I may so call them, and then I left him, and went to my own rooms to sit up for my lord, and tell him what I had done.

" Of course, it was all right; and neither my lord nor I could sleep for wondering how Madame de Crequy would bear her awakening. I had engaged the doctor, to whose face and voice she was accustomed, to remain with her all night: the nurse was experienced, and Clement was within call. But it was with the greatest relief that I heard from my own woman, when she brought me my chocolate, that Madame de Crequy (Monsieur had said) had awakened more tranquil than she had been for many days. To be sure, the whole aspect of the bed-chamber must have been more familiar to her than the miserable place where I had found her, and she must have intuitively felt herself among friends.

" My lord was scandalized at Clement's dress, which, after the first moment of seeing him,

I had forgotten, in thinking of other things, and for which I had not prepared Lord Ludlow. He sent for his own tailor, and bade him bring patterns of stuffs, and engage his men to work night and day till Clement could appear as became his rank. In short, in a few days so much of the traces of their flight were removed, that we had almost forgotten the terrible causes of it, and rather felt as if they had come on a visit to us than that they had been compelled to fly their country. Their diamonds, too, were sold well by my lord's agents, though the London shops were stocked with jewellery, and such portable valuables, some of rare and curious fashion, which were sold for half their real value by emigrants who could not afford to wait. Madame de Crequy was recovering her health, although her strength was sadly gone, and she would never be equal to such another flight, as the perilous one which she had gone through, and to which she could not bear the slightest reference. For some time things continued in this state ;—the De Crequys still our honoured visitors, —many houses besides our own, even among our own friends, open to receive the poor flying nobility of France, driven from their country by the brutal republicans, and every freshly-arrived emigrant bringing new tales of horror, as if these revolutionists were drunk with blood, and mad to devise new atrocities. One day Clement;—I should tell you he had been presented to our good King George and the sweet Queen, and they had accosted him most graciously, and his beauty and elegance, and some of the circumstances attendant on his flight, made him be received in the world quite like a hero of romance : he might have been on intimate terms in many a distinguished house, had he cared to visit much; but he accompanied my lord and me with an air of indifference and languor, which I sometimes fancied, made him be all the more sought after: Monkshaven (that was the title my eldest son bore) tried in vain to interest him in all young men's sports. But no! it was the same through all. His mother took far more interest in the on-dits of the London world, into which she was far too great an invalid to venture, than he did in the absolute events themselves, in which he might have been an actor. One day, as I was saying, an old Frenchman of a humble class presented himself to our servants, several of whom understood French ; and, through Medlicott, I learnt that he was in some way connected with the De Crequys; not with their Paris-life ; but I fancy he had been intendant of their estates in the country ; estates which were more useful as hunting-grounds than as adding to their income. However, there was the old man ; and with him, wrapped round his person, he had brought the long parchment rolls, and deeds relating to their property. These he would deliver up to none but Monsieur de Crequy, the rightful owner; and Cle'ment was out with Monkshaven, so the old man waited; and when Clement came in, I told him of the steward's arrival, and how he had been cared for by my people. Clement went directly to see him. He was a long time away, and I was waiting for him to drive out with me, for some purpose or another, I scarce know what, but I remember I was tired of waiting, and was just in the act of ringing the bell to desire that he might be reminded of his engagement with me, when he came in, his face as white as the powder in his hair, his beautiful eyes dilated with horror. I saw that he had heard something that touched him even more closely than the usual tales which every fresh emigrant brought.

"«What is it, Clement ?' I asked.

"He clasped his hands,, and looked as though he tried to speak, but could not bring out the words.

" ' They have guillotined my uncle F said he at last. Now, I knew that there was a Count de Crequy; but I had always understood that the elder branch held very little communication with him ; in fact, that he was a vaurien of some kind, and rather a disgrace than otherwise to the family. So, perhaps, I was hard-hearted ; but I was a little surprised at this excess of emotion, till I saw that peculiar look in his eyes that many people have when there is more terror in their hearts than they dare put into words. He wanted me to understand something without his saying it; but how could I ? I had never heard of a Mademoiselle de Crequy.

" * Virginie!' at last he uttered. In an instant I understood it all, and remembered that, if Urian had lived, he too might have been in love.

" 'Your uncle's daughter?' I inquired.

" ' My cousin he replied.

" I did not say, ; your betrothed,' but I had no doubt of it. I was mistaken, however.

" ' O madame !' he continued, ' her mother died long ago—her father now—and she is in daily fear, alone, deserted '

"«Is she in the Abbaye ?' asked I.

"' No! She is in hiding with the widow of her father's old concierge. Any day they may search the house for aristocrats. They are seeking them everywhere. Then, not her life alone, but that of the old woman, her hostess, is sacrificed. The old woman knows this, and trembles with fear. Even if she is brave enough to be faithful, her fears would betray her, should the house be searched. Yet, there is no one to help Virginie to escape. She is alone in Paris.'

" I saw what was in his mind. He was fretting and chafing to go to his cousin's assistance ; but the thought of his mother restrained him. I would not have kept back Urian from such an errand at such a time. How should I restrain him ? And yet, perhaps, I did wrong in not urging the chances of danger more. Still, if it

was danger to him, was it not the same or even greater danger to her ?for the French spared neither age nor sex in those wicked days of terror. So I rather fell in with his wish, and encouraged him to think how best and most prudently it might be fulfilled; never doubting, as I have said, that he and his cousin were troth-plighted.

" But when I went to Madame de Crequy—after he had imparted his, or rather our plan to her—I found out my mistake. She, who was in general too feeble to walk across the room save slowly, and with a stick, was going from end to end with quick, tottering steps ; and, if now and then she sank upon a chair, it seemed as if she could not rest, for she was up again in a moment, pacing along, wringing her hands, and speaking rapidly to herself. When she saw me, she stopped : ' Madame,' she said, 'you have lost your own boy. You might have left me mine.'

"I was so astonished—I hardly knew what to say. I had spoken to Clement as if his mother's consent were secure (as I had felt my own would have been if Urian had been alive to ask it). Of course, both he and I knew that his mother's consent must be asked and obtained, before he could leave her to go on such an undertaking; but, somehow, my blood always rose at the sight or sound of danger; perhaps, because my

life had been so peaceful. Poor Madame de Crequy! it was otherwise with her; she despaired while I hoped, and Clement trusted.

fc<' Dear Madame de Crequy said I, ' he will return safely to us; every precaution shall be taken, that either he or you, or my lord, or Monkshaven can think of; but he cannot leave a girl—his nearest relation save you—his betrothed, is she not ?'

" c His betrothed!' cried she, now at the utmost pitch of her excitement. 'Virginie betrothed to Clement ?—no! thank heaven, not so bad as that! Yet it might have been. But Mademoiselle scorned my son! She would have nothing to do with him. Now is the time for him to have nothing to do with her!'

"Clement had entered at the door behind his mother as she thus spoke. His face was set and pale, till it looked as gray and immovable as if it had been carved in stone. He came forward and stood before his mother. She stopped her walk, threw back her haughty head, and the two looked each other steadily in the face. After a minute or two in this attitude, her proud and resolute gaze never flinching or wavering, he went down upon one knee, and, taking her hand her hard, stony hand, which never closed on his, but remained straight and stiff:

"' Mother,' he pleaded, ' withdraw your 'prohibition. Let me go!'

"'What were her words?' Madame de Crequy replied, slowly, as if forcing her memory to the extreme of accuracy. ' My cousin,' she said, ' when I marry, I marry a man, not a petit-maitre. I marry a man who, whatever his rank may be, will add dignity to the human race by his virtues, and not be content to live in an effeminate court on the traditions of past grandeur.' She borrowed her words from the infamous Jean-Jacques Rousseau, the friend of her scarce less infamous father, nay! I will say it,if not her words, she borrowed her principles. And my son to request her to marry him!'

" * It was my father's written wish,' said Clement.

"' But did you not love her? You plead your father's words,words written twelve years before, and as if that were your reason for being indifferent to my dislike to the alliance. But you requested her to marry you,—and she refused you with insolent contempt; and now you are ready to leave me,leave me desolate in a foreign land—'

"' Desolate! my mother! and the Countess Ludlow stands there!'

"' Pardon, madame! But all the earth, 'though it were full of kind hearts, is but a desolation and a

desert place to a mother when her only child is absent. And you, Clement, would leave me for this Virginie, this degenerate De Cre'quy, tainted with the atheism of the Encyclopedistes! She is only reaping some of the fruit of the harvest whereof her friends have sown the seed. Let her alone! Doubtless she has friends—it may be lovers—among these demons, who, under the cry of liberty, commit every licence. Let her alone, Clement! She refused you with scorn: be too proud to notice her now.'

"' Mother, I cannot think of myself; only of her.' " 'Think of me, then! I, your mother, forbid you to go.'

"Clement bowed low, and went out of the room instantly, as one blinded. She saw his groping movement, and, for an instant, I think her heart was touched. But she turned to me, and tried to exculpate her past violence by dilating upon her wrongs, and they certainly were many. The Count, her husband's younger brother, had invariably tried to make mischief between husband and wife. He had been the cleverer man of the two, and had possessed extraordinary influence over her husband. She suspected him of having instigated that clause in her husband's will, by which the Marquis expressed his wish for the marriage of the cousins. The Count had had some interest in the management of the De Crequy property during her son's minority. Indeed, I remembered then, that it was through Count de Crequy that Lord Ludlow had first heard of the apartment which we afterwards took in the Hotel de Crequy ; and then the recollection of a past feeling came distinctly out of the mist, as it were; and I called to mind how, when we first took up our abode in the Hotel de Crequy, both Lord Ludlow and I imagined that the arrangement was displeasing to our hostess; and how it had taken us a considerable time before we had been able to establish relations of friendship with her. Years after our visit, she began to suspect that Clement (whom she could not forbid to visit at his uncle's house, considering the terms on which his father had been with his brother; though she herself never set foot over the Count de Cre'quy's threshold) was attaching himself to Mademoiselle, his cousin; and she made cautious inquiries as to the appearance, character, and disposition of the young lady. Mademoiselle was not handsome, they said; but of a fine figure, and generally considered as having a very noble and attractive presence. In character she was daring and wilful (said one set); original and independent (said another). She was much indulged by her father, who had given her something of a man's education, and selected for her intimate friend a young lady below her in rank, one of the Bureaucracie, a Mademoiselle Necker, daughter of the Minister of Finance. Mademoiselle de Crequy was thus introduced into all the free-thinking salons of Paris; among people who were always full of plans for subverting society. * And did Clement affect such people ?' Madame de Crequy had asked, with some anxiety. No ! Monsieur de Crequy had neither eyes nor ears, nor thought for anything but his cousin, while she was by. And she ? She hardly took notice of his devotion, so evident to every one else. The proud creature! But perhaps that was her haughty way of concealing what she felt. And so Madame de Crequy listened, and questioned, and learnt nothing decided, until one day she surprised Clement with the note in his hand, of which she remembered the stinging words so well, in which Vir-ginie had said, in reply to a proposal Clement had sent her through her father, that * When she married she married a man, not a petit-maitre.'

" Clement was justly indignant at the insulting nature of the answer Virginie had sent to a proposal, respectful in its tone, and which was, after all, but the cool, hardened lava over a burning heart. He acqui-' esced in his mother's desire, that he should not again present himself in his uncle's salons; but he did not forget Virginie, though he never mentioned her name.

" Madame de Crequy and her son were among the earliest proscrits, as they were of the strongest possible royalists, and aristocrats, as it was the custom of the horrid Sansculottes to term those who adhered to the habits of expression and action in which it was their pride to have been educated. They had left Paris some weeks before they had arrived in England, and Clement's belief at the time of quitting the Hotel de Crequy had certainly been, that his uncle was not merely safe, but rather a popular man with the party in power. And, as all communication having relation to private individuals of a reliable kind was intercepted, Monsieur de Crequy had felt but little anxiety for his uncle and cousin, in comparison with what he did for many other friends of very different opinions in politics, until the day when he was stunned by the fatal information that even his progressive uncle was guillotined, and learnt that his cousin was imprisoned by the licence of the mob, whose rights (as she called them) she was always advocating.

" When I had heard all this story, I confess I lost in sympathy for Clement what I gained for his mother. Virginie's life did not seem to me worth the risk that Clement's would run. But when I saw him—sad, depressed, nay, hopeless—going about like one oppressed by a heavy dream which he cannot shake off; caring neither to eat, drink, nor sleep, yet bearing all with silent dignity, and even trying to force a poor, faint smile when he caught my anxious eyes; I turned round again, and wondered how Madame de Crequy could resist this mute pleading of her son's altered appearance. As for my Lord Ludlow and Monks-haven, as soon as they understood the case, they were indignant that any mother should attempt to keep a son out of honourable danger; and it was honourable, and a clear duty (according to them) to try to save the life of a helpless orphan girl, his next of kin. None but a Frenchman, said my lord, would hold himself bound by an old woman's whimsies and fears, even though she were his mother. As it was, he was chafing himself to death under the restraint. If he went, to be sure, the wretches might make an end of him, as they had done of many a fine fellow; but my lord would take heavy odds that, instead of being guillotined, he would save the girl, and bring her safe to England, just desperately in love with her preserver, and then we would have a jolly wedding down at Monkshaven. My lord repeated his opinion so often, that it became a certain prophecy in his mind of what was to take place; and, one day seeing VOL. I.

Clement look even paler and thinner than he had ever done before, he sent a message to Madame de Crequy, requesting permission to speak to her in private.

"' For, by George!' said he, ' she shall hear my opinion, and not let that lad of hers kill himself by fretting. He's too good for that. If he had been an English lad, he would have been off to his sweetheart long before this, without saying with your leave or by your leave; but being a Frenchman, he is all for ^Eneas and filial piety,—filial fiddle-sticks!' (My lord had run away to sea, when a boy, against his father's consent, I am sorry to say; and, as all had ended well, and he had come back to find both his parents alive, I do not think he was ever as much aware of his fault as he might have been under other circumstances.) ' No, my lady/ he went on, < don't come with me. A woman can manage a man best when he has a fit of obstinacy, and a man can persuade a woman out of her tantrums, when all her own sex, the whole army of them, would fail. Allow me to go alone to my tete-a-tete with madame.'

" What he said, what passed, he never could repeat; but he came back graver than he went. However, the point was gained; Madame de Crequy withdrew her prohibition, and had given him leave to tell Clement as much.

"' But she is an old Cassandra/ said he. ( Don't let the lad be much with her; her talk would destroy the courage of the bravest man; she is so given over to superstition.' Something that she had said had touched a chord in my lord's nature which he inherited from his Scotch ancestors. Long afterwards, I heard what this was. Medlicott told me.

" However, my lord shook off all fancies that told against the fulfilment of Clement's wishes. All that afternoon we three sat together, planning; and Monkshaven passed in and out, executing our commissions, and preparing everything. Towards nightfall all was ready for Clement's start on his journey towards the coast

" Madame had declined seeing any of us since my lord's stormy interview with her. She sent word that she was fatigued, and desired repose. But, of course, before Clement set off, he was bound to wish her farewell, and to ask for her blessing. In order to avoid an agitating conversation between mother and son, my lord and I resolved to be present at the interview. Clement was already in his travelling-dress, that of a Norman fisherman, which Monkshaven had, with infinite trouble, discovered in the possession of one of the emigres who thronged London, and who had made his escape from the shores of France in this disguise. Clement's plan was, to go down to the Coast of Sussex, and get some of the fishing or smuggling boats to take him across to the French Coast near Dieppe. There again he would have to change his dress. O, it was so well planned! His mother was startled by his disguise (of which we had not thought to forewarn her) as he entered her apartment. And either that, or the being suddenly roused from the heavy slumber into which she was apt to fall when she was left alone, gave her manner an air of wildness that was almost like insanity.

"' Go, go !' she said to him, almost pushing him away as he knelt to kiss her hand. ' Virginie is beckoning to you, but you don't see what kind of a bed it is '

"( Clement, make haste !' said my lord, in a hurried manner, as if to interrupt madame. 'The time is later than I thought, and you must not miss the morning's tide. Bid your mother good-bye at once, and let us be off.' For my lord and Monkshaven were to ride with him to an inn near the shore, from whence he was to walk to his destination. My lord almost took him by the arm to pull him away; and they were gone, and I was left alone with Madame de Crequy. When she heard the horses' feet, she seemed to find out the truth, as if for the first time. She set her teeth together. * He has left me for her !' she almost screamed. 'Left me for her!' she kept muttering; and then, as the wild look came back into her eyes, she said, almost with exultation, ' But I did not give him my blessing 1" :

## CHAPTER VI.

" ALL night Madame de Crequy raved in delirium. If I could, I would have sent for Clement back again. I did send off one man, but I suppose my directions were confused, or they were wrong, for he came back after my lord's return, on the following afternoon. By this time Madame de Crequy was quieter: she was, indeed, asleep from exhaustion when Lord Ludlow and Monkshaven came in. They were in high spirits, and their hopefulness brought me round to a less dispirited state. All had gone, well: they had accompanied Clement on foot along the shore, until they had met with a lugger, which my lord had hailed in good nautical language. The captain had responded to these freemason terms by sending a boat to pick up his passenger, and by an invitation to breakfast sent through a speaking-trumpet. Monkshaven did not approve of either the meal or the company, and had returned to the inn, but my lord had gone with Clement, and breakfasted on board, upon grog, biscuit, fresh-caught fish—' the best breakfast he ever ate/ he said, but that was probably owing to the appetite his night's ride had given him. However, his good fellowship had evidently won the captain's heart, and Clement had set sail under the best auspices. It was agreed that I should tell all this to Madame de Crequy, if she inquired ; otherwise, it would be wiser not to renew her agitation by alluding to her son's journey.

"I sat with her constantly for many days; but she never spoke of Clement. She forced herself to talk of the little occurrences of Parisian society in former days : she tried to be conversational and agreeable, and to betray no anxiety or even interest in the object of Clement's journey; and, as far as unremitting efforts could go, she succeeded. But the tones of her voice were sharp and yet piteous, as if she were in constant pain ; and the glance of her eye hurried and fearful, as if she dared not let it rest on any object.

" In a week we heard of Clement's safe arrival on the French coast. He sent a letter to this effect by the captain of the smuggler, when the latter returned. We hoped to hear again; but week after week elapsed, and there was no news of Clement. I had told Lord Ludlow, in Madame de Crequy's presence, as he and I had arranged, of the note I had received from her son, informing us of his landing in France. She heard, but she took no notice. Yet now, evidently, she began to wonder that we did not mention any further intelligence of him in the same manner before her; and daily I began to fear that her pride would give way, and that she would supplicate for news before I had any to give her.

"One morning, on my awakening, my maid told me that Madame de Crequy had passed a wretched night, and had bidden Medlicott (whom, as understanding French, and speaking it pretty well, though with that horrid German accent, I had put about her) request that I would go to madame's room as soon as I was dressed.

" I knew what was coming, and I trembled all the time they were doing my hair, and otherwise arranging me. I was not encouraged by my lord's speeches. He had heard the message, and kept declaring that he would rather be shot than have to tell her that there was no news of her son ; and yet he said, every now and then, when I was at the lowest pitch of uneasiness, that he never expected to hear again : that some day soon we should see him walking in, and introducing Mademoiselle de Crequy to us.

" However, at last 1 was ready, and go I must.

" Her eyes were fixed on the door by which I entered. I went up to the bedside. She was not rouged,

—she had left it off now for several days,—she no longer attempted to keep up the vain show of not feeling, and loving, and fearing.

" For a moment or two she did not speak, and I was glad of the respite.

" ' Clement ?' she said at length, covering her mouth with a handkerchief the minute she had spoken, that I might not see it quiver.

" * There has been no news since the first letter, saying how well the voyage was performed, and how safely he had landed,—near Dieppe, you know,' I replied as cheerfully as possible. ' My lord does not expect that we shall have another letter; he thinks that we shall see him soon.'

" There was no answer. As I looked, uncertain whether to do or say more, she slowly turned herself in bed, and lay with her face to the wall; and, as if that did not shut out the light of day and the busy, happy world enough, she put out her trembling hands, and covered her face with her handkerchief. There was no violence : hardly any sound.

" I told her what my lord had said about Clement's coming in some day, and taking us all by surprise. I did not believe it myself, but it was just possible,—and I had nothing else to say. Pity, to one who was striving so hard to conceal her feelings, would have

been impertinent. She let me talk; but she did not reply. She knew that my words were vain and idle, and had no root in my belief, as well as I did myself.

" I was very thankful when Medlicott came in with Madame's breakfast, and gave me an excuse for leaving.

" But I think that conversation made me feel more anxious and impatient than ever. I felt almost pledged to Madame de Crequy for the fulfilment of the vision I had held out. She had taken entirely to her bed by this time; not from illness, but because she had no hope within her to stir her up to the effort of dressing. In the same way she hardly cared for food. She had no appetite,—why eat to prolong a life of despair ? But she let Medlicott feed her, sooner than take the trouble of resisting.

" And so it went on,—for weeks, months,—I could hardly count the time, it seemed so long. Medlicott told me she noticed a preternatural sensitiveness of ear in Madame de Crequy, induced by the habit of listening silently for the slightest unusual sound in the house. Medlicott was always a minute watcher of any one whom she cared about; and, one day, she made me notice by a sign madame's acuteness of hearing, although the quick expectation was but evinced for a moment in the turn of the eye, the hushed breath—and

then, when the unusual footstep turned into my lord's apartments, the soft quivering sigh, and the closed eyelids.

" At length the intendant of the De Crequy estates,—the old man, you will remember, whose information respecting Virginie de Crequy first gave Clement the desire to return to Paris,—came to St. James's Square, and begged to speak to me. I made haste to go down to him in the housekeeper's room, sooner than that he should be ushered into mine, for fear of madame hearing any sound.

" The old man stood—I see him now—with his hat held before him in both his hands; he slowly bowed till his face touched it when I came in. Such long excess of courtesy augured ill. He waited for me to speak

" ' Have you any intelligence ?' I inquired. He had been often to the house before, to ask if we had received any news ; and once or twice I had seen him, but this was the first time he had begged to see me.

" ' Yes, madame,' he replied, still standing with his head bent down, like a child in disgrace.

" ' And it is bad!' I exclaimed.

"' It is bad.' For a moment I was angry at the cold tone in which my words were echoed; but directly afterwards I saw the large, slow, heavy tears of

age falling down the old man's cheeks, and on to the sleeves of his poor, thread-bare coat.

" I asked him how he had heard it: it seemed as though I could not all at once bear to hear what it was. He told me that the night before, in crossing Long Acre, he had stumbled upon an old acquaintance of his; one who, like himself, had been a dependant upon the De Crequy family, but had managed their Paris affairs, while FUchier had taken charge of their estates in the country. Both were now emigrants, and living on the proceeds of such small available talents as they possessed. Flechier, as I knew, earned a very fair livelihood by going about to dress salads for dinner parties. His compatriot, Le Febvre, had begun to give a few lessons as a dancing-master. One of them took the other home to his lodgings; and there, when their most immediate personal adventures had been hastily talked over, came the inquiry from Flechier as to Monsieur de Crequy.

"'Clement was dead—guillotined. Virginie was dead—guillotined.'

" When Flechier had told me thus much, he could not speak for sobbing; and I, myself, could hardly tell how to restrain my tears sufficiently, until I could go to my own room and be at liberty to give way. He asked my leave to bring in his friend Le Febvre, who

was walking in the square, awaiting a possible summons to tell his story. I heard afterwards a good many details, which filled up the account, and made me feel —which brings me back to the point I started from— how unfit the lower orders are for being trusted indiscriminately with the dangerous powers of education. I have made a long preamble, but now I am coming to the moral of my story."

My lady was trying to shake off the emotion which she evidently felt in recurring to this sad history of Monsieur de Crequy's death. She came behind me, and arranged my pillows, and then, seeing I had been crying—for, indeed, I was weak-spirited at the time, and a little served to unloose my tears—she stooped down, and kissed my forehead, and said " Poor child !" almost as if she thanked me for feeling that old grief of hers.

" Being once in France, it was no difficult thing for Clement to get into Paris. The difficulty in those days was to leave, not to enter. He came in dressed as a Norman peasant, in charge of a load of fruit and vegetables, with which one of the Seine barges was freighted. He worked hard with his companions in landing and arranging their produce on the quays; and then, when they dispersed to get their breakfasts at some of the estaminets near the old

MY LADY LUDLOW.

Marche aux Fleurs, he sauntered up a street which conducted him, by many an odd turn, through the Quartier Latin to a horrid back alley, leading out of the Rue l'Ecole de Medecine ; some atrocious place, as I have heard, not far from the shadow of that terrible Abbaye, where so many of the best blood of France awaited their deaths. But here some old man lived on whose fidelity Clement thought that he might rely. I am not sure if he had not been gardener in those very gardens behind the Hotel Crequy where Clement and Urian used to play together years before. But, whatever the old man's dwelling might be, Clement was only too glad to reach it, you may be sure. He had been kept in Normandy, in all sorts of disguises, for many days after landing in Dieppe, through the difficulty of entering Paris unsuspected by the many ruffians who were always on the look-out for aristocrats.

"The old gardener was, I believe, both faithful and tried, and sheltered Clement in his garret as well as might be. Before he could stir out, it was necessary to procure a fresh disguise; and one more in character with an inhabitant of Paris than that of a Norman carter was procured; and, after waiting in-doors for one or two days, to see if any suspicion was excited, Clement set off to discover Virginie.

"He found her at the old concierge's dwelling.

Madame Babette was the name of this woman, who must have been a less faithful—or rather, perhaps I should say, a more interested—friend to her guest than the old gardener Jacques was to Clement.

" I have seen a miniature of Virginie, which a French lady of quality happened to have in her possession at the time of her flight from Paris, and which she brought with her to England unwittingly ; for it belonged to the Count de Crequy, with whom she was slightly acquainted. I should fancy from it, that Virginie was taller and of a more powerful figure for a woman than her cousin Clement was for a man. Her dark-brown hair was arranged in short curls—the way of dressing the hair announced the politics of the individual, in those days, just as patches did in my grandmother's time; and Virginie's hair was not to my taste, or according to my principles ; it was too classical. Her large, black eyes looked out at you steadily. One cannot judge of the shape of a nose from a full-face miniature, but the nostrils were clearly cut and largely opened. I do not fancy her nose could have been pretty; but her mouth had a character all its own, and which would, I think, have redeemed a plainer face. It was wide and deep set into the cheeks at the corners; the upper lip was very much arched, and hardly closed over the teeth; so that' the whole face

looked (from the serious, intent look in the eyes, and the sweet intelligence of the month) as if she were listening eagerly to something to which her answer was quite ready, and would come out of those red, opening lips as soon as ever you had done speaking, and you longed to know what she would say.

" Well; this Virginie de Crequy was living with Madame Babette in the conciergerie of an old French inn, somewhere to the north of Paris, so, far enough from Clement's refuge. The inn had been frequented by farmers from Brittany and such kind of people, in the days when that sort of intercourse went on between Paris and the provinces which had nearly stopped now. Few Bretons came near it now, and the inn had fallen into the hands of Madame Babette's brother, as payment for a bad wine debt of the last proprietor. He put his sister and her child in, to keep it open, as it were, and sent all the people he could to occupy the half-furnished rooms of the house. They paid Babette for their lodging every morning as they went out to breakfast, and returned or not as they chose, at night. Every three days, the wine-merchant or his son came to Madame Babette, and she accounted to them for the money she had received. She and her child occupied the porter's office (in which the lad slept at nights) and a lit'tle, miserable bed-room which opened

out of it, and received all the light and air that was admitted through the door of communication, which was half glass. Madame Babette must have had a kind of attachment for the De Crequys—her De Crequys, you understand—Virginie's father, the Count; for, at some risk to herself, she had warned both him and his daughter of the danger impending over them. But he, infatuated, would not believe, that his dear Human Race could ever do him harm; and, as long as he did not fear, Virginie was not afraid. It was by some ruse, the nature of which I never heard, that Madame Babette induced Virginie to come to her abode at the very hour in which the Count had been recognised in the streets, and hurried off to the Lanterne. It was after Babette had got her there, safe shut up in the little back den, that she told her what had befallen her father. From that day, Virginie had never stirred out of the gates, or crossed the threshold of the porter's lodge. I do not say that Madame Babette was tired of her continual presence, or regretted the impulse which had made her rush to the De Crequy's well-known house—after being compelled to form one of the mad crowds that saw the Count de Crequy seized and hung—and hurry his daughter out, through alleys and back-ways, until at length she had the orphan safe in her own dark sleeping-room, and could tell her tale of

horror: but Madame Babette was poorly paid for her porter's work by her avaricious brother; and it was hard enough to find food for herself and her growing boy; and, though the poor girl ate little enough, I dare say, yet there seemed no end to the burthen that Madame Babette had imposed upon herself: the De Crequys were plundered, ruined, had become an extinct race, all but a lonely, friendless girl, in broken health and spirits; and, though she lent no positive encouragement to his suit, yet, at the time, when Clement reappeared in Paris, Madame Babette was beginning to think that Virginie might do worse than encourage the attentions of Monsieur Morin Fils, her nephew, and the wine-merchant's son. Of course, he and his father had the entree into the conciergerie of the hotel that belonged to them, in right of being both proprietors and relations. The son, Morin, had seen Virginie in this manner. He was fully aware that she was far above him in rank, and guessed from her whole aspect that she had lost her natural protectors by the terrible guillotine ; but he did not know her exact name or station, nor could he persuade his aunt to tell him. However, he fell head over ears in love with her, whether she were princess or peasant; and, though at first there was something about her which made his passionate love conceal itself with shy, awkward

reserve, and then, made it only appear in the guise of deep, respectful devotion; yet, by-and-by,—by the same process of reasoning I suppose that his aunt had gone through even before him—Jean Morin began to let Hope oust Despair from his heart. Sometimes he thought—perhaps years hence—that solitary, friendless lady, pent up in squalor, might turn to him as to a

friend and comforter — and then—and then .

Meanwhile Jean Morin was most attentive to his aunt; whom he had rather slighted before. He would linger over the accounts; would bring her little presents; and, above all, he made a pet and favourite of Pierre, the little cousin who could tell him about all the ways of going on of Mam'selle Cannes, as Virginie was called. Pierre was thoroughly aware of the drift and cause of his cousin's inquiries; and was his ardent partisan, as I have heard, even before Jean Morin had exactly acknowledged his wishes to himself.

"It must have required some patience and much diplomacy, before Clement de Crequy found out the exact place where his cousin was hidden. The old gardener took the cause very much to heart; as, judging from my recollections, I imagine he would have forwarded any fancy, however wild, of Monsieur Clement's. (I will tell you afterwards how I came to know all these particulars so well)

" After Clement's return, on two succeeding days, from his dangerous search, without meeting with any good result, Jacques entreated Monsieur de Crequy to let him take it in hand. He represented that he, as gardener for the space of twenty years and more at the Hotel de Crequy, had a right to be acquainted with all the successive concierges at the Count's house ; that he should not go among them as a stranger, but as an old friend, anxious to renew pleasant intercourse; and that if the Intendant's story, which he^had told Monsieur de Crequy in England, was true, that Mademoiselle was in hiding at the house of a former concierge, why, something relating to her would surely drop out in the course of conversation. So he persuaded Clement to remain in-doors, while he set off on his round, with no apparent object but to gossip.

" At night he came home,—having seen Mademoiselle. He told Clement much of the story relating to Madame Babette that I have told to you. Of course, he had heard nothing of the ambitious hopes of Morin Fils,—hardly of his existence, I should think. "Madame Babette had received him kindly; although, for some time, she had kept him standing in the carriage gateway outside her door. But, on his complaining of the draught and his rheumatism, she had asked him in: first looking round with some anxiety, to see who was

in the room behind her. No one was there when he entered and sat down. But, in a minute or two, a tall, thin young lady, with great, sad eyes, and pale cheeks, came from the inner room, and, seeing him, retired. 'It is Mademoiselle Cannes,' said Madame Babette, rather unnecessarily; for, if he had not been on the watch for some sign of Mademoiselle de Crequy, he would hardly have noticed the entrance and withdrawal.

" Clement and the good old gardener were always rather perplexed by Madame Babette's evident avoidance of all mention of the De Crequy family. If she were so much interested in one member as to be willing to undergo the pains and penalties of a domiciliary visit, it was strange that she never inquired after the existence of her charge's friends and relations from one who might very probably have heard something of them. They settled that Madame Babette must believe that the Marquise and Clement were dead; and admired her for her reticence in never speaking of Virginie. The truth was, I suspect, that she was so desirous of her nephew's success by this time, that she did not like letting any one into the secret of Virginie's whereabouts who might interfere with their plan. However, it was arranged between Clement and his humble friend, th t the former, dressed in the peasant's clothes

in which he had entered Paris, but smartened up in one or two particulars, as if, although a countryman, he had money to spare, should go and engage a sleeping-room in the old Breton Inn; where, as I told you, accommodation for the night was to be had. This was accordingly done, without exciting Madame Babette's suspicions, for she was unacquainted with the Normandy accent, and consequently did not perceive the exaggeration of it which Monsieur de Crequy adopted in order to disguise his pure Parisian. But after he had for two nights slept in a queer, dark closet, at the end of one of the numerous short galleries in the Hotel Duguesclin, and paid his money for such accommodation each morning at the little bureau under the window of the conciergerie, he found himself no nearer to his object. He stood outside in the gateway: Madame Babette opened a pane in her window, counted out the change, gave polite thanks, and shut to the pane with a clack, before he could ever find out what to say that might be the means of opening a conversation. Once in the streets, he was in danger from the bloodthirsty mob, who-were ready in those days to hunt to death every one who looked like a gentleman, as an aristocrat: and Clement, depend upon it, looked a gentleman, whatever dress he wore. Yet it was unwise to traverse Paris to his old friend the gardener's grenier, so he

had to loiter about, where I hardly know. Only he did leave the Hotel Duguesclin, and he did not go to old Jacques, and there was not another house in Paris open to him. At the end of two days, he had made out Pierre's existence; and he began to try to make friends with the lad. Pierre was too sharp and shrewd not to suspect something from the confused attempts at friendliness. It was not for nothing that the Norman farmer lounged in the court and doorway, and brought home presents of galette. Pierre accepted the galette, reciprocated the civil speeches, but kept his eyes open. Once, returning home pretty late at night, he surprised the Norman studying the shadows on the blind, which was drawn down when Madame Babette's lamp was lighted. On going in, he found Mademoiselle Cannes with his mother, sitting by the table, and helping in the family mending.

" Pierre was afraid that the Norman had some view upon the money which his mother, as concierge, collected for her brother. But the money was all safe next evening when his cousin, Monsieur Morin Fils, came to collect it. Madame Babette asked her nephew to sit down, and skilfully barred the passage to the inner door, so that Virginie, had she been ever so much disposed, could not have retreated. She sat silently sewing. All at once the little party were startled by

a very sweet tenor voice, just close to the street window, singing one of the airs out of Beaumarchais* operas, which, a few years before, had been popular all over Paris. But after a few moments of silence, and one or two remarks, the talking went on again. Pierre, however, noticed an increased air of abstraction in Virginie, who, I suppose, was recurring to the last time that she had heard the song, and did not consider, as her cousin had hoped she would have done, what were the words set to the air, which he imagined she would remember, and which would have told her so much. For, only a few years before, Adam's opera of Richard le Roi had made the story of the Minstrel Blondel and our English Coeur de Lion familiar to all the opera-going part of the Parisian public, and Clement had bethought him of establishing a communication with Virginie by some such means.

" The next night, about the same hour, the same voice was singing outside the window again. Pierre, who had been irritated by the proceeding the evening before, as it had diverted Virginie's attention from his cousin, who had been doing his utmost to make himself agreeable, rushed out to the door, just as the Norman was ringing the bell to be admitted for the night. Pierre looked up and down the street; no one else was to be seen. The next day, the Norman mollified

him somewhat by knocking at the door of the con-ciergerie, and begging Monsieur Pierre's acceptance of some knee-buckles, which had taken the country farmer's fancy the day before, as he had been gazing into the shops, but which, being too small for his purpose, he took the liberty of offering to Monsieur Pierre. Pierre, a French boy, inclined to foppery, was charmed, ravished by the beauty of the present arid with monsieur's goodness, and he began to adjust them to his breeches immediately, as well as he could, at least, in his mother's absence. The Norman, whom Pierre kept carefully on the outside of the threshold, stood by, as if amused at the boy's eagerness.

" ' Take care,' said he, clearly and distinctly; * take care, my little friend, lest you become a fop; and, in that case, some day, years hence, when your heart is devoted to some young lady, she may be inclined to say to you'—here he raised his voice—' No, thank you; when I marry, I marry a man, not a petit-mattre; I marry a man, who, whatever his position may be, will add dignity to the human race by his virtues.' Farther than that in his quotation Clement dared not go. His sentiments (so much above the apparent occasion) met with applause from Pierre, who liked to contemplate himself in the light of a lover, even though it should be a rejected one, and who hailed the mention of the words 'virtues' and 'dignity of the human race' as belonging to the cant of a good citizen.

" But Clement was more anxious to know how the invisible lady took his speech. There was no sign at the time. But when he returned at night, he heard a voice, low singing, behind Madame Babette, as she handed him his candle, the very air he had sung without effect for two nights past. As if he had caught it up from her murmuring voice, he sang it loudly and clearly as he crossed the court.

"'Here is our opera-singer!' exclaimed Madame Babette. 'Why, the Norman grazier sings like Boupre,' naming a favourite singer at the neighbouring theatre.

" Pierre was struck by the remark, and quietly resolved to look after the Norman; but again, I believe, it was more because of his mother's deposit of money than with any thought of Virginie.

" However, the next morning, to the wonder of both mother and son, Mademoiselle Cannes proposed, with much hesitation, to go out and make some little purchase for herself. A month or two ago, this was what Madame Babette had been never weary of urging. But now she was as much surprised as if she had expected Virginie to remain a prisoner in her rooms all the rest of her life. I suppose she had hoped that her first time of quitting it would be when she left it for Monsieur's Morin's house as his wife.

" A quick look from Madame Babette towards Pierre was all that was needed to encourage the boy to follow her. He went out cautiously. She was at the end of the street. She looked up and down, as if waiting for some one. No one was there. Back she came, so swiftly that she nearly caught Pierre before he could retreat through the porte-cochere. There he looked out again. The neighbourhood was low and wild, and strange; and some one spoke to Virginie,—nay, laid his hand upon her arm,—whose dress and aspect (he had emerged out of a side-street) Pierre did not know ; but, after a start, and (Pierre could fancy) a little scream, Virginie recognised the stranger, and the two turned up the side street whence the man had come. Pierre stole swiftly to the corner of this street; no one was there : they had disappeared up some of the alleys. Pierre returned home to excite his mother's infinite surprise. But they had hardly done talking, when Virginie returned, with a colour and a radiance in her face, which they had never seen there since her father's death.

## CHAPTER VII.

" I HAVE told you that I heard much of this story from a friend of the Intendant of the De Cre'quys, whom he met with in London. Some years afterwards—the summer before my lord's death—I was travelling with him in Devonshire, and we went to see the French prisoners of war on Dartmoor. We fell into conversation with one of them, whom I found out to be the very Pierre of whom I had heard before, as having been involved in the fatal story of Clement and Virginie, and by him I was told much of their last days, and thus I learnt how to have some sympathy with all those who were concerned in those terrible events; yes, even with the younger Morin himself, on whose behalf Pierre spoke warmly, even after so long a time had elapsed.

" For when the younger Morin called at the porter's lodge, on the evening of the day when Virginie had gone out for the first time after so many months' confinement to the conciergerie, he was struck with the improvement in her appearance. It seems to have hardly been that he thought her beauty greater; for, in addition to the fact that she was not beautiful, Morin had arrived at that point of being enamoured when it does not signify whether the beloved one is plain or handsome —she has enchanted one pair of eyes, which henceforward see her through their own medium. But Morin noticed the faint increase of colour and light in her countenance. It was as though she had broken through her thick cloud of hopeless sorrow, and was dawning forth into a happier life. And so, whereas during her grief, he had revered and respected it even to a point of silent sympathy, now that she was gladdened, his heart rose on the wings of strengthened hopes. Even in the dreary monotony of this existence in his Aunt Babette's conciergerie, Time had not failed in his work, and now, perhaps, soon he might humbly strive to help Time. The very next day he returned—on some pretence of business—to the Hotel Duguesclin, and made his aunt's room, rather than his aunt herself, a present of roses and geraniums tied up in a bouquet with a tricolor ribbon. Virginie was in the room, sitting at the coarse sewing she liked to do for Madame Babette. He saw her eyes brighten at the sight of the flowers : she asked his aunt to let her arrange them ; he saw her untie the ribbon, and with a gesture of dislike,

throw it on the ground, and give it a kick with her little foot, and even in this girlish manner of insulting his dearest prejudices, he found something to admire.

" As he was coming out, Pierre stopped him. The lad had been trying to arrest his cousin's attention by futile grimaces and signs played off behind Virginie's back ; but Monsieur Morin saw nothing but Mademoiselle Cannes. However, Pierre was not to be baffled, and Monsieur Morin found him in waiting just outside the threshold. With his finger on his lips, Pierre walked on tiptoe by his companion's side till they would have been long past sight or hearing of the conciergerie, even had the inhabitants devoted themselves to the purposes of spying or listening.

" * Chut!' said Pierre, at last. c She goes out walking.'

"' Well ?' said Monsieur Morin, half curious, half annoyed at being disturbed in the delicious reverie of the future into which he longed to fall.

" * Well! It is not well. It is bad.'

" ' Why ? I do not ask who she is, but I have my ideas. She is an aristocrat. Do the people about here begin to suspect her ?'

" < No, no !' said Pierre. * But she goes out walking. She has gone these two mornings. I have watched her. She meets a man—she is friends with him, for

she talks to him as eagerly as he does to her—mamma cannot tell who he is.'

" ' Has my aunt seen him ?'

"' No, not so much as a fly's wing of him. I myself have only seen his back. It strikes me like a familiar back, and yet I cannot think who it is. But they separate with sudden darts, like two birds who have been together to feed their young ones. One moment they are in close talk, their heads together chuckotting the next he has turned up some bye-street, and Mademoiselle Cannes is close upon me—has almost caught me.'

"'But she did not see you?' inquired Monsieur Morin, in so altered a voice that Pierre gave him one of his quick penetrating looks. He was struck by the way in which his cousin's features—always coarse and common-place—had become contracted and pinched; struck, too, by the livid look on his sallow complexion. But as if Morin was conscious of the manner in which his face belied his feelings, he made an effort, and smiled, and patted Pierre's head, and thanked him fo r his intelligence, and gave him a five-franc piece, and bade him go on with his observations of Mademoiselle Cannes' movements, and report all to him.

" Pierre returned home with a light heart, tossing up his five-franc piece as he ran. Just as he was a

the conciergerie door, a great tall man bustled past him, and snatched his money away from him, looking hack with a laugh, which added insult to injury. Pierre had no redress; no one had witnessed the impudent theft, and if they had, no one to be seen in the street was strong enough to give him redress. Besides, Pierre had seen enough of the state of the streets of Paris at that time to know that friends, not enemies, were required, and the man had a bad air about him. But all these considerations did not keep Pierre from bursting out into a fit of crying when he was once more under his mother's roof; and Virginie, who was alone there (Madame Babette having gone out to make her daily purchases), might have imagined him pommeled to death by the loudness of his sobs.

"' What is the matter ?' asked she. ' Speak, my child. What hast thou done ?'

"' He has robbed me ! he has robbed me !' was all Pierre could gulp out.

"' Eobbed thee! and of what, my poor boy ?' said Virginie, stroking his hair gently.

"' Of my five-franc piece—of a five-franc piece,' said Pierre, correcting himself, and leaving out the word my, half fearful lest Virginie should inquire how he became possessed of such a sum, and for what services it had been given him. But, of course, no such idea came into her head, for it would have been impertinent, and she was gentle-born.

"' Wait a moment, my lad,' and, going to the one small drawer in the inner apartment, which held all her few possessions, she brought back a little ring—a ring just with one ruby in it—which she had worn in the days when she cared to wear jewels. ' Take this,' said she, ' and run with it to a jeweller's. It is but a poor, valueless thing, but it will bring you in your five francs at any rate. Go ! I desire you.'

"' But I cannot,' said the boy, hesitating; some dim sense of honour flitting through his misty morals.

"' Yes ; you must!' she continued, urging him with her hand to the door. ' Run ! if it brings in more than five francs, you shall return the surplus to me.'

"Thus tempted by her urgency, and, I suppose, reasoning with himself to the effect that he might as well have the money, and then see whether he thought it right to act as a spy upon her or not—the one action did not pledge him to the other, nor yet did she make any conditions with her gift—Pierre went off with her ring; and, after repaying himself his five francs, he was enabled to bring Virginie back two more, so well had he managed his affairs. But, although the whole transaction did not leave him bound, in any way, to discover or forward Virginie's

II 3

wishes, it did leave him pledged, according to his code, to act according to her advantage, and he considered himself the judge of the best course to he pursued to this end. And, moreover, this little kindness attached him to her personally. He began to think how pleasant it would be to have so kind and generous a person for a relation; how easily his troubles might be borne if he had always such a ready helper at hand; how much he should like to make her like him, and come to him for the protection of his masculine power! First of all his duties, as her self-appointed squire, came the necessity of finding out who her strange new acquaintance was. Thus, you see, he arrived at the same end, via supposed duty, that he was previously pledged to via interest. I fancy a good number of us, when any line of action will promote our own interest, can make ourselves believe that reasons exist which compel us to it as a duty.

" In the course of a very few days, Pierre had so circumvented Virginie as to have discovered that her new friend was no other than the Norman farmer in a different dress. This was a great piece of knowledge to impart to Morin. But Pierre was not prepared for the immediate physical effect it had on his cousin. Morin sat suddenly down on one of the seats in the Boulevards—it was there Pierre had met with him accidentally—when he heard who it was that Virginie met. I do not suppose the man had the faintest idea of any relationship or even previous acquaintanceship between Clement and Virginie. If he thought of anything beyond the mere fact presented to him, that his idol was in communication with another, younger, handsomer man than himself, it must have been that the Norman farmer had seen her at the con-ciergerie, and had been attracted by her, and, as was but natural, had tried to make her acquintance, and had succeeded. But, from what Pierre told me, I should not think that even this much thought passed through Morin's mind. He seems to have been a man of rare and concentrated attachments; violent, though restrained and undemonstrative passions ; and, above all, a capability of jealousy, of which his dark oriental complexion must have been a type. I could fancy that if he had married Virginie, he would have coined his life-blood for luxuries to make her happy ; would have watched over and petted her, at every sacrifice to himself, as long as she would have been content to live for him alone. But, as Pierre expressed it to me : ' When I saw what my cousin was, when I learned his nature too late, I perceived that he would have strangled a bird if she whom he loved was attracted by it from him.'

" When Pierre had told Morin of his discovery, Morin sat down, as I have said, quite suddenly, as if he had been shot. He found out that the first meeting between the Norman and Virginie was no accidental, isolated circumstance. Pierre was torturing him with his accounts of daily rendezvous : if but for a moment, they were seeing each other every day, sometimes twice a day. And Virginie could speak to this man, though to himself she was so coy and reserved as hardly to utter a sentence. Pierre caught these broken words while his cousin's complexion grew more and more livid, and then purple, as if some great effect were produced on his circulation by the news he had just heard. Pierre was so startled by his cousin's wandering, senseless eyes, and otherwise disordered looks, that he rushed into a neighbouring cabaret for a glass of absinthe, which he paid for, as he recollected afterwards, with a portion of Virginie's five francs. By-and-by Morin recovered his natural appearance; but he was gloomy and silent; and all that Pierre could get out of him was, that the Norman farmer should not sleep another night at the Hotel Dugues-clin, giving him such opportunities of passing and repassing by the conciergerle door. He was too much absorbed in his own thoughts to repay Pierre the half-franc he had spent on the absinthe, which Pierre per-

ceived, and seems to have noted down in the ledger of his mind as on Virginie's balance of favour.

"Altogether, he was so much disappointed at his cousin's mode of receiving intelligence, which the lad thought worth another five-franc piece at least; or, if not paid for in money, to be paid for in open-mouthed confidence and expression of feeling, that he was for a time, so far a partisan of Virginie's—unconscious Virginie—against his cousin, as to feel regret when the Norman returned no more to his night's lodging, and when Virginie's eager watch at the crevice of the closely-drawn blind ended only with a sigh of disappointment. If it had not been for his mother's presence at the time, Pierre thought he should have told her all. But how far was his mother in his cousin's confidence as regarded the dismissal of the Norman ?

" In a few days, however, Pierre felt almost sure that they had established some new means of communication. Virginie went out for a short time every day ; but, though Pierre followed her as closely as he could without exciting her observation, he was unable to discover what kind of intercourse she held with the Norman. She went, in general, the same short round among the little shops in the neighbourhood; not entering any, but stopping at two or three. Pierre afterwards remembered that she had invariably paused at the nosegays displayed in a certain window, and studied them long; but, then, she stopped and looked at caps, hats, fashions, confectionery (all of the humble kind common in that quarter), so how should he have known that any particular attraction existed among the flowers? Morin came more regularly than ever to his aunt's; but Virginie was apparently unconscious that she was the attraction. She looked healthier and more hopeful than she had done for months, and her manners to all were gentler and not so reserved. Almost as if she wished to manifest her gratitude to Madame Babette for her long continuance of a kindness, the necessity for which was nearly enaed, Virginie showed an unnusual alacrity in rendering the old woman any little service in her power, and evidently tried to respond to Monsieur Morin's civilities, he being Madame Babette's nephew, with the soft graciousness which must have made one of her principal charms; for all who knew her speak of the fascination of her manners, so winning and attentive to others, while yet her opinions, and often her actions, were of so decided a character. For, as I have said, her beauty was by no means great; yet every man who came near her seems to have fallen into the sphere of her influence. Monsieur Morin was deeper than ever in love with her during these last few

days: he was worked up into a state capable of any sacrifice, either of himself or others, so that he might obtain her at last. He sat' devouring her with his eyes ' (to use Pierre's expression) whenever she could not see him; but, if she looked towards him, he looked to the ground—anywhere—away from her, and almost stammered in his replies if she addressed any question to him.'

" He had been, I should think, ashamed of his extreme agitation on the Boulevards, for Pierre thought that he absolutely shunned him for these few succeeding days. He must have believed that he had driven the Norman (my poor Clement!) off the field, by banishing him from his inn ; and thought that the intercourse between him and Virginie, which he had thus interrupted, was of so slight and transient a character as to be quenched by a little difficulty.

" But he appears to have felt that he made but little way, and he awkwardly turned to Pierre for help—not yet confessing his love, though; he only tried to make friends again with the lad after their silent estrangement. And Pierre for some time did not choose to perceive his cousin's advances. He would reply to all the roundabout questions Morin put to him respecting household conversations when he was not present, or household occupations and tone of thought, without

mentioning Virginie's name any more than his questioner did. The lad would seem to suppose, that his cousin's strong interest in their domestic ways of going on was all on account of Madame Babette. At last he worked his cousin up to the point of making him a confidant; and then the boy was half frightened at the torrent of vehement words he had unloosed. The lava came down with a greater rush for having been pent up so long. Morin cried out his words in a hoarse, passionate voice, clenched his teeth, his fingers, and seemed almost convulsed, as he spoke out his terrible love for Virginie, which would lead him to kill her sooner than see her another's; and if another stepped in between him and her!—and then he smiled a fierce, triumphant smile, but did not say any more.

"Pierre was, as I said, half-frightened; but also half-admiring. This was really love—a ' grande passion,'—a really fine, dramatic thing,—like the plays they acted at the little theatre yonder. He had a dozen times the sympathy with his cousin now that he had had before, and readily swore by the infernal gods, for they were far too enlightened to believe in one God, or Christianity, or anything of the kind,— that he would devote himself, body and soul, to forwarding his cousin's views. Then his cousin took him to a shop, and bought him a smart second-hand watch, on which they scratched the word Fidelite, and thus was the compact sealed. Pierre settled in his own mind, that if he were a woman, he should like to be beloved as Virginie was, by his cousin, and that it would be an extremely good thing for her to be the wife of so rich a citizen as Morin Fils,—and for Pierre himself, too, for doubtless their gratitude would lead them to give him rings and watches ad infinitum.

"A day or two afterwards, Virginie was taken ill. Madame Babette said it was because she had persevered in going out in all weathers, after confining herself to two warm rooms for so long; and very probably this was really the cause, for, from Pierre's account, she must have been suffering from a feverish cold, aggravated, no doubt, by her impatience at Madame Babette's familiar prohibitions of any more walks until she was better. Every day, in spite of her trembling, aching limbs, she would fain have arranged her dress for her walk at the usual time ; but Madame Babette was fully prepared to put physical obstacles in her way, if she was not obedient in remaining tranquil on the little sofa by the side of the fire. The third day, she called Pierre to her, when his mother was not attending (having, in fact, locked up Mademoiselle Cannes' out-of-door things).

"'See, my child,' said Virginie. 'Thou must do me a great favour. Go to the gardener's shop in the Rue des Bons-Enfans, and look at the nosegays in the window. I long for pinks; they are my favourite flower. Here are two francs. If thou seest a nosegay of pinks displayed in the window, if it be ever so faded,—nay, if thou seest two or three nosegays of pinks, remember, buy them all, and bring them to me, I have so great a desire for the smell.' She fell back weak and exhausted. Pierre hurried out. Now was the time; here was the clue to the long inspection of the nosegay in this very shop.

"Sure enough, there was a drooping nosegay of pinks in the window. Pierre went in, and, with all his impatience, he made as good a bargain as he could, urging that the flowers were faded, and good for nothing. At last he purchased them at a very moderate price. And now you will learn the bad consequences of teaching the lower orders anything beyond what is immediately necessary to enable them to earn their daily bread! The silly Count de Crequy,—he who had been sent to his bloody rest, by the very canaille of whom he thought so much,—he who had made Virginie (indirectly, it is true) reject such a man as her cousin Clement, by inflating her mind with his bubbles of theories,—this Count de Crequy had long ago taken a fancy to Pierre, as he saw the bright sharp child playing about his court-yard. Monsieur de Cre'quy had even begun to educate the boy himself, to try to work out certain opinions of his into practice,— but the drudgery of the affair wearied him, and, beside? Babette had left his employment. Still the Count took a kind of interest in his former pupil; and made some sort of arrangement by which Pierre was to be taught reading and writing, and accounts, and Heaven knows what besides,—Latin, I dare say. So Pierre, instead of being an innocent messenger, as he ought to have been—(as Mr. Horner's little lad Gregson ought to have been this morning)—could read writing as well as either you or I. So what does he do, on obtaining the nosegay, but examine it well. The stalks of the flowers were tied up with slips of matting in wet moss. Pierre undid the strings, unwrapped the moss, and out fell a piece of wet paper, with the writing all blurred with moisture. It was but a torn piece of writing-paper apparently, but Pierre's wicked mischievous eyes read what was written on it,—written so as to look like a fragment,—' Ready, every and any night at nine. All is prepared. Have no fright. Trust one who, whatever hopes he might once have had, is content now to serve you as a faithful cousin,' and a place was named, which I forget, but which Pierre did not, as it was evidently the rendezvous. After the lad had studied every word, till he could say it off by heart, he placed the paper where he had found it, enveloped it in moss, and tied the whole up again carefully. Virginie's face coloured scarlet as she received it. She kept smelling at it, and trembling: but she did not untie it, although Pierre suggested how much fresher it would be if the stalks were immediately put into water. But once, after his back had been turned for a minute, he saw it untied when he looked round again, and Virginie was blushing, and hiding something in her bosom.

"Pierre was now all impatience to set off and find his cousin. But his mother seemed to want him for small domestic purposes even more than usual; and he had chafed over a multitude of errands connected with the Hotel before he could set off and search for his cousin at his usual haunts. At last the two met; and Pierre related all the events of the morning to Morin. He said the note off word by word. (That lad this morning had something of the magpie look of Pierre —it made me shudder to see him, and hear him repeat the note by heart.) Then Morin asked him to tell him all over a^ain. Pierre was struck by Morin's heavy sighs as he repeated the story. When he came the second time to the note, Morin tried to write the words down; but either he was not a good, ready scholar, or his fingers trembled too much. Pierre hardly remembered, but, at any rate, the lad had to do it, with his wicked reading and writing. When this was done, Morin sat heavily silent. Pierre would have preferred the expected outburst, for this impenetrable gloom perplexed and baffled him. He had even to speak to his cousin to rouse him; and when he replied, what he said had so little apparent connection with the subject which Pierre had expected to find uppermost in his mind, that he was half afraid that his cousin had lost his wits.

" ' My Aunt Babette is out of coffee/

" * I am sure I do not know,' said Pierre.

" ' Yes, she is. I heard her say so. Tell her that a friend of mine has just opened a shop in the Rue Saint Antoine, and that if she will join me there in an hour, I will supply her with a good stock of coffee, just to give my friend encouragement. His name is Antoine Meyer, Number One hundred and Fifty, at the sign of the Cap of Liberty/

"' I could go with you now. I can carry a few pounds of coffee better than my mother,' said Pierre, all in good faith. He told me he should never forget the look on his cousin's face, as he turned round, and bade him begone, and give his mother the messa ge without another word. It had evidently sent him home promptly to obey his cousin's command. Morin's message perplexed Madame Babette.

" ' How could he know I was out of coffee ?" said she. ' I am; but I only used the last up this morning. How could Victor know about it ? ;

" ' I am sure I can't tell/ said Pierre, who by this time had recovered his usual self-possession. ' All I know is, that Monsieur is in a pretty temper, and that if you are not sharp to your time at this Antoine Meyer's you are likely to come in for some of his black looks.'

" * Well, it is very kind of him to offer to give me some coffee, to be sure ! But how could he know I was out ?'

" Pierre hurried his mother off impatiently, for he was certain that the offer of the coffee was only a blind to some hidden purpose on his cousin's part; and he made no doubt that when his mother had been informed of what his cousin's real intention was, he, Pierre, could extract it from her by coaxing or bullying. But he was mistaken. Madame Babette returned home, grave, depressed, silent, and loaded with the best coffee. Some time afterwards he learnt why his cousin had sought for this interview. It was to extract from her, by promises and threats, the real name of Mam'selle Cannes, which would give him a clue to the true appellation of The Faithful Cousin. He concealed this second purpose from his aunt, who had been quite unaware of his jealousy of the Norman farmer, or of his identification of him with any relation of VirgnnVs. But Madame Babette instinctively shrank from giving him any information: she must have felt that, in the lowering mood in which she found him,—his desire for greater knowledge of Virginie's antecedents boded her no good. And yet he made his aunt his confidante—told her what she had only suspected before—that he was deeply enamoured of Mam'selle Cannes, and would gladly marry her. He spoke to Madame Babette of his father's hoarded riches; and of the share which he, as partner, had in them at the present time; and of the prospect of the succession to the whole, which he had, as an only child. He told his aunt of the provision for her (Madame Babette's) life, which he would make on the day when he married Mam'selle Cannes. And yet—and yet— Babette saw that in his eye and look which made her more and more reluctant to confide in him. By-and-by he tried threats. She should leave the coriciergerie, and find employment where she liked. Still silence. Then he grew angry, and swore that he would inform

against her at the bureau of the Directory, for harbouring an aristocrat; an aristocrat he knew Mademoiselle was, whatever her real name might be. His aunt should have a domiciliary visit, and see how she liked that. The officers of the Government were the people for finding out secrets. In vain she reminded him that, by so doing, he would expose to imminent danger the lady whom he had professed to love. He told her, with a sullen relapse into silence after his vehement outpouring of passion, never to trouble herself about that. At last he wearied out the old woman, and, frightened alike of herself, and of him, she told him all,—that Mam'selle Cannes was Mademoiselle Virginie de Crequy, daughter of the Count of that name. Who was the Count? Younger brother of the Marquis. Where was the Marquis ? Dead long ago, leaving a widow and child. A son? (eagerly). Yes, a son. Where was he ? Parbleu! how should she know ?— for her courage returned a little as the talk went away from the only person of the De Crequy family that she cared about. But, by dint of some small glasses out of a bottle of Antoine Meyer's, she told him more about the De Crequys than she liked afterwards to remembe'r. For the exhilaration of the brandy lasted but a very short time, and she came home, as I have said, depressed, with a presentiment of coming evil.

She would not answer Pierre, but cuffed him about in a manner to which the spoilt boy was quite unaccustomed. His cousin's short, angry words, and sudden withdrawal of confidence,—his mother's unwonted crossness and fault-finding, all made Virginie's kind, gentle treatment more than ever charming to the lad. He half resolved to tell her how he had been acting as a spy upon her actions, and at whose desire he had done it. But he was afraid of Morin, and of the vengeance which he was sure would fall upon him for any breach of confidence. Towards half-past eight that evening—Pierre, watching, saw Virginie arrange several little things—she was in the inner room, but he sat where he could see her through the glazed partition. His mother sat—apparently sleeping—in the great easy chair; Virginie moved about softly, for fear of disturbing her. She made up one or two little parcels of the few things she could call her own: one packet she concealed about herself,—the others she directed, and left on the shelf. " She is going," thought Pierre, and (as he said in giving me the account) his heart gave a spring, to think that he should never see her again. If either his mother or his cousin had been more kind to him, he might have endeavoured to intercept her; but as it was, he held his breath, and when she came out he pretended to read, scarcely

knowing whether he 'wished her to succeed in the purpose which he was almost sure she entertained, or not. She stopped by him, and passed her hand over his hair. He told me that his eyes filled with tears at this caress. Then she stood for a moment, looking at the sleeping Madame

Babette, and stooped down and softly kissed her on the forhead. Pierre dreaded lest his mother should awake (for by this time the wayward, vacillating boy must have been quite on Virginie's side), but the brandy she had drank made her slumber heavily. Virginie went. Pierre's heart beat fast. He was sure his cousin would try to intercept her; but how, he could not imagine. He longed to run out and see the catastrophe,—but he had let the moment slip; he was also afraid of reawakening his mother to her unusual state of anger and violence."

## CHAPTER VIII.

" PIERRE went on pretending to read, but in reality listening with acute tension of ear to every little sound. His perceptions became so sensitive in this respect that he was incapable of measuring time, every moment had seemed so full of noises, from the beating of his heart up to the roll of the heavy carts in the distance. He wondered whether Virginie would have reached the place of rendezvous, and yet he was unable to compute the passage of minutes. His mother slept soundly: that was well. By this time Virginie must have met the ' faithful cousin:' if, indeed, Morin had not made his appearance.

" At length, he felt as if he could no longer sit still, awaiting the issue, but must run out and see what course -events had taken. In vain his mother, half-rousing herself, called after him to ask whither he was going: he was already out of hearing before she had ended her sentence, and he ran on until stopped by the sight of

I 2

Mademoiselle Cannes walking along at so swift a pace that it was almost a run; while at her side, resolutely keeping by her, Morin was striding abreast. Pierre had just turned the corner of the street, when he came upon them. Virginie would have passed him without recognising him, she was in such passionate agitation, but for Moriri's gesture, by which he would fain have kept Pierre from interrupting them. Then, when Virginie saw the lad, she caught at his arm, and thanked God, as if in that boy of twelve or fourteen she held a protector. Pierre felt her tremble from head to foot, and was afraid lest she would fall, there where she stood, in the hard rough street.

" 'Begone, Pierre !' said Morin.

*"I cannot/ replied Pierre, who indeed was held firmly by Virginie. 'Besides, I won't,' he added. 'Who has been frightening Mademoiselle in this way ?' asked he, very much inclined to brave his cousin at all hazards.

"' Mademoiselle is not accustomed to walk in the streets alone,' said Morin, sulkily. ' She came upon a crowd attracted by the arrest of an aristocrat, and their cries alarmed her. I offered to take charge of her home. Mademoiselle should not walk in these streets alone. We are not like the cold-blooded people of the Faubourg Saint Germain.'

"Virginia did not speak. Pierre doubted if she heard a word of what they were saying. She leant upon him more and more heavily.

" ' Will Mademoiselle condescend to take my arm ?' said Morin, with sulky, and yet humble, uncouthness. I dare say he would have given worlds if he might have had that little hand within his arm; but, though she still kept silence, she shuddered up away from him, as you shrink from touching a toad. He had said something to her during that walk, you may be sure, which had made her loathe him. He marked and understood the gesture. He held himself aloof while Pierre gave her all the assistance he could in their slow progress homewards. But Morin accompanied her all the same. He had played too desperate a game to be baulked now. He had given information against the c^i-devant Marquis de Crequy, as a returned emigre, to be met with at such a time, in such a place. Morin had hoped that all sign of the arrest would have been cleared away before Virginie reached the spot—so swiftly were terrible deeds done in those days. But

Clement defended himself desperately: Virginie was punctual to a second; and, though the wounded man was borne off to the Abbaye, amid a crowd of the unsympathising jeerers who mingled with the armed officials of the Directory, Morin feared lest Virginie had recognised him ; and he would have preferred that she should have thought that the * faithful cousin' was faithless, than that she should have seen him in bloody danger on her account. I suppose he fancied that, if Virginie never saw or heard more of him, her imagination would not dwell on his simple disappearance, as it would do if she knew what he was suffering for her sake.

" At any rate, Pierre saw that his [cousin was deeply mortified by the whole tenor of his behaviour during their walk home. When they arrived at Madame Babette's, Virginie fell fainting on the floor; her strength had but just sufficed for this exertion of reaching the shelter of the house. Her first sign of restoring consciousness consisted in avoidance of Morin. He had been most assiduous in his efforts to bring her round; quite tender in his way, Pierre said ; and this marked, instinctive repugnance to him evidently gave him extreme pain. I suppose Frenchmen are more demonstrative than we are ; for Pierre declared that he saw his cousin's eyes fill with tears, as she shrank away from his touch, if he tried to arrange the shawl they had laid under her head like a pillow, or as she shut her eyes when he passed before her. Madame Babette was urgent with her to go and lie down on the bed in the inner room; but it was some time before she was strong enough to rise and do this.

" When Madame Babette returned from arranging the girl comfortably, the three relations sat down in silence ; a silence which Pierre thought would never be broken. He wanted his mother to ask his cousin what had happened. But Madame Babette was afraid of her nephew, and thought it more discreet to wait for such crumbs of intelligence as he might think fit to throw to her. But, after she had twice reported Virginie to be asleep, without a word being uttered in reply to her whispers by either of her companions, Morin's powers of self-containment gave way.

" < It is hard !' he said.

" < What is hard ?' asked Madame Babette, after she had paused for a time, to enable him to add to, or to finish, his sentence, if he pleased.

" ' It is hard for a man to love a woman as I do,' he went on. ' I did not seek to love her, it came upon me before I was aware—before I had ever thought about it at all, I loved her better than all the world beside. All my life before I knew her, seems a dull blank. I neither know nor care for what I did before then. And now there are just two lives before me. Either I have her, or I have not. That is all: but that is everything. And what can I do to make her have me? Tell me, aunt,' and he caught at Madame Babette's arm, and gave it so sharp a shake, that she half screamed out,

Pierre said, and evidently grew alarmed at her nephew's excitement.

"' Hush, Victor!' said she. ' There are other women in the world, if this one will not have you.'

" < None other for me,' he said, sinking back as if hopeless. ' I am plain and coarse, not one of the scented darlings of the aristocrats. Say that I am ugly, brutish; I did not make myself so, any more than I made myself love her. It is my fate. But am I to submit to the consequences of my fate without a struggle ? Not I. As strong as my love is, so strong is my will. It can be no stronger,' continued he, gloomily, 'Aunt Babette, you must help me—you must make her love me.' He was so fierce here, that Pierre said he did not wonder that his mother was frightened.

"'I, Victor!' she exclaimed. 'I make her love you? How can I? Ask me to speak for you to Mademoiselle Didot, or to Mademoiselle Cauchois even, or to such as they, and I'll do it, and welcome. But to Mademoiselle de Crequy, why you don't know the difference! Those people—the old nobility I mean—why they don't know a man from a dog, out of their own rank! And no wonder, for the young gentlemen of quality are treated differently to us from their very birth. If she had you to-morrow, you would be miserable. Let me alone for knowing the aristocracy. I have not been a concierge to a duke and three counts for nothing. I tell you, all your ways are different to her ways.'

"' I would change " my ways," as you call them.'

" ' Be reasonable, Victor.'

"' No, I will not be reasonable, if by that you mean giving her up. I tell you two lives are before me; one with her, one without her. But the latter will be but a short career for both of us. You said, aunt, that the talk went in the conciergerie of her father's hotel, that she would have nothing to do with this cousin whom I put out of the way to-day ?'

" ' So the servants said. How could I know ? All I know is, that he left off coming to our hotel, and that at one time before then he had never been two days absent.'

" ' So much the better for him. He suffers now for having come between me and my object—in trying to snatch her away out of my sight. Take you warning, Pierre ! I did not like your meddling to-night.' And so he went off, leaving Madame Babette rocking herself backwards and forwards, in all the depression of spirits consequent upon the reaction after the brandy, and upon her knowledge of her nephew's threatened purpose combined.

" In telling you most of this, I have simply repeated Pierre's account, which I wrote down at the time. But here what he had to say came to a sudden break; for, the next morning, when Madame Babette rose, Virginie was missing, and it was some time before either she, or Pierre, or Morin, could get the slightest clue to the missing girl.

" And now I must take up the story as it was told to the Intendant Flechier by the old gardener Jacques, with whom Clement had been lodging on his first arrival in Paris. The old man could not, I dare say, remember half as much of what had happened as Pierre did; the former had the dulled memory of age, while Pierre had evidently thought over the whole series of events as a story—as a play, if one may call it so— during the solitary hours in his after-life, wherever they were passed, whether in lonely camp watches, or in the foreign prison where he had to drag out many years. Clement had, as I said, returned to the gardener's garret after he had been dismissed from the Hotel Duguesclin. There were several reasons for his thus doubling back. One was, that he put nearly the whole breadth of Paris between him and an enemy; though why Morin was an enemy, and to what extent he carried his dislike or hatred, Clement could not tell, of course. The next reason for returning to Jacques was, no doubt, the conviction that, in multiplying his residences, he multiplied the chances against his being suspected and recognised. And then, again, the old man was in his secret, and his ally, although perhaps but a feeble kind of one. It was through Jacques that the plan of communication, by means of a nosegay of pinks, had been devised; and it was Jacques who procured him the last disguise that Clément was to use in Paris—as he hoped and trusted. It was that of a respectable shopkeeper of no particular class; a dress that would have seemed perfectly suitable to the young man who would naturally have worn it; and yet, as Clement put it on, and adjusted it—giving it a sort of finish and elegance which I always noticed about his appearance, and which I believed was innate in the wearer—I have no doubt it seemed like the usual apparel of a gentleman. No coarseness of texture, nor clumsiness of cut could disguise the nobleman of thirty descents, it appeared; for immediately on arriving at the place of rendezvous, he was recognised by the men placed there on Morin's information to seize him. Jacques, following at a little distance, with a bundle under his arm containing articles of feminine disguise for Virginie, saw four men attempt Clement's arrest—

saw him, quick as lightning, draw a sword hithert concealed in a clumsy stick—saw his agile figure spring to his guard,—and saw him defend himself with the rapidity and art of a man skilled in arms. But what good did it do? as Jacques piteously used to ask, Monsieur Flechier told me. A great blow from a heavy club on the sword-arm of Monsieur de Crequy laid it helpless and immoveable by his side. Jacques always thought that that blow came from one of the spectators, who by this time had collected round the scene of the affray. The next instant, his master,—his little marquis was down among the feet of the crowd, and though he was up again before he had received much damage so active and light was my poor Clement—it was not before the old gardener had hobbled forwards, and, with many an old-fashioned oath and curse, proclaimed himself a partizan of the losing side a follower of a c,i-devant aristocrat. It was quite enough. He received one or two good blows, which were, in fact, aimed at his master; and then, almost before he was aware, he found his arms pinioned behind him with a woman's garter, which one of the viragos in the crowd had made no scruple of pulling off in public, as soon as she heard for what purpose it was wanted. Poor Jacques was stunned and unhappy, his master was out of sight, on before; and the old gardener scarce knew whither they were taking him. His head ached from the blows which had fallen upon it; it was growing dark,—June day though it was,

and when first he seems to have become exactly aware of what had happened to him, it was when he was turned into one of the larger rooms of the Abbaye, in which all were put who had no other allotted- place wherein to sleep. One or two iron lamps hung from the ceiling by chains, giving a dim light for a little circle. Jacques stumbled forwards over a sleeping body lying on the ground. The sleeper wakened up enough to complain: and the apology of the old man in reply caught the ear of his master, who, until this time, could hardly have been aware of the straits and difficulties of his faithful Jacques. And there they sat,—against a pillar, the live-long night, holding one another's hands, and each restraining expressions of pain, for fear of adding to the other's distress. That nighf, made them intimate friends, in spite of the difference of age and rank. The disappointed hopes, the acute suffering of the present, the apprehensions of the future, made them seek solace in talking of the past. Monsieur de Crequy and the gardener found themselves disputing with interest in which chimney of the stack the starling used to build,—the starling whose nest Clement sent to Urian, you remember,and discussing the merits of different espalier-pears which grew, and may grow still, in the old garden of the Hotel de Crequy. Towards morning both fell asleep. The old

man wakened first. His frame was deadened to suffering, I suppose, for he felt relieved of his pain; but Clement moaned and cried in feverish slumber. His broken arm was beginning to inflame his blood. He was, besides, much injured by some kicks from the crowd as he fell. As the old man looked sadly on the white, baked lips, and the flushed cheeks, contorted with suffering even in his sleep, Clement gave a sharp cry, which disturbed his miserable neighbours, all slumbering around in uneasy attitudes. They bade him with curses be silent; and then turning round, tried again to forget their own misery in sleep. For you see, the bloodthirsty canaille had not been sated with guillotining and hanging all the nobility they could find, but were now informing, right and left, even against each other; and when Clement and Jacques were in the prison, there were few of gentle blood in the place, and fewer still of gentle manners. At the sound of the angry words and threats, Jacques thought it best to awaken his master from his feverish uncomfortable sleep, lest he should provoke more enmity; and, tenderly lifting him up, he tried to adjust his own body, so that it should serve as a rest and a pillow for the younger man. The motion aroused Clement, and he began to talk in a strange, feverish way, of Virginie, too,—whose name he would not have breathed in such

a place had he been quite himself. But Jacques had as much delicacy of feeling as any lady in the land, although, mind you, he knew neither how to read nor write,—and bent his head low down, so that his master might tell him in a whisper what messages he was to take to Mademoiselle de Cre'quy, in case Poor Clement, he knew it must come to that! No escape for him now, in Norman disguise or otherwise! Either by gathering fever or guillotine, death was sure of his prey. Well! when that happened, Jacques was to go and find Mademoiselle de Crequy, and tell her that her cousin loved her at the last as he had loved her at the first; but that she should never have heard another word of his attachment from his living lips; that he knew he was not good enough for her, his queen; and that no thought of earning her love by his devotion had prompted his return to France, only that, if possible, he might have the great privilege of serving her whom he loved. And then he went off into rambling talk about petit-maitres, and such kind of expressions, said Jacques to Fle'chier, the intendant, little knowing what a clue that one word gave to much of the poor lad's suffering.

" The summer morning came slowly on in that dark prison, and when Jacques could look round—his master was now sleeping on his shoulder, still the uneasy,

starting sleep of fever, he saw that there were many women among the prisoners. (I have heard some of those who have escaped from the prisons say, that the look of despair and agony that came into the faces of the prisoners on first wakening, as the sense of their situation grew upon them, was what lasted the longest in the memory of the survivors. This look, they said, passed away from the women's faces sooner than it did from those of the men.

" Poor old Jacques kept falling asleep, and plucking himself up again for fear lest, if he did not attend to his master, some harm might come to the swollen, helpless arm. Yet his weariness grew upon him in spite of all his efforts, and at last he felt as if he must give way to the irresistible desire, if only for five minutes. But just then there was a bustle at the door. Jacques opened his eyes wide to look.

"' The gaoler is early with breakfast,' said some one, lazily.

"' It is the darkness of this accursed place that makes us think it early,' said another.

" All this time a parley was going on at the door. Some one came in; not the gaoler—a woman. The door was shut to and locked behind her. She only advanced a step or two ; for it was too sudden a change, out of the light into that dark shadow, for any one to

MY LADY LUDLOW.

see clearly for the first few minutes. Jacques had his eyes fairly open now; and was wide awake. It was Mademoiselle de Crequy, looking bright, clear, and resolute. The faithful heart of the old man read that look like an open page. Her cousin should not die there on her behalf, without at least the comfort of her sweet presence.

"' Here he is he whispered, as her gown would have touched him in passing, without her perceiving him, in the heavy obscurity of the place.

' " The good God bless you, my friend!' she murmured, as she saw the attitude of the old man, propped against a pillar, and holding Clement in his arms, as if the young man had been a helpless baby, while one of the poor gardener's hands supported the broken limb in the easiest position. Virginie sat down by the old man, and held out her arms. Softly she moved Clement's head to her own shoulder; softly she transferred the task of holding the arm to herself. Clement lay on the floor, but she supported him, and Jacques was at liberty to arise and stretch and shake his stiff, weary old body. He then sat down at a little distance, and watched the pair until he fell asleep. Clement had muttered i Virginie,' as they half-roused him by their movements out of his stupor; but Jacques thought he was only dreaming; nor did he seem fully awake

when once his eyes opened, and he looked full at Virginie's face bending over him, and growing crimson under his gaze, though she never stirred, for fear of hurting him if she moved.

Clement looked in silence, until his heavy eyelids came slowly down, and he fell into his oppressive slumber again. Either he did not recognise her, or she came in too completely as a part of his sleeping visions for him to be disturbed by her appearance there.

" When Jacques awoke it was full daylight—at least as full as it would ever be in that place. His breakfast —the gaol-allowance of bread and vin ordinaire—was by his side. He must have slept soundly. He looked for his master. He and Virginie had recognised each other now,—hearts, as well as appearance. They were smiling into each other's faces, as if that dull, vaulted room in the grim Abbaye were the sunny gardens of Versailles, with music and festivity all abroad. Apparently they had much to say to each other ; for whispered questions and answers never ceased.

"Virginie had made a sling for the poor broken arm; nay, she had obtained two splinters of wood in some way, and one of their fellow-prisoners—having, it appeared, some knowledge of surgery—had set it. Jacques felt more desponding by far than they did, for he was suffering from the night he had passed, which

told upon his aged frame ; while they must have heard some good news, as it seemed to him, so bright and happy did they look. Yet Clement was still in bodily pain and suffering, and Virginie, by her own act and deed, was a prisoner in that dreadful Abbaye, whence the only issue was the guillotine. But they were together : they loved: they understood each other at length.

" When Virginie saw that Jacques was awake, and languidly munching his breakfast, she rose from the wooden stool on which she was sitting, and went to him, holding out both hands, and refusing to allow him to rise, while she thanked him with pretty eagerness for all his kindness to Monsieur. Monsieur himself came towards him, following Virginie, but with tottering steps, as if his head was weak and dizzy, to thank the poor old man, who, now on his feet, stood between them, ready to cry while they gave him credit for faithful actions which he felt to have been almost involuntary on his part, for loyalty was like an instinct in the good old days, before your educational cant had come up. And so two days went on. The only event was the morning call for the victims, a certain number of whom were summoned to trial every day. And to be tried was to be condemned. Every one of the prisoners became grave, as the hour for their summons approached. Most of the victims went to their doom

with uncomplaining resignation, and for awhile after their departure there was comparative silence in the prison. But, by-and-by, so said Jacques, the conversation or amusements began again. Human nature cannot stand the perpetual pressure of such keen anxiety, without an effort to relieve itself by thinking of something else. Jacques said that Monsieur and Mademoiselle were for ever talking together of the past days,—it was ' Do you remember this ?' or, ' Do you remember that ?' perpetually. He sometimes thought they forgot where they were, and what was before them. But Jacques did not, and every day he trembled more and more as the list was called over.

" The third morning of their incarceration, the gaoler brought in a man whom Jacques did not recognise, and therefore did not at once observe ; for he was waiting, as in duty bound, upon his master and his sweet young lady (as he always called her in repeating the story). He thought that the new introduction was some friend of the gaoler, as the two seemed well acquainted, and the latter stayed a few minutes talking with his visitor before leaving him in the prison. So Jacques was surprised when, after a short time had elapsed, he looked round, and saw the fierce stare with which the stranger was regarding Monsieur and Mademoiselle de Crequy, as the pair sat

at breakfast,—the said breakfast being laid as well as Jacques knew how, on a bench fastened into the prison wall,—Virginie sitting on her low stool, and Clement half lying on the ground by her side, and submitting gladly to be fed by her pretty white fingers; for it was one of her fancies, Jacques said, to do all she could for him, in consideration of his broken arm. And, indeed, Clement was wasting away daily; for he had received other injuries, internal and more serious than that to his arm, during the mêle'e which had ended in his capture. The stranger made Jacques conscious of his presence by a sigh, which was almost a groan. All three prisoners looked round at the sound. Clement's face expressed little but scornful indifference; but Virginie's face froze into stony hate. Jacques said he never saw such a look, and hoped that he never should again. Yet after that first revelation of feeling, her look was steady and fixed in another direction to that in which the stranger stood, still motionless—still watching. He came a step nearer at last.

"' Mademoiselle he said. Not the quivering of an eyelash showed that she heard him. 'Mademoiselle!' he said again, with an intensity of beseeching that made Jacques—not knowing who he was—almost pity him, when he saw his young lady's obdurate face.

" There was perfect silence for a space of time which Jacques could not measure. Then again the voice, hesitatingly, saying, 'Monsieur!' Clement could not hold the same icy countenance as Virginie; he turned his head with an impatient gesture of disgust; but even that emboldened the man.

"' Monsieur, do ask Mademoiselle to listen to me,— just two words!'

" < Mademoiselle de Crequy only listens to whom she chooses.' Very haughtily my Clement would say that, I am sure.

"' But, Mademoiselle, lowering his voice, and coming a step or two nearer. Virginie must have felt his approach, though she did not see it; for she drew herself a little on one side, so as to put as much space as possible between him and her. 'Mademoiselle, it is not too late. I can save you; but to-morrow your name is down on the list. I can save you, if you will listen.'

" Still no word or sign. Jacques did not understand the affair. Why was she so obdurate to one who might be ready to include Clement in the proposal, as far as Jacques knew?

" The man withdrew a little, but did not offer to leave the prison. He never took his eyes off Virginie; he seemed to be suffering from some acute and terrible pain as he watched her.

" Jacques cleared away the breakfast-things as well as he could. Purposely, as I suspect, he passed near the man.

" ' Hist!' said the stranger. ' You are Jacques, the gardener, arrested for assisting an aristocrat. I know the gaoler. You shall escape,, if you will. Only take this message from me to Mademoiselle. You heard. She will not listen to me: I did not want her to come here. I never knew she was here, and she will die to-morrow. They will put her beautiful, round throat under the guillotine. Tell her, good old man, tell her how sweet life is; and how I can save her; and how I will not ask for more than just to see her from time to time. She is so young; and death is annihilation, you know. Why does she hate me so? I want to save her; I have done her no harm. Good old man, tell her how terrible death is; and that she will die to-morrow, unless she listens to me.'

" Jacques saw no harm in repeating this message. Cle'ment listened in silence, watching Virginie with an air of infinite tenderness.

" Will you not try him, my cherished one?' he said. ' Towards you he may mean well' (which makes me think that Virginie had never repeated to Clement the conversation which she had overheard that last night at Madame Babette's); ' you would be in no worse a situation than you were before!'

"' No worse, Clement! and I should have known what you were, and have lost you. My Clement!' said she, reproachfully.

" ' Ask him,' said she, turning to Jacques, suddenly, 4 if he can save Monsieur de Crequy as well,—if he can ?O Cle'ment, we might escape to England; we are but young.' And she hid her face on his shoulder.

" Jacques returned to the stranger, and asked him Virginie's question. His eyes were fixed on the cousins; he was very pale, and the twitchings or contortions, which must have been involuntary whenever he was agitated, convulsed his whole body.

" He made a long pause. ' I will save mademoiselle and monsieur, if she will go straight from prison to the mairie, and be my wife.'

"' Your wife!' Jacques could not help exclaiming. ' That she will never be—never!'

"' Ask her !' said Morin, hoarsely.

" ' But almost before Jacques thought he could have fairly uttered the words, Clement caught their meaning.

" ' Begone !' said he ; ' not one word more.' Virginie touched the old man as he was moving away. 4 Tell him he does not know how he makes me welcome Death.' And smiling, as if triumphant, she turned again to Clement.

" The stranger did not speak as Jacques gave him

the meaning, not the words of their replies. He was going away, but stopped. A minute or two afterwards, he beckoned to Jacques. The old gardener seems to have thought it undesirable to throw away even the chance of assistance from such a man as this, for he went forwards to speak to him.

" ' Listen! I have influence with the gaoler. He shall let thee pass out with the victims to-morrow.

No one will notice it, or miss thee, . They will

be led to trial,even at the last moment, I will save her, if she sends me word she relents. Speak to her, as the time draws on. Life is very sweet,tell her how sweet. Speak to him ; he will do more with her than thou canst. Let him urge her to live. Even at the last, I will be at the Palais de Justice,at the Greve. I have followers,I have interest. Come among the crowd that follow the victims,I shall see thee. It will be no worse for him, if she escapes '

" ' Save my master, and I will do all,' said Jacques.

"' Only on my one condition,' said Morin, doggedly ; and Jacques was hopeless of that condition ever being fulfilled. But he did not see why his own life might not be saved. By remaining in prison until the next day, he should have rendered every service in his power x to his master and the young lady. He, poor fellow, shrank from death; and he agreed with

Morin to escape, if he could, by the means Morin suggested, and to bring him word if Mademoiselle de Crequy relented. (Jacques had no expectation that she would; but I fancy he did not think it necessary to tell Morin of this conviction of his.) This bargaining with so base a man for so slight a thing as life, was the only flaw that I heard of in the old gardener's behaviour. Of course, the mere reopening of the subject was enough to stir Virginie to displeasure. Clement urged her, it is true; but the light he had gained upon Morin's motions, made him rather try to set the case before her in as fair a manner as possible than use any persuasive arguments. And, even as it was, what he said on the subject made Virginie shed tears —the first that had fallen from her since she entered the prison. So, they were summoned and went together, at the fatal call of the muster-roll of victims the next morning. He, feeble from his wounds and his injured health; she, calm and serene, only petitioning to be allowed to walk next] to him, in order that she might hold him up when he turned faint and giddy from his extreme suffering.

" Together they stood at the bar; together they were condemned. As the words of judgment were pronounced, Virginie turned to Clement, and embraced him with passionate fondness. Then, making him lean on her, they marched out towards the Place de la Greve.

" Jacques was free now. He had told Morin how fruitless his efforts at persuasion had been; and, scarcely caring to note the effect of his information upon the man, he had devoted himself to watching Monsieur and Mademoiselle de Crequy. And now he followed them to the Place de la Greve. He saw them mount the platform; saw them kneel down together till plucked up by the impatient officials; could see that she was urging some request to the executioner; the end of which seemed to be, that Clement advanced first to the guillotine, was executed (and just at this moment there was a stir among the crowd, as of a man pressing forward towards the scaffold). Then she, standing with her face to the guillotine, slowly made the sign of the cross, and knelt down.

"Jacques covered his eyes, blinded with tears. The report of a pistol made him look up. She was gone—another victim in her place and where there hao been the little stir in the crowd not five minutes before, some men were carrying off a dead body. A man had shot himself, they said. Pierre told me who that man was."

CHAPTER IX.

AFTER a pause, I ventured to ask what became of Madame de Crequy, Clement's mother.

"She never made any inquiry about him again," said my lady. " She must have known that he was dead; though how, we never could tell. Medlicott remembered afterwards that it was about, if not on— Medlicott to this day declares that it was on the very Monday, June the nineteenth, when her son was executed, that Madame de Cre'quy left off her rouge, and took to her bed, as one bereaved and hopeless. It certainly was about that time; and Medlicott who was deeply impressed by that dream of Madame de Crequy's (the relation of which I told you had had such an effect on my lord), in which she had seen .the figure of Virginie as the only light object amid much surrounding darkness as of night, smiling and beckoning Clement on on till at length the bright phantom stopped, motionless, and Madame de Crequy's eyes

began to penetrate the murky darkness, and f to see closing around her the gloomy dripping walls which she had once seen and never forgotten the walls of the vault of the chapel of the De Crequys in Saint Germain 1'Auxerrois; and there the two last of the Crequys laid them down among their forefathers, and Madame de Crequy had wakened to the sound of the great door, which led to the open air, being locked upon her I say Medlicott, who was predisposed by this dream to look out for the supernatural, always declared that Madame de Crequy was made conscious, in some mysterious way, of her son's death, on the very day and hour when it occurred, and that after that she had no more anxiety, but was only conscious of a kind of stupefying despair."

" And what became of her, my lady ?" asked I, repeating my question.

" What could become of her ?" replied Lady Lud-low. "She never could be induced to rise again, though she lived more than a year after her son's departure. She kept her bed; her room darkened, her face turned towards the wall, whenever any one besides Medlicott was in the room. She hardly ever spoke, and would have died of starvation but for Med-licott's tender care, in putting a morsel to her lips every now and then, feeding her, in, fact, just as an

old bir,d feeds her young ones, In the height of summer my lord and I left London. We would fain have taken her with us into Scotland, but the doctor (we had the old doctor from Leicester Square) forbade her removal; and this time he gave such good reasons against it that I acquiesced. Medlicott and a maid were left with her. Every care was taken of her. She survived till our return. Indeed, I thought she was in much the same state as I had left her in, when I came back to London. But Medlicott spoke of her as much weaker; and one morning on awakening, they told me she was- dead. I sent for Medlicott, who was in sad distress, she had become so fond of her charge. She said that, about two o'clock, she had been awakened by unusual restlessness on Madame de Crequy's part; that she had gone to her bedside, and found the poor lady feebly but perpetually moving her wasted arm up and down—and saying to herself in a wailing voice: ' I did not bless him when he left me—I did not bless him when he left me !' Medlicott gave her a spoonful or two of jelly, and sat by her, stroking her hand, and soothing her till she seemed to fall asleep. But in the morning she was dead."

" It is a sad story, your ladyship," said I, after a while.

" Yes it is. people seldom arrive at my age without having watched the beginning, middle, and end of many lives and many fortunes. We do not talk about them, perhaps; for they are often so sacred to us, from having touched into the very quick of our own hearts, as it were, or into those of others who are dead and gone, and veiled over from human sight, that we cannot tell the tale as if it was a mere story. But young people should remember that we have had this solemn experience of life, on which to base our opinions and form our judgments, so that they are not mere untried theories. I am not alluding to Mr. Homer just now, for he is nearly as old as I am—within ten years, I daresay—but I am thinking of Mr. Gray, with his endless plans for some new thing—schools, education, Sabbaths, and what not. Now he has not seen what all this leads to."

" It is a pity he has not heard your ladyship tell the story of poor Monsieur de Crequy."

" Not at all a pity, my dear. A young man like him, who, both by position and age must have had his experience confined to a very narrow circle, ought not to set up his opinion against mine; he ought not to require reasons from me, nor to need such explanation of my arguments (if I condescend to argue), as going into relation of the circumstances on which my arguments are based in my own mind, would be."

"But, my lady, it might convince him," I said, with perhaps injudicious perseverance.

"And why should he be convinced?" she asked, with gentle inquiry in her tone. "He has only to acquiesce. Though he is appointed by Mr. Croxton, I am the lady of the manor, as he must know. But it is with Mr. Horner that I must have to do about this unfortunate lad Gregson. I am afraid there will be no method of making him forget his unlucky knowledge. His poor brains will be intoxicated with the sense of his powers, without any counterbalancing principles to guide him. Poor fellow ! I am quite afraid it will end in his being hanged!"

The next day Mr. Horner came to apologise and explain. He was evidently—as I could tell from his voice, as he spoke to my lady in the next" room—extremely annoyed at her ladyship's discovery of the education he had been giving to this boy. My lady spoke with great authority, and with reasonable grounds of complaint. Mr. Horner was well acquainted with her thoughts on the subject, and had acted in defiance of her wishes. He acknowledged as much, and should on no account have done it, in any other instance, without her leave.

" Which I could never have granted you,' said my lady.

But this boy had extraordinary capabilities ; would, in fact, have taught himself much that was bad, if he not been rescued, and another direction given to his powers. And in all Mr. Horner had done, he had had her ladyship's service in view. The business was getting almost beyond his power, so many letters and so much account-keeping was required by the complicated state in which things were.

Lady Ludlow felt what was coming—a reference to the mortgage for the benefit of my lord's Scottish estates, which, she was perfectly aware, Mr. Horner considered as having been a most unwise proceeding— and she hastened to observe :

" All this may be very true, Mr. Horner, and I am sure I should be the last person to wish you to overwork or distress yourself; but of that we will talk another time. What I am now anxious to remedy is, if possible, the state of this poor little Gregson's mind. Would not hard work in the fields be a wholesome and excellent way of enabling him to forget ?"

"I was in hopes, my lady, that you would have permitted me to bring him up to act as a kind of clerk," said Mr. Horner, jerking out his project abruptly.

" A what?" asked my lady, in infinite surprise.

" A kind of—of assistant, in the way of copying letters and doing up accounts. He is already an excellent penman and very quick at figures."

"Mr. Homer," said my lady, with dignity, "the son of a poacher and vagabond ought never to have been able to copy letters relating to the Hanbury estates; and, at any rate, he shall not. I wonder how it is that, knowing the use he has made of his power of reading a letter, you should venture to propose such an employment for him as would require his being in your confidence, and you the trusted agent of this family. Why, every secret (and every ancient and honourable family has its secrets, as you know, Mr. Homer!) would be learnt off by heart, and repeated to the first comer!"

" I should have hoped to have trained him, my lady, to understand the rules of discretion."

" Trained! Train a barn-door fowl to be a pheasant, Mr. Horner! That would be the easier task. But you did right to speak of discretion rather than honour. Discretion looks to the consequences of actions—honour looks to the action itself, and is an instinct rather than a virtue. After all, it is possible, you might have trained him to be discreet."

Mr. Horner was silent. My lady was softened by his not replying, and began, as she always did in such cases, to fear lest she had been too harsh. I could tell that by her voice and by her next speech, as well as if I had seen her face.

" But I am sorry you are feeling the pressure of the affairs; I am quite aware that I have entailed much additional trouble upon you by some of my measures ; I must try and provide you with some suitable assistance. Copying letters and doing up accounts, I think you said ?"

Mr. Horner had certainly had a distant idea of turning the little boy, in process of time, into a clerk ; but he had rather urged this possibility of future usefulness beyond what he had at first intended, in speaking of it to my lady as a palliation of his offence, and he certainly was very much inclined to retract his statement that the letter-writing, or any other business, had increased, or that he was in the slightest want of help of any kind, when my lady, after a pause of consideration, suddenly said:

" I have it. Miss Galindo will, I am sure, be glad to assist you. I will speak to her myself. The payment we should make to a clerk would be of real service to her!"

I could hardly help echoing Mr. Homer's tone of surprise as he said

" Miss Galindo!"

For, you must be told who Miss Galindo was; at least, told us much as I know. Miss Galindo had lived in the village for many years, keeping house on the smallest possible means, yet always managing to maintain a servant. And this servant was invariably chosen because she had some infirmity that made her undesirable to every one else. I believe Miss Galindo had had lame and blind and hump-backed maids. She had even at one time taken in a girl hopelessly gone in consumption, because if not she would have had to go to the workhouse, and not have had enough to eat. Of course the poor creature could not perform a single duty usually required of a servant, and Miss Galindo herself was both servant and nurse.

Her present maid was scarcely four feet high, and bore a terrible character for ill-temper. Nobody but Miss Galindo would have kept her; but, as it was, mistress and servant squabbled perpetually, and were, at heart, the best of friends. For it was one of Miss Galindo's peculiarities to do all manner of kind and self-denying actions, and to say all manner of provoking things. Lame, blind, deformed, and dwarf, all came in for scoldings without number: it was only the consumptive girl that never had heard a sharp word. I don't think any of her servants liked her the worse for her peppery temper, and passionate odd ways, for they knew her real and beautiful kindness of heart;

and, besides, she had so great a turn for humour, that very often her speeches amused as much or more than they irritated; and, on the other side, a piece of witty impudence from her servant would occasionally tickle her so much and so suddenly, that she would burst out laughing in the middle of her passion.

But the talk about Miss Gralindo's choice and management of her servants was confined to village gossip, and had never reached my Lady Ludlow's ears, though doubtless Mr. Horner was well acquainted with it. What my lady knew of her amounted to this. It was the custom in those days for the wealthy ladies of the county to set on foot a repository, as it was called, in the assize-town. The ostensible manager of this repository was generally a decayed gentlewoman, a clergyman's widow, or so forth. She was, however, controlled by a committee of ladies; and paid by them in proportion to the amount of goods she sold; and these goods were the small manufactures of ladies of little or no fortune, whose names, if they chose it, were only signified by initials.

Poor water-colour drawings, in indigo and Indian ink ; screens, ornamented with moss and dried leaves; paintings on velvet, and such faintly ornamental works were displayed on one side of the shop. It was always reckoned a mark of characteristic gentility in the

repository, to have only common heavy framed sash-windows, which admitted very little light, so I never was quite certain of the merit of these Works of Art as they were entitled. But, on the other side, where the Useful Work placard was put up, there was a great variety of articles, of whose unusual excellence every one might judge. Such fine sewing, and stitching, and button-holing! Such bundles of soft delicate knitted stockings and socks; and, above all, in Lady Ludlow's eyes, such hanks of the finest spun flaxen thread!

And the most delicate dainty work of all was done by Miss Galindo, as Lady Ludlow very well knew. Yet, for all their fine sewing, it sometimes happened that Miss Galindo's patterns were of an old-fashioned kind; and the dozen night-caps, may-be, on the materials for which she had expended bona-fide money, and on the making-up, no little time and eye-sight, would lie for months in a yellow neglected heap; and at such times, it was said, Miss Galindo was more amusing than usual, more full of dry drollery and humour; just as at the times when an order came in to,X. (the initial she had chosen) for a stock of well-paying things, she sat and stormed at her servant as she stitched away. She herself explained her practice in this way :

MY LADY LUDLOW.

" When everything goes wrong, one would give up breathing if one could not lighten one's heart by a joke. But when I've to sit still from morning till night, I must have something to stir my blood, or I should go off into an apoplexy, so I set to, and quarrel with Sally."

Such were Miss Galindo's means and manner of living in her own house. Out of doors, and in the village, she was not popular, although she would have been sorely missed had she left the place. But she asked too many home questions (not to say impertinent) respecting the domestic economies (for even the very poor like to spend their bit of money their own way), and would open cupboards to find out hidden extravagances, and question closely respecting the weekly amount of butter, till one day she met with what would have been a rebuff to any other person, but which she rather enjoyed than otherwise.

She was going into a cottage, and in the doorway met the good woman chasing out a duck, and apparently unconscious of her visitor.

" Get out, Miss Galindo !" she cried addressing the duck. " Get out! O, I ask your pardon," she continued, as if seeing the lady for the first time. " It's only that weary duck that will come in. Get out, Miss Gal " (to the duck).

" And so you call it after me, do you ?" inquired her visitor.

" O, yes, ma'am, my master would have it so, for he said, sure enough the unlucky bird was always poking herself where she was not wanted."

" Ha, ha! very good! And so your master is a wit, is he ? Well! tell him to come up and speak to me to-night about my parlour chimney, for there is no one like him for chimney doctoring."

And the master went up, and was so won over by Miss Galindo's merry ways, and sharp insight into the mysteries of his various kinds of business (he was a mason, chimney-sweeper, and ratcatcher), that he came home and abused his wife the next time she called the duck the name by which he himself had christened her.

But odd as Miss Galindo was in general, she could be as well-bred a lady as any one when she chose. And choose she always did when my Lady Ludlow was by. Indeed, I don't know the man, woman, or child, that did not instinctively turn out its best side to her ladyship. So she had no notion of the qualities which, I am sure, made Mr. Horner think that Miss Galindo would be most unmanageable as a clerk, and heartily wish that the idea had never come into my lady's head. But there it was; and he had annoyed her ladyship already more than he liked to-day, so he could not directly contradict her, but only urge difficulties which he hoped might prove insuperable. But every one of them Lady Ludlow knocked down. Letters to copy ? Doubtless. Miss Galindo could come up to the hall; she should have a room to herself; she wrote a beautiful hand; and writing would save her eyesight " Capability with regard to accounts ?" My lady would anwer for that too; and for more than Mr. Horner seemed to think it necessary to inquire about. Miss Galindo was by birth and breeding a lady of the strictest honour, and would, if possible, forget the substance of any letters that passed through her hands; at any rate, no one would ever hear of them again from her. " Remuneration ?" Oh ! as for that, Lady Ludlow would herself take care that it was managed in the most delicate manner possible. She would send to invite Miss Galindo to tea at the Hall that very afternoon, if Mr. Horner would only give her ladyship the slightest idea of the average length of time that my lady was to request Miss Galindo to sacrifice to her daily, " Three hours! Very well." Mr. Horner looked very grave as he passed the windows of the room where I lay. I don't think he liked the idea of Miss Galindo as a clerk.

Lady Ludlow's invitations were like royal commands. Indeed, the village was too quiet to allow the inhabit-

ants to have many evening engagements of any kind. Now and then, Mr. and Mrs. Horner gave a tea and supper to the principal tenants and their wives, to which the clergyman was invited, and Miss Galindo, Mrs. Medlicott, and one or two other spinsters and widows. The glory of the supper-table on these occasions was invariably furnished by her ladyship: it was a cold roasted peacock, with his tail stuck out as if in life. Mrs. Medlicott would take up the whole morning arranging the feathers in the proper semicircle, and was always pleased with the wonder and admiration it excited. It was considered a due reward and fitting compliment to her exertions that Mr. Horner always took her in to supper, and placed her opposite to the magnificent dish, at which she sweetly smiled all the time they were at table. But since Mrs. Homer had had the paralytic stroke these parties had been given up; and Miss Galindo wrote a note to Lady Ludlow in reply to her invitation, saying that she was entirely disengaged, and would have great pleasure in doing herself the honour of waiting upon her ladyship. Whoever visited my lady took their meals with her, sitting on the dais, in the presence of all my former companions. So I did not see Miss Galindo until some time after tea; as the young gentlewomen had had to bring her their sewing and spinning, to hear the remarks of so competent a judge. At length her ladyship brought her visitor into the room where I lay,—it was one of my bad days, I remember,—in order to have her little bit of private conversation. Miss Galindo was dressed in her best gown, I am sure, but I had never seen anything like it except in a picture, it was so old-fashioned. She wore a white muslin apron, delicately embroidered, and put on a little crookedly, in order, as she told us, even Lady Ludlow, before the evening was over, to conceal a spot whence the colour had been discharged by a lemon-stain. This crookedness had an odd effect, especially when I saw that it was intentional; indeed, she was so anxious about her apron's right adjustment in the wrong place, that she told us straight out why she wore it so, and asked her ladyship if the spot was properly hidden, at the same time lifting up her apron and showing her how large it was.

" When my father was alive, I always took his right arm, so, and used to remove any spotted or discoloured breadths to the left side, if it was a walking-dress. That's the convenience of a gentleman. But widows and spinsters must do what they can. Ah, my dear (to me)! when you are reckoning up the blessings in your lot,—though you may think it a hard one in some respects,—don't forget how little your stockings want darning, as you are obliged to lie down so much! I would rather knit two pairs of stockings than darn one, any day."

" Have you been doing any of your beautiful knitting lately ?" asked my lady, who had now arranged Miss Galindo in the pleasantest chair, and taken her own little wicker-work one, and, having her work in her hands, was ready to try and open the subject.

" No, and alas! your ladyship. It is partly the hot weather's fault, for people seem to forget that winter must come; and partly, I suppose, that every one is stocked who has the money to pay four-and-sixpence a pair for stockings."

"Then may I ask if you have any time in your active days at liberty ?" said my lady, drawing a little nearer to her proposal, which I fancy she found it a little awkward to make.

"Why, the village keeps me busy, your ladyship, when I have neither knitting or sewing to do. You know I took X. for my letter at the repository, because it stands for Xantippe, who was a great scold in old times, as I have learnt. But I'm sure I don't know how the world would get on without scolding, your ladyship. It would go to sleep, and the sun would stand still."

" I don't think I could bear to scold, Miss Galindo," said her ladyship, smiling.

" No ! because your ladyship has people to do it for you. Begging your pardon, my lady, it seems to me the generality of people may be divided into saints scolds, and sinners. Now, your ladyship is a saint, because you have a sweet and holy nature, in the first place ; and have people to do your anger and vexation for you, in the second place. And Jonathan Walker is a sinner, because he is sent to prison. But here am I, half way, having but a poor kind of disposition at best, and yet hating sin, and all that leads to it, such as wasting and extravagance, and gossiping,—and yet all this lies right under my nose in the village, and I am not saint enough to be vexed at it; and so I scold. And though I had rather be a saint, yet I think I do good in my way."

" No doubt you do, dear Miss Galindo," said Lady Ludlow. " But I am sorry to hear that there is so much that is bad going on in the village,very sorry."

" O, your ladyship! then I am sorry I brought it out. It was only by way of saying, that when I have no particular work to do at home, I take a turn abroad, and set my neighbours to rights, just by way of steering clear of Satan.

For Satan finds some mischief still For idle hands to do,

you know, my lady."

There was no leading into the subject by delicate degrees, for Miss Galindo was evidently so fond of talking, that, if asked a question, she made her answer so long, that before she came to an end of it, she had wandered far away from the original starting point So Lady Ludlow plunged at once into what she had to say.

" Miss Galindo, I have a great favour to ask of you."

"My lady, I wish I could tell you what a pleasure it is to hear you say so," replied Miss Galindo, almost with tears in her eyes; so glad were we all to do anything for her ladyship, which could be called a free service and not merely a duty.

" It is this. Mr. Homer tells me that the business-letters, relating to the estate, are multiplying so much that he finds it impossible to copy them all himself, and I therefore require the services of some confidential and discreet person to copy these letters, and occasionally to go through certain accounts. Now, there is a very pleasant little sitting-room very near to Mr. Homer's office (you know Mr. Homer's office ? on the • other side of the stone hall?) and if I could prevail 1 upon you to come here to breakfast and afterwards sit there for three hours every morning, Mr. Horner should bring or send you the papers "

Lady Ludlow stopped. Miss Galindo's countenance

had fallen. There was some great obstacle in her mind to her wish for obliging Lady Ludlow.

"What would Sally do?" she asked at length. Lady Ludlow had not a notion who Sally was. Nor if she had had a notion, would she have had a conception of the perplexities that poured into Miss Galindo's mind, at the idea of leaving her rough forgetful dwarf without the perpetual monitorship of her mistress. Lady Ludlow, accustomed to a household where everything went on noiselessly, perfectly, and by clock-work, conducted by a number of highly-paid, well-chosen, and accomplished servants, had not a conception of the nature of the rough material from which her servants came. Besides, in her establishment, so that the result was good, no one inquired if the small economies had been observed in the production. Whereas every penny—every halfpenny, was of consequence to Miss Galindo ; and visions of squandered drops of milk and wasted crusts of bread filled her mind with dismay. But she swallowed all her apprehensions down, out of her regard for Lady Ludlow, and desire to be of service to her. No one knows how great a trial it was to her when she thought of Sally, unchecked and un-scolded for three hours every morning. But all she said was,—

" ' Sally, go to the Deuce.' I beg your pardon, my

lady, if I was talking to myself; it's a habit I have got into of keeping ray tongue in practice, and I am not quite aware when I do it. Three hours every morning ! I shall be only too proud to do what I can for your ladyship ; and I hope Mr. Horner will not be too impatient with me at first. You know, perhaps, that I was nearly being an authoress once, and that seems as if I was destined to 'employ my time in writing.'"

" No, indeed ; we must return to the subject of the clerkship r afterwards, if you please. An authoress, Miss Galindo ! You surprise me !"

" But, indeed, I was. All was quite ready. Doctor Burney used to teach me music: not that I ever could learn, but it was a fancy of my poor father's. And his daughter wrote a book, and they said she was but a very young lady, and nothing but a music-master's daughter; so why should not I try ?"

-Well?"

" Well! I got paper and half-a-hundred good pens, a bottle of ink, all ready "

" And then "

" O, it ended in my having nothing to say, when I sat down to write. But sometimes, when I get hold of a book, I wonder why I let such a poor reason stop me. It does not others."

" But I think it was very well it did, Miss Galindo," said her ladyship. " I am extremely against women usurping men's employments, as they are very apt to do. But perhaps, after all, the notion of writing a book improved your hand. It is one of the most legible I ever saw."

"I despise z's without tails," said Miss Galindo, with a good deal of gratified pride at my lady's praise. Presently, my lady took her to look at a curious old cabinet, which Lord Ludlow had picked up at the Hague; and while they were out of the room on this errand, I suppose the question of remuneration was settled, for I heard no more of it.

When they came back, they were talking of Mr. Gray. Miss Galindo was unsparing in her expressions of opinion about him: going much farther than my lady—in her language, at least.

" A little blushing man like him, who can't say bo to a goose without hesitating and colouring, to come to this village—which is as good a village as ever lived and cry us down for a set of sinners, as if we had all committed murder and that other thing! I have no patience with him, my lady. And then, how is he to help us to heaven, by teaching us our a b, ab—b a, ba ? And yet, by all accounts, that's to save poor children's souls. O, I knew your ladyship would agree with me.

I am sure my mother was as good a creature as ever breathed the blessed air; and if she's not gone to heaven, I don't want to go there; and she could not spell a letter decently. And does Mr. Gray think God took note of that ?"

" I was sure you would agree with me, Miss Ga-lindo," said my lady. " You and I can remember how this talk about education—Rousseau, and his writings—stirred up the French people to their Reign of Terror, and all those bloody scenes."

" I'm afraid that Rousseau and Mr. Gray are birds of a feather," replied Miss Galindo, shaking her head. "And yet there is some good in the young man, too. He sat up all night with Billy Davis, when his wife was fairly worn out with nursing him."

" Did he, indeed!" said my lady, her face lighting up, as it always did when she heard of any kind or generous action, no matter who performed it. " What a pity he is bitten with these new revolutionary ideas, and is so much for disturbing the established order of society!"

When Miss Galindo went, she left so favourable an impression of her visit on my lady, that she said to me with a pleased smile:

" I think I have provided Mr. Homer with a far better clerk than he would have made of that lad

Gregson in twenty years. And I will send the lad to my lord's grieve, in Scotland, that he may be kept out of harm's way."

But something happened to the lad before this purpose could be accomplished.

CHAPTER X.

THE next morning, Miss Galindo made her appearance, and, by some mistake, unusual in my lady's well-trained servants, was shown into the room where I was trying to walk; for a certain amount of exercise was prescribed for me, painful although the exertion had become.

She brought a little basket along with her; and while the footman was gone to inquire my lady's wishes (for I don't think that Lady Ludlow expected Miss Galindo so soon to assume her clerkship; nor, indeed, had Mr. Homer any work of any kind ready for his new assistant to do), she launched out into conversation with me.

" It was a sudden summons, my dear ! However, as I have often said to myself, ever since an occasion long ago, if Lady Ludlow ever honours me by asking for my right hand, I'll cut it off, and wrap the stump up so tidily she shall never find out it bleeds. But, if I had had a little more time, I could have mended my pens better.

You see, I have had to sit up pretty late to get these sleeves made "—and she took out of her basket a pair of brown-holland over-sleeves, very much such as a grocer's apprentice wears—" and I had only time to make seven or eight pens, out of some quills Farmer Thomson gave me last autumn. As for ink, I'm thankful to say, that's always ready; an ounce of steel filings, an ounce of nut-gall, and a pint of water (tea, if you're extravagant, which, thank Heaven I I'm not), put all in a bottle, and hang it up behind the house door, so that the whole gets a good shaking every time you slam it to—and even if you are in a passion and bang it, as Sally and I often do, it is all the better for it—and there's my ink ready for use; ready to write my lady's will with, if need be."

" O, Miss Galindo!" said I, " don't talk so; my lady's will! and she not dead yet."

" And if she were, what would be the use of talking of making her will! Now, if you were Sally, I should say, ' Answer me that, you goose ?' But, as you're a relation of my lady's, I must be civil, and only say, ' I can't think how you can talk so like a fool!' To be sure, poor thing, you're lame !"

I do not know how long she would have gone on; but my lady came in, and I, released from my duty of entertaining Miss Galindo, made my limping way into the next room. To tell the truth, I was rather afraid of Miss Galindo's tongue, for I never knew what she would say next.

After a while my lady came, and began to look in the bureau for k something; and as she looked she said :

u I think Mr. Horner must have made some mistake, when he said he had so much work that he almost required a clerk, for this morning he cannot find anything for Miss Galindo to do; and there she is, sitting with her pen behind her ear, waiting for something to write. I am come to find her my mother's letters, for I should like to have a fair copy made of them. O, here they are! don't trouble yourself, my dear child."

When my lady returned again, she sat down and began to talk of Mr. Gray.

" Miss Galindo says she saw him going to hold a prayer-meeting in a cottage. Now, that really makes me unhappy, it is so like what Mr. Wesley used to do in my younger days; and since then we have had rebellion in the American colonies and the French revolution. You may depend upon it, my dear, making religion and education common—vulgarising them, as it were—is a bad thing for a nation. A man who hears prayers read in the cottage where he has just supped on bread and bacon, forgets the respect due to a

church: he begins to think that one place is as good as another, and, by-and-hy, that one person is as good as another; and after that, I always find that people begin to talk of their rights, instead of thinking of their duties. I wish Mr. Gray had been more tractable, and had left well alone. What do you think I heard this morning? Why, that the Home Hill estate, which niches into the Hanbury property, was bought by a Baptist baker from Birmingham !"

" A Baptist baker !" I exclaimed. I had never seen a Dissenter, to my knowledge ; but, having always heard them spoken of with horror, I looked upon them almost as if they were rhinoceroses. I wanted to see a live Dissenter, I believe, and yet I wished it were over. I was almost surprised when I heard that any of them were engaged in such peaceful occupations as baking.

" Yes! so Mr. Homer tells me. A Mr. Lambe, I believe. But, at any rate, he is a Baptist, and has been in trade. What with his schismatism and Mr. Gray's methodism, I am afraid all the primitive character of this place will vanish."

From what I could hear, Mr. Gray seemed to be taking his own way; at any rate, more than he had done when he first came to the village, when his natural timidity had made him defer to my lady, and seek her consent and sanction before embarking in any new

plan. But newness was a quality Lady Ludlow especially disliked. Even in the fashions of dress and furniture, she clung to the old, to the modes which had prevailed when she was young; and, though she had a deep personal regard for Queen Charlotte (to whom, as I have already said, she had been maid-of-honour), yet there was a tinge of Jacobitism about her, such as made her extremely dislike to hear Prince Charles Edward called the Young Pretender, as many loyal people did in those days, and made her fond of telling of the thorn-tree in my lord's park in Scotland, which had been planted by bonny Queen Mary herself, and before which every guest in the Castle of Monks-haven was expected to stand bare-headed, out of respect to the memory and misfortunes of the royal planter.

We might play at cards, if we so chose, on a Sunday; at least, I suppose we might, for my lady and Mr. Mountford used to do so often when I first went. But we must neither play cards, nor read, nor sew on the fifth of November and on the thirtieth of January, but must go to church, and meditate all the rest of the day—and very hard work meditating was. I would far rather have scoured a room. That was the reason, I suppose, why a passive life was seen to be better discipline for me than an active one.

But I am wandering away from my lady, and her dislike to all innovation. Now, it seemed to me, as far as I heard, that Mr. Gray was full of nothing but new things, and that what he first did was to attack all our established institutions, both in the village and the parish, and also in the nation. To be sure, I heard of his ways of going on principally from Miss Galindo, who was apt to speak more strongly than accurately.

" There he goes," she said, " clucking up the children just like an old hen, and trying to teach them about their salvation and their souls, and I don't know what—things that it is just blasphemy to speak about out of church. And he potters old people about reading their Bibles. I am sure I don't want to speak disrespectfully about the Holy Scriptures, but I found old Job Horton busy reading his Bible yesterday. Says I, ' What are you reading, and where did you get it, and who gave it you ?' So he made answer, ' That he was reading Susannah and the Elders, for that he had read Bel and the Dragon till he could pretty near say it off by heart, and they were two as pretty stories as ever he had read, and that it was a caution to him what bad old chaps there were in the world.' Now, as Job is bed-ridden, I don't think he is likely to meet with the Elders, and I say that I think repeating his Creed, the Commandments, and the Lord's Prayer, and, maybe,

throwing in a verse of the Psalms, if he wanted a bit of a change, would have done him far more good than his pretty stories, as he called them. And what's the next thing our young parson does ? Why he tries to make us all feel pitiful for the black slaves, and leaves little pictures of negroes about, with the question printed below,' Am I not a man and a brother ?' just as if I was to be hail-fellow-well-met with every negro footman. They do say he takes no sugar in his tea, because he thinks he sees spots of blood in it. Now I call that superstition."

The next day it was a still worse story.

" Well, my dear! and how are you ? My lady sent me in to sit a bit with you, while Mr. Homer looks out some papers for me to copy. Between ourselves, Mr. Steward Homer does not like having me for a clerk. It is all very well, he does not; for, if he were decently civil to me, I might want a chaperone, you know, now poor Mrs. Horner is dead." This was one of Miss Galindo's grim jokes. " As it is, I try to make him forget I'm a woman, I do everything as ship-shape as a masculine man-clerk. I see he can't find a fault— writing good, spelling correct, sums all right. And then he squints up at me with the tail of his eye, and looks glummer than ever, just because I'm a woman— as if I could help that. I have gone good lengths to

set his mind at ease. I have stuck my pen behind my ear, I have made him a bow instead of a curtsey, I have whistled—not a tune, I can't pipe up that—nay, if you won't tell my lady, I don't mind telling you that I have said ' Confound it!' and ' Zounds !' I can't get any farther. For all that, Mr. Horner won't forget I am a lady, and so I am not half the use I might be, and if it were not to please my Lady Ludlow, Mr. Horner and his books might go hang (see how natural that came out 1). And there is an order for a dozen nightcaps for a bride, and I am so afraid I shan't have time to do them. Worst of all, there's Mr. Gray taking advantage of my absence to seduce Sally!"

« To seduce Sally! Mr. Gray!"

" Pooh, pooh, child! There's many a kind of seduction. Mr. Gray is seducing Sally to want to go to church. There has he been twice at my house, while I have been away in the mornings, talking to Sally about the state of her soul and that sort of thing. But when I found the meat all roasted to a cinder, I said, 'Come, Sally, let's have no more praying when beef is down at the fire. Pray at six o'clock in the morning and nine at night, and I won't hinder you.' So she sauced me, and said something about Martha and. Mary, implying that, because she had let the beef get so overdone that I declare I could hardly find a bit fit for

Nancy Pole's sick grandchild, she had chosen the better part. I was very much put about, I own, and perhaps you'll be shocked at what I said—indeed, I don't know if it was right myself—

but I told her I had a soul as well as she, and if it was to be saved by my sitting still and thinking about salvation and never doing my duty, I thought I had as good a right as she had to be Mary, and save my soul. So, that afternoon I sat quite still, and it was really a comfort, for I am often too busy, I know, to pray as I ought. There is first one person wanting me, and then another, and the house and the food and the neighbours to see after. So, when tea-time comes, there enters my maid with her hump on her back, and her soul to be saved. ' Please, ma'am, did you order the pound of butter ?No, Sally,' I said, shaking my head, ' this morning I did not go round by Hale's farm, and this afternoon I have been employed in spiritual things.'

"Now, our Sally likes tea and bread-and-butter above everything, and dry bread was not to her taste.

"' I'm thankful,' said the impudent hussy, ' that you have taken a turn towards godliness. It will be my prayers, I trust, that's given it you.'

"I was determined not to give her an opening towards the carnal subject of butter, so she lingered still, longing to ask leave to run for it. But I gave her none, and munched my dry bread myself, thinking what a famous cake I could make for little Ben Pole with the bit of butter we were saving ; and when Sally had had her butterless tea, and was in none of the best of tempers because Martha had not bethought herself of the butter, I just quietly said:

"' Now, Sally, to-morrow we'll try to hash that beef well, and to remember the butter, and to work out our salvation all at the same time, for I don't see why it can't all be done, as God has set us to do it all.' But I heard her at it again about Mary and Martha, and I have no doubt that Mr. Gray will teach her to consider me a lost sheep."

I had heard so many little speeches about Mr. Gray from one person or another, all' speaking against him, as a mischief-maker, a setter-up of new doctrines, and of a fanciful standard of life (and you may be sure that, where Lady Ludlow led, Mrs. Medlicott and Adams were certain to follow, each in their different ways showing the influence my lady had over them), that I believe I had grown to consider him as a very instrument of evil, and to expect to perceive in his face marks of his presumption, and arrogance, and impertinent interference. It was now many weeks since I had seen him, and when he was one morning shown into the blue drawing-room (into which I had been removed for a change), I was quite surprised to see how innocent and awkward a young man he appeared, confused even more than I was at our unexpected tete-a-tete. He looked thinner, his eyes more eager, his expression more anxious, and his colour came and went more than it had done when I had seen him last. I tried to make a little conversation, as I was, to my own surprise, more at my ease than he was; but his thoughts were evidently too much preoccupied for him to do more than answer me with monosyllables.

Presently my lady came in. Mr. Gray twitched and coloured more than ever; but plunged into the middle of his subject at once.

" My lady, I cannot answer it to my conscience, if I allow the children of this village to go on any longer the little heathens that they are. I must do something to alter their condition. I am quite aware that your ladyship disapproves of many of the plans which have suggested themselves to me; but nevertheless I must do something, and I am come now to your ladyship to ask respectfully, but firmly, what you would advise me to do."

His eyes were dilated, and I could almost have said they were full of tears with his eagerness. But I am sure it is a bad plan to remind people of decided opinions which they have once expressed, if you wish them to modify those opinions. Now, Mr. Gray had done this with my lady; and though I do not mean to say she was obstinate, yet she was not one to retract.

She was silent for a moment or two before she replied.

" You ask me to suggest a remedy for an evil of the existence of which I am not conscious," was her answer —very coldly, very gently given. " In Mr. Mount-ford's time I heard no such complaints: whenever I see the village children (and they are not unfrequent visitors at this house, on one pretext or another), they are well and decently behaved." T"Oh, madam, you cannot judge," he broke in. " They are trained to respect you in word and deed; you are the highest they ever look up to; they have no notion of a higher."

" Nay, Mr. Gray," said my lady, smiling, " they are as loyally disposed as any children can be. They come up here every fourth of June, and drink his Majesty's health, and have buns, and (as Margaret Dawson can testify) they take a great and respectful interest in all the pictures I can show them of the Royal family."

" But, madam, I think of something higher than any earthly dignities."

My lady coloured at the mistake she had made; for she herself was truly pious. Yet when she resumed

the subject, it seemed to me as if her tone was a little sharper than before.

"Such want of reverence is, I should say, the clergyman's fault. You must excuse me, Mr. Gray, if I speak plainly."

" My lady, I want plain-speaking. I myself am not accustomed to those ceremonies and forms which are, I suppose, the etiquette in your ladyship's rank of life, and which seem to hedge you in from any power of mine to touch, you. Among those with whom I have passed my life hitherto, it has been the custom to speak plainly out what we have felt earnestly. So, instead of needing any apology from your ladyship for straightforward speaking, I will meet what you say at once, and admit that it is the clergyman's fault, in a great measure, when the children of his parish swear, and curse, and are brutal, and ignorant of all saving grace ; nay, some of them of the very name of God. And because this guilt of mine, as the clergyman of this parish, lies heavy on my soul, and every day leads but from bad to worse, till I am utterly bewildered how to do good to children who escape from me as if I were a monster, and who are growing up to be men fit for and capable of any crime, but those requiring wit or sense, I come to you, who seem to me all-powerful, as far as material power goes—for your ladyship only knows

MY LADY LUDLOW.

the surface of things, and barely that, that pass in your village—to help me with advice, and such outward help as you can give."

Mr. Gray had stood up and sat down once or twice while he had been speaking, in an agitated, nervous kind of way, and now he was interrupted by a violent fit of coughing, after which he trembled all over.

My lady rang for a glass of water, and looked much distressed.

" Mr. Gray," said she, " I am sure you are not well; and that makes you exaggerate childish faults into positive evils. It is always the case with us when we are not strong in health. I hear of you exerting yourself in every direction: you over-work yourself, and the consequence is, that you imagine us all worse people than we are."

And my lady smiled very kindly and pleasantly at him, as he sat, a little panting, a little flushed, trying to recover his breath. I am sure that now they were brought face to face, she had quite forgotten all the offence she had taken at his doings when she heard of them from others ; and, indeed, it was enough to soften any one's heart to see that young, almost boyish face, looking in such anxiety and distress.

" O, my lady, what shall I do ?" he asked, as soon as he could recover breath, and with such an air of humility that I am sure no one who had seen it could have ever thought him conceited again. " The evil of this world is too strong for me. I can do so little. It is all in vain. It was only to-day " And again the cough and agitation returned.

" My dear Mr. Gray," said my lady (the day before, I could never have believed she could have called him My dear), " you must take the advice of an old woman about yourself. You are not fit to do anything just now but attend to your own health: rest, and see a doctor (but, indeed, I will take care of that), and when you are pretty strong again, you will find that you have been magnifying evils to yourself."

" But, my lady, I cannot rest. The evils do exist, and the burden of their continuance lies on my shoulders. I have no place to gather the children together in, that I may teach them the things necessary to salvation. The rooms in my own house are too small; but I have tried them. I have money of iny own; and, as your ladyship knows, I tried to get a piece of leasehold property on which to build a school-house at my own expense. Your ladyship's lawyer comes forward, at your instructions, to enforce some old feudal right, by which no building is allowed on leasehold property without the sanction of the Lady of the Manor. It may be all very true; but it was a cruel thing to do,—that is, if your ladyship had known (which I am sure you do not) the real moral and spiritual state of my poor parishioners. And now I come to you to know what I am to do ? Kest! I cannot rest, while children whom I could possibly save are being left in their ignorance, their blasphemy, their uncleanness, their cruelty. It is known through the village that your ladyship disapproves of my efforts, and opposes all my plans. If you think them wrong, foolish, ill-digested (I have been a student, living in a college, and eschewing all society but that of pious men, until now: I may not judge for the best, in my ignorance of this sinful human nature), tell me of better plans and wiser projects for accomplishing my end; but do not bid me rest, with Satan compassing me round, and stealing souls away."

" Mr. Gray," said my lady, " there may be some truth in what you have said. I do not deny it, though I think, in your present state of indisposition and excitement, you exaggerate it much. I believe—nay, the experience of a pretty long life has convinced me— that education is a bad thing, if given indiscriminately. It unfits the lower orders for their duties, the duties to which they are called by God, of submission to those placed in authority over them, of contentment with that state of life to which it has pleased God to call them, and of ordering themselves lowly and reverently to all their betters. I have made this conviction of mine tolerably evident to you; and have expressed distinctly my disapprobation of some of your ideas. You may imagine, then, that I was not well pleased when I found that you had taken a rood or more of Farmer Hale's land, and were laying the foundations of a school-house. You had done this without asking for my permission, which, as Farmer Hale's liege lady, ought to have been obtained legally, as well as asked for out of courtesy. I put a stop to what I believed to be calculated to do harm to a village, to a population in which, to say the least of it, I may be supposed to take as much interest as you can do. How can reading and writing, and the multiplication-table (if you choose to go so far), prevent blasphemy, and uncleanness and cruelty ? Really, Mr. Gray, I hardly like to express myself to strongly on the subject in your present state of health, as I should do at any other time. It seems to me that books do little; character much ; and character is not formed from books."

" I do not think of character: I think of souls. I must get some hold upon these children, or what will become of them in the next world ? I must be found to have some power beyond what they have, and which they are rendered capable of appreciating, before they will listen to me. At present, physical force is all they look up to; and I have none."

" Nay, Mr. Gray, by your own admission, they look up to me."

" They would not do anything your ladyship disliked if it was likely to come to your knowledge; but if they could conceal it from you, the knowledge of your dislike to a particular line of conduct would never make them cease from pursuing it."

" Mr. Gray "—surprise in her air, and some little indignation—" they and their fathers have lived on the Hanbury lands for generations!"

" I cannot help it, madam. I am telling you the truth, whether you believe me or not." There was a pause; my lady looking perplexed, and somewhat ruffled; Mr. Gray as though hopeless and wearied out. " Then, my lady," said he, at last, rising as he spoke, " you can suggest nothing to ameliorate the state of things which, I do assure you, does exist on your lands, and among your tenants. Surely, you will not object to my using Farmer Hale's great barn every Sabbath ? He will allow me the use of it, if your ladyship will grant your permission."

" You are not fit for any extra work at present," (and indeed he had been coughing very much all through the conversation). " Give me time to consider

of it. Tell me what you wish to teach. You will be able to take care of your health * and grow stronger while I consider. It shall not be the worse for you, if you leave it in my hands for a time."

My lady spoke very kindly; but he was in too excited a state to recognise the kindness, while the idea of delay was evidently a sore irritation. I heard him say: " And I have so little time in which to do my work. Lord! lay not this sin to my charge."

But my lady was speaking to the old butler, for whom, at her sign, I had rung the bell some little time before. Now she turned round.

" Mr. Gray, I find I have some bottles of Malmsey, of the vintage of seventeen hundred and seventy-eight, yet left Malmsey, as perhaps you know, used to be considered a specific for coughs arising from weakness. You must permit me to send you half-a-dozen bottles, and, depend upon it, you will take a more cheerful view of life and its duties before you have finished them, especially if you will be so kind as to see Doctor Trevor, who is coming to see me in the course of the week. By the time you are strong enough to work, I will try and find some means of preventing the children from using such bad language, and otherwise annoying you."

" My lady, it is the sin, and not the annoyance. I wish I could make you understand." He spoke with

some impatience; poor fellow, he was too weak, exhausted, and nervous. " I am perfectly well; I can set to work to-morrow; I will do anything not to be oppressed with the thought of how little I am doing. I do not want your wine. Liberty to act in the manner I think right, will do me far more good. But it is of no use. It is preordained that I am to be nothing but a cumberer of the ground. I beg your ladyship's pardon for this call."

He stood up, and then turned dizzy. My lady looked on, deeply hurt, and not a little offended. He held out his hand to her, and I could see that she had a little hesitation before she took it. He then saw me, I almost think, for the first time; and put out his hand once more, drew it back, as if undecided, put it out again, and finally took hold of mine for an instant in his damp, listless hand, and was gone.

Lady Ludlow was dissatisfied with both him and herself, I was sure. Indeed, I was dissatisfied with the result of the interview myself. But my lady was not one to speak out her feelings on the subject; nor was I one to forget myself, and begin on a topic which she did not begin. She came to me, and was very tender with me; so tender, that that, and the thoughts of Mr. Gray's sick, hopeless, disappointed look, nearly made me cry.

"You are tired, little one," said my lady. "Go and lie down in my room, and hear what Medlicott and I can decide upon in the way of strengthening dainties for that poor '.young man, who is killing himself with his over-sensitive conscientiousness."

"O, my lady!" said I, and then I stopped.

"Well. What?" asked she.

"If you would but let him have Farmer Hale's barn at once, it would do him more good than all."

"Pooh, pooh, child!" though I don't think she was displeased, "he is not fit for more work just now. I shall go and write for Doctor Trevor."

And, for the next half-hour, we did nothing but arrange physical comforts and cures for poor Mr. Gray. At the end of the time, Mrs. Medlicott said:

"Has your ladyship heard that Harry Gregson has fallen from a tree, and broken his thigh-bone, and is like to be a cripple for life?"

"Harry Gregson! That black-eyed lad who read my letter? It all comes from over-education!"

CHAPTER XI.

BUT I don't see how my lady could think it was over education that made Harry Gregson break his thigh, for the manner in which he met with the accident was this:— »

Mr. Horner, who had fallen sadly out of health since his wife's death, had attached himself greatly to Harry Gregson. Now, Mr. Horner had a cold manner to every one, and never spoke more than was necessary, at the best of times. And, latterly, it had not been the best of times with him. I dare say, he had had some causes for anxiety (of which I knew nothing) about my lady's affairs; and he was evidently annoyed by my lady's whim (as he once inadvertently called it) of placing Miss Galindo under him in the position of a clerk. Yet he had always been friends, in his quiet way, with Miss Galindo, and she devoted herself to her new occupation with diligence and punctuality, although more than once she had moaned to me over the orders

for needlework which had been sent to her, and which, owing to her occupation in the service of Lady Ludlow, she had been unable to fulfil.

The only living creature to whom the staid Mr. Horner could be said to be attached, was Harry Gregson. To my lady he was a faithful and devoted servant, looking keenly after her interests, and anxious to forward them at any cost of trouble to himself But the more shrewd Mr. Horner was, the more probability was there of his being annoyed at certain peculiarities of opinion which my lady held with a quiet, gentle pertinacity; against which no arguments, based on mere worldly and business calculations, made any way. This frequent opposition to views which Mr. Horner entertained, although it did not interfere with the sincere respect which the lady and the steward felt for each other, yet prevented any warmer feeling of affection from coming in. It seems strange to say it, but I must repeat it—the only person for whom, since his wife's death, Mr. Horner seemed to feel any love, was the little imp Harry Gregson, with his bright, watchful eyes, his tangled hair hanging right down to his eyebrows, for all the world like a Skye terrier. This lad, half gipsy and whole poacher, as many people esteemed him, hung about the silent, respectable, staid Mr. Horner, and followed his steps with

something of the affectionate fidelity of the dog which he resembled* I suspect, this demonstration of attachment to his person on Harry Gregson's part was what won Mr. Horner's regard. In the first instance, the steward had only chosen the lad out as the cleverest instrument he could find for his purpose; and I don't mean to say that, if Harry had not been almost as shrewd as Mr. Homer himself was, both by original disposition and subsequent experience, the steward would have taken to him as he did, let the lad have shown ever so much affection for him.

But even to Harry Mr. Horner was silent. Still, it was pleasant to find himself in many ways so readily understood; to perceive that the crumbs of knowledge he let fall were picked up by his little follower, and hoarded like gold; that here was one to hate the persons and things whom Mr. Horner coldly disliked, and to reverence and admire all those for whom he had any regard. Mr. Horner had never had a child, and unconsciously, I suppose, something of the paternal feeling had begun to develop itself in him towards Harry Gregson. I heard one or two things from different people, which have always made me fancy that Mr. Horner secretly and almost unconsciously hoped that Harry Gregson might be trained so as to be first his clerk, and next his assist-ant, and finally his successor in his stewardship to the Hanbury estates.

Harry's disgrace with my lady, in consequence of his reading the letter, was a deeper blow to Mr. Horner than his quiet manner would ever have led any one to suppose, or than Lady Ludlow ever dreamed of inflicting, I am sure.

Probably Harry had a short, stern, rebuke from Mr. Horner at the time, for his manner was always hard even to those he cared for the most. But Harry's love was not to be daunted or quelled by a few sharp words. I dare say, from what I heard of them afterwards, that Harry accompanied Mr. Horner in his walk over the farm the very day of the rebuke; his presence apparently unnoticed by the agent, by whom his absence would have been painfully felt nevertheless. That was the way of it, as I have been told. Mr. Horner never bade Harry go with him ; never thanked him for going, or being at his heels ready to run on any errands, straight as the crows flies to his point, and back to heel in as short a time as possible. Yet, if Harry were away, Mr. Horner never inquired the reason from any of the men who might be supposed to know whether he was detained by his father, or otherwise engaged ; he never asked Harry himself where he had been. But Miss Galindo said that those labourers

^who knew Mr. Homer well, told her that he was always more quick-eyed to short-comings, more savage-like in fault-finding, on those days when the lad was absent.

Miss Galindo, indeed, was my great authority for most of the village news which I heard. She it was who gave me the particulars of poor Harry's accident.

"You see, my dear," she said, "the little poacher has taken some unaccountable fancy to my master." (This was the name by which Miss Galindo always spoke of Mr. Homer to me, ever since she had been, as she called it, appointed his clerk.)

" Now, if I had twenty hearts to lose, I never could spare a bit of one of them for that good, grey, square severe man. But different people have different tastes, and here is that little imp of a gipsy-tinker ready to turn slave for my master; and, odd enough, my master,—who, I should have said before-hand, would have made short work of imp, and imp's family, and have sent Hall, the Bang-beggar, after them in no time—my master, as they tell me, is in his way quite fond of the lad, and if he could, without vexing my lady too much, he would have made him what the folks here call a Latiner. However, last night, it seems that there was a letter of some importance forgotten (I can't tell you what it was about, my dear, though I

know perfectly well, but ' service oblige, 1 as well as 4 noblesse,' and you must take my word for it that it was important, and one that I am surprised my master could forget), till too late for the post. (The poor, good, orderly man is not what he was before his wife's death.) Well, it seems that he was sore annoyed by his forgetfulness, and well he might be. And it was all the more vexatious, as he had no one to blame but himself. As for that matter, I always scold somebody else when I'm in fault; but I suppose my master would never think of doing that, else it's a mighty relief. However, he could eat no tea, and was altogether put out and gloomy. And the little faithful imp-lad, perceiving all this, I suppose, got up like a page in an old ballad, and said he would run for his life across country to Comberford, and see if he could not get there before the bags were made up. So my master gave him the letter, and nothing more was heard of the poor fellow till this morning, for the father thought his son was sleeping in Mr. Homer's barn, as he does occasionally it seems, and my master, as was very natural, that he had gone to his father's,"

" And he had fallen down the old stone quarry, had he not?"

" Yes, sure enough. Mr. Gray had been up here fretting my lady with some of his new-fangled schemes,

MY LADY LUDLOW

and because the young man could not have it all his own way, from what I understand, he was put out, and thought he would go home by the back lane, instead of through the village, where the folks would notice if the parson looked glum. But, however, it was a mercy, and I don't mind saying so, ay, and meaning it too, though it may be like methodism, for, as Mr. Gray walked by the quarry, he heard a groan, and at first he thought it was a lamb fallen down; and he stood still, and then he heard it again; and then, I suppose, he looked down and saw Harry. So he let himself down by the boughs of the trees to the ledge where Harry lay half-dead, and with his poor thigh broken. There he had lain ever since the night before: he had been returning to tell the master that he had safely posted the letter, and the first words he said, when they recovered him from the exhausted state he was in, were " (Miss Galindo tried hard not to whimper, as she said it), " 'It was in time, sir. I see'd it put in the bag with my own eyes.'"

" But where is he ?" asked I. " How did Mr. Gray get him out ?"

" Ay! there it is, you see. Why the old gentleman (I daren't say Devil in Lady Ludlow's house) is not so black as he is painted; and Mr. Gray must have a deal of good in him, as I say at times; and then at

others, when he has gone against me, I can't bear him, and think hanging too good for him. But he lifted the poor lad, as if he had been a baby, I suppose, and carried him up the great ledges that were formerly used for steps; and laid him soft and easy on the wayside grass, and ran home and got help and a door, and had him carried to his house, and laid on his bed; and then somehow, for the first time either he or any one else perceived it, he himself was all over blood his own blood he had broken a blood-vessel; and there he lies in the little dressing-room, as white and as still as if he were dead; and the little imp in Mr. Gray's own bed, sound asleep, now his leg is set, just as if linen sheets and a feather bed were his native element, as one may say. Really, now he is doing so well, I've no patience with him, lying there where Mr. Gray ought to be. It is just what my lady always prophesied would come to pass, if there was any confusion of ranks."

" Poor Mr. Gray!" said I, thinking of his flushed face, and his feverish, restless ways, when he had been calling on my lady not an hour before his exertions on Harry's behalf. And I told Miss Galindo how ill I had thought him.

" Yes," said she. " And that was the reason my lady had sent for Doctor Trevor. Well, it has fallen

out admirably, for he looked well after that old donkey of a Prince, and saw that he made no blunders."

Now "that old donkey of a Prince" meant the village surgeon, Mr. Prince, between whom and Miss Galindo there was war to the knife, as they often met in the cottages, when there was illness, and she had her queer, odd recipes, which he, with his grand pharmacopoeia, held in infinite contempt, and the consequence of their squabbling had been, not long before this very time, that he had established a kind of rule, that into whatever sick-room Miss Galindo was admitted, there he refused to visit. But Miss Galindo's prescriptions and visits cost nothing, and were often backed by kitchen-physic; so, though it was true that she never came but she scolded about something or other, she was generally preferred as medical attendant to Mr. Prince.

"Yes, the old donkey is obliged to tolerate me, and be civil to me; for, you see, I got there first, and had possession, as it were, and yet my lord the donkey likes the credit of attending the parson, and being in consultation with so grand a county-town doctor as Doctor Trevor. And Doctor Trevor is an old friend of mine" (she sighed a little, some time I may tell you why), "and treats me with infinite bowing and respect; so the donkey, not to be out of medical fashion, bows too, though it is sadly against the grain: and he pulled a face as if he had heard a slate-pencil gritting against a slate, when I told Doctor Trevor I meant to sit up with the two lads, for I call Mr. Gray little more than a lad, and a pretty conceited one, too, at times."

"But why should you sit up, Miss Galindo? It will tire you sadly."

"Not it. You see, there is Gregson's mother to keep quiet; for she sits by her lad, fretting and sobbing, so that I'm afraid of her disturbing Mr. Gray; and there's Mr. Gray to keep quiet, for Doctor Trevor says his life depends on it; and there is medicine to be given to the one, and bandages to be attended to for the other; and the wild horde of gipsy brothers and sisters to be turned out, and the father to be held in from showing too much gratitude to Mr. Gray, who can't bear it,—and who is to do it all but me? The only servant is old lame Betty, who once lived with me, and would leave me because she said I was always bothering—(there was a good deal of truth in what she said, I grant, but she need not have said it; a good deal of truth is best let alone at the bottom of the well), and what can she do,—deaf as ever she can be, too?"

So Miss Galindo went her ways; but not the less was she at her post in the morning; a little crosser and more silent than usual; but the first was not to be wondered at, and the last was rather a blessing.

Lady Ludlow had been extremely anxious both about Mr. Gray and Harry Gregson. Kind and thoughtful in any case of illness and accident, she always was; but somehow, in this, the feeling that she was not quite what shall I call it? "friends" seems hardly the right word to use, as to the possible feeling between the Countess Ludlow and the little vagabond messenger, who had only once been in her presence,— that she had hardly parted from either as she could have wished to do, had death been near, made her more than usually anxious. Doctor Trevor was not to spare obtaining the best medical advice the county could afford; whatever he ordered in the way of diet, was to be prepared under Mrs. Medlicott's own eye, and sent down from the Hall to the Parsonage. As Mr. Horner had given somewhat similar directions, in the case of Harry Gregson at least, there was rather a multiplicity of counsellors and dainties, than any lack of them. And, the second night, Mr. Horner insisted on taking the superintendence of the nursing himself, and sat and snored by Harry's bedside, while the poor, exhausted mother lay by her child,—thinking that she watched him, but in reality fast asleep, as Miss Galindo told us; for, distrusting any one's powers of watching and nursing but her own, she had stolen across the quiet village street in cloak and dressing-gown, and

found Mr. Gray in vain trying to reach the cup of barley-water which Mr. Homer had placed just beyond his reach.

In consequence of Mr. Gray's illness, we had to have a strange curate to do duty; a man who dropped his h's, and hurried through the service, and yet had time enough to stand in my lady's way, bowing to her as she came out of church, and so subservient in manner, that I believe that sooner than remain unnoticed by a countess, he would have preferred being scolded, or even cuffed. Now I found out, that great as was my lady's liking and approval of respect, nay, even reverence, being paid to her as a person of quality, —a sort of tribute to her Order, which she had no individual right to remit, or, indeed, not to exact,—yet she, being personally simple, sincere, and holding herself in low esteem, could not endure anything like the servility of Mr. Crosse, the temporary curate. She grew absolutely to loathe his perpetual smiling and bowing; his instant agreement with the slightest opinion she uttered; his veering round as she blew the wind. I have often said that my lady did not talk much, as she might have done had she lived among her equals. But we all loved her so much, that we had learnt to interpret all her little ways pretty truly; and I knew what particular turns of her head, and

contractions of her delicate fingers meant, as well as if she had expressed herself in words. I began to suspect that my lady would be very thankful to have Mr. Gray about again, and doing his duty even with a conscientiousness that might amount to worrying himself, and fidgeting others; and although Mr. Gray might hold her opinions in as little esteem as those of any simple gentlewoman, she was too sensible not to feel how much flavour there was in his conversation, compared to that of Mr. Crosse, who was only her tasteless echo.

As for Miss Galindo, she was utterly and entirely a partisan of Mr. Gray's, almost ever since she had begun to nurse him during his illness.

" You know, I never set up for reasonableness, my lady. So I don't pretend to say, as I might do if I were a sensible woman and all that,—that I am convinced by Mr. Gray's arguments of this thing or t'other. For one thing, you see, poor fellow! he has never been able to argue, or hardly indeed to speak, for Doctor Trevor has been very peremptory. So there's been no scope for arg ing! But what I mean is this:—When I see a sick man thinking always of others, and never of himself; patient, humble—a trifle too much at times, for I've caught him praying to be forgiven for having neglected his work as a parish priest," (Miss

Galindo was making horrible faces, to keep back tears, squeezing up her eyes in a way which would have amused me at any other time, but when she was speaking of Mr. Gray); " when I see a downright good, religious man, I'm apt to think he's got hold of the right clue, and that I can do no better than hold on by the tails of his coat and shut my eyes, if we've got to go over doubtful places on our road to Heaven. So, my lady, you must excuse me, if, when he gets about again, he is all agog about a Sunday-school, for if he is, I shall be agog too, and perhaps twice as bad as him, for, you see, I've a strong constitution compared to his, and strong ways of speaking and acting. And I tell your ladyship this now, because I think from your rank—and still more, if I may say so, for all your kindness to me long ago, down to this very day—you've a right to be first told of anything about me. Change of opinion I can't exactly call it, for I don't see the good of schools and teaching ABC, any more than I did before, only Mr. Gray does, so I'm to shut my eyes, and leap over the ditch to the side of education. I've told Sally already, that if she does not mind her work, but stands gossiping with Nelly Mather, I'll teach her her lessons; and I've never caught her with old Nelly since."

I think Miss Galindo's desertion to Mr. Gray's opinions in this matter hurt my lady just a little bit; but she only said :

" Of course, if the parishioners wish for it, Mr. Gray must have his Sunday-school. I shall, in that case, withdraw my opposition. I am sorry I cannot change my opinions as easily as you."

My lady made herself smile as she said this. Miss Galindo saw it was an effort to do so. She thought a minute before she spoke again.

Your ladyship has not seen Mr. Gray as intimately as I have done. That's one thing. But, as for the parishioners, they will follow your ladyship's lead in everything; so there is no chance of their wishing for a Sunday-school."

" I have never done anything to make them follow my lead, as you call it, Miss Galindo," said my lady, gravely.

"Yes, you have," replied Miss Galindo, bluntly. And then, correcting herself, she said, " Begging your ladyship's pardon, you have. Your ancestors have lived here time out of mind, and have owned the land i on which their forefathers have lived ever since there were forefathers. You yourself were born amongst them, and have been like a little queen to them ever since, I might say, and they've never known your ladyship do anything but what was kind and gentle;

but I'll leave fine speeches about your ladyship to Mr. Crosse. Only you, my lady, lead the thoughts of the parish; and save some of them a world of trouble, for they could never tell what was right if they had to think for themselves. It's all quite right that they should be guided by you, my lady,—if only you would agree with Mr. Gray."

" Well/' said my lady, " I told him only the last day that he was here, that I would think about it. I do believe I could make up my mind on certain subjects better if I were left alone, than while being constantly talked to about them."

My lady said this in her usual soft tones; but the words had a tinge of impatience about them ; indeed, she was more ruffled than I had often seen her; but, checking herself in an instant, she said:

" You don't know how Mr. Horner drags in this subject of education apropos of everything. Not that he says much about it at any time : it is not his way. But he cannot let the thing alone."

" I know why, my lady," said Miss Galindo. " That poor lad, Harry Gregson, will never be able to earn his livelihood in any active way, but will be lame for life. Now, Mr. Horner thinks more of Harry than of any one else in the world,—except, perhaps, your ladyship." Was it not a pretty companionship for my

lady ? " And he has schemes of his own for teaching Harry; and if Mr. Gray could but have his school, Mr. Horner and he think Harry might be schoolmaster, as your ladyship would not like to have him coming to you as steward's clerk. I wish your ladyship would fall into this plan; Mr. Gray has it so at heart."

Miss Galindo looked wistfully at my lady, as she said this. But my lady only said, drily, and rising at the same time, as if to end the conversation :

" So! Mr. Horner and Mr. Gray seem to have gone a long way in advance of my consent to their plans."

" There !" exclaimed Miss Galindo, as my lady left the room, with an apology for going away; " I have gone and done mischief with my long, stupid tongue. To be sure, people plan a long way ahead of to-day; more especially when one is a sick man, lying all through the weary day on a sofa."

" My lady will soon get over her annoyance," said I, as it were apologetically. I only stopped Miss Galindo's self-reproaches to draw down her wrath upon myself.

" And has not she a right to be annoyed with me, if she likes, and to keep annoyed as long as she likes ? Am I complaining of her, that you need tell me that ? Let me tell you, I have known my lady these thirty

years; and if she were to take me by the shoulders, and turn me out of the house, I should only love her the more. So don't you think to come between us with any little mincing, peace-making speeches. I have been a mischief-making parrot, and I like her the better for being vexed with me. So good-bye to you, Miss; and wait till you know Lady Ludlow as well as I do, before you next think of telling me she will soon get over her annoyance !" And off Miss Galindo went.

I could not exactly tell what I had done wrong; but I took care never again to come in between my lady and her by any remark about the one to the other; for I saw that some most powerful bond of grateful affection made Miss Galindo almost worship my lady.

Meanwhile, Harry Gregson was limping a little about in the village, still finding his home in Mr. Gray's house ; for there he could most conveniently be kept under the doctor's eye, and receive the requisite care, and enjoy the requisite nourishment. As soon as he was a little better, he was to go to Mr. Horner's house ; but, as the steward lived some distance out of the way, and was much from home, he had agreed to leave Harry at the house to which he had first been taken, until he was quite strong again; and the more willingly, I suspect, from what I heard afterwards, because Mr. Gray gave up all the little strength of speaking which he had, to caching Harry in the very manner which Mr. Horner most desired.

As for Gregson the father—he—wild man of the woods, poacher, tinker, jack-of-all-trades—was getting tamed by this kindness to his child. Hitherto his hand lad been against every man, as every man's had been against him. That affair before the justice, which I told you about, when Mr. Gray and even my lady had nterested themselves to get him released from unjust mprisonment, was the first bit of justice he had ever met with ; it attracted him to the people, and attached lim to the spot on which he had but squatted for a ime. I am not sure if any of the villagers were grateful to him for remaining in their neighbourhood, nstead of decamping as he had often done before, for rood reasons, doubtless, of personal safety. Harry was only one out of a brood of ten or twelve children, some jof whom had earned for themselves no good character jin service : one, indeed, had been actually transported, jfor a robbery committed in a distant part of the Bounty ; and the tale was yet told in the village of ihow Gregson the father came back from the trial in a 'state of wild rage, striding through the place, and Buttering oaths of vengeance to himself, his great black iieyes gleaming out of his matted hair, and his arms working by his side, and now and then tossed up in his impotent despair. As I heard the account, his wife followed him, child-laden and weeping. After this, they had vanished from the country for a time, leaving their mud hovel locked up, and the door-key, as the neighbours said, buried in a hedge bank. The Gregsons had reappeared much about the same time that Mr. Gray came to Hanbury. He had either never heard of their evil character, or considered that it gave them all the more claims upon his Christian care, and the end of it was that this rough, untamed, strong giant of a heathen was loyal slave to the weak, hectic, nervous, self-distrustful parson. Gregson had also a kind of grumbling respect for Mr. Horner: he did not quite like the steward's monopoly of his Harry: the mother submitted to that with a better grace, swallowing down her maternal jealousy in the prospect of her child's advancement to a better and more respectable position than that in which his parents had struggled through life. But Mr. Horner, the steward, and Gregson, the poacher and squatter, had come into disagreeable contact too often in former days for them to be perfectly cordial at any future time. Even now, when there was no immediate cause for anything but gratitude for his child's sake on Gregson's part, he would skulk out of Mr. Horner's way, if he saw him coming; and it took all Mr. Horner's natural reserve and acquired self-restraint to keep him from occasionally holding up his father's life as a warning to Harry. Now Gregson had nothing of this desire for avoidance with regard to Mr. Gray. The poacher had a feeling of physical protection towards the parson; while the latter had shown the moral courage, without which Gregson would never have respected him, in coming right down upon him more than once in the exercise of unlawful pursuits, and simply and boldly telling him he was doing wrong, with such a quiet reliance upon Gregson's better feeling, at the same time, that the strong poacher could not have lifted a finger against Mr. Gray, though it had been to save himself from being apprehended and taken to the lockups the very next hour. He had rather listened to the parson's bold words with an approving smile, much as Mr. Gulliver might have hearkened to a lecture from a Lilliputian. But when brave words passed into kind deeds, Gregson's heart mutely acknowledged its master and keeper. And the beauty of it all was, that Mr. Gray knew nothing of the good work he had done, or recognised himself as the instrument which God had employed. He thanked God, it is true, fervently and often, that the work was done; and loved the wild man for his rough gratitude ; but it never occurred to the poor young clergyman, lying on his sick-bed, and

praying, as Miss Galindo had told us he did, to be forgiven for his unprofitable life, to think of Gregson's reclaimed soul as anything with which he had had to do. It was now more than three months since Mr. Gray had been at Hanbury Court During all that time, he had been confined to his house, if not to his sick-bed, and he and my lady had never met since their last discussion and difference about Farmer Hale's barn.

This was not my dear lady's fault; no one could have been more attentive in every way to the slightest possible want of either of the invalids, especially of Mr. Gray. And he would have gone to see him at his own house, as she sent him word, but that her foot had slipped upon the polished oak staircase, and her ancle had been sprained.

So we had never seen Mr. Gray since his illness, when one November day he was announced as wishing to speak to my lady. She was sitting in her room— the room in which I lay now pretty constantly—and I remember she looked startled, when word was brought to her of Mr. Gray's being at the Hall.

She could not go to him, she was too lame for that, so she bade him be shown into where she sat.

" Such a day for him to go out!" she exclaimed, looking at the fog which had crept up to the windows, and was sapping the little remaining life in the brilliant

Virginian creeper leaves that draperied the house on the terrace side.

He came in white, trembling, his large eyes wild and dilated. He hastened up to Lady Ludlow's chair, and, to my surprise, took one of her hands and kissed it, without speaking, yet shaking all over.

" Mr. Gray!" said she, quickly, with sharp, tremulous apprehension of some unknown evil. " What is it ? There is something unusual ahcut you."

"Something unusual has occurred," replied he, forcing his words to be calm, as with a great effort. " A gentleman came to my house, not half-an-hour ago —a Mr. Howard. He came straight from Vienna."

" My son !" said my dear lady, stretching out her arms in dumb questioning attitude.

" The Lord gave and the Lord taketh away. Blessed be the name of the Lord."

But my poor lady could not echo the words. He was the last remaining child. And once she had been the joyful mother of nine.

CHAPTER XII.

I AM ashamed to say what feeling become strongest in my mind about this time. Next to the sympathy we all of us felt for my dear lady in her deep sorrow, I mean. For that was greater and stronger than anything else, however contradictory you may think it, when you hear all.

It might arise from my being so far from well at the time, which produced a diseased mind in a diseased body; but I was absolutely jealous for my father's memory, when I saw how many signs of grief there were for my lord's death, he having done next to nothing for the village and parish, which now changed, as it were, its daily course of life, because his lordship died in a far-off city. My father had spent the best years of his manhood in labouring hard, body and soul, for the people amongst whom he lived. His family, of course, claimed the first place in his heart; he would have been good for little, even in the way of benevolence, if they had not. But close after them he cared

for his parishioners and neighbours. And yet, when he died, though the church-hells tolled, and smote upon our hearts with hard, fresh pain at every beat, the sounds of every-day life still went on, close pressing around us,—carts and carriages, street-cries, distant barrel-organs (the kindly neighbours kept them out of our street): life, active, noisy life, pressed on our acute consciousness of Death, and jarred upon it as on a quick nerve.

And when we went to church,—my father's own church,—though the pulpit-cushions were black, and many of the congregation had put on some humble sign of mourning, yet it did not alter the whole material aspect of the place. And yet what was Lord Ludlow's relation to Hanbury, compared to my father's work and place in ?

O I it was very wicked in me ! I think if I had seen my lady,—if I had dared to ask to go to her, I should not have felt so miserable, so discontented. But she sat in her own room, hung with black, all, even over the shutters. She saw no light but that which was artificial—candles, lamps, and the like, for more than a month. Only Adams went near her. Mr. Gray was not admitted, though he called daily. Even Mrs. Medlicott did not see her for near a fortnight. The sight of my lady's griefs, or rather the recollection of

it, made Mrs. Medlicott talk far more than was her wont. She told us, with many tears, and much gesticulation, even speaking German at times, when her English would not flow, that my lady sat there, a white figure in the middle of the darkened room; a shaded lamp near her, the light of which fell on an open Bible,—the great family Bible. It was not opened at any chapter, or consoling verse ; but at the page whereon were registered the births of her nine children. Five had died in infancy,—sacrificed to the cruel system which forbade the mother to suckle her babies. Four had lived longer; Urian had been the first to die, Ughtred-Mortimar, Earl Ludlow, the last.

My lady did not cry, Mrs. Medlicott said. She was quite composed; very still, very silent. She put aside everything that savoured of mere business; sent people to Mr. Homer for that. But she was proudly alive to every possible form which might do honour to the last of her race.

In those days, expresses were slow things, and forms still slower. Before my lady's directions could reach Vienna, my lord was buried. There was some talk (so Mrs. Medlicott said) about taking the body up, and bringing him to Hanbury. But his executors,—connections on the Ludlow side,—demurred to this. If he were removed to England, he must be carried on to

Scotland, and interred with his Monkshaven forefathers. My lady, deeply hurt, withdrew from the discussion before it degenerated to an unseemly contest. But all the more, for this understood mortification of my lady's, did the whole village and estate of Hanbury assume every outward sign of mourning. The church-bells tolled morning and evening. The church itself was draped in black inside. Hatchments were placed everywhere, where hatchments could be put. All the tenantry spoke in hushed voices for more than a week, scarcely daring to observe that all flesh, even that of an Earl Ludlow, and the last of the Hanburys, was but grass after all. The very Fighting Lion closed its front door, front shutters it had none, and those who needed drink stole in at the back, and were silent and maudlin over their cups, instead of riotous and noisy. Miss Galindo's eyes were swollen up with crying, and she told me, with a fresh burst of tears, that even humpbacked Sally had been found sobbing over her Bible, and using a pocket-handkerchief for the first time in her life; her aprons having hitherto stood her in the necessary stead, but not being sufficiently in accordance with etiquette, to be used when mourning over an earl's premature decease.

If it was in this way out of the Hall, " you might work it by the rule of three," as Miss Galindo used to

say, and judge what it was in the Hall. We none of us spoke but in a whisper: we tried not to eat; and indeed the shock had been so really great, and we did really care so much for my lady, that for some days we had but little appetite. But after that, I fear our sympathy grew weaker, while our flesh grew stronger. But we still spoke low, and our hearts ached whenever we thought of my lady sitting there alone in the darkened room, with the light ever falling on that one solemn

We wished, O how I wished that she would see Mr. Gray! But Adams said, she thought my lady ought to have a bishop come to see her. Still no one had authority enough to send for one.

Mr. Horner all this time was suffering as much as any one. He was too faithful a servant of the great Hanbury family, though now the family had dwindled down to a fragile old lady, not to mourn acutely over its probable extinction. He had, besides, a deeper sympathy and reverence with, and for, my lady in all things, than probably he ever cared to show, for his manners were always measured and cold. He suffered from sorrow. He also suffered from wrong. My lord's executors kept writing to him continually. My lady refused to listen to mere business, saying she intrusted all to him. But the " all" was more complicated than I

ever thoroughly understood. As far as I comprehended the case, it was something of this kind:—There had been a mortgage raised on my lady's property of Han-bury, to enable my lord, her husband, to spend money in cultivating his Scotch estates, after some new fashion that required capital. As long as my lord, her son, lived, who was to succeed to both the estates after her death, this did not signify; so she had said and felt; and she had refused to take any steps to secure the repayment of capital, or even the payment of the interest of the mortgage from the possible representatives and possessors of the Scotch estates, to the possible owner of the Hanbury property; saying it ill became her to calculate on the contingency of her son's deatn.

But he had died, childless, unmarried. The heir of the Monkshaven property was an Edinburgh advocate, a far-away kinsman of my lord's: the Hanbury property, at my lady's death, would go to the descendants of a third son of the Squire Hanbury in the days of Queen Anne.

This complication of affairs was most grievous to Mr. Homer. He had always been opposed to the mortgage ; had hated the payment of the interest, as obliging my lady to practise certain economies which, though she took care to make them as personal as possible, he

disliked as derogatory to the family. Poor Mr. Homer! He was so cold and hard in his manner, so curt and decisive in his speech, that I don't think we any of us did him justice. Miss Galindo was almost the first, at this time, to speak a kind word of him, or to take thought of him at all, any farther than to get out of his way when we saw him approaching.

" I don't think Mr. Horner is well," she said one day, about three weeks after we had heard of my lord's death. " He sits resting his head on his hand, and hardly hears me when I speak to him."

But I thought no more of it, as Miss Galindo did not name it again. My Lady came amongst us once more. From elderly she had become old; a little, frail, old lady, in heavy black drapery, never speaking about nor alluding to her great sorrow ; quieter, gentler, paler than ever before; and her eyes dim with much weeping, never witnessed by mortal.

She had seen Mr. Gray at the expiration of the month of deep retirement. But I do not think that even to him she had said one word of her own particular individual sorrow. All mention of it seemed buried deep for evermore. One day, Mr. Horner sent word that he was too much indisposed to attend to his usual business at the Hall; but he wrote down some directions and requests to Miss Galindo, saying that he

would be at his office early the next morning. The next morning he was dead!

Miss Galindo told my lady. Miss Galindo herself cried plentifully, but my lady, although very much distressed, could not cry. It seemed a physical impossibility, as if she had shed all the tears in her power. Moreover, I almost think her wonder was far greater that she herself lived than that Mr. Homer died. It was almost natural that so faithful a servant should break his heart, when the family he belonged to lost their stay, their heir and their last hope.

Yes! Mr. Homer was a faithful servant. I do not think there are many so faithful now; but, perhaps, that is an old woman's fancy of mine. When his will came to be examined, it was discovered that, soon after Harry Gregson's accident, Mr. Homer had left the few thousands (three, I think,) of which he was possessed, in trust for Harry's benefit, desiring his executors to see that the lad was well educated in certain things, for which Mr. Horner had thought that he had shown especial aptitude; and there was a kind of implied apology to* my lady in one sentence, where he stated that Harry's lameness would prevent his being ever able to gain his living by the exercise of any mere bodily faculties, " as had been wished by a lady whose wishes " he, the testator, " was bound to regard."

But there was a codicil to the will, dated since Lord Ludlow's death—feebly written by Mr. Homer himself, as if in preparation only for some more formal manner of bequest; or, perhaps, only as a mere temporary arrangement till he could see a lawyer, and have a fresh will made. In this he revoked his previous bequest to Harry Gregson. He only left two hundred pounds to Mr. Gray to be used, as that gentleman thought best, for Henry Gregson's benefit. With this one exception, he bequeathed all the rest of his savings to my lady, with a hope that they might form a nest-egg, as it were, towards the paying off of the mortgage which had been such a grief to him during his life. I may not repeat all this in lawyer's phrase; I heard it through Miss Galindo, and she might make mistakes. Though, indeed, she was very clear-headed, and soon earned the respect of Mr. Smithson, my lady's lawyer from Warwick. Mr. Smithson knew Miss Galindo a little before, both personally and by reputation; but I don't think he was prepared to find her installed as steward's clerk, and, at first, he was inclined to treat her, in this capacity, with polite contempt. But Miss Galindo was both a lady and a spirited, sensible woman, and she could put aside her self-indulgence in eccentricity of speech and manner whenever she chose. Nay more; she was usually so talkative, that if she

had not been amusing and warm-hearted, one might have thought her wearisome occasionally. But, to meet Mr. Sinithson, she came out daily in her Sunday gown; she said no more than was required in answer to his questions; her books and papers were in thorough order, and methodically kept; her statements of matters-of fact accurate, and to be relied on. She was amusingly conscious of her victory over his contempt of a woman-clerk and his preconceived opinion of her unpractical eccentricity.

" Let me alone," said she, one day when she came in to sit awhile with me. " That man is a good man —a sensible man—and, I have no doubt, he is a good lawyer ; but he can't fathom women yet. I make no doubt he'll go back to Warwick, and never give credit again to those people who made him think me half-cracked to begin with. O, my dear, he did! He showed it twenty times worse than my poor dear master ever did. It was a form to be gone through to please my lady, and, for her sake, he would hear my statements and see my books. It was keeping a woman out of harm's way, at any rate, to let her fancy herself useful. I read the man. And, I am thankful to say, he cannot read me. At least, only one side of me. When I see an end to be gained, I can behave myself accordingly. Here was a man who thought

that a woman in a black silk gown was a respectable, orderly kind of person; and I was a woman in a black silk gown. He believed that a woman could not write straight lines, and required a man to tell her that two and two made four. I was not above ruling my books, and had Cocker a little more at my fingers' ends than he had. But my greatest triumph has been holding my tongue. He would have thought nothing of my books, or my sums, or my black silk gown, if I had spoken unasked. So I have buried more sense in my bosom these ten days than ever I have uttered in the whole course of my life before. I have been so curt, so abrupt, so abominably dull, that I'll answer for it he thinks me worthy to be a man. But I must go back to him, my dear, so goodbye to conversation and you."

But though Mr. Smithson might be satisfied with Miss Galindo, I am afraid she was the only part of the affair with which he was content. Everything else went wrong. I could not say who told me so—but the conviction of this seemed to pervade the house. I never knew how much we had all looked up to the silent, gruff Mr. Homer for decisions, until he was gone. My lady herself was a pretty good woman of business, as women of business go. Her father, seeing that she would be the heiress of the Hanbury property, had

given her a training which was thought unusual in those days, and she liked to feel herself queen regnant, and to have to decide in all cases between herself and her tenantry. But, perhaps, Mr. Homer would have done it more wisely ; not but what she always attended to him at last. She would begin by saying, pretty clearly and promptly, what she would have done, and what she would net have done. If Mr. Homer approved of it, he bowed, and set about obeying her directly; if he disapproved of it, he bowed, and lingered so long before he obeyed her, that she forced his opinion out of him with her " Well, Mr. Horner! and what have you to say against it?" For she always understood his silence as well as if he had spoken. But the estate was pressed for ready money, and Mr. Horner had grown gloomy and languid since the death of his wife, and even his own personal affairs were not in the order in which they had been a year or two before, for his old clerk had gradually become superannuated, or, at any rate, unable by the superfluity of his own energy and wit to supply the spirit that was wanting in Mr. Horner.

Day after day Mr. Smithson seemed to grow more iidgety, more annoyed at the state of affairs. Like every one else employed by Lady Ludlow, as far as I could learn, he had an hereditary tie to the Hanbury

family. As long as the Smithsons had been lawyers, they had been lawyers to the Hanburys; always coming in on all great family occasions, and better able to understand the characters, and connect the links of what had once been a large and scattered family, than any individual thereof had ever been.

As long as a man was at the head of the Hanburys, the lawyers had simply acted as servants, and had only given their advice when it was required. But they had assumed a different position on the memorable occasion of the mortgage : they had remonstrated against it. My lady had resented this remonstrance, and a slight, unspoken coolness had existed between her and the father of this Mr. Smithson ever since.

I was very sorry for my lady. Mr. Smithson was inclined to blame Mr. Homer /or the disorderly state in which he found some of the outlying farms, and for the deficiencies in the annual payment of rents. Mr. Smithson had too much good feeling to put this blame into words ; but my lady's quick instinct led her to reply to a thought, the existence of which she perceived; and she quietly told the truth, and explained how she had interfered repeatedly to prevent Mr. Homer from taking certain desirable steps, which were discordant to her hereditary sense of right and wrong between landlord and tenant. She also spoke

of the want of ready money as a misfortune that could be remedied, by more economical personal expenditure on her own part; by which individual saving, it was possible that a reduction of fifty pounds a year might have been accomplished. But as soon as Mr. Smithson touched on larger economies, such as either affected the welfare of others, or the honour and standing of the great House of Hanbury, she was inflexible. Her establishment consisted of somewhere about forty servants, of whom nearly as many as twenty were unable to perform their work properly, and yet would have been hurt if they had been dismissed; so they had the credit of fulfilling duties, while my lady paid and kept their substitutes. Mr. Smithson made a calculation, and would have saved some hundreds a year by pensioning off these old servants. But my lady would not hear of it. Then, again, I know privately that he urged her to allow some of us to return to our homes. Bitterly we should have regretted the separation from Lady Ludlow; but we would have gone back gladly, had we known at the time that her circumstances required it: but she would not listen to the proposal for a moment.

" If I cannot act justly towards every one, I will give up a plan which has been a source of much satisfaction ; at least, I will not carry it out to such an extent

in future. But to these young ladies, who do me the favour to live with me at present, I stand pledged. I cannot go back from my word, Mr. Smithson. We had better talk no more of this."

As she spoke, she entered the room where I lay. She and Mr. Smithson were coming for some papers contained in the bureau. They did not know I was there, and Mr. Smithson started a little when he saw me, as he must have been aware that I had overheard something. But my lady did not change a muscle of her face. All the world might overhear her kind, just, pure sayings, and she had no fear of their misconstruction. She came up to me, and kissed me on the forehead, and then went to search for the required papers.

" I rode over the Conington farms yesterday, my lady. I must say I was quite grieved to see the condition they are in; all the land that is not waste is utterly exhausted with working successive white crops. Not a pinch of manure laid on the ground for years. I must say that a greater contrast could never have been presented than that between Harding's farm and the next fields—fences in perfect order, rotation crops, sheep eating down the turnips on the waste lands— everything that could be desired."

" Whose farm is that ?" asked my lady.

"Why, I am sorry to say, it was on none of your

ladyship's that I saw such good methods adopted. I hoped it was, I stopped my horse to inquire. A queer-looking man, sitting on his horse like a tailor, watching his men with a couple of the sharpest eyes I ever saw, and dropping his h's at every word, answered my question, and told me it was his. I could not go on asking him who he was; but I fell into conversation with him, and I gathered that he had earned some money in trade in Birmingham, and had bought the estate (five hundred acres, I think he said,) on which he was born, and now was setting himself to cultivate it in downright earnest, going to Holkham and Woburn, and half the country over, to get himself up on the subject."

" It would be Brooke, that dissenting baker from Birmingham," said my lady in her most icy tone. " Mr. Smithson, I am sorry I have been detaining you so long, but I think these are the letters you wished to see."

If her ladyship thought Jby this speech to quench Mr. Smithson she was mistaken. Mr. Smithson just looked at the letters, and went on with the old subject.

" Now, my lady, it struck me that if you had such a man to take poor Horner's place, he would work the rents and the land round most satisfactorily. I should not despair of inducing this very man to undertake the work. I should not mind speaking to him myself on

the subject, for we got capital friends over a snack of luncheon that he asked me to share with him."

Lady Ludlow fixed her eyes on Mr. Smithson as he spoke, and never took them off his face until he had ended. She was silent a minute before she answered.

" You are very good, Mr. Smithson, but I need not trouble you with any such arrangements. I am going to write this afternoon to Captain James, a friend of one of my sons, who has, I hear, been severely wounded at Trafalgar, to request him to honour me by accepting Mr. Homer's situation."

"A Captain James! A captain in the navy! going to manage your ladyship's estate!"

"If he will be so kind. I shall esteem it a condescension on his part; but I hear that he will have to resign his profession, his state of health is so bad, and a country life is especially prescribed for him. I am in some hopes of tempting him here, as I learn he has but little to depend on if he gives up his profession."

"A Captain James! an invalid captain!"

"You think I am asking too great a favour," continued my lady. (I never could tell how far it was simplicity, or how far a kind of innocent malice, that made her misinterpret Mr. Smithson's words and looks as she did.) "But he is not a post-captain, only a commander, and his pension will be but small. I may be able, by offering him country air and a healthy occupation, to restore him to health."

"Occupation! My lady, may I ask how a sailor is to manage land? Why, your tenants will laugh him to scorn."

"My tenants, I trust, will not behave so ill as to laugh at any one I choose to set over them. Captain James has had experience in managing men. He has remarkable practical talents, and great common sense, as I hear from every one. But, whatever he may be, the affair rests between him and myself. I can only say I shall esteem myself fortunate if he comes."

There was no more to be said, after my lady spoke in this manner. I had heard her mention Captain James before, as a middy who had been very kind to her son Urian. I thought I remembered then, that she had mentioned that his family circumstances were not very prosperous. But, I confess, that little as I knew of the management of land, I quite sided with Mr. Smithson. He, silently prohibited from again speaking to my lady on the subject, opened his mind to Miss Galindo, from whom I was pretty sure to hear all the opinions and news of the household and village. She had taken a great fancy to me, because she said I talked so agreeably. I believe it was because I listened so well.

"Well, have you heard the news," she began, "about this Captain James? A sailor,—with a wooden leg, I have no doubt. What would the poor, dear, deceased master have said to it, if he had known who was to be his successor? My dear, I have often thought of the postman's bringing me a letter as one of the pleasures I shall miss in heaven. But, really, I think Mr. Horner may be thankful he has got out of the reach of news; or else he would hear of Mr. Smithson's having made up to the Birmingham baker, and of this one-legged Captain, coming to dot-and-go-one over the estate. I suppose he will look after the labourers through a spy-glass. I only hope he won't stick in the mud with his wooden leg; for I, for one, won't help him out. Yes, I would," said she, correcting herself; "I would, for my lady's sake."

"But are you sure he has a wooden leg?" asked I. "I heard Lady Ludlow tell Mr. Smithson about him, and she only spoke of him as wounded."

"Well, sailors are almost always wounded in the leg. Look at Greenwich Hospital! I should say there were twenty one-legged pensioners to one without an arm there. But say he has got half-a-dozen legs, what is he to do with managing land? I shall think him very impudent if he comes, taking advantage of my lady's kind heart."

However, come he did. In a month from that time, the carriage was sent to meet Captain James; just as three years before it had been sent to meet me. His coming had been so much talked about that we were all as curious as possible to see him, and to know how so unusual an experiment, as it seemed to us, would answer. But, before I tell you anything about our new agent, I must speak of something quite as interesting, and I really think quite as important. And this was my lady's making friends with Harry Gregson. I do believe she did it for Mr. Homer's sake; but, oj course, I can only conjecture why my lady did anything. But I heard one day, from

Mary Legard, that my lady had sent for Harry to come and see her, if he was well enough to walk so far; and the next day he was shown into the room he had been in once before under such unlucky circumstances.

The lad looked pale enough, as he stood propping himself up on his crutch, and the instant my lady saw him, she bade John Footman place a stool for him to sit down upon while she spoke to him. It might be his paleness that gave his whole face a more refined and gentle look; but I suspect it was that the boy was apt to take impressions, and that Mr. Homer's grave, dignified ways, and Mr. Gray's tender and quiet manners, had altered him; and then the thoughts of

illness and death seem to turn many of us into gentlemen, and gentlewomen, as long as such thoughts are in our minds. We cannot speak loudly or angrily at such times ; we are not apt to be eager about mere worldly things, for our very awe at our quickened sense of the nearness of the invisible world, makes us calm and serene about the petty trifles of to-day. At least, I know that was the explanation Mr. Gray once gave me of what we all thought the great improvement in Harry Gregson's way of behaving.

My lady hesitated so long about what she had best say, that Harry grew a little frightened at her silence. A few months ago it would have surprised me more than it did now; but since my lord her son's death, she had seemed altered in many ways,—more uncertain and distrustful of herself, as it were.

At last she said, and I think the tears were in her eyes : " My poor little fellow, you have had a narrow escape with your life since I saw you last."

To this there was nothing to be said but " Yes;" and again there was silence.

" And you have lost a good, kind friend, in Mr. Horner."

The boy's lips worked, and I think he said, " Please, don't." But I can't be sure ; at any rate, my lady went on :

" And so have I,—a good, kind friend, he was to both of us; and to you he wished to show his kindness in even a more generous way than he has done. Mr. Gray has told you about his legacy to you, has he not ?"

There was no sign of eager joy on the lad's face, as if he realised the power and pleasure of having what to him must have seemed like a fortune.

" Mr. Gray said as how he had left me a matter of money."

" Yes, he has left you two hundred pounds."

" But I would rather have had him alive, my lady," he burst out, sobbing as if his heart would break.

"My lad, I believe you. We would rather have had our dead alive, would we not ? and there is nothing in money that can comfort us for their loss. But you know—Mr. Gray has told you—who has appointed us all our times to die. Mr. Homer was a good, just man; and has done well and kindly, both by me and you. You perhaps do not know " (and now I understood what my lady had been making up her mind to say to Harry, all the time she was hesitating how to begin) " that Mr. Horner, at one time, meant to leave you a great deal more; probably all he had, with the exception of a legacy to his old clerk, Morrison. But he knew that this estate—on which my forefathers had lived for six hundred years—was in debt, and that

I had no immediate chance of paying off this debt; and yet he felt that it was a very sad thing for an old property like this to belong in part to those other men, who had lent the money. You understand me, I think, my little man ?" said she, questioning Harry's face.

He had left off crying, and was trying to understand, with all his might and main; and I think he had got a pretty good general idea of the state of affairs; though probably he was puzzled by the term "the estate being in debt." But he was sufficiently interested to want my lady to go on

; and he nodded his head at her, to signify this to her.

"So Mr. Horner took the money which he once meant 'to be yours, and has left the greater part of it to me, with the intention of helping me to pay off this debt I have told you about. It will go a long way, and I shall try hard to save the rest, and then I shall die happy in leaving the land free from debt." She paused. " But I shall not die happy in thinking of you. I do not know if having money, or even having a great estate and much honour, is a good thing for any of us. But God sees fit that some of us should be called to this condition, and it is our duty then to stand by our posts, like brave soldiers. Now, Mr. Horner intended you to have this money first. I shall only call it borrowing it from you, Harry Gregson, if I I take it and use it to pay off the debt. I shall pay I Mr. Gray interest on this money, because he is to I stand as your guardian, as it were, till you come of I age; and he must fix what ought to be done with it, I so as to fit you for spending the principal rightly when I the estate can repay it you. I suppose, now, it will be I .right for you to be educated. That will be another I snare that will come with your money. But have I courage, Harry. Both education and money may be f used rightly, if we only pray against the temptations I they bring with them."

Harry could make no answer, though I am sure he I understood it all. My lady wanted to get him to talk to her a little, by way of becoming acquainted with ; what was passing in his mind; and she asked him what he would like to have done with his money, if he j could have part of it now ? To such a simple question, involving no talk about feelings, his answer came 1 readily enough.

"Build a cottage for father, with stairs in it, and j give Mr. Gray a school-house. O, father does so | want Mr. Gray for to have his wish! Father saw all .1 the stones lying quarried and hewn on Farmer Hale's ! land; Mr. Gray had paid for them all himself. And i father said he would work night and day, and little Tommy should carry mortar, if the parson would let him, sooner than that he should be fretted and frabbed as he was, with no one giving him a helping hand or a kind word."

Harry knew nothing of my lady's part in the affair ; that was very clear. My lady kept silence.

" If I might have a piece of my money, I would buy land from Mr. Brooke : he has got a bit to sell just at the corner of Hendon Lane, and I would give it to Mr. Gray; and, perhaps, if your ladyship thinks I may be learned again, I might grow up into the schoolmaster."

" You are a good boy," said my lady. " But there are more things to be thought of, in carrying out such a plan, than you are aware of. However, it shall be tried."

" The school, my lady ?" I exclaimed, almost thinking she did not know what she was saying.

" Yes, the school. For Mr. Horner's sake, for Mr. Gray's sake, and last, not least, for this lad's sake, I will give the new plan a trial. Ask Mr. Gray to come up to me this afternoon about the land he wants. He need not go to a Dissenter for it. And tell your father he shall have a good share in the building of it, and Tommy shall carry the mortar."

"And I may be schoolmaster?" asked Harry, eagerly.

MY LADY LUDLOW.

We'll " It will see about that," said my lady, amused, some time before that plan comes to pass, my little fallow."

And to return to Captain James. My first account c/f him was from Miss Galindo.

He/s not above thirty; and I must just pack up my p^ns and my paper, and be off; for it would be the Height of impropriety for me to be staying here as his cWk. It was all very well in the old master's days. But here am I, not fifty till next May, and this young| unmarried man, who is not even a widower! O, thdre would be no end of gossip. Besides, he looks as askance at me as I do at him. My black silk gown had no efreot. Bt's afraid I shall marry him. But I won't; he may feel himself quite safe from that. And Mr. Smithson has been recommending a clerk to my lady. She would far rather keep me on; but I can't stop. I really could not think it proper."

" What sort of a looking man is he ?"

" O, nothing particular. Short, and brown, and sunburnt. I did not think it became me to look at him. Well, now for the nightcaps. I should have grudged any one else doing them, for I have got such a pretty pattern!"

But, when it came to Miss Galindo's leaving, there was a great misunderstanding between her and my

lady. Miss Galindo had imagined that my lady had asked her as a favour to copy the letters, and enter the accounts, and had agreed to do the work without a notion of being paid for so doing. She had, now and then, grieved over a very profitable order for needlework passing out of her hands on account of her not having time to do it, because of her occupation at the Hall; but she had never hinted this to my lady, but gone on cheerfully at her writing as long as her clerkship was required. My lady was annoyed that she had not made her intention of paying Miss Galindo more clear, in the first conversation she had had with her; but I suppose that she had been too delicate to be very explicit with regard to money matters; and now Miss Galindo was quite hurt at my lady's wanting to pay her for what she had done in such right-down goodwill.

"No," Miss Galindo said; "my own dear lady, you may be as angry with me as you like, but don't offer me money. Think of six-and-twenty years ago, and poor Arthur, and as you. were to me then! Besides, I wanted money—I don't disguise it—for a particular purpose; and when I found that (God bless you for asking me !) I could do you a service, I turned it over in my mind, and I gave up one plan and took up another, and it's all settled now. Bessy is to leave

school and come and live with me. Don't, please, offer me money again. You don't know how glad I have been to do anything for you. Have not I, Margaret Dawson ? Did you not hear me say, one day, I would cut off my hand for my lady ; for am I a stock or a stone, that I should forget kindness ? O, I have been so glad to work for you. And now Bessy is coming here; and no one knows anything about her —as if she had done anything wrong, poor child!"

" Dear Miss Galindo," replied my lady, " I will never ask you to take money again. Only I thought it was quite understood between us. And, you know, you have taken money for a set of morning wrappers, before now."

"Yes, my lady; but that was not confidential. Now I was so proud to have something to do for you confidentially."

" But who is Bessy ?" asked my lady. " I do not understand who she is, or why'she is to come and live with you. Dear Miss Galindo, you must honour me by being confidential with me in your turn!"

CHAPTER XIII.

I HAD always understood that Miss Galindo had once been in much better circumstances, but I had never liked to ask any questions respecting her. But about this time many things came out respecting her former life, which I will try and arrange; not, however, in the order in which I heard them, but rather as they occurred.

Miss Galindo was the daughter of a clergyman in Westmoreland. Her father was the younger brother of a baronet, his ancestor having been one of those of James the First's creation. This baronet-uncle of Miss Galindo was one of the queer, out-of-the-way people who were bred at that time, and in that northern district of England. I never heard much of him from any one, besides this one great fact: that he had early disappeared from his family, which indeed only consisted of a brother and sister who died unmarried, and lived no one knew where,—somewhere on the Continent it was supposed, for he had never returned from the grand tour which he had been

sent to make, according to the general fashion of the day, as soon as he left Oxford. He corresponded occasionally with his brother the clergyman; but the letters passed through a banker's hands; the banker being pledged to secrecy, and, as he told Mr. Galindo, having the penalty, if he broke his pledge, of losing the whole profitable business, and of having the management of the baronet's affairs taken out of his hands* without any advantage accruing to the inquirer, for Sir Lawrence had told Messrs. Graham that, in case his place of residence was revealed by them, not only would he cease to bank with them, but instantly take measures to baffle any future inquiries as to his whereabouts, by removing to some distant country.

Sir Lawrence paid a certain sum of money to his brother's account every year; but the time of this payment varied, and it was sometimes eighteen or nineteen months between the deposits; then, again, it would not be above a quarter of the time, showing that he intended it to be annual, but, as this intention was never expressed in words, it was impossible to rely upon it, and a great deal of this money was swallowed up by the necessity Mr. Galindo felt himself under of living in the large, old, rambling family mansion, which had been one of Sir Lawrence's rarely expressed desires. Mr. and Mrs. Galindo often planned to live

upon their own small fortune and the income derived from the living (a vicarage, of which the great tithes went to Sir Lawrence as lay impropriator), so as to put-by the payments made by the baronet, for the benefit of Laurentia—our Miss Galindo. But I suppose they found it difficult to live economically in a large house, even though they had it rent free. They had to keep up with hereditary neighbours and friends, and could hardly help doing it in the hereditary manner.

One of these neighbours, a Mr. Gibson, had a son a few years older than Laurentia. The families were sufficiently intimate for the young people to see a good deal of each other: and I was told that this young Mr. Mark Gibson was an unusually prepossessing man (he seemed to have impressed every one who spoke of him to me as being a handsome, manly, kind-hearted fellow), just what a girl would be sure to find most agreeable. The parents either forgot that their children were growing up to man's and woman's estate, or thought that the intimacy and probable attachment would be no bad thing, even if it did lead to a marriage. Still, nothing was ever said by young Gibson till later on, when it was too late, as it turned out. He went to and from Oxford ; he shot and fished with Mr. Galindo, or came to the Mere

to skate in winter-time; was asked to accompany Mr. Galindo to the Hall, as the latter returned to the quiet dinner with his wife and daughter; and so, and so, it went on, nobody much knew how, until one day, when Mr. Galindo received a formal letter from his brother's bankers, announcing Sir Lawrence's death, of malaria fever, at Albano, and congratulating Sir Hubert on his accession to the estates and the baronetcy. The king is dead—" Long live the king !" as I have since heard that the French express it.

Sir Hubert and his wife were greatly surprised. Sir Lawrence was but two years older than his brother ; and they had never heard of any illness till they heard of his death. They were sorry ; very much shocked ; but still a little elated at the succession to the baronetcy and estates. The London bankers had managed everything well. There was a large sum of ready money in their hands, at Sir Hubert's service, until he should touch his rents, the rent-roll being eight thousand a-year. And only Laurentia to inherit it all! Her mother, a poor clergyman's daughter, began to plan all sorts of fine marriages for her; nor was her father much behind his wife in his ambition. They took her up to London, when they went to buy new carriages, and dresses, and furniture. And it was then and there she made my lady's ac-

quaintance. How it was that they came to take a fancy to each other, I cannot say. My lady was of the old nobility, — grand, composed, gentle, and stately in her ways. Miss Galindo must always have been hurried in her manner, and her energy must have shown itself in inquisitiveness and oddness even in her youth. But I don't pretend to account for things : I only narrate them. And the fact was this: —that the elegant, fastidious Countess was attracted to the country girl, who on her part almost worshipped my lady. My lady's notice of their daughter made her parent's think, I suppose, that there was no match that she might not command; she, the heiress of eight thousand a-year, and visiting about among earls and dukes. So when they came back to their old Westmoreland Hall, and Mark Gibson rode over to offer his hand and his heart, and prospective estate of nine hundred a-year to his old companion and playfellow, Laurenti a, Sir Hubert and Lady Galindo made very short work of it. They refused him plumply them-%elves, and when he begged to be allowed to speak to Laurentia, they found some excuse for refusing him the opportunity of so doing, until they had talked to her themselves, and brought up every argument and fact in their power to convince her—a plain girl, and conscious of her plainness—that Mr. Mark Gibson

had never thought of her in the way of marriage till after her father's accession to his fortune ; and that it was the estate—not the young lady—that he was in love with. I suppose it will never be known in this world how far this supposition of theirs was true. My Lady Ludlow had always spoken as if it was; but perhaps events, which came to her knowledge about this time, altered her opinion. At any rate, the end of it was, Laurentia refused Mark, and almost broke her heart in doing so. He discovered the suspicions of Sir Hubert and Lady Galindo, and that they had persuaded their daughter to share in them. So he flung off with high words, saying that they did not know a true heart when they met with one; and that, although he had never offered till after Sir Lawrence's death, yet that his father knew all along that he had been attached to Laurentia, only that he, being the eldest of five children, and having as yet no profession, had had to conceal, rather than to express, an attachment, which, in those days, he had believed was reciprocated. He had always meant to study for the bar, and the end of all he had hoped for had been to earn a moderate income, which he might ask Laurentia to share. This, or something like it, was what he said. But his reference to his father cut two ways. Old Mr. Gibson was known to be very

keen about money. It was just as likely that he would urge Mark to make love to the heiress, now she was an heiress, as that he would have restrained him previously, as Mark said he had done. When this was repeated to Mark, he became proudly reserved, or sullen, and said that Laurentia, at any rate, might have known him better. He left the country, and went up to London to study law soon afterwards ; and Sir Hubert and Lady Galindo thought they were well rid of him. But Laurentia never ceased reproaching herself, and never did to her dying day, as I believe. The words, " she might have known me better," told to her by some kind friend or other, rankled in her mind, and were never forgotten. Her father and mother took her up to London the next year; but she did not care to visit—dreaded going out even for a drive, lest she should see Mark Gibson's reproachful eyes—pined and lost her health. Lady Ludlow saw this change with regret, and was told the cause by Lady Galindo, who, of course, gave her own version of Mark's conduct and motives. My lady never spoke to Miss Galindo about it, but tried constantly to interest and please her. It was at this time that my lady told Miss Galindo so much about her own early life, and about Hanbury, that Miss Galindo resolved, if ever she could, she would go and see the old place which her friend loved so well. The end of it all was, that she came to live there, as we know.

But a great change was to come first Before Sir Hubert and Lady Galindo had left London on this, their second visit, they had a letter from the lawyer, whom they employed, saying that Sir Lawrence had left an heir, his legitimate child by an Italian woman of low rank; at least, legal claims to the title and property had been sent into him on the boy's behalf. Sir Lawrence had always been a man of adventurous and artistic,' rather than of luxurious tastes; and it was supposed, when all came to be proved at the trial, that he was captivated by the free, beautiful life they lead in Italy, and had married this Neapolitan fisherman's daughter, who had people about her shrewd enough to see that the ceremony was legally performed. She and her husband had wandered about the shores of the Mediterranean for years, leading a happjr, careless, irresponsible life, unencumbered by any duties except those connected with a rather numerous family. It was enough for her that they never wanted money, and that her husband's love was always continued to her. She hated the name of England—wicked, cold, heretic England— and avoided the mention of any subjects connected with her husband's early life. So that, when he died at

MY LADY LUDLOW.

Albano, she was almost roused out of her vehement grief to anger with the Italian doctor, who declared that he must write to a certain address to announce the death of Lawrence Galindo. For some time, she feared lest English barbarians might come down upon her, making a claim to the children. She hid herself and them in the Abruzzi, living upon the sale of what furniture and jewels Sir Lawrence had died possessed of. When these failed, she returned to Naples, which she had not visited since her marriage. Her father was dead ; but her brother inherited some of his keenness. He interested the priests, who made inquiries and found that the Galindo succession was worth securing to an heir of the true faith. They stirred about it, obtained advice at the English Embassy; and hence that letter to the lawyers, calling upon Sir Hubert to relinquish title and property, and to refund what money he had expended. He was vehement in his opposition to this claim. He could not bear to think of his brother having married a foreigner—a papist, a fisherman's daughter; nay, of his having become a papist himself. He was in despair at the thought of his ancestral property going to the issue of such a marriage. He fought tooth and nail, making enemies of his relations, and losing almost all his own private property; for he would go on against the lawyer's advice, long after every one was convinced except himself and his wife. At last he was conquered. He gave up his living in gloomy despair. He would have changed his name if he could, so desirous was he to obliterate all tie between himself and the mongrel papist baronet and his Italian mother, and all the succession of children and nurses who came to take possession of the Hall soon after Mr. Hubert Galindo's departure, stayed there one winter, and then flitted back to Naples with gladness and delight. Mr. and Mrs, Hubert Galindo lived in London. He had obtained a curacy somewhere in the city. They would have been thankful now if Mr. Mark Gibson had renewed his offer. No one could accuse him of mercenary motives if he had done so. Because he did not come forward, as they wished, they brought his silence up as a justification of what they had previously attributed to him. I don't know what Miss Galindo thought herself; but Lady Ludlow has told me how she shrank from hearing her parents abuse him. Lady Ludlow supposed that he was aware that they were living in London. His father must have known the fact, and it was curious if he had never named it to his son. Besides, the name was very uncommon ; and it was unlikely that it should never come across him, in the advertisements of charity sermons which the new and rather eloquent curate of Saint Mark's East was asked to preach. All this time

Lady Ludlow never lost sight of them, for Miss Galindo's sake. And when the father and mother died, it was my lady who upheld Miss Galindo in her determination not to apply for any provision to her cousin, the Italian baronet, but rather to live upon the hundred a-year which had been settled on her mother and the children of his son Hubert's marriage by the old grandfather, Sir Lawrence.

Mr. Mark Gibson had risen to some eminence as a barrister on the Northern Circuit; but had died unmarried in the lifetime of his father, a victim (so people said) to intemperance. Doctor Trevor, the physician who had been called in to Mr. Gray and Harry Gregson, had married a sister of his. And that was all my lady knew about the Gibson family. But who was Bessy ?

That mystery and secret came out, too, in process of time. Miss Galindo had been to Warwick, some years before I arrived at Hanbury, on some kind of business or shopping, which can only be transacted in a county town. There was an old Westmoreland connection between her and Mrs. Trevor, though I believe the latter was too young to have been made aware of her brother's offer to Miss Galindo at the time when it took place; and such affairs, if they are unsuccessful, are seldom spoken about in the gentleman's family afterwards. But the Gibsons and Galindos had been

county neighbours too long for the connection not to be kept up between two members settled far away from their early homes. Miss Galindo always desired her parcels to be sent to Doctor Trevor's, when she went to Warwick for shopping purchases. If she were going any journey, and the coach did not come through Warwick as soon as she arrived (in my lady's coach or otherwise) from Hanbury, she went to Doctor Trevor's to wait. She was as much expected to sit down to the household meals as if she had been one of the family ; and in after-years it was Mrs. Trevor who managed her repository business for her.

So, on the day I spoke of, she had gone to Doctor Trevor's to rest, and possibly to dine. The post in those times came in at all hours of the morning; and Doctor Trevor's letters had not arrived until after his departure on his morning round. Miss Galindo was sitting down to dinner with Mrs. Trevor and her seven children, when the Doctor came in. He was flurried and uncomfortable, and hurried the children away as soon as he decently could. Then (rather feeling Miss Galindo's presence an advantage, both as a present restraint on the violence of his wife's grief, and as a consoler when he was absent on his afternoon round), he told Mrs. Trevor of her brother's death. He had been taken ill on circuit, and had hurried back to his

chambers in London, only to die. She cried terribly ; but Doctor Trevor said afterwards, he never noticed that Miss Galindo cared much about it one way or another. She helped him to soothe his wife, promised to stay with her all the afternoon instead of returning to Hanbury, and afterwards offered to remain with her while the Doctor went to attend the funeral. When they heard of the old love-story between the dead man and Miss Galindo,—brought up by mutual friends in Westmoreland, in the review which we are all inclined to take of the events of a man's life when he comes to die,—they tried to remember Miss Galindo's speeches and ways of going on during this visit. She was a little pale, a little silent; her eyes were sometimes swollen, and her nose red ; but she was at an age when such appearances are generally attributed to a bad cold in the head, rather than to any more sentimental reason. They felt towards her as towards an old friend, a kindly, useful, eccentric old maid. She did not expect more, or wish them to remember that she might once have had other hopes, and more youthful feelings. Doctor Trevor thanked her very warmly for staying with his wife, when he returned home from London (where the funeral had taken place). He begged Miss Galindo to stay with them, when the children were gone to bed, and she was preparing to leave the husband and wife by themselves. He told her and his wife many particulars—then paused—then went on—

"And Mark has left a child—a little girl "

" But he never was married," exclaimed Mrs. Trevor.

" A little girl," continued her husband, " whose mother, I conclude, is dead. At any rate, the child was in possession of his chambers; she and an old nurse, who seemed to have the charge of everything, and has cheated poor Mark, I should fancy, not a little."

"But the child!" asked Mrs. Trevor, still almost breathless with astonishment. " How do 'you know it is his ?"

" The nurse told me it was, with great appearance of indignation at my doubting it. I asked the little thing her name, and all I could get was ' Bessy!' and a cry of ' Me wants papa!' The nurse said the mother was dead, and she knew no more about it than that Mr. Gibson had engaged her to take care of the little girl, calling it his child. One or two of his lawyer friends, whom I met with at the funeral, told me they were aware of the existence of the child."

" What is to be done with her ?" asked Mrs. Gibson.

" Nay, I don't know," replied he. " Mark has hardly left assets enough to pay his debts, and your father is not inclined to come forward."

That night, as Doctor Trevor sat in his study, after his wife had gone to bed, Miss Galindo knocked at his door. She and he had a long conversation. The result was that he accompanied Miss Galindo up to town the next day; that they took possession of the little Bessy, and she was brought down, and placed at nurse at a farm in the country near Warwick, Miss Galindo undertaking to pay one-half the expense, and to furnish her with clothes, and Dr. Trevor undertaking that the remaining half should be furnished by the Gibson family, or by himself in their default.

Miss Galindo was not fond of children, and I daresay she dreaded taking this child to live with her for more reasons than one. My Lady Ludow could not endure any mention of illegitimate children. It was a principle of hers that society ought to ignore them. And I believe Miss Galindo had always agreed with her until now, when the thing came home to her womanly heart. Still she shrank from having this child of some strange woman under her roof. She went over to see it from time to time ; she worked at its clothes long after every one thought she was in bed; and, when the time came for Bessy to be sent to school, Miss Galindo laboured away more diligently than ever, in order to pay the increased expense. For the Gibson family had, at first, paid their part of the compact, but with unwillingness and grudging hearts; then they had left it off altogether, and it fell hard on Doctor Trevor with his twelve children; and, latterly, Miss Galindo had taken upon herself almost all the burden. One can hardly live and labour, and plan and make sacrifices, for any human creature, without learning to love it. And Bessy loved Miss Galindo, too, for all the poor girl's scanty pleasures came from her, and Miss Galindo had always a kind word, and, latterly, many a kind caress, for Mark Gibson's child; whereas, if she went to Doctor Trevor's for her holiday, she was overlooked and neglected in that bustling family, who seemed to think that if she had comfortable board and lodging under their roof, it was enough.

I am sure, now, that Miss Galindo had often longed to have Bessy to live with her ; but, as long as she could pay for her being at school, she did not like to take so bold a step as bringing her home, knowing what the effect of the consequent explanation would be on my lady. And as the girl was now more than seventeen, and past the age when young ladies are usually kept at school, and as there was no great demand for governesses in those days, and as Bessy had never been taught any trade by which to earn her own living, why I don't exactly see what could have been done but for Miss Galindo to bring her to her own home in Hanbury. For, although the child had grown up lately, in a kind of unexpected manner, into a young woman, Miss Galindo might have kept her at school for a year longer, if she could have afforded it; but this was impossible when she became Mr. Homer's clerk, and relinquished all the payment of her repository work; and perhaps, after all, she was not sorry to be compelled to take the step she was longing for. At any rate, Bessy came to live with Miss Galindo, in a very few weeks from the time when Captain James set Miss Galindo free to superintend her own domestic economy again.

For a long time, I knew nothing about this new inhabitant of Hanbury. My lady never mentioned her in any way. This was in accordance with Lady Ludlow's well-known principles. She neither saw nor heard, nor was in any way cognisant of the existence of those who had no legal right to exist at all. If Miss Galindo had hoped to have an exception made in Bessy's favour, she was mistaken. My lady sent a note inviting Miss Galindo herself to tea one evening, about a month after Bessy came; but Miss Galindo "had a cold and could not come." The next time she was invited, she " had an engagement at home "— a step nearer to the absolute truth. And the third time, she " had a young friend staying with her whom she was unable to leave." My lady accepted every excuse as bona fide, and took no further notice. I missed Miss Galindo very much; we all did; for, in the days when she was clerk, she was sure to come in and find the opportunity of saying something amusing to some of us before she went away. And I, as an invalid, or perhaps from natural tendency, was particularly fond of little bits of village gossip. There was no Mr. Horner—he even had come in, now and then, with formal, stately pieces of intelligence—and there was no Miss Galindo, in these days. I missed her much. And so did my lady, I am sure. Behind all her quiet, sedate manner, I am certain her heart ached sometimes for a few words from Miss Galindo, who seemed to have absented herself altogether from the Hall now Bessy was come.

Captain James might be very sensible, and all that; but not even my lady could call him a substitute for the old familiar friends. He was a thorough sailor, as sailors were in those days— swore a good deal, drank a good deal (without its ever affecting him in the least), and was very prompt and kind-hearted in all his actions; but he was not accustomed to women, as my lady once said, and would judge in all things for himself. My lady had expected, I think, to find some one who would take his notions on the management of her estate from her u ladyship's own self; but he spoke as if he were responsible for the good management of the whole, and must, consequently, be allowed full liberty of action. He had been too long in command over men at sea to like to be directed by a woman in anything he undertook, even though that woman was my lady. I suppose this was the common-sense my lady spoke of; but when common-sense goes against us, I don't think we value it quite so much as we ought to do.

Lady Ludlow was proud of her personal superintendence of her own estate. She liked to tell us how her father used to take her with him in his rides, and bid her observe this and that, and on no account to allow such and such things to be done. But I have heard that the first time she told all this to Captain James, he told her point-blank that he had heard from Mr. Smithson that the farms were much neglected and the rents sadly behind-hand, and that he meant to set to in good earnest and study agriculture, and see how he could remedy the state of things. My lady would, I am sure, be greatly surprised, but what could she do? Here was the very man she had chosen herself, setting to with all his energy to conquer the defect of ignorance, which was all that those who had presumed to offer her ladyship advice had ever had to say against him. Captain James read Arthur Young's < Tours' in all his spare time, as long as he was an invalid; and

shook his head at my la'dy's accounts as to how the land had been cropped or left fallow from time immemorial. Then he set to, and tried too many new experiments at once. My lady looked on in dignified silence; but all the farmers and tenants were in an uproar, and prophesied a hundred failures. Perhaps fifty did occur; they were only half as many as Lady Ludlow had feared; but they were twice as many, four, eight times as many as the captain had anticipated. His openly-expressed disappointment made him popular again. The rough country people could not have understood silent and dignified regret at the failure of his plans; but they sympathised with a man who swore at his ill success—sympathised, even while they chuckled over his discomfiture. Mr. Brooke, the retired tradesman, did not cease blaming him for not succeeding, and for swearing. "But what could you expect from a sailor?" Mr. Brooke asked, even in my lady's hearing; though he might have known Captain James was my lady's own personal choice, from the old friendship Mr. Urian had always shown for him. I think it was this speech of the Birmingham baker's that made my lady determine to stand by Captain James, and encourage him to try again. For she would not allow that her choice had been an unwise one, at the bidding (as it were) of a Dissenting tradesman; the

MY LADY LUDLOW.

only person in the neighbourhood, too, who had flaunted about in coloured clothes, when all the world was in mourning for my lady's only son.

Captain James would have thrown the agency up at once, if my lady had not felt herself bound to justify the wisdom of her choice, by urging him to stay. He was much touched by her confidence in him, and swore a great oath, that the next year he would make the land such as it had never been before for produce. It was not my lady's way to repeat anything she had heard, especially to another person's disadvantage. So I don't think she ever told Captain James of Mr. Brooke's speech about a sailor's being likely to mismanage the property; and the captain was too anxious to succeed in this, the second year of his trial, to be above going to the flourishing, shrewd Mr. Brooke, and asking for his advice as to the best method of working the estate. I dare say, if Miss Galindo had been as intimate as formerly at the Hall, we should all of us have heard of this new acquaintance of the agent's long before we did. As it was, I am sure my lady never dreamed that the captain, who held opinions that were even more Church and King than her own, could ever have made friends with a Baptist baker from Birmingham, even to serve her ladyship's own interests in the most loyal manner.

We heard of it first from Mr. Gray, who came now often to see my lady, for neither he nor she could forget the solemn tie which the fact of his being the person to acquaint her with my lord's death had created between them. For true and holy words spoken at that time, though having no reference to aught below the solemn subjects of life and death, had made her withdraw her opposition to Mr. Gray's wish about establishing a village school. She had sighed a little, it is true, and was even yet more apprehensive than hopeful as to the result; but, almost as if as a memorial to my lord, she had allowed a kind of rough school-house to be built on the green, just by the church; and had gently used the power she undoubtedly had, in expressing her strong wish that the boys might only be taught to read and write, and the first four rules of arithmetic; while the girls were only to learn to read, and to add up in their heads, and the rest of the time to work at mending their own clothes, knitting stockings and spinning. My lady presented the school with more spinning-wheels than there were girls, and requested that there might be a rule that they should have spun so many hanks of flax, and knitted so many pairs of stockings, before they ever were taught to read at all. After all, it was but making the best of a bad job with my poor lady—but life was not what it had

MY LADY LUDLOW.

been to her. I remember well the day that Mr. Gray pulled some delicately fine yarn (and I was a good judge of those things) out of his pocket, and laid it and a capital pair of knitted stockings before my lady, as the first-fruits, so to say, of his school. I recollect seeing her put on her spectacles, and carefully examine both productions. Then she passed them to me.

"This is well, Mr. Gray. I am much pleased. You are fortunate in your schoolmistress. She has had both proper knowledge of womanly things and much patience. Who is she ? One out of our village ?"

" My lady," said Mr. Gray, stammering and colouring in his old fashion, " Miss Bessy is so very kind as to teach all those sorts of things—Miss Bessy, and Miss Galindo, sometimes."

My lady looked at him "over her spectacles: but she only repeated the words " Miss Bessy," and paused, as if trying to remember who such a person could be; and he, if he had then intended to say more, was quelled by her manner, and dropped the subject. He went on to say, that he had thought it his duty to decline the subscription to his school offered by Mr. Brooke, because he was a Dissenter; that he (Mr, Gray) feared that Captain James, through whom Mr. Brooke's offer of money had been made, was offended at his refusing to accept it from a man who

held heterodox opinions; nay, whom Mr. Gray suspected of being infected by Dodwell's heresy.

"I think there must be some mistake," said my lady, "or I have misunderstood you. Captain James would never be sufficiently with a schismatic to be employed by that man Brooke in distributing his charities. I should have doubted, until now, if Captain James knew him." *

" Indeed, my lady, he not only knows him, but is intimate with him, I regret to say. 1 have repeatedly seen the captain and Mr. Brooke walking together; going through the fields together; and people do say "

My lady looked up in interrogation at Mr. Gray's pause.

" I disapprove of gossip, and it may be untrue; but people do say that Captain James is very attentive to Miss Brooke."

" Impossible!" said my lady, indignantly. " Captain Jaines is a loyal and religious man. I beg your pardon, Mr. Gray, but it is impossible."

CHAPTER XIV.

LIKE many other things which have been declared to be impossible, this report of Captain James being attentive to Miss Brooke turned out to be very true.

The mere idea of her agent being on the slightest possible terms of acquaintance with the Dissenter, the tradesman, the Birmingham democrat, who had come to settle in our good, orthodox, aristocratic, and agricultural Hanbury, made my lady very uneasy. Miss Galindo's misdemeanor in having taken Miss Bessy to live with her, faded into a mistake, a mere error of judgment, in comparison with Captain James's intimacy at Yeast House, as the Brookes called their ugly square-built farm. My lady talked herself quite into complacency with Miss Galindo, and even Miss Bessy was named by her, the first time I had ever been aware that my lady recognised her existence; but—I recollect it was a long rainy afternoon, and I sat with her ladyship, and we had time and opportunity for a long uninterrupted talk—whenever we had been silent for a

little while, she began again, with something like a wonder how it was that Captain James could ever have commenced an acquaintance with " that man Brooke." My lady recapitulated all the times she could remember, that anything had occurred, or been said by Captain James which she could now understand as throwing light upon the subject.

" He said once that he was anxious to bring in the Norfolk system of cropping, and spoke a good deal about Mr. Coke of Holkham (who, by the way, was no more a Coke than I am—collateral in the female line —which counts for little or nothing among the great old commoners' families of pure blood), and his new ways of cultivation ; of course new men bring in new ways, but it does not follow that either are better than the old ways. However, Captain James has been very anxious to try turnips and bone manure, and he really is a man of such good sense and energy, and was so sorry last year about the failure, that I consented; and now I begin to see my error. I have always heard that town bakers adulterate their flour with bone-dust; and, of course, Captain James would be aware of this, and go to Brooke to inquire where the article was to be purchased."

My lady always ignored the fact which had sometimes, I suspect, been brought under her very eyes

MY LADY LUDLOW.

during her drives, that Mr. Brooke's few fields were in a state of far higher cultivation than her own; so she could not, of course, perceive that there was any wisdom to be gained from asking the advice of the tradesman turned farmer.

But by-and-bj this fact of her agent's intimacy with the person whom in the whole world she most disliked (with that sort of dislike in which a large amount of uncomfortableness is combined—the dislike which conscientious people sometimes feel to another without knowing why, and yet which they cannot indulge in with comfort to themselves without having a moral reason why), came before my lady in many shapes. For, indeed, I am sure that Captain James was not a man to conceal or be ashamed of one of his actions. I cannot fancy his ever lowering his strong loud clear voice, or having a confidential conversation with any one. When his crops had failed, all the village had known it. He complained, he regretted, he

was angry, or owned himself a fool, all down the

village street; and the consequence was that, although he was a far more passionate man than Mr. Horner, all the tenants liked him far better. People, in general, take a kindlier interest in any one, the workings of whose mind and heart they can watch and understand, than in a man who only lets you know what he has

been thinking about and feeling, by what he does. But Harry Gregson was faithful to the memory of Mr. Horner. Miss Galindo has told me that she used to watch him hobble out of the way of Captain James, as if to accept his notice, however good-naturedly given, would have been a kind of treachery to his former benefactor. But Gregson (the father) and the new agent rather took to each other; and one day, much to my surprise, I heard that the "poaching, tinkering vagabond," as people used to call Gregson when I first had come to live at Hanbury, had been appointed gamekeeper ; Mr. Gray standing godfather, as it were, to his trustworthiness, if he were trusted with anything : which I thought at the time was rather an experiment, only it answered, as many of Mr. Gray's deeds of daring did. It was curious how he was growing to be a kind of autocrat in the village ; and how unconscious he was of it. He was as shy and awkward and nervous as ever in any affair that was not of some moral consequence to him. But as soon as he was convinced that a thing was right, he " shut his eyes and ran and butted at it like a ram," as Captain James once expressed it, in talking over something Mr. Gray had done. People in the village said, " they never knew what the parson would be at next;" or they might have said " where his reverence would next turn up.

For I have heard of his inarching right into the middle of a set of poachers, gathered together for some desperate midnight enterprise, or walking into a public-house that lay just beyond the bounds of my lady's estate, and in that extra-parochial piece of ground I named long ago, and which was considered the rendezvous of all the ne'er-do-weel characters for miles round, and where a parson and a constable were held in much the same kind of esteem, as unwelcome visitors. And yet Mr. Gray had his long fits of depression, in which he felt a§ if he were doing nothing, making no way in his work, useless and unprofitable, and better out of the world than in it. In comparison with the work he had set himself to do, what he did seemed to be nothing. I suppose it was constitutional, those attacks of lowness of spirits which he had about this time ; perhaps a part of the nervousness which made him always so awkward when he came to the Hall. Even Mrs. Medlicott, who almost worshipped the ground he trod on, as the saying is, owned that Mr. Gray never entered one of my lady's rooms without knocking down something, and too often breaking- it. He would much sooner have faced a desperate poacher than a young lady any day. At least so we thought.

I do not know how it was that it came to pass that my lady became reconciled to Miss Galindo about this time. Whether it was that her ladyship was weary of the unspoken coolness with her old friend ; or that the specimens of delicate sewing and fine spinning at the school had mollified her towards Miss Bessy; but I was surprised to learn one day that Miss Galindo and her young friend were coming that very evening to tea at the Hall. This information was given me by Mrs. Medlicott, as a message from my lady, who further went on to desire that certain little preparations should be made in her own private sitting-room, in which the greater part of my days were spent. From the nature of these preparations, I became quite aware that my lady intended to do honour to her expected visitors. Indeed Lady Ludlow never forgave by halves, as I have known some people do. Whoever was coming as a visitor to my lady, peeress, or poor nameless girl, there was a certain amount of preparation required, in order to do them fitting honour. I do not mean to say that the preparation was of the same degree of importance in each case. I dare say, if a peeress had come to visit us at the Hall, the covers would have been taken off the furniture in the white drawing-room (they never were uncovered all the time I stayed at the Hall), because my lady would wish to offer her the ornaments and luxuries which this grand visitor (who never came— I wish she had! I did so want to see that furniture

MY LADY LUDLOW.

uncovered!) was accustomed to at home, and to present them to her in the best order in which my lady could. The same rule, modified, held good with Miss Galindo. Certain things, in which my lady knew she took an interest, were laid out ready for her to examine on this very day; and, what was more, great hooks of prints were laid out, such as I remembered my lady had had brought forth to beguile my own early days of illness, Mr. Hogarth's works, and the like,which I was sure were put out for Miss Bessy.

No one knows how curious I was to see this mysterious Miss Bessy—twenty times more mysterious, of course, for want of her surname. And then again (to try and account for my great curiosity, of which in recollection I am more than half ashamed), I had been leading the quiet monotonous life of a crippled invalid for many years,—shut up from any sight of new faces; and this was to be the face of one whom I had thought about so much and so long,Oh ! I think I might be excused.

Of course, they drank tea in the great hall, with the four young gentlewomen, who, with myself, formed the small bevy now under her ladyship's charge. Of those who were at Hanbury when first I came, none remained ; all were married, or gone once more to live at some home which could be called their own, whether

the ostensible head were father or brother. I myself was not without some hopes of a similar kind. My brother Harry was now a curate in Westmoreland, and wanted me to go and live with him, as eventually I did for a time. But that is neither here nor there at present. What I am talking about is Miss Bessy.

After a reasonable time had elapsed, occupied as I well knew by the meal in the great hall,—the measured, yet agreeable conversation afterwards,and a certain promenade around the hall, and through the drawing-rooms, with pauses before different pictures, the history or subject of each of which was invariably told by my lady to every new visitor,a sort of giving them the freedom of the old family-seat, by describing the kind and nature of the great progenitors who had lived there before the narrator,I heard the steps approaching my lady's room where I lay. I think I was in such a state of nervous expectation, that if I could have moved easily, I should have got up and run away. And yet I need not have been, for Miss Galindo was not in the least altered (her nose a little redder, to be sure, but then that might only have had a temporary cause in the private crying I know she would have had before coming to see her dear Lady Ludlow once again.) But I could almost have pushed Miss Galindo away, as she intercepted me in my view of the mysterious Miss Bessy.

MY LADY LUDLOW.

Miss Bessy was, as I knew, only about eighteen, but she looked older. Dark hair, dark eyes, a tall, firm figure, a good, sensible face, with a serene expression, not in the least disturbed by what I had been thinking must be such awful circumstances as a first introduction to my lady, who had so dissapproved of her very existence : those are the clearest impressions I remember of my first interview with Miss Bessy. She seemed to observe us all, in her quiet manner, quite as much as 1 did her; but she spoke very little; occupied herself, indeed, as my lady had planned, with looking over the great books of engravings. I think I must have (foolishly) intended to make her feel at her ease, by my patronage ; but she was seated far away from my sofa, in order to command the light, and really seemed so unconcerned at her unwonted circumstances, that she did not need my countenance or kindness. One thing I did like—her watchful look at Miss Galindo from time to time: it showed that her thoughts and sympathy were ever at Miss Galindo's service, as indeed they well might be. When Miss Bessy spoke, her voice was full and clear, and what she said, to the purpose, though there was a slight provincial accent in her way of speaking. After a while, my lady set us two to play at chess, a game which I had lately learnt at Mr. Gray's suggestion. Still we did not talk much together,

though we were becoming attracted towards each other, I fancy.

" You will play well," said she. " You have only learnt about six months, have you ? And yet you can nearly beat me, who have been at it as many years."

U I began to learn last November. I remember Mr. Gray's bringing me ' Philidor on Chess,' one very foggy, dismal day."

What made her look up so suddenly, with bright inquiry in her eyes? What made her silent for a moment, as if in thought, and then go on with something, I know not what, in quite an altered tone ?

My lady and Miss Galindo went on talking, while I sat thinking. I heard Captain James's name mentioned pretty frequently ; and at last my lady put down her work, and said, almost with tears in her eyes:

"I could not—I cannot believe it. He must be aware she is a schismatic; a baker's daughter; and he is a gentleman by virtue and feeling, as well as by his profession, though his manners may be at times a little rough. My dear Miss Galindo, what will this world come to?"

Miss Galindo might possibly be aware of her own share in bringing the world to the pass which now dismayed my lady,—for, of course, though all was now over and forgiven, yet Miss Bessy's being received into a respectable maiden lady's house, was one of the portents as to the world's future which alarmed her ladyship; and Miss Galindo knew this,—but, at any rate, she had too lately been forgiven herself not to plead for mercy for the next offender against my lady's delicate sense of fitness and propriety,—so she replied: "Indeed, my lady, I have long left off trying to conjecture what makes Jack fancy Gill, or Gill Jack. It's best to sit down quiet under the belief that marriages are made for us, somewhere out of this world, and out of the range of this world's reasons and laws. I'm not so sure that I should settle it down that they were made in Heaven; t'other place seems to me as likely a workshop; but, at any rate, I've given up troubling my head as to why they take place. Captain James is a gentleman; I make no doubt of that ever since I saw him stop to pick up old Goody Blake (when she tumbled down on the slide last winter) and then swear at a little lad who was laughing at her, and cuff him till he tumbled down crying; but we must have bread somehow, and though I like it better baked at home in a good sweet brick oven, yet, as some folks never can get it to rise, I don't see why a man may not be a baker. You see, my lady, I look upon baking as a simple trade, and as such lawful. There is no machine comes in to take away a man's or woman's power of earning their living,, like the spinning-jenny (the old busybody that she is), to knock up all our good old women's livelihood, and send them to their graves before their time. There's an invention of the enemy, if you will!"

"That's very true!" said my lady, shaking her head.

"But baking bread is wholesome, straight-forward elbow-work. They, have not got to inventing any contrivance for that yet, thank Heaven! It does not seem to me natural, nor according to Scripture, that iron and steel (whose brows can't sweat) should be made to do man's work. And so I say, all those trades where iron and steel do the work ordained to man at the Fall, are unlawful, and I never stand up for them. But say this baker Brooke did knead his bread, and make it rise, and then that people, who had, perhaps, no good ovens, came to him, and bought his good light bread, and in this manner he turned an honest penny, and got rich; why, all I say, my lady, is this,—I dare say he would have been born a Hanbury, or a lord, if he could ; and if he was not, it is no fault of his, that I can see, that he made good bread (being a baker by trade), and got money, and bought his land. It was his misfortune, not his fault, that he was not a person of quality by birth."

"That's very true," said my lady, after a moment's pause for consideration. "But, although he was a baker, he might have been a Churchman. Even your eloquence, Miss Galindo, shan't convince me that that is riot his own fault."

"I don't see even that, begging your pardon, my lady," said Miss Galindo, emboldened by the first success of her eloquence. "When a Baptist is a baby, if I understand their creed aright, he is not baptized; and, consequently, he can have no godfathers and godmothers to do anything for him in his baptism; you agree to that, my lady?"

My lady would rather have known what her acquiescence would lead to, before acknowledging that she could not dissent from this first proposition; still she gave her tacit agreement by bowing her head.

" And, you know, our godfathers and godmothers are expected to promise and vow three things in our name, when we are little babies, and can do nothing but squall for ourselves. It is a great privilege, but don't let us be hard upon those who have not had the chance of godfathers and godmothers. Some people, we know, are born with silver spoons,that's to say, a godfather to give one things, and teach one one's catechism, and see that we're confirmed into good church-going Christians,and others with wooden ladles in their mouths. These poor last folks must just be content to be godfatherless orphans, and Dissenters, all their lives: and if they are tradespeople into the bargain, so much the worse for them; but let us be humble Christians, my dear lady, and not hold our heads too high because we were born orthodox quality."

" You go on too fast, Miss Galindo ! I can't follow you. Besides, I do believe dissent to be an invention of the Devil's. Why can't they believe as we do? It's very wrong. Besides, it's schism and heresy, and, you know, the Bible says that's as bad as witchcraft."

My lady was not convinced, as I could see. After Miss Galindo had gone, she sent Mrs. Medlicott for certain books out of the great old library up stairs, and had them made up into a parcel under her own eye.

" If Captain James comes to-morrow, I will speak to him about these Brookes. I have not hitherto liked to speak to him, because I did not wish to hurt him, by supposing there could be any truth in the reports about his intimacy with them. But now I will try and do my duty by him and them. Surely, this great body of divinity will bring them back to the true church."

I could not tell, for though my lady read me over the titles, I was not any the wiser as to their contents. Besides, I was much more anxious to consult my lady as to my own change of place. I showed her the letter I had that day received from Harry; and we once more talked over the expediency of my going to live with him, and trying what entire change of air would do to re-establish my failing health. I could say anything to my lady, she was so sure to understand me rightly. For one thing, she never thought of herself, so I had no fear of hurting her by stating the truth. I told her how happy my years had been while passed under her roof; but that now I had begun to wonder whether I had not duties elsewhere, in making a home for Harry,—and whether the fulfilment of these duties, quiet ones they must needs be in the case of such a cripple as myself, would not prevent my sinking into the querulous habit of thinking and talking into which I found myself occasionally falling. Add to which, there was the prospect of benefit from the more bracing air of the north.

It was then settled that my departure from Hanbury, my happy home for so long, was to take place before many weeks had passed. And as, when one period of life is about to be shut up for ever, we are sure to look back upon it with fond regret, so I, happy enough in my future prospects, could not avoid recurring to all the days of my life in the Hall, from the time when I came to it, a shy, awkward girl, scarcely past childhood, to now, when a grown woman, past childhood—almost, from the very character of my illness, past youth, I was looking forward to leaving my lady's house (as a residence) for ever. As it has turned out, I never saw either her or it again. Like a piece of sea-wreck, I have drifted away from those days: quiet, happy, eventless days, very happy to rememher!

I thought of good, jovial Mr. Mountford, and his regrets that he might not keep a pack, " a very small pack," of harriers, and his merry ways, and his love of good eating; of the first coming of Mr. Gray, and my lady's attempt to quench his sermons, when they tended to enforce any duty connected with education. And now we had an absolute school-house in the village; and since Miss Bessy's drinking tea at the Hall, my lady had been twice inside it, to give directions about some fine yarn she was having spun for table-napery. And her ladyship had so outgrown her old custom of dispensing with sermon or discourse, that even during the temporary preaching of Mr. Crosse, she had never had recourse to it, though I believe she would have had all the congregation on her side if she had.

And Mr. Horner was dead, and Captain James reigned in his stead. Good, steady, severe, silent Mr. Horner! with his clock-like regularity, and his snuff-coloured clothes, and silver buckles! I have often wondered which one misses most when they are dead and gone, the bright creatures full of life, who are hither and thither and everywhere, so that no one can reckon upon their coming and going, with whom stillness and the long quiet of the grave seems utterly irreconcilable, so full are they of vivid motion and passion, or the slow, serious people, whose movements nay, whose very words, seem to go by clock-work; who never appear much to affect the course of our life while they are with us, but whose methodical ways show themselves, when they are gone, to have been intertwined with our very roots of daily existence. I think I miss these last the most, although I may have loved the former best. Captain James never was to me what Mr. Homer was, though the latter had hardly changed a dozen words with me at the day of his death. Then Miss Galindo! I remembered the time, as if it had been only yesterday, when she was but a name—and a very odd one—to me ; then she was a queer, abrupt, disagreeable, busy old maid. Now I loved her dearly, and I found out that I was almost jealous of Miss Bessy.

Mr. Gray I never thought of with love; the feeling was almost reverence with which I looked upon him. I have not wished to speak much of myself, or else I could have told you how much he had been to me during these long, weary years of illness. But he was almost as much to every one, rich and poor, from my lady down to Miss Galindo's Sally.

The village, too, had a different look about it. I am sure I could not tell you what caused the change; but there were no more lounging young men to form a group at the cross-road, at a time of day when young men ought to be at work. I don't say this was all Mr. Gray's doing, for there really was so much to do in the fields that there was but little time for lounging now-a days. And the children were hushed up in school, and better behaved out of it, too, than in the days when I used to be able to go my lady's errands in the village. I went so little about now, that I am sure I can't tell who Miss Galindo found to scold; and yet she looked so well and so happy that I think she must have had her accustomed portion of that wholesome exercise.

Before I left Hanbury, the rumour that Captain James was going to marry Miss Brooke, Baker Brooke's eldest daughter, who had only a sister to share his property with her, was confirmed. He himself announced it to my lady; nay, more, with a courage, gained, I suppose, in his former profession, where, as I have heard, he had led his ship into many a post of danger, he asked her ladyship, the Countess Ludlow, if he might bring his bride elect (the Baptist baker's daughter !) and present her to my lady!

I am glad I was not present when he made this request; I should have felt so much ashamed for him,

MY LADY LUDLOW.

and I could not have helped being anxious till I heard my lady's answer, if I had been there. Of course she acceded; but I can fancy the grave surprise of her look. I wonder if Captain James noticed it.

I hardly dared ask my lady, after the interview had taken place, what she thought of the bride elect; but I hinted my curiosity, and she told me, that if the young person had applied to Mrs. Medlicott, for the situation of cook, and Mrs. Medlicott had engaged her, she thought that it would have been a very suitable arrangement. I understood from this how little she thought a marriage with Captain James, R.N., suitable.

About a year after I left Hanbury, I received a letter from Miss Galindo, I think I can find it.—Yes, this is it.

'Hanbury, May 4, 1811.

' DEAE MAKGAKET,

" You ask for news of us all. Don't you know there is no news in Hanbury? Did you ever hear of an event here ? Now, if you have answered "Yes," in your own mind to these questions, you have fallen into my trap, and never were more mistaken in your life. Hanbury is full of news; and we have more events on our hands than we know what to do with. I will take them in the order of the newspapers—births, deaths, and marriages. In the matter of births, Jenny Lucas has had twins not a week ago. Sadly too much of a

i good thing, you'll say. Very true: but then they ' died; so their birth did not much signify. My cat has ' kittened, too ; she has had three kittens, which again ' you may observe is too much of a good thing ; and so ' it would be, if it were not for the next item of intelligence I shall lay before you. Captain and Mrs. ' James have taken the old house next Pearson's ; and

the house is overrun with mice, which is just as 'fortunate for me as the King of Egypt's rat-ridden 'kingdom was to Dick Whittington. For my cat's ' kittening decided me to go and call on the bride, in

hopes she wanted a cat; which she did, like a sensible 1 woman, as I do believe she is, in spite of Baptism, ' Bakers, Bread, and Birmingham, and something worse ' than all, which you shall hear about, if you'll only be ' patient. As I had got my best bonnet on—the one I ; bought when poor Lord Ludlow was last at Hanbury ' in '99—I thought it a great condescension in myself 4 (always remembering the date of the Galindo Ba-' ronetcy) to go and call on the bride; though I don't ' think so much of myself in my every-day clothes, as ' you know. But who should I find there but my Lady ' Ludlow! She looks as frail and delicate as ever, but 'is, I think, in better heart ever since that old city ' merchant of a Hanbury took it into his head that he ' was a cadet of the Hanburys of Hanbury, and left ' her that handsome legacy. I'll warrant you the ' mortgage was paid off pretty fast; and Mr. Homer's 'money—or my lady's money, or Harry Gregson's

MY LADY LUDLOW.

money, call it which you will,is invested in his name, all right and tight, and they do talk of his being captain of his school, or Grecian, or something, and going to college, after all! Harry Gregson the ' poacher's son! Well! to be sure, we are living in ' strange times!

But I have not done with the marriages yet. Cap-1 tain James's is all very well, but no one cares for it now, we are all so full of Mr. Gray's. Yes, indeed, Mr. Gray is going to be married, and to nobody else but my little Bessy ! I tell her she will have to nurse him half the days of her life, he is such a frail little body. But she says she does not care for that, so that

his body holds his soul, it is enough for her. She has 1 a good spirit, and a brave heart, has my Bessy ! It is a great advantage that she won't have to mark her clothes over again ; for when she had knitted herself her last set of stockings, I told her to put G for Galindo, if she did not choose to put it for Gibson, for she should be my child if she was no one else's.

And now, you see, it stands for Gray. So there are two marriages, and what more would you have ? And she promises to take another of my kittens.

Now, as to deaths, old Farmer Hale is dead—poor old man, I should think his wife thought it a good 4 riddance, for he beat her every day that he was drunk, and he never was sober, in spite of Mr. Gray. 1 don't think (as I tell him) that Mr. Gray would ever have found courage to speak to Bessy as long

' as Farmer Hale lived, he took the old gentleman's sins so much to heart, and seemed to think it was all his fault ' for not being able to make a sinner into a saint. The parish bull is dead too. I never was so glad in my life.

* But they say we are to have a new one in his place. ' In the meantime I cross the common in peace, which ' is convenient just now, when I have so often to go to ' Mr. Gray's to see about furnishing.

t Now you think I have told you all the Hanbury news, ' don't you ? Not so. The very greatest thing of all is ' to come. I won't tantalize you, but just out with it,

* for you would never guess it. My Lady Ludlow has given a party, just like any plebeian amongst us. We ' had tea and toast in the blue drawing-room, old John 4Footman waiting, with Tom Diggles, the lad that 6 used to frighten away crows in Farmer Bale's fields, following in my lady's livery, hair powdered and 4 everything. Mrs. Medlicott made tea in my lady's 'own room. My lady looked like a splendid fairy 'queen of mature age, in black velvet, and the old lace, which I have never seen her wear before since ' my lord's death. But the company ? you'll say. Why we had the parson of Clove, and the parson of Head-'leigh, and the parson of Merribank, and the three ' parsonesses; and Farmer Donkin and two Miss ' Donkins ; and Mr. Gray (of course), and myself and ' Bessy; and Captain and Mrs. James; yes, and Mr.

' and Mrs. Brooke : think of that! I am not so sure ' the parsons liked it; but he was there. For he has

MY LADY LUDLOW.

' been helping Captain James to get my lady's land ' into order; and then his daughter married the agent; ' and Mr. Gray (who ought to know) says, after all, ' Baptists are not such bad people; and he was right ' against them at one time, as you may remember. ' Mrs. Brooke is a rough diamond, to be sure. People ' have said that of me, I know. But, being a Galindo, ' I learnt manners in my youth, and can take them up ' when I choose. But Mrs. Brooke never learnt * manners, I'll be bound. When John Footman handed ' her the tray with the tea-cups, she looked up at him ' as if she were sorely puzzled by that way of going on. 4 1 was sitting next to her, so I pretended not to see ' her perplexity, and put her cream and sugar in for ' her, and was all ready to pop it into her hands,— 'when who should come up, but that impudent lad 'Tom Diggles (I call him lad, for all his hair is pow-1 dered, for you know that it is not natural grey hair), ' with his tray full of cakes and what not, all as good ' as Mrs. Medlicott could make them. By this time, I ' should tell you, all the parsonesses were looking at ' Mrs. Brooke, for she had shown her want of breeding ' before; and the parsonesses, who were just a step ' above her in manners, were very much inclined to ' smile at her doings and sayings. Well! what does ' she do but pull out a clean Bandanna pocket-handker-' chief, all red and yellow silk, spread it over her best ' silk gown; it was, like enough, a new one, for I had ' it from Sally, who had it from her cousin Molly, who

MY LADY LUDLOW.

is dairy-woman at the Brookes', that the Brookes were mighty set-up with an invitation to drink tea at the Hall. There we were, Tom Diggles even on the grin (I wonder how long it is since he was own brother to a scarecrow, only not so decently dressed) and Mrs. Parsoness of Headleigh,I forget her name, and it's no matter, for she's an ill-bred creature, I hope Bessy will behave herself better,was right-down bursting with laughter, and as near a hee-haw as ever a donkey was, when what does my lady do ? Ay ! there's my own dear Lady Ludlow, God bless her! She takes out her own pocket-handkerchief, all snowy cambric, and lays it softly down on her velvet lap, for all the world as if she did it every day of her life, just like Mrs. Brooke, the baker's wife ; and when the one got up to shake the crumbs into the fire-place, the other did just the same. But with such a grace ! and such a look at us all! Tom Diggles went red all over ; and Mrs. Parsoness of Headleigh scarce spoke for the rest of the evening; and the tears came into my old silly eyes; and Mr. Gray, who was before silent and awkward, in a way which I tell Bessy she must cure him of, was made so happy by this pretty action of my lady's, that he talked away all the rest of the evening, and was the life of the company.

Oh! Margaret Dawson, I sometimes wonder if you're the better off for leaving us. To be sure, you're with your brother, and blood is blood. But when I look at my lady and Mr. Gray, for all they're so

MY LADY LUDLOW.

' different, I would not change places with any in ' England.'

Alas! alas ! I never saw my dear lady again. She died in eighteen hundred and fourteen, and Mr. Gray did not long survive her. As I dare say you know the Reverend Henry Gregson is now vicar of Hanbury, and his wife is the daughter of Mr. Gray and Miss Bessy.

As any one may guess, it had taken Mrs. Dawson several Monday evenings to narrate all this history of the days of her youth. Miss Duncan thought it would be a good exercise for me, both in memory and composition, to write out on Tuesday mornings all that I had heard the night before; and thus it came to pass that I have the manuscript of " My Lady Ludlow " now lying by me.

END OF VOL. I.

# ROUND THE SOFA.

BY THE AUTHOR OF
"Mary Barton," "Life of Charlotte Brontë," &c. &c.

TWO VOLUMES.

VOL. II.

LONDON:
SAMPSON LOW, SON & CO., 47 LUDGATE HILL.
1859.

## CONTENTS OF VOL. II.

|  | PAGE |
|---|---|
| THE ACCURSED RACE | 3 |
| THE DOOM OF THE GRIFFITHS | 32 |
| HALF A LIFE-TIME AGO | 97 |
| THE POOR CLARE | 179 |
| THE HALF-BROTHERS | 277 |

# ROUND THE SOFA.

MR. DAWSON had often come in and out of the room during the time that his sister had been telling us about Lady Ludlow. He would stop, and listen a little, and smile or sigh as the case might be. The Monday after the dear old lady had wound up her tale (if tale it could be called), we felt rather at a loss what to talk about, we had grown so accustomed to listen to Mrs. Dawson. I remember I was saying, " Oh, dear \ I wish some one would tell us another story!" when her brother said, as if in answer to my speech, that he had drawn up a paper all ready for the Philosophical Society, and that perhaps we might care to hear it before it was sent off: it was in a great measure compiled from a French book, published by one of the Academies, and rather dry in itself; but to which Mr. Dawson's attention had been directed, after a tour he

ROUND .THE SOFA.

had made in England during the past year, in which he had noticed small walled-up doors in unusual parts of some old parish churches, and had been told that they had formerly been appropriated to the use of some half-heathen race, who, before the days of gipsies, held the same outcast pariah position in most of the countries of western Europe. Mr. Dawson had been recommended to the French book which he named, as containing the fullest and most authentic account of this mysterious race, the Cagots. I did not think I should like hearing this paper as much as a story; but, of course, as he meant it kindly, we were bound to submit, and I found it, on the whole, more interesting than I anticipated.

AN ACCURSED RACE.

WE have our prejudices in England. Or, if that assertion offends any of my readers, I will modify it: we have had our prejudices in England. We have tortured Jews; we have burnt Catholics and Protestants, to say nothing of a few witches and wizards. We have satirised Puritans, and we have dressed-up Guys. But, after all, I do not think we have been so bad as our Continental friends. To be sure, our insular position has kept us free, to a certain degree, from the inroads of alien races; who, driven from one land of refuge, steal into another equally unwilling to receive them; and where, for long centuries, their presence is barely endured, and no pains is taken to conceal the repugnance which the natives of "pure blood " experience towards them.There yet remains a remnant of the miserable people called Cagots in the valleys of the Pyrenees ; in the Landes near Bourdeaux ; and, stretching up on the west side of France, their numbers become larger in Lower Brittany. Even now, the origin of these families is a word of shame to them among their neighbours; although they are protected by the law, which confirmed them in the equal rights of citizens about the end of the last century. Before then they had lived, for hundreds of years, isolated from all those who boasted of pure blood, and they had been, all this time, oppressed by cruel local edicts. They were truly what they were popularly called, The Accursed Race.

All distinct traces of their origin are lost. Even at the close of that period which we call the Middle Ages, this was a problem which no one could solve; and as the traces, which even then were faint and uncertain, have vanished away one by one, it is a complete mystery at the present day. Why they were accursed in the first instance, why isolated from their kind, no one knows. From the earliest accounts of their state that are yet remaining to us, it seems that the names which they gave each other were ignored by the population they lived amongst, who spoke of them as Crestiaa, or Cagots, just as we speak of animals by

their generic names. Their houses or huts were always placed at some distance out of the villages of the country-folk, who unwillingly called in the services of the Cagots as carpenters, or tilers, or slaters—trades which seemed appropriated by this unfortunate race who were forbidden to occupy land, or to bear arms, the usual occupations of those times. They had some small right of pasturage on the common lands, and in the forests: but the number of their cattle and livestock was strictly limited by the earliest laws relating to the Cagots. They were forbidden by one act to have more than twenty sheep, a pig, a ram, and six geese. The pig was to be fattened and killed for winter food; the fleece of the sheep was to clothe them; but, if the said sheep had lambs, they were forbidden to eat them. Their only privilege arising from this increase was, that they might choose out the strongest and finest in preference to keeping the old sheep. At Martinmas the authorities of the commune came round, and counted over the stock of each Cagot. If he had more than his appointed number, they were forfeited; half went to the commune, and half to the baillie, or chief magistrate of the commune. The poor beasts were limited as to the amount of common land which they might stray over in search of grass. While the cattle of the inhabitants of the commune

might wander hither and thither in search of the sweetest herbage, the deepest shade, or the coolest pool in which to stand on the hot days, and lazily switch their dappled sides, the Cagot sheep and pig had to learn imaginary bounds, beyond which if they strayed, any one might snap them up, and kill them, reserving a part of the flesh for his own use, but graciously restoring the inferior parts to their original owner. Any damage done by the sheep was, however, fairly appraised, and the Cagot paid no more for it than any other man would have done.

Did a Cagot leave his poor cabin, and venture into the towns, even to render services required of him in the way of his trade, he was bidden, by all the municipal laws, to stand by and remember his rude old state. In all the towns and villages in the large districts extending on both sides of the Pyrenees—in all that part of Spain— they were forbidden to buy or sell anything eatable, to walk in the middle (esteemed the better) part of the streets, to come within the gates before sunrise, or to be found after sunset within the walls of the town. But still, as the Cagots were good-looking men, and (although they bore certain natural marks of their caste, of which I shall speak by-and-by) were not easily distinguished by casual passers-by from other men, they were compelled to wear some distinct-

ive peculiarity which should arrest the eye ; and, in the greater number of towns, it was decreed that the outward sign of a Cagot should be a piece of red cloth sewed conspicuously on the front of his dress. In other towns, the mark of Cagoterie was the foot of a duck or a goose hung over their left shoulder, so as to be seen by any one meeting them. After a time, the more convenient badge of a piece of yellow cloth cut out in the shape of a duck's foot, was adopted. If any Cagot was found in any town or village without his badge, he had to pay a fine of five sous, and to lose his dress. He was expected to shrink away from any passer-by, for fear that their clothes should touch each other; or else to stand still in some corner or by-place. If the Cagots were thirsty during the days which they passed in those towns where their presence was barely suffered, they had no means of quenching their thirst, for they were forbidden to enter into the little cabarets or taverns. Even the water gushing out of the common fountain was prohibited to them. Far away, in their own squalid village, there was the Cagot fountain, and they were not allowed to drink of any other water. A Cagot woman having to make purchases in the town, was liable to be flogged out of it if she went to buy anything except on a Monday a day on which all other people who could, kept their houses for fear of coming in contact with the accursed race. In the Pays Basque, the prejudices and for some time the laws ran stronger against them than any which I have hitherto mentioned. The Basque Cagot was not allowed to possess sheep. He might keep a pig for provision, but his pig had no right of pasturage. He might cut and carry grass for the ass, which was the only other animal he was permitted to own; and this ass was permitted, because its existence was rather an advantage to the oppressor, who constantly availed himself of the Cagot's mechanical skill, and was glad to have him and his tools easily conveyed from one place to another.

The race was repulsed by the State. Under the small local governments they could hold no post whatsoever. And they were barely tolerated by the Church, although they were good Catholics, and zealous frequenters of the mass. They might only enter the churches by a small door set apart for them, through which no one of the pure race ever passed. This door was low, so as to compel them to make an obeisance. It was occasionally surrounded by sculpture, which invariably represented an oak-branch with a dove above it. When they were once in, they might not go to the holy water used by others. They had a benitier of their own; nor were they allowed to share in the consecrated bread when that was handed round to the believers of the pure race. The Cagots stood afar off, near the door. There were certain boundaries imaginary lines on the nave and in the aisles which they might not pass. In one or two of the more tolerant of the Pyrenean villages, the blessed bread was offered to the Cagots, the priest standing on one side of the boundary, and giving the pieces of bread on a long wooden fork to each person successively.

When the Cagot died, he was interred apart, in a plot of burying-ground on the north side of the cemetery. Under such laws and prescriptions as I have described, it is no wonder that he was generally too poor to have much property for his children to inherit; but certain descriptions of it were forfeited to the commune. The only possession which all who were not of his own race refused to touch, was his furniture. That was tainted, infectious, unclean—fit for none but Cagots.

When such were, for at least three centuries, the prevalent usages and opinions with regard to this oppressed race, it is not surprising that we read of occasional outbursts of ferocious violence on their part. In the Basses-Pyrenees, for instance, it is only about a hundred years since, that the Cagots of Rehouilhes rose up against the inhabitants of the neighbouring town of Lourdes, and got the better of them, by their magical powers, as it is said. The people of Lourdes were conquered and slain, and their ghastly, bloody heads served the triumphant Cagots for balls to play at ninepins with ! The local parliaments had begun, by this time, to perceive how oppressive was the ban of public opinion under which the Cagots lay, and were not inclined to enforce too severe a punishment. Accordingly, the decree of the parliament of Toulouse condemned only the leading Cagots concerned in this affray to be put to death, and that henceforward and for ever no Cagot was to be permitted to enter the town of Lourdes by any gate but that called Capdet-pourtet: they were only to be allowed to walk under the rain-gutters, and neither to sit, eat, nor drink in the town. If they failed in observing any of these rules, the parliament decreed, in the spirit of Shylock, that the disobedient Cagots should have two strips of flesh, weighing never more than two ounces a-piece, cut out from each side of their spines.

In the fourteenth, fifteenth, and sixteenth centuries, it was considered no more a crime to kill a Cagot than to destroy obnoxious vermin. A " nest of Cagots," as the old accounts phrase it, had assembled in a deserted castle of Mauvezin, about the year sixteen hundred; and, certainly, they made themselves not very agreeable neighbours, as they seemed to enjoy their reputation of magicians ; and, by some acoustic secrets which were known to them, all sorts of moanings and groanings were heard in the neighbouring forests, very much to the alarm of the good people of the pure race ; who could not cut off a withered branch for firewood, but some unearthly sound seemed to fill the air, nor drink water which was not poisoned, because the Cagots would persist in filling their pitchers at the same running stream. Added to these grievances, the various pilferings perpetually going on in the neighbourhood made the inhabitants of the adjacent towns and hamlets believe that they had a very sufficient cause for wishing to murder all the Cagots in the Chateau de Mauvezin. But it was surrounded by a moat, and only accessible by a drawbridge; besides which, the Cagots were fierce and vigilant. Some one, however, proposed to get into their confidence; and for this purpose he pretended to fall ill close to their path, so that on returning to their stronghold they perceived him, and took him in, restored him to health, and made a friend of him. One day, when they were all playing at ninepins in the woods, their treacherous friend left the party on pretence of being thirsty, and went back into the castle, drawing up the bridge after he had passed

over it, and so cutting off their means of escape into safety. Then, going up to the highest part of the castle, he blew a horn, and the pure race, who were lying in wait on the watch for some such signal, fell upon the Cagots at their games, and slew them all. For this murder I find no punishment decreed in the parliament of Toulouse, or elsewhere.

As any intermarriage with the pure race was strictly forbidden, and as there were books kept in every commune in which the names and habitations of the reputed Cagots were written, these unfortunate people had no hope of ever becoming blended with the rest of the population. Did a Cagot marriage take place, the couple were serenaded with satirical songs. They also had minstrels, and many of their romances are still current in Brittany; but they did not attempt to make any reprisals of satire or abuse. Their disposition was amiable, and their intelligence great Indeed, it required both these qualities, and their great love of mechanical labour, to make their lives tolerable.

At last, they began to petition that they might receive some protection from the laws ; and, towards the end of the seventeenth century, the judicial power took their side. But they gained little by this. Law could not prevail against custom: and, in the ten or twenty years just preceding the first French revolution, the prejudice

in France against the Cagots amounted to fierce and positive abhorrence.

At the beginning of the sixteenth century, the Cagots of Navarre complained to the Pope, that they were excluded from the fellowship of men, and accursed by the Church, because their ancestors had given help to a certain Count Raymond of Toulouse in his revolt against the Holy See, They entreated his holiness not to visit upon them the sins of their fathers. The Pope issued a bull—on the thirteenth of May, fifteen hundred and fifteen—ordering them to be well-treated and to be admitted to the same privileges as other men. He charged Don Juan de Santa Maria of Pampeluna . to see to the execution of this bull. But Don Juan was slow to help, and the poor Spanish Cagots grew impatient, and resolved to try the secular power. They accordingly applied to the cortes of Navarre, and were opposed on a variety of grounds. First, it was stated that their ancestors had had " nothing to do with Raymond Count of Toulouse, or with any such knightly personage ; that they were in fact descendants of Gehazi, servant of Elisha (second book of Kings, fifth chapter, twenty-seventh verse), who had been accursed by his master for his fraud upon Naaman, and doomed, he and his descendants, to be lepers for evermore. Name, Cagots or Gahets ; Gahets, Gehazites. What can be

more clear ? And if that is not enough, and you tell us that the Cagots are not lepers now; we reply that there are two kinds of leprosy, one perceptible and the other imperceptible, even to the person suffering from it. Besides, it is the country talk, that where the Cagot treads, the grass withers, proving the unnatural heat of his body. Many credible and trustworthy witnesses will also tell you that, if a Cagot holds a freshly-gathered apple in his hand, it will shrivel and wither up in an hour's time as much as if it had been kept for a whole winter in a dry room. They are born with tails; although the parents are cunning enough to pinch them off immediately. Do you doubt this? If it is not true, why do the children of the pure race delight in sewing on sheep's tails to the dress of any Cagot who is so absorbed in his work as not to perceive them? And their bodily smell is so horrible and detestable that it shows that they must be heretics of some vile and pernicious description, for do we not read of the incense of good workers, and the fragrance of holiness?"

Such were literally the arguments by which the Cagots were thrown back into a worse position than ever, as far as regarded their rights as citizens. The Pope insisted that they should receive all their ecclesiastical privileges. The Spanish priests said nothing; but tacitly refused to allow the Cagots to mingle with

the rest of the faithful, either dead or alive. The accursed race obtained laws in their favour from the Emperor Charles the Fifth; which, however, there was no one to carry into effect. As a sort of revenge for their want of submission, and for their impertinence in daring to complain, their tools were all taken away from them by the local authorities: an old man and all his family died of starvation, being no longer allowed to fish.

They could not emigrate. Even to remove their poor mud habitations, from one spot to another, excited anger and suspicion. To be sure, in sixteen hundred and ninety-five, the Spanish government ordered the alcaldes to search out all the Cagots, and to expel them before two months had expired, under pain of having fifty ducats to pay for every Cagot remaining in Spain at the expiration of that time. The inhabitants of the villages rose up and flogged out any of the miserable race who might be in their neighbourhood; but the French were on their guard against this enforced irruption, and refused to permit them to enter France. Numbers were hunted up into the inhospitable Pyrenees, and there died of starvation, or became a prey to wild beasts. They were obliged to wear both gloves and shoes when they were thus put to flight, otherwise the stones and herbage they trod upon, and the balustrades

of the bridges that they handled in crossing, would, according to popular belief, have become poisonous.

And all this time, there was nothing remarkable or disgusting in the outward appearance of this unfortunate people. There was nothing about them to countenance the idea of their being lepers— the most natural mode of accounting for the abhorrence in which they were held. They were repeatedly examined by learned doctors, whose experiments, although singular and rude, appear to have been made in a spirit of humanity. For instance, the surgeons of the king of Navarre, in sixteen hundred, bled twenty-two Cagots, in order to examine and analyse their blood. They were young and healthy people of both sexes; and the doctors seem to have expected that they should have been able to extract some new kind of salt from their blood which might account for the wonderful heat of their bodies. But their blood was just like that of other people. Some of these medical men have left us a description of the general appearance of this unfortunate race, at a time when they were more numerous and less intermixed than they are now. The families existing in the south and west of France, who are reputed to be of Cagot descent at this day, are, like their ancestors, tall, largely made, and powerful in frame; fair and ruddy in complexion, with gray-blue eyes, in

which some observers see a pensive heaviness of look. Their lips are thick, but well-formed. Some of the reports name their sad expression of countenance with surprise and suspicion—" They are not gay, like other folk." The wonder would be if they were. Dr. Guy on, the medical man of the last century who has left the clearest report on the health of the Cagots, speaks of the vigorous old age they attain to. In one family alone, he found a man of seventy-four years of age ; a woman as old, gathering cherries; and another woman, aged eighty-three, was lying on the grass, having her hair combed by her great-grandchildren. Dr. Guyon and other surgeons examined into the subject of the horribly infectious smell which the Cagots were said to leave behind them, and upon everything they touched ; but they could perceive nothing unusual on this head. They also examined their ears, which, according to common belief (a belief existing to this day), were differently shaped from those of other people; being round and gristly, without the lobe of flesh into which the earring is inserted. They decided that most of the Cagots whom they examined had the ears of this round shape; but they gravely added, that they saw no reason why this should exclude them from the good-will of men, and from the power of holding office in Church and State. They recorded the fact, that the children of the towns

ran baaing after any Cagot who had been compelled to come into the streets to make purchases, in allusion to this peculiarity of the shape of the ear, which bore some resemblance to the ears of the sheep as they are cut by the shepherds in this district. Dr. Guyon names the case of a beautiful Cagot girl, who sang most sweetly, and prayed to be allowed to sing canticles in the organ-loft. The organist, more musician than bigot, allowed her to come ; but the indignant congregation, finding out whence proceeded that clear, fresh voice, rushed up to the organ-loft, and chased the girl out, bidding her "remember her ears," and not commit the sacrilege of singing praises to God along with the pure race.

But this medical report of Dr. Guyon's—bringing facts and arguments to confirm his opinion, that there was no physical reason why the Cagots should not be received on terms of social equality by the rest of the world — did no more for his clients than the legal decrees promulgated two centuries before had done. The French proved the truth of the saying in Hudibras,

He that's convinced against his will Is of the same opinion still.

And, indeed, the being convinced by Dr. Guyon that they ought to receive Cagots as fellow-creatures, only made them more rabid in declaring that they would not.

One or two little occurrences which are recorded, show that the bitterness of the repugnance to the Cagots was in full force at the time just preceding the first French revolution. There was a M. d'Abedos, the curate of Lourbes, and brother to the seigneur of the neighbouring castle, who was living in seventeen hundred and eighty ; he was well-educated for the time, a travelled man, and sensible and moderate in all respects but that of his abhorrence of the Cagots : he would insult them from the very altar, calling out to them, as they stood afar off, " Oh! ye Cagots, damned for evermore I" One day, a half-blind Cagot stumbled and touched the censer borne before this Abbe de Lourbes. He was immediately turned out of the church, and forbidden ever to re-enter it. One does not know how to account for the fact, that the very brother of this bigoted abbe, the seigneur of the village, went and married a Cagot girl; but so it was, and the abbe brought a legal process against him, and had his estates taken from him, solely on account of his marriage, which reduced him to the condition of a Cagot, against whom the old law was still in force. The descendants of this Seigneur de Lourbes are simple peasants at this very day, working on the lands which belonged to their grandfather. -

This prejudice against mixed marriages remained

prevalent until very lately. The tradition of the Cagot descent lingered among the people, long after the laws against the accursed race were abolished. A Breton girl, within the last few years, having two lovers each of reputed Cagot descent, employed a notary to examine their pedigrees, and see which of the two had least Cagot in him; and to that one she gave her hand. In

Brittany the prejudice seems to have been more virulent than anywhere else. M. Emile Souvestre records proofs of the hatred borne to them in Brittany so recently as in eighteen hundred and thirty-five. Just lately a baker at Hennebon, having married a girl of Cagot descent, lost all his custom. The godfather and godmother of a Cagot child became Cagots themselves by the Breton laws, unless, indeed, the poor little baby died before attaining a certain number of days. They had to eat the butchers' meat condemned as unhealthy; but, for some unknown reason, they were considered to have a right to every cut loaf turned upside down, with its cut side towards the door, and might enter any house in which they saw a loaf in this position, and carry it away with them. About thirty years ago, there was the skeleton of a hand hanging up as an offering in a Breton Church near Quim-perle, and the tradition was, that it was the hand of a rich Cagot who had dared to take holy water out of

the usual benitier, some time at the beginning of the reign of Louis the Sixteenth ; which an old soldier witnessing, he lay in wait, and the next time the offender approached the benitier he cut off his hand, and hung it up, dripping with blood, as an offering to the patron saint of the church. The poor Cagots in Brittany petitioned against their opprobrious name, and begged to be distinguished by the appellation of Malandrins. To English ears one is much the same as the other, as neither conveys any meaning; but, to this day, the descendants of the Cagots do not like to have this name applied to them, preferring that of Malandrin.

The French Cagots tried to destroy all the records of their pariah descent, in the commotions of seventeen hundred and eighty-nine; but if writings have disappeared, the tradition yet remains, and points out such and such a family as Cagot, or Malandrin, or Oiselier, according to the old terms of abhorrence.

There are various ways in which learned men have attempted to account for the universal repugnance in which this well-made, powerful race are held. Some say that the antipathy to them took its rise in the days when leprosy was a dreadfully prevalent disease : and that the Cagots are more liable than any other men to a kind of skin disease, not precisely leprosy, but resem-

bling it in some of its symptoms; such as dead whiteness of complexion, and swellings of the face and extremities. There was also some resemblance to the ancient Jewish custom in respect to'Jepers, in the habit of the people ; who, on meeting a Cagot, called out, "Cagote? Cagote?" to which they were bound to reply, " Perlute ! perlute !" Leprosy is not properly an infectious complaint, in spite of the horror in which the Cagot furniture, and the cloth woven by them, are held in some places; the disorder is hereditary, and hence (say this body of wise men, who have troubled themselves to account for the origin of Cagoterie) the reasonableness and the justice of preventing any mixed marriages, by which this terrible tendency to leprous complaints might be spread far and wide. Another authority says, that though the Cagots are fine-looking men, hard-working, and good mechanics, yet they bear in their faces, and show in their actions, reasons for the detestation in which they are held : their glance, if you meet it, is the jettatura, or evil-eye, and they are spiteful, and cruel, and deceitful above all other men. All these qualities they derive from their ancestor Gehazi, the servant of Elisha, together with their tendency to leprosy.

Again, it is said that they are descended from the Arian Goths, who were permitted to live in certain places

in Guienne and Languedoc, after their defeat by King Clovis, on condition that they abjured their heresy, and kept themselves separate from all other men for ever. The principal reason alleged in support of this supposition of their Gothic descent, is the specious one of derivation,—Chiens Gots, Cans Gots, Cagots, equivalent to Dogs of Goths.

Again, they were thought to be Saracens, coming from Syria. In confirmation of this idea, was the belief that all Cagots were possessed by a horrible smell. The Lombards, also, were an unfragrant race, or so reputed among the Italians: witness Pope Stephen's letter to Charlemagne, dissuading him from marrying Bertha, daughter of Didier, King of Lombardy. The Lombards boasted of Eastern descent, and were noisome. The Cagots were noisome, and therefore must be of Eastern descent. What could be clearer ? In addition, there was the proof to be derived from the name Cagot, which those maintaining the opinion of their Saracen descent held to be Chiens, or Chasseurs des Gots, because the Saracens chased the Goths out of Spain. Moreover, the Saracens were originally Mahometans, and as such obliged to bathe seven times a-day : whence the badge of the duck's foot. A duck was a water-bird: Mahometans bathed in the water. Proof upon proof!

In Brittany the common idea was, they were of Jewish descent. Their unpleasant smell was again pressed into the service. The Jews, it was well known, had this physical infirmity, which might be cured either by bathing in a certain fountain in Egypt—which was a long way from Brittany—or by anointing themselves with the blood of a Christian child. Blood gushed out of the body of every Cagot on Good Friday. No wonder, if they were of Jewish descent. It was the only way of accounting for so portentous a fact. Again; the Cagots were capital carpenters, which gave the Bretons every reason to believe that their ancestors were the very Jews who made the cross. When first the tide of emigration set from Brittany to America, the oppressed Cagots crowded to the ports, seeking to go to some new country, where their race might be unknown. Here was another proof of their descent from Abraham and his nomadic people ; and, the forty years' wandering in the wilderness and the Wandering Jew himself, were pressed into the service to prove that the Cagots derived their restlessness and love of change from their ancestors, the Jews. The Jews, also, practised arts-magic, and the Cagots sold bags of wind to the Breton sailors, enchanted maidens to love them— maidens who never would have cared for them, unless they had been previously enchanted—made hollow

rocks and trees give out strange and unearthly noises, and sold the magical herb called bon-succes. It is true enough that, in all the early acts of the fourteenth century, the same laws apply to Jews as to Cagots, and the appellations seem used indiscriminately ; but their fair complexions, their remarkable devotion to all the ceremonies of the Catholic Church, and many other circumstances, conspire to forbid our believing them to be of Hebrew descent.

Another very plausible idea is, that they are the descendants of unfortunate individuals afflicted with goitres, which is, even to this day, not an uncommon disorder in the gorges and valleys of the Pyrenees. Some have even derived the word goitre from Got, or Goth; but their name, Crestiaa, is not unlike Cretin, and the same symptoms of idiotism were not unusual among the Cagots; although sometimes, if old tradition is to be credited, their malady of the brain took rather the form of violent delirium, which attacked them at new and full moons. Then the workmen laid down their tools, and rushed off from their labour to play mad pranks up and down the country. Perpetual motion was required to alleviate the agony of fury that seized upon the Cagots at such times. In this desire for rapid movement, the attack resembled the Neapolitan tarantella ; while in the mad deeds they per-

formed during such attacks, they were not unlike the northern Berserker. In Beam especially, those suffering from this madness were dreaded by the pure race ; the Bearnais, going to cut their wooden clogs in the great forests that lay around the base of the Pyrenees, feared above all things to go too near the periods when the Cagoutelle seized on the oppressed and accursed people; from whom it was then the oppressors' turn to fly. A man was living within the memory of some, who had married a Cagot wife; he used to beat her right soundly when he saw the first symptoms of the Cagoutelle, and, having reduced her to a wholesome state of exhaustion and insensibility, he locked her up until the moon had altered her shape in the heavens. If he had not taken such decided steps, say the oldest inhabitants, there is no knowing what might have happened.

From the thirteenth to the end of the nineteenth century, there are facts enough to prove the universal abhorrence in which this unfortunate race was held; whether called Cagots, or Gahets in Pyrenean districts, Caqueaux in Brittany, or Vaqueros in Asturias. The great French revolution brought some good out of its fermentation of the people: the more intelligent among them tried to overcome the prejudice against the Cagots.

In seventeen hundred and eighteen, there was a famous cause tried at Biarritz relating to Cagot rights and privileges. There was a wealthy miller, Etienne Arnauld by name, of the race of Gotz, Quagotz, Bi-sigotz, Astragotz, or Gahetz, as his people are described in the legal document He married an heiress a Gotte (or Cagot) of Biarritz ; and the newly-married, well-to-do couple saw no reason why they should stand near the door in the church, nor why he should not hold some civil office in the commune, of which he was the principal inhabitant. Accordingly, he petitioned the law that he and his wife might be allowed to sit in the gallery of the church, and that he might be relieved from his civil disabilities. This wealthy white miller, Etienne Arnauld, pursued his rights with some vigour against the Baillie of Labourd, the dignitary of the neighbourhood. Whereupon the inhabitants of Biarritz met in the open air, on the eighth of May, to the number of one hundred and fifty ; approved of the conduct of the Baillie in rejecting Arnauld, made a subscription, and gave all power to their lawyers to defend the cause of the pure race against Etienne Arnauld— " that stranger," who, having married a girl of Cagot blood, ought also to be expelled from the holy places. This lawsuit was carried through all the local courts, and ended by an appeal to the highest court in Paris ;

c2

where a decision was given against Basque superstitions ; and Etienne Arnauld was thenceforward entitled to enter the gallery of the church.

Of course, the inhabitants of Biarritz were all the more, ferocious for having been conquered ; and, four years later, a carpenter, Miguel Legaret, suspected of Cagot descent, having placed himself in church among other people, was dragged out by the abbe and two of the jurats of the parish. Legaret defended himself with a sharp knife at the time, and went to law afterwards ; the end of which was, that the abbe and his two accomplices were condemned to a public confession of penitence, to be uttered while on their knees at the church door, just after high-mass. They appealed to the parliament of Bourdeaux against this decision, but met with no better success than the opponents of the miller Arnauld. Legaret was confirmed in his right of standing where he would in the parish church. That a living Cagot had equal rights with other men in the town of Biarritz seemed now ceded to them ; but a dead Cagot was a different thing. The inhabitants of pure blood struggled long and hard to be interred apart from the abhorred race. The Cagots were equally persistent in claiming to have a common bury ing-ground. Again the texts of the old Testament were referred to, and the pure blood quoted triumphantly the precedent of Uzziah the leper (twenty-sixth chapter of the second book of Chronicles), who was buried in the field of the Sepulchres of the Kings, not in the sepulchres themselves. The Cagots pleaded that they were healthy and able-bodied; with no taint of leprosy near them. They were met by the strong argument so difficult to be refuted, which I have quoted before. Leprosy was of two kinds, perceptible and imperceptible. If the Cagots were suffering from the latter kind, who could tell whether they were free from it or not? That decision must bereft to the judgment of others.

One sturdy Cagot family alone, Belone by name, kept up a lawsuit, claiming the privilege of common sepulture, for forty-two years; although the cure of Biarritz had to pay one hundred livres for every Cagot not interred in the right place. The inhabitants indemnified the curate for all these fines.

M. de Romagne, Bishop of Tarbes, who died in seventeen hundred and sixty-eight, was the first to allow a Cagot to fill any office in the Church. To be sure, some were so spiritless as to reject office when it was offered to them, because, by.so claiming their equality, they had to pay the same taxes as other men, instead of the Rancale or poll-tax levied on the Cagots ; the collector of which had also a right to claim a piece of bread of a certain size for his dog at every Cagot dwelling.

Even in the present century, it has been necessary in some churches for the archdeacon of the district, followed by all his clergy, to pass out of the small door previously appropriated to the Cagots, in order to mitigate the superstition which, even so lately, made the people refuse to mingle with them in the house of God. A Cagot once played the congregation at Larroque a trick suggested by what I have just named. He slily locked the great parish-door of the church, while the greater part of the inhabitants were assisting at mass inside ; put gravel into the lock itself, so as to prevent the use of any duplicate key,— and had the pleasure of seeing the proud pure-blooded people file out with bended head, through the small low door used by the abhorred Cagots.

We are naturally shocked at discovering, from facts such as these, the causeless rancour with which innocent and industrious people were so recently persecuted. The moral of the history of the accursed race may, perhaps, be best conveyed in the words of an epitaph on Mrs. Mary Hand, who lies buried in the churchyard of Stratford-on-Avon.

What faults you saw in me,
Pray strive to shun; And look at home: there's
Spmething to be done.

FOR some time past I had observed that Miss Duncan made a good deal of occupation for herself in writing, but that she did not like me to notice her employment. Of course, this made me all the more curious ; and many were my silent conjectures—some of them so near the truth that I was not much surprised when, after Mr. Dawson had finished reading his Paper to us, she hesitated, coughed, and abruptly introduced a little formal speech, to the effect that she had noted down an old Welsh story, the particulars of which had often been told her in her youth, as she lived close to the place where the events occurred. Everybody pressed her to read the manuscript, which she now produced from her reticule; but, when on the point of beginning, her nervousness seemed to overcome her, and she made so many apologies for its being the first and only attempt she had ever made at that kind of composition, that I began to wonder if we should ever arrive at the story at all. At length, in a high-pitched, ill-assured voice, she read out the title :

"THE DOOM OF THE GRIFFITHS."

THE DOOM OF THE GRIFFITHS.

CHAPTER I.

I HAVE always been much interested by the traditions which are scattered up and down North Wales relating to Owen Glendower (Owain Glendwr is the national spelling of the name), and I fully enter into the feeling which makes the Welsh peasant still look upon him as the hero of his country. There was great joy among many of the inhabitants of the principality, when the subject of the Welsh prize poem at Oxford, some fifteen or sixteen years ago, was announced to be "Owain Glendwr." It was the most proudly national subject that had been given for years.

Perhaps, some may not be aware that this redoubted chieftain is, even in the present days of enlightenment, as famous among his illiterate countrymen for his magical powers as for his patriotism. He says him-

self—or Shakspeare says it for him, which is much the same thing—

* At my nativity The front of heaven was full of fiery shapes

Of burning cressets

.... I can call spirits from the vasty deep.'

And few among the lower orders in the principality would think of asking Hotspur's irreverent question in reply.

Among other traditions preserved relative to this part of the Welsh hero's character, is the old family prophecy which gives a title to this tale. When Sir David Gam, " as black a traitor as if he had been born in Builth," sought to murder Owen at Machynlleth, there was one with him whose name Glendwr little dreamed of having associated with his enemies. Rhys ap Gryfydd, his " old familiar friend," his relation, his more than brother, had consented unto his blood. Sir David Gam might be forgiven, but one whom he had loved, and who had betrayed him, could never be forgiven. Glendwr was too deeply read in the human heart to kill him. No, he let him live on, the loathing and scorn of his compatriots, and the victim of bitter remorse. The mark of Cain was upon him.

But before he went forth—while yet he stood a prisoner, cowering beneath his conscience before Owain

Glendwr—that chieftain passed a doom upon him and his race:

" I doom thee to live, because I know thou wilt pray for death. Thou shalt live on beyond the natural term of the life of man, the scorn of all good men. The very children shall point to thee with hissing tongue, and say, * There goes one who would have shed a brother's blood!' For I loved thee more than a brother, oh Rhys ap Gryfydd! Thou shalt live on to see all of thy house, except the weakling in arms, perish by the sword. Thy race shall be accursed. Each generation shall see their lands melt away like snow ; yea, their wealth shall vanish, though they may labour night and day to heap up gold. And when nine generations have passed from the face of the earth, thy blood shall no longer flow in the veins of any human being. In those days the last male of thy race shall avenge me. The son shall slay the father."

Such was the traditionary account of Owain Glen-dwr's speech to his once-trusted friend. And it was declared that the doom had been fulfilled in all things ; that, live in as miserly a manner as they would, the Griffiths never were wealthy and prosperous—indeed, that their worldly stock diminished without any visible cause.

But the lapse of many years had almost deadened

the wonder-inspiring power of the whole curse. It was only brought forth from the hoards of Memory when some untoward event happened to the Griffiths family; and in the eighth generation the faith in the prophecy was nearly destroyed, by the marriage of the Griffiths of that day, to a Miss Owen, who, unexpectedly, by the death of a brother, became an heiress—to no considerable amount, to be sure, but enongh to make the prophecy appear reversed. The heiress and her husband removed from his small patrimonial estate in Merionethshire, to her heritage in Caenarvonshire, and for a time the prophecy lay dormant.

If you go from Tremadoc to Criccaeth you pass by the parochial church of Ynysynhanarn, situated in a boggy valley running from the mountains, which shoulder up to the Rivals, down to Cardigan Bay. This tract of land has every appearance of having been redeemed at no distant period of time from the sea, and has all the desolate rankness often attendant upon such marshes. But the valley beyond, similar in character, had yet more of gloom at the time of which I write. In the higher part there were large plantations of firs, set too closely to attain to any size, and remaining stunted in height and scrubby in appearance. Indeed, many of the smaller and more weakly had died, and the bark had fallen down on the brown soil

neglected and unnoticed. These trees had a ghastly appearance, with their white trunks, seen by the dim light which struggled through the thick boughs above. Nearer to the sea, the valley assumed a more open, though hardly a more cheerful character; it looked dank and overhung by sea-fog through the greater part of the year, and even a farm-house, which usually imparts something of cheerfulness to a landscape, failed to do so here. This valley formed the greater part of the estate to which Owen Griffiths became entitled by right of his wife. In the higher part of the valley was situated the family mansion, or rather dwelling-house, for " mansion," is too grand a word to apply to the clumsy, but substantially-built Bodowen. It was square and heavy-looking, with just that much pretension to ornament necessary to distinguish it from the mere farm-house.

In this dwelling Mrs. Owen Griffiths bore her husband two sons—Llewellyn, the future Squire, and Robert, who was early destined for the Church. The only difference in their situation, up to the time when Robert was entered at Jesus College, was that the elder was invariably indulged by all around him, while Robert was thwarted and indulged by turns; that Llewellyn never learned anything from the poor Welsh parson who was nominally his private tutor; while occa-

sionally Squire Griffiths made a great point of enforcing Robert's diligence, telling him that, as he had his bread to earn, he must pay attention to his learning* There is no knowing how far the very irregular education he had received would have carried Robert through his college examinations; but, luckily for him in this respect, before such a trial of his learning came round, he heard of the death of his elder brother, after a short illness, brought on by a hard-drinking bout. Of course, Robert was summoned home, and it seemed quite as much of course, now that there was no necessity for him to " earn his bread by his learning," that he should not return to Oxford. So the half-educated, but not unintelligent, young man continued at home, during the short remainder of his parent's lifetime.

His was not an uncommon character. In general he was mild, indolent, and easily managed; but once thoroughly roused, his passions were vehement and fearful. He seemed, indeed, almost afraid of himself, and in common hardly dared to give way to justifiable anger — so much did he dread losing his self-control. Had he been judiciously educated, he would, probably, have distinguished himself in those branches of literature which call for taste and imagination, rather than any exertion of reflection or judgment. As it was, his literary taste showed itself in making collections of

Cambrian antiquities of every description, till his stock of Welsh MSS. would have excited the envy of Dr. Pugh himself, had he been alive at the time of which I write.

There is one characteristic of Robert Griffiths which 1 have omitted to note, and which was peculiar among his class. He was no hard drinker; whether it was that his head was very easily affected, or that his partially-refined taste led him to dislike intoxication and its attendant circumstances, I cannot say; but at five-and-twenty Robert Griffiths was habitually sober—a thing so rare in Llyn, that he was almost shunned as a churlish, unsocial being, and passed much of his time in solitude.

About this time, he had to appear in some case that was tried at the Caernarvon assizes ; and while there, was a guest at the house of his agent, a shrewd, sensible Welsh attorney, with one daughter, who had charms enough to captivate Robert Griffiths. Though he remained only a few days at her father's house, they were sufficient to decide his affections, and short was the period allowed to elapse before he brought home a mistress to Bodowen. The new Mrs. Griffiths was a gentle, yielding person, full of love toward her husband, of whom, nevertheless, she stood something in awe, partly arising from the difference in their ages, partly from his devoting much time to studies of which she could understand nothing.

She soon made him the father of a blooming little daughter, called Augharad after her mother. Then there came several uneventful years in the household of. Bodoweu; and when the old women had one and all declared that the cradle would not rock again, Mrs. Griffiths bore the son and heir. His birth was soon followed by his mother's death : she had been ailing and low-spirited during her pregnancy, and she seemed to lack the buoyancy of body and mind requisite to bring her round after her time of trial. Her husband, who loved her all the more from having few other claims on his affections, was deeply grieved by her early death, and his only comforter was the sweet little boy whom she had left behind. That part of the Squire's character, which was so tender, and almost feminine, seemed called forth by the helpless situation of the little infant, who stretched out his arms to his father with the same earnest cooing that happier children make use of to their mother alone. Augharad was almost neglected, while the little Owen was king of the house ; still, next to his father, none tended him so lovingly as his sister. She was so accustomed to give way to him that it was no longer a hardship. By night and by day Owen was the constant companion of his father, and increasing years seemed only to confirm the custom. It was an unnatural , life for the child, seeing no bright little faces peering into his own (for Augharad was, as I said before, five or six years older, and her face, poor motherless girl, was often anything but bright), hearing no din of clear ringing voices, but day after day sharing the otherwise solitary hours of his father, whether in the dim room, surrounded by wizard-like antiquities, or pattering his little feet to keep up with his "tada" in his mountain rambles or shooting excursions. When the pair came to some little foaming brook, where the stepping-stones were far and wide, the father carried his little boy across with the tenderest care; when the lad was weary, they rested, he cradled in his father's arms, or the Squire would lift him up and carry him to his home again. The boy was indulged (for his father felt flattered by the desire) in his wish of sharing his meals and keeping the same hours. All this indulgence did not render Owen unamiable, but it made him wilful, and not a happy child. He had a thoughtful look, not common to the face of a young boy. He knew no games, no merry sports; his information was of an imaginative and speculative character. His father delighted to interest him in his own studies, without considering how far they were healthy for so young a mind.

Of course Squire Griffiths was not unaware of the prophecy which was to be fulfilled in his generation. He would occasionally refer to it when among his friends, with sceptical levity; but in truth it lay nearer to his heart than he chose to acknowledge. His strong imagination rendered him peculiarly impressible on such subjects ; while his judgment, seldom exercised or fortified by severe thought, could not prevent his continually recurring to it. He used to gaze on the half-sad countenance of the child, who sat looking up into his face with his large dark eyes, so fondly yet so inquiringly, till the old legend swelled around his heart, and became too painful for him not to require sympathy. Besides, the overpowering love he bore to the child seemed to demand fuller vent than tender words; it made him like, yet dread, to upbraid its object for the fearful contrast foretold. Still Squire Griffiths told the legend, in a half-jesting manner, to his little son, when they were roaming over the wild heaths in the autumn days, " the saddest of the year," or while they sat in the oak-wainscoted room, surrounded by mysterious relics that gleamed strangely forth by the flickering fire-light. The legend was wrought into the boy's mind, and he would crave, yet tremble to hear it told over and over again, while the words were intermingled with caresses and questions as to his love. Occasionally his loving words and actions were cut short by his father's light yet bitter speech— " Get thee away, my lad; thou knowest what is to come of all this love."

When Augharad was seventeen, and Owen eleven or twelve, the rector of the parish in which Bodowen was situated, endeavoured to prevail on Squire Griffiths to send the boy to school. Now, this rector had many congenial tastes with his parishioner, and was his only intimate ; and, by repeated arguments, he succeeded in convincing the Squire that the unnatural life Owen was leading was in every way injurious. Unwillingly was the father wrought to part from his son; but he did at length send him to the Grammar School at Bangor, then under the management of an excellent classic. Here Owen showed that he had more talents than the rector had given him credit for, when he affirmed that the lad had been completely stupified by the life he led at Bodowen. He bade fair to do credit to the school in the peculiar branch of learning for which it was famous. But he was not popular among his schoolfellows. He was wayward, though, to a certain degree, generous and unselfish ; he was reserved but gentle, except when the tremendous bursts of passion (similar in character to those of his father) forced their way.

On his return from school one Christmas time, when he had been a year or so at Bangor, he was stunned by hearing that the undervalued Augharad was about to be married to a gentleman of South Wales, residing near Aberystwith. Boys seldom appreciate their sisters; but Owen thought of the many slights with which he had requited the patient Augharad, and he gave way to bitter regrets, which, with a selfish want of control over his words, he kept expressing to his father, until the Squire was thoroughly hurt and chagrined at the repeated exclamations of " What shall we do when Augharad is gone ?" " How dull we shall be when Augharad is married!" Owen's holidays were prolonged a few weeks, in order that he might be present at the wedding; [and when all the festivities were over, and the bride and bridegroom had left Bodowen, the boy and his father really felt how much they missed the quiet, loving Augharad. She had performed so many thoughtful, noiseless little offices, on which their daily comfort depended; and now she was gone, the household seemed to miss the spirit that peacefully kept it in order; the servants roamed about in search of commands and directions, the rooms had no longer the un-obtrusive ordering of taste to make them cheerful, the very fires burned dim, and were always sinking down into dull heaps of gray ashes. Altogether Owen did not regret his return to Bangor, and this also the mortified parent perceived. Squire Griffiths was a selfish parent.

Letters in those days were a rare occurrence. Owen usually received one during his half-yearly absences from home, and occasionally his father paid him a visit. This half-year the boy had no visit, nor even a letter, till very near the time of his leaving school, and then he was astounded by the intelligence that his father was married again.

Then came one of his paroxysms of rage ; the more disastrous in its effects upon his character because it could find no vent in action. Independently of the slight to the memory of the first wife, which children are so apt to fancy such an action implies, Owen had hitherto considered himself (and with justice) the first object of his father's life. They had been so much to each other; and now a shapeless, but too real something had come between him and his father there for ever. He felt as if his permission should have been asked, as if he should have been consulted. Certainly he ought to have been told of the intended event. So the Squire felt, and hence his constrained letter, which had so much increased the bitterness of Owen's feelings.

With all this anger, when Owen saw his stepmother, he thought he had never seen so beautiful a woman for her age; for she was no longer in the bloom of youth, being a widow when his father married her. Her manners, to the Welsh lad, who had seen little of female grace among the families of the few antiquarians with whom his father visited, were so fascinating that he watched her with a sort of breathless admiration. Her measured grace, her faultless movements, her tones of voice, sweet, till the ear was sated with their sweetness, made Owen less angry at his father's marriage. Yet he felt, more than ever, that the cloud was between him and his father; that the hasty letter he had sent in answer to the announcement of his wedding was not forgotten, although no allusion was ever made to it. He was no longer his father's confidant—hardly ever his father's companion, for the newly-married wife was all in all to the Squire, and his son felt himself almost a cipher, where he had so long been everything. The lady herself had ever the softest consideration for her stepson; almost too obtrusive was the attention paid to his wishes, but still he fancied that the heart had no part in the winning advances. There was a watchful glance of the eye that Owen once or twice caught when she had imagined herself unobserved, and many other nameless little circumstances, that gave him a strong feeling of want of sincerity in his stepmother. Mrs. Owen brought with her into the family her little child by her first husband, a boy nearly three years old. He was one of those elfish, observant, mocking children, over whose feelings you seem to have no control: agile and mischievous, his little practical jokes, at first performed in ignorance of the pain he gave, but afterward proceeding to a malicious pleasure in suffering, really seemed to afford some ground to the superstitious notion of some of the common people that he was a fairy changeling.

Years passed on ; and as Owen grew older he became more observant. He saw, even in his occasional visits at home (for from school he had passed on to college), that a great change had taken place in the outward manifestations of his father's character ; and, by degrees, Owen traced this change to the influence of his stepmother ; so slight, so imperceptible to the common observer, yet so resistless in its effects. Squire Griffiths caught up his wife's humbly advanced opinions, and, unawares to himself, adopted them as his own, defying all argument and opposition. It was the same with her wishes ; they met with their fulfilment, from the extreme and delicate art with which she insinuated them into her husband's mind, as his own. She sacrificed the show of authority for the power. At last, when Owen perceived some oppressive act in his father's conduct toward his dependants, or some unaccountable thwarting of his own wishes, he fancied he saw his stepmother's secret influence thus displayed, however much she might regret the injustice of his father's actions in her conversations with him when they were alone. His father was fast losing his temperate habits, and frequent intoxication soon took its usual effect upon the temper. Yet even here was the spell of his wife upon him. Before her he placed a restraint upon his passion, yet she was perfectly aware of his irritable disposition, and directed it hither and thither with the same apparent ignorance of the tendency of her words.

Meanwhile Owen's situation became peculiarly mortifying to a youth whose early remembrances afforded such a contrast to his present state. As a child, he had been elevated to the consequence of a man before his years gave any mental check to the selfishness which such conduct was likely to engender ; he could remember when his will was law to the servants and dependants, and his sympathy necessary to his father: now he was as a cipher in his father's house ; and the Squire, estranged in the first instance by a feeling of the injury he had done his son in not sooner acquainting him with his purposed marriage, seemed rather to avoid than to seek him as a companion, and too frequently showed the most utter indifference to the feelings and wishes which a young man of a high and independent spirit might be supposed to indulge.

Perhaps Owen was not fully aware of the force of all these circumstances ; for an actor in a family drama is seldom unimpassioned enough to be perfectly observant. But he became moody and soured; brooding over his unloved existence, and craving with a human heart after sympathy.

This feeling took more full possession of his mind when he had left college, and returned home to lead an idle and purposeless life. As the heir, there was no worldly necessity for exertion : his father was too much of a Welsh squire to dream of the moral necessity, and he himself had not sufficient strength of mind to decide r at once upon abandoning a place and mode of life which abounded in daily mortifications ; yet t© this course his judgment was slowly tending, when some circumstances occurred to detain him at Bodowen.

It was not to be expected that harmony would long be preserved, even in appearance, between an unguarded and soured young man, such as Owen, and his wary stepmother, when he had once left college, and come, not as a visitor, but as the heir to his father's house.

Some cause of difference occurred, where the woman subdued her hidden anger sufficiently to become convinced that Owen was not entirely the dupe she had believed him to be. Henceforward there was no peace between them. Not in vulgar altercations did this show itself; but in moody reserve on Owen's part, and in undisguised and contemptuous pursuance of her own plans by his stepmother. Bodowen was no longer a place where, if Owen was not loved or attended to, he could at least find peace, and care for himself: he was thwarted at every step, and in every wish, by his father's desire apparently, while the wife sat by with a smile of triumph on her beautiful lips.

So Owen went forth at the early day dawn, sometimes roaming about on the shore or the upland, shooting or fishing, as the season might be, but oftener " stretched in indolent repose " on the short, sweet grass, indulging in gloomy and morbid reveries. He would fancy that this mortified state of existence was a dream, a horrible dream, from which he should awake and find himself again the sole object and darling of his father. And then he would start up and strive to shake off the incubus. There was the molten sunset of his childish memory; the gorgeous crimson piles of glory in the west, fading away into the cold, calm light of the rising moon, while here and there a cloud floated across the western

heaven, like a seraph's wing, in its flaming beauty; the earth was the same as in his childhood's days, full of gentle evening sounds, and the harmonies of twilight —the breeze came sweeping low over the heather and blue-bells by his side, and the turf was sending up its evening incense of perfume. But life, and heart, and hope were changed for ever since those bygone days!

Or he would seat himself in a favourite niche of the rocks on Moel Gest, hidden by a stunted growth of the whitty, or mountain-ash, from general observation, with a rich-tinted cushion of stone-crop for his feet, and a straight precipice of rock rising just above. Here would he sit for hours, gazing idly at the bay below with its back-ground of purple hills, and the little fishing-sail on its bosom, showing white in the sunbeam, and gliding on in such harmony with the quiet beauty of the glassy sea; or he would pull out an old school-volume, his companion for years, and in morbid accordance with the dark legend that still lurked in the recesses of his mind—a shape of gloom in those innermost haunts awaiting its time to come forth in distinct outline—would he turn to the old Greek dramas which treat of a family foredoomed by an avenging Fate. The worn page opened of itself at the play of the (Edipus Tyrannus, and Owen dwelt with the craving of disease upon the prophecy so nearly resembling that which concerned himself.

With his consciousness of neglect, there was a sort of self-flattery in the consequence which the legend gave him. He almost wondered how they durst, with slights and insults, thus provoke the Avenger.

The days drifted onward. Often he would vehemently pursue some sylvan sport, till thought and feeling were lost in the violence of bodily exertion. Occasionally his evenings were spent at a small public-house, such as" stood by the unfrequented wayside, where the welcome, hearty though bought, seemed so strongly to contrast with the gloomy negligence of home—unsym-pathizing home.

One evening (Owen might be four or five-and-twenty), wearied with a day's shooting on the Clenneny Moors, he passed by the open door of " The Goat" at Penmorfa. The light and the cheeriness within tempted, him, poor self-exhausted man, as it has done many a one more wretched in worldly circumstances, to step in, and take his evening meal where at least his presence was of some consequence. It was a busy day in that little hostel. A flock of sheep, amounting to some hundreds, had arrived at Penmorfa, on their road to England, and thronged the space before the house. Inside was the shrewd, kind-hearted hostess, bustling to and fro, with merry greetings for every tired drover who was to pass the night in her house, while the sheep were penned in

a field close by. Ever and anon, she kept attending to the second crowd of guests, who were celebrating a rural wedding in her house. It was busy work to Martha Thomas, yet her smile never flagged ; and when Owen Griffiths had finished his evening meal she was there, ready with a hope that it had done him good, and was to his mind, and a word of intelligence that the wedding-folk were about to dance in the kitchen, and the harper was the famous Edward of Corwen.

Owen, partly from good-natured compliance with his hostess's implied wish, and partly from curiosity, lounged to the passage which led to the kitchen—not the every-day, working, cooking kitchen which was beyond, but a good-sized room where the mistress sat when her work was done, and where the country people were commonly entertained at such merry-makings as the present. The lintels of the door formed a frame for the animated picture which Owen saw within, as he leaned against the wall in the dark passage. The red light of the fire, with every now and then a falling piece of turf sending forth a fresh blaze, shone full upon four young men who were dancing a measure something like a Scotch reel, keeping admirable time in their rapid movements to the capital tune the harper was playing. They had their hats on when Owen first took his stand, but as they grew more and more animated they flung

them away, and presently their shoes were kicked off with like disregard to the spot where they might happen to alight. Shouts of applause followed any remarkable exertion of agility, in which each seemed to try to excel his companions. At length, wearied and exhausted, they sat down, and the harper gradually changed to one of those wild, inspiring national airs for which he was so famous. The thronged audience sat earnest and breathless, and you might have heard a pin drop, except when some maiden passed hurriedly, with flaring candle and busy look, through to the real kitchen beyond. When he had finished playing his beautiful theme on " The march of the men of Harlech," he changed the measure again to " Tri chant o' bunnan " (Three hundred pounds), and immediately a most unmusical-looking man began chanting " Pennillion," or a sort of recitative stanzas, which were soon taken up by another, and this amusement lasted so long that Owen grew weary, and was thinking of retreating from his post by the door, when some little bustle was occasioned, on the opposite side of the room, by the entrance of a middle-aged man, and a young girl, apparently his daughter. The man advanced to the bench occupied by the seniors of the party, who welcomed him with the usual pretty Welsh greeting, " Pa sut mae dy galon ?" (" How is thy heart ?") and drinking his health, passed on to him

the cup of excellent cwrw. The girl, evidently a village belle, was as warmly greeted by the young men, while the girls eyed her rather askance with a half-jealous look, which Owen set down to the score of her extreme prettiness. Like most Welsh women, she was of middle size as to height, but beautifully made, with the most perfect yet delicate roundness in every limb. Her little mob-cap was carefully adjusted to a face which was excessively pretty, though it never could be called handsome. It also was round, with the slightest tendency to the oval shape, richly coloured, though somewhat olive in complexion, with dimples in cheek and chin, and the most scarlet lips Owen had ever seen, that were too short to meet over the small pearly teeth. The nose was the most defective feature; but the eyes were splendid. They were so long, so lustrous, yet at times so very soft under their thick fringe of eyelash! The nut-brown hair was carefully braided beneath the border of delicate lace : it was evident the little village beauty knew how to make the most of all her attractions, for the gay colours which were displayed in her neckerchief were in complete harmony with the complexion.

Owen was much attracted, while yet he was amused, by the evident coquetry the girl displayed, collecting around her a whole bevy of young fellows, for each of whom she seemed to have some gay speech, some attractive look or action. In a few minutes, young Griffiths of Bodowen was at her side, brought thither by a variety of idle motives, and as her undivided attention was given to the Welsh heir, her admirers, one by one, dropped off, to seat themselves by some less facinating but more attentive fair one. The more Owen conversed with the girl, the more he was taken ; she had more wit and talent than he had fancied possible; a self-abandon and thoughtfulness, to boot, that seemed full of charms ; and then her voice was so clear and sweet, and her actions so full of grace, that Owen was fascinated before he was well aware, and kept looking into her bright, blushing face, till her uplifted flashing eye fell beneath his earnest gaze.

While it thus happened that they were silent—she from confusion at the unexpected warmth of his admiration, he from an unconsciousness of anything but the beautiful changes in her flexile countenance—the man whom Owen took for her father came up and addressed some observation to his daughter, from whence he glided into some common-place yet respectful remark to Owen, and at length engaging him in some slight, local conversation, he led the way to the account of a spot on the peninsula of Penthryn where teal abounded, and concluded with begging Owen to allow him to show him the exact place, saying that whenever the young Squire felt so inclined, if he would honour him by a call at his house, he would take him across in his boat. While Owen listened, his attention was not so much absorbed as to be unaware that the little beauty at his side was refusing one or two who endeavoured to draw her from her place by invitations to dance. Flattered by his own construction of her refusals, he again directed all his attention to her, till she was called away by her father, who was leaving the scene of festivity. Before he left he reminded Owen of his promise, and added,

" Perhaps, Sir, you do not know me. My name is Ellis Pritchard, and I live at Ty Glas, on this side of Moel Gest; any one can point it out to you."

When the father and daughter had left, Owen slowly prepared for his ride home; but, encountering the hostess, he could not resist asking a few questions relative to Ellis Pritchard and his pretty daughter. She answered shortly but respectfully, and then said rather hesitatingly—

" Master Griffiths, you know the triad, ' Tri pheth tebyg y naill i'r Hall, ysgnbwr heb yd, mail deg heb ddiawd, a merch deg heb ei geirda' (Three things are alike: a fine barn without corn, a fine cup without drink, a fine woman without her reputation.)" She hastily quitted him, and Owen rode slowly to his unhappy home.

Ellis Pritchard, half farmer and half fisherman, was shrewd, and keen, and worldly; yet he was good-natured, and sufficiently generous to have become rather a popular man among his equals. He had been struck with the young Squire's attention to his pretty daughter, and was not insensible to the advantages to be derived from it. Nest would not be the first peasant girl, by any means, who had been transplanted to a Welsh manor-house as its mistress; and, accordingly, her father had shrewdly given the admiring young man some pretext for further opportunities of seeing her.

As for Nest herself, she had somewhat of her father's worldliness, and was fully alive to the superior station of her new admirer, and quite prepared to slight all her old sweethearts on his account. But then she had something more of feeling in her reckoning; she had not been insensible to the earnest yet comparatively refined homage which Owen paid her; she had noticed his expressive and occasionally handsome countenance with admiration, and was flattered by his so immediately singling her out from her companions. As to the hint which Martha Thomas had thrown out, it is enough to say that Nest was very giddy, and that she was motherless. She had high spirits and a great love of

admiration, or, to use a softer term, she loved to please; men, women, children, all, she delighted to gladden with her smile and her voice. She coquetted, and flirted, and went to the extreme lengths of Welsh courtship, till the seniors of the village shook their heads, and cautioned their daughters against her acquaintance. If not absolutely guilty, she had too frequently been on the verge of guilt.

Even at the time, Martha Thomas's hint made but little impression on Owen, for his senses were otherwise occupied; but in a few days the recollection thereof had wholly died away, and one warm glorious summer's day, he bent his steps toward Ellis Pritchard's with a beating heart; for, except some very slight flirtations at Oxford, Owen had never been touched; his thoughts, his fancy had been otherwise engaged.

Ty Glas was built against one of the lower rocks of Moel Gest, which, indeed, formed a side to the low, lengthy house. The materials of the cottage were the shingly stones which had fallen from above, plastered rudely together, with deep recesses for the small oblong windows. Altogether, the exterior was much ruder than Owen had expected; but inside there seemed no lack of comforts. The house was divided into two apartments, one large, roomy, and dark, into which Owen entered immediately; and before the

blushing Nest came from the inner chamber (for she had seen the young Squire coming, and hastily gone to make some alteration in her dress), he had had time to look around him, and note the various little particulars of the room. Beneath the window (which commanded a magnificent view) was an oaken dresser, replete with drawers and cupboards, and brightly polished to a rich dark colour. In the farther part of the room, Owen could at first distinguish little, entering as he did from the glaring sunlight, but he soon saw that there were two oaken beds, closed up after the manner of the Welsh: in fact, the dormitories of Ellis Pritchard and the man who served under him, both on sea and on land. There was the large wheel used for spinning wool, left standing on the middle of the floor, as if in use only a few minutes before; and around the ample chimney hung flitches of bacon, dried kids'-flesh, and fish, that was in process of smoking for winter's store.

Before Nest had shyly dared to enter, her father, who had been mending his nets down below, and seen Owen winding up to the house, came in and gave him a hearty yet respectful welcome; and then Nest, downcast and blushing, full of the consciousness which her father's advice and conversation had not failed to inspire, ventured to join them. To Owen's mind this reserve and shyness gave her new charms.

It was too bright, too hot, too anything, to think of going to shoot teal till later in the day, and Owen was delighted to accept a hesitating invitation to share the noonday meal. Some ewemilk cheese, very hard and dry, oat-cake, slips of the dried kids'-flesh broiled, after having been previously soaked in water for a few minutes, delicious butter and fresh buttermilk, with a liquor called " diod griafol " (made from the berries of the Sorbus aucuparia, infused in water and then fermented), composed the frugal repast; but there was something so clean and neat, and withal such a true welcome, that Owen had seldom enjoyed a meal so much. Indeed, at that time of day the Welsh squires differed from the farmers more in the plenty and rough abundance of their manner of living than in the refinement of style of their table.

At the present day, down in Llyn, the Welsh gentry are not a whit behind their Saxon equals in the expensive elegances of life; but then (when there was but one pewter-service in all Northumberland) there was nothing in Ellis Pritchard's mode of living that grated on the young Squire's sense of refinement.

Little was said by that young pair of wooers during the meal: the father had all the conversation to himself, apparently heedless of the ardent looks and inattentive mien of his guest. As Owen became more

serious in his feelings, he grew more timid in their expression, and at night, when they returned from their shooting-excursion, the caress he gave Nest was almost as bashfully offered as received.

This was but the first of a series of days devoted to Nest in reality, though at first he thought some little disguise of his object was necessary. The past, the future, was all forgotten in those happy days of love.

And every worldly plan, every womanly wile was put in practice by Ellis Pritchard and his daughter, to render his visits agreeable and alluring. Indeed, the very circumstance of his being welcome was enough to attract the poor young man, to whom the feeling so produced was new and full of charms. He left a home where the certainty of being thwarted made him chary in expressing his wishes, where no tones of love ever fell on his ear, save those addressed to others, where his presence or absence was a matter of utter indifference ; and when he entered Ty Glas, all, down to the little cur which, with clamorous barkings, claimed a part of his attention, seemed to rejoice. His account of his day's employment found a willing listener in Ellis; and when he passed on to Nest, busy at her wheel or at her churn, the deepened colour, the conscious eye, and the gradual yielding of herself up to his lover-like caress, had worlds of charms. Ellis

Pritchard was a tenant on the Bodowen estate, and therefore had reasons in plenty for wishing to keep the young Squire's visits secret; and Owen, unwilling to disturb the sunny calm of these halcyon days by any storm at home, was ready to use all the artifice which Ellis suggested as to the mode of his calls at Ty Glas.

Nor was he unaware of the probable, nay, the hoped-for termination of these repeated days of happiness. He was quite conscious that the father wished for nothing better than the marriage of his daughter to the heir of Bodowen ; and when Nest had hidden her face in his neck, which was encircled by her clasping arms, and murmured into his ear her acknowledgment of love, he felt only too desirous of finding some one to love him for ever. Though not highly principled, he would not have tried to obtain Nest on other terms save those of marriage; he did so pine after enduring love, and fancied he should have bound her heart for evermore to his, when they had taken the solemn oaths of matrimony.

There was no great difficulty attending a secret marriage at such a place and at such a time. One gusty autumn day, Ellis ferried them round Penthryn to Llandutrwyn, and there saw his little Nest become future lady of Bodowen.

How often do we see giddy, coquetting, restless

girls become sobered by marriage ! A great object in life is decided ; one on which their thoughts have been running in all their vagaries, and they seem to verify the beautiful fable of Undine. A new soul beams out in the gentleness and repose of their future lives. An indescribable softness and tenderness takes place of the wearying vanity of their former endeavours to attract admiration. Something of this sort took place in Nest Pritchard. If at first she had been anxious to attract the young Squire of Bodowen, long before her marriage this feeling had merged into a truer love than she had ever felt before; and now that he was her own, her husband, her whole soul was bent toward making him amends, as far as in her lay, for the misery which, with a woman's tact, she saw that he had to endure at his home. Her greetings were abounding in delicately-expressed love; her study of his tastes unwearying, in the arrangement of her dress, her time, her very thoughts.

No wonder that he looked back on his wedding-day with a thankfulness which is seldom the result of unequal marriages. No wonder that his heart beat aloud as formerly when he wound up the little path to Ty Glas, and saw—keen though the winter's wind might be—that Nest was standing out at the door to watch for his dimly-seen approach, while the candle

flared in the little window as a beacon to guide him aright.

The angry words and unkind actions of home fell deadened on his heart; he thought of the love that was surely his, and of the new promise of love that a short time would bring forth, and he could almost have smiled at the impotent efforts to disturb his peace.

A few more months, and the young father was greeted by a feeble little cry, when he hastily entered Ty Glas, one morning early, in consequence of a summons conveyed mysteriously to Bodowen; and the pale mother, smiling, and feebly holding up her babe to its father's kiss, seemed to him even more lovely than the bright gay Nest who had won his heart at the little inn of Penmorfa.

But the curse was at work! The fulfilment of the prophecy was nigh at hand!

CHAPTER II.

IT was the autumn after the birth of their boy: it had been a glorious summer, with bright, hot, sunny weather; and now the year was fading away as seasonably into mellow days, with mornings of silver mists and clear frosty nights. The blooming look of the time of flowers was past and gone; but instead there were even richer tints abroad in the sun-coloured leaves, the lichens, the golden-blossomed furze: if it was the time of fading, there was a glory in the decay.

Nest, in her loving anxiety to surround her dwelling with every charm for her husband's sake, had turned gardener, and the little corners of the rude court before the house were filled with many a delicate mountain-flower, transplanted more for its beauty than its rarity. The sweetbrier bush may even yet be seen, old and gray, which she and Owen planted a green slipling beneath the window of her Mttle chamber.

In those moments Owen forgot all besides the present; all the cares and griefs he had known in the past, and all that might await him of woe and death in the future. The boy, too, was as lovely a child as the fondest parent was ever blessed with ; and crowed with delight, and clapped his little hands, as his mother held him in her arms at the cottage-door to watch his father's ascent up the rough path that led to Ty Glas, one bright autumnal morning; and when the three entered the house together, it was difficult to say which was the happiest. Owen carried his boy, and tossed and played with him, while Nest sought out some little article of work, and seated herself on the dresser beneath the window, where now busily plying the needle, and then again looking at her husband, she eagerly told him the little pieces of domestic intelligence, the winning ways of the child, the result of yesterday's fishing, and such of the gossip of Penmorfa as came to the ears of the now retired Nest. She noticed that, when she mentioned any little circumstance which bore the slightest reference to Bodowen, her husband appeared chafed and uneasy, and at last avoided anything that might in the least remind him of home. In truth, he had been suffering much of late from the irritability of his father, shown in trifles to be sure, but not the less galling on that account.

While they were thus talking, and caressing each other and the child, a shadow darkened the room, and before they could catch a glimpse of the object that had occasioned it, it vanished, and Squire Griffiths lifted the door-latch and stood before them. He stood and looked—first on his son, so different, in his buoyant expression of content and enjoyment, with his noble child in his arms, like a proud and happy father, as he was, from the depressed, moody young man he too often appeared at Bodowen; then on Nest—poor, trembling, sickened Nest!—who dropped her work, but yet durst not stir from her seat on the dresser, while she looked to her husband as if for protection from his father.

The Squire was silent, as he glared from one to the other, his features white with restrained passion. When he spoke, his words came most distinct in their forced composure. It was to his son he addressed himself:

" That woman ! who is she ?"

Owen hesitated one moment, and then replied, in a steady, yet quiet voice :

" Father, that woman is my wife."

He would have added some apology for the long concealment of his marriage; have appealed to his father's forgiveness; but the foam flew from Squire

Owen's lips as he burst forth with invective against Nest :—

"You have married her! It is as they told me! Married Nest Pritchard yr buten! And you stand there as if you had not disgraced yourself for ever and ever with your accursed wiving! And the fair harlot sits there, in her mocking modesty, practising the mimming airs that will become her state as future lady of Bodowen. But I will move heaven and earth before that false woman darken the doors ( of my father's house as mistress!"

All this was said with such rapidity that Owen had no time for the words that thronged to his lips. " Father!" (he burst forth at length) " Father, whosoever told you that Nest Pritchard was a harlot told you a lie as false as hell! Ay! a lie as false as hell!" he added, in a voice of thunder, while he advanced a step or two nearer to the Squire. And then, in a lower tone, he said:

" She is as pure as your own wife ; nay, God help me! as the dear, precious mother who brought me forth, and then left me—with no refuge in a mother's heart—to struggle on through life alone. I tell you Nest is as pure as that dear, dead mother!"

" Fool—poor fool!"

At this moment the child—the little Owen—who

had kept gazing from one angry countenance to the other, and with earnest look, trying to understand what had brought the fierce glare into the face where till now he had read nothing but love, in some way attracted the Squire's attention, and increased his wrath.

"Yes!" he continued, "poor, weak fool that you are, hugging the child of another as if it were your own offspring!" Owen involuntarily caressed the affrighted child, and half smiled at the implication of his father's words. This the Squire perceived, and raising his voice to a scream of rage, he went on:

" I bid you, if you call yourself my son, to cast away that miserable, shameless woman's offspring; cast it away this instant—this instant!"

In his ungovernable rage, seeing that Owen was far from complying with his command, he snatched the poor infant from the loving arms that held it, and throwing it to its mother, left the house inarticulate with fury.

Nest—who had been pale and still as marble during this terrible dialogue, looking on and listening as if fascinated by the words that smote her heart—opened her arms to receive and cherish her precious babe ; but the boy was not destined to reach the white refuge of

her breast. The furious action of the Squire had been almost without aim, and the infant fell against the sharp edge of the dresser down on to the stone floor.

Owen sprang up to take the child, but he lay so still, so motionless, that the awe of death came over the father, and he stooped down to gaze more closely. At that moment, the upturned, filmy eyes rolled convulsively—a spasm passed along "the body—and the lips, yet warm with kissing, quivered into everlasting rest.

A word from her husband told Nest all. She slid down from her seat, and lay by her little son as corpse-like as he, unheeding all the agonizing endearments and passionate adjurations of her husband. And that poor, desolate husband and father! Scarce one little quarter of an hour, and he had been so blessed in his consciousness of love! the bright promise of many years on his infant's face, and the new, fresh soul beaming forth in its awakened intelligence. And there it was; the little clay image, that would never more gladden up at the sight of him, nor stretch forth to meet his embrace; whose inarticulate, yet most eloquent cooings might haunt him in his dreams, but would never more be heard in waking life again! And by the dead babe, almost as utterly insensate, the poor mother had fallen in a merciful faint—the slandered,

heart-pierced Nest! Owen struggled against the sickness that came over him, and busied himself in vain attempts at her restoration.

It was now near noon-day, and Ellis Pritchard came home, little dreaming of the sight that awaited him; but, though stunned, he was able to take more effectual measures for his poor daughter's recovery than Owen had done.

By-and-by she showed symptoms of returning sense, and was placed in her own little bed in a darkened room, where, without ever waking to complete consciousness, she fell asleep. Then it was that her husband, suffocated by pressure of miserable thought, gently drew his hand from her tightened clasp, and printing one long soft kiss on her white waxen forehead, hastily stole out of the room, and out of the house.

Near the base of Moel Gest—it might be a quarter of a mile from Ty Glas—was a little neglected solitary copse, wild and tangled with the trailing branches of the dog-rose and the tendrils of the white bryony. Toward the middle of this thicket lay a deep crystal pool—a clear mirror for the blue heavens above—and round the margin floated the broad green leaves of the water-lily, and when the regal sun shone down in his noonday glory the flowers arose from their cool depths

to welcome and greet him. The copse was musical with many sounds ; the warbling of birds rejoicing in its shades, the ceaseless hum of the insects that hovered over the pool, the chime of the distant waterfall, the occasional bleating of the sheep from the mountain-top, were all blended into the delicious harmony of nature.

It had been one of Owen's favourite resorts when he had been a lonely wanderer—a pilgrim in search of love in the years gone by. And thither he went, as if by instinct, when he left Ty Glas; quelling the uprising agony till he should reach that little solitary spot.

It was the time of day when a change in the aspect of the weather so frequently takes place ; and the little pool was no longer the reflection of a blue and sunny sky; it sent back the dark and slaty clouds above, and, every now and then, a rough gust shook the painted autumn leaves from their branches, and all other music was lost in the sound of the wild winds piping down from the moorlands, which lay up and beyond the clefts in the mountain-side. Presently the rain came on and beat down in torrents.

But Owen heeded it not. He sat on the dank ground, his face buried in his hands, and his

whole strength, physical and mental, employed in quelling
the rush of blood, which rose and boiled and gurgled in his brain as if it would madden him.

The phantom of his dead child rose ever before him, and seemed to cry aloud for vengeance. And when the poor young man thought upon the victim whom he required in his wild longing for revenge, he shuddered, for it was his father!

Again and again he tried not to think; but still the circle of thought came round, eddying through his brain. At length he mastered his passions, and they were calm; then he forced himself to arrange some plan for the future.

He had not, in the passionate hurry of the moment, seen that his father had left the cottage before he was aware of the fatal accident that befell the child. Owen thought he had seen all; and once he planned to go to the Squire and tell him of the anguish of heart he had wrought, and awe him, as it were, by the dignity of grief. But then again he durst not he distrusted his self-control— the old prophecy rose up in its horror— he dreaded his doom.

At last he determined to leave his father for ever;to take Nest to some distant country where she might forget her first-born, and where he himself might gain a livelihood by his own exertions. But when he tried to descend to the various little arrangements which were involved in the execution of this plan, he remembered that all his money (and in this respect Squire Griffiths was no niggard) was locked up in his escritoire at Bodowen. In vain he tried to do away with this matter-of-fact difficulty; go to Bodowen he must; and his only hope nay his determination was to avoid his father.

He rose and took a by-path to Bodowen. The house looked even more gloomy and desolate than usual in the heavy down-pouring rain, yet Owen gazed on it with something of regret—for sorrowful as his days in it had been, he was about to leave it for many, many years, if not for ever. He entered by a side-door, opening into a passage that led to his own room, where he kept his books, his guns, his fishing-tackle, his writing-materials, etc.

Here he hurriedly began to select the few articles he intended to take; for, besides the dread of interruption, he was feverishly anxious to travel far that very night, if only Nest was capable of performing the journey. As he was thus employed, he tried to conjecture what his father's feelings would be on finding that his once-loved son was gone away for ever. Would he then awaken to regret for the conduct which had driven him from home, and bitterly think on the loving and caressing boy who haunted his footsteps in former days?

Or, alas! would he only feel that an obstacle to his daily happiness—to his contentment with his wife, and his strange, doting affection for her child was taken away? Would they make merry over the heir's departure? Then he thought of Nest the young childless mother, whose heart had not yet realized her fullness of desolation. Poor Nest! so loving as she was, so devoted to her child—how should he console her? He pictured her away in a strange land, pining for her native mountains, and refusing to be comforted because her child was not.

Even this thought of the home-sickness that might possibly beset Nest hardly made him hesitate in his determination; so strongly had the idea taken possession of him that only by putting miles and leagues between him and his father could he avert the doom which seemed blending itself with the very purposes of his life as long as he stayed in proximity with the slayer of his child.

He had now nearly completed his hasty work of preparation, and was full of tender thoughts of his wife, when the door opened, and the elfish Robert peered in, in search of some of his brother's possessions. On seeing Owen he hesitated, but then came boldly forward, and laid his hand on Owen's arm, saying,

"Nesta yr buten! How is Nest yr buten?"

He looked maliciously into Owen's face to mark the effect of his words, but was terrified at the expression he read there. He started off and ran to the door, while Owen tried to check himself, saying continually, "He is but a child. He does not understand the meaning of what he says. He is but a child!" Still Rojbert, now in fancied security, kept calling out his insulting words, and Owen's hand was on his gun, grasping it as if to restrain his rising fury.

But when Robert passed on daringly to mocking words relating to the poor dead child, Owen could bear it no longer; and before the boy was well aware, Owen was fiercely holding him in an iron clasp with one hand, while he struck him hard with the other.

In a minute he checked himself. He paused, relaxed his grasp, and, to his horror, he saw Robert sink to the ground; in fact, the lad was half-stunned, half-frightened, and thought it best to assume insensibility.

Owen—miserable Owen—seeing him lie there prostrate, was bitterly repentant, and would have dragged him to the carved settle, and done all he could to restore him to his senses, but at this instant the Squire came in.

Probably, when the household at Bodowen rose that morning, there was but one among them ignorant of the heir's relation to Nest Pritchard and her child:

for secret as he had tried to make his visits to Ty Glas, they had been too frequent not to be noticed, and Nest's altered conduct—no longer frequenting dances and merry-makings—was a strongly corroborative circumstance. But Mrs. Griffiths' influence reigned paramount, if unacknowledged, at Bodowen, and till she sanctioned the disclosure, none would dare to tell the Squire.

Now, however, the time drew near when it suited her to make her husband aware of the connection his son had formed; so, with many tears, and much seeming reluctance, she broke the intelligence to him—taking good care, at the same time, to inform him of the light character Nest had borne. Nor did she confine this evil reputation to her conduct before her marriage, but insinuated that even to this day she was a "woman of the grove and brake"—for centuries the Welsh term of opprobrium for the loosest female characters.

Squire Griffiths easily tracked Owen to Ty Glas; and without any aim but the gratification of his furious anger, followed him to upbraid as we have seen. But he left the cottage even more enraged against his son than he had entered it, and returned home to hear the evil suggestions of the stepmother. He had heard a slight scuffle in which he caught the tones of Robert's voice, as he passed along the hall, and an instant after-

wards he saw the apparently lifeless body of his little favourite dragged along by the culprit Owen—the marks of strong passion yet visible on his face. Not loud, but bitter and deep were the evil words which the father bestowed on the son; and as Owen stood proudly and sullenly silent, disdaining all exculpation of himself in the presence of one who had wrought him so much graver—so fatal an injury—Robert's mother entered the room. At sight of her natural emotion the wrath of the Squire was redoubled, and his wild suspicions that this violence of Owen's to Robert was a premeditated act appeared like the proven truth through the mists of rage. He summoned domestics as if to guard his own and his wife's life from the attempts of his son; and the servants stood wondering around—now gazing at Mrs. Griffiths, alternately scolding and sobbing, while she tried to restore the lad from his really bruised and half-unconscious state; now at the fierce and angry Squire; and now at the sad and silent Owen. And he—he was hardly aware of their looks of wonder and terror; his father's words fell on a deadened ear; for before his eyes there rose a pale dead babe, and in that lady's violent sounds of grief he heard the wailing of a more sad, more hopeless mother. For by this time the lad Robert had opened his eyes, and though evidently suffering a good deal from the effects of Owen's blows, was fully conscious of all that was passing around him.

Had Owen been left to his own nature, his heart would have worked itself to doubly love the boy whom he had injured ; but he was stubborn from injustice, and hardened by suffering. He refused to vindicate himself; he made no effort to resist the imprisonment the Squire had decreed, until a surgeon's opinion of the real extent of Robert's injuries was made known. It was not until the door was locked and barred, as if upon some wild and furious beast, that the recollection of poor Nest, without his comforting presence, came into his mind. Oh! thought he, how she would be wearying, pining for his tender sympathy; if, indeed, she had recovered the shock of mind sufficiently to be sensible of consolation! What would she think of his absence ? Could she imagine he believed his father's words, and had left her, in this her sore trouble and bereavement ? The thought maddened him, and he looked around for some mode of escape.

He had been confined in a small unfurnished room on the first floor, wainscoted, and carved all round, with a massy door, calculated to resist the attempts of a dozen strong men, even had he afterward been able to escape from the house unseen, unheard. The window was placed (as is common in old Welsh houses) over the fire-place; with branching chimneys on either hand, forming a sort of projection on the outside. By this outlet his escape was easy, even had he been less determined and 'desperate than he was. And when he had descended, with a little care, a little winding, he might elude all observation and pursue his original intention of going to Ty Glas.

The storm had abated, and watery sunbeams were gilding the bay, as Owen descended from the window, and, stealing along in the broad afternoon shadows, made his way to the little plateau of green turf in the garden at the top of a steep precipitous rock, down the abrupt face of which he had often dropped, by means of a well-secured rope, into the small sailing-boat (his father's present, alas! in days gone by) which lay moored in the deep sea-water below. He had always kept his boat there, because it was the nearest available spot to the house ; but before he could reach the place —unless, indeed, he crossed a broad sun-lighted piece of ground in full view of the windows on that side of the house, and without the shadow of a single sheltering tree or shrub—he had to skirt round a rude semicircle of underwood, which would have been considered as a shrubbery had any one taken pains with it. Step by step he stealthily moved along—hearing voices now, again seeing his father and stepmother in no distant walk, the Squire evidently caressing and consoling his wife, who seemed to be urging some point with great vehemence, again forced to crouch down to avoid being seen by the cook, returning from the rude kitchen-garden with a handful of herbs. This was the way the doomed heir of Bodowen left his ancestral house for ever, and hoped to leave behind him his doom. At length he reached the plateau—he breathed more freely. He stooped to discover the hidden coil of rope, kept safe and dry in a hole under a great round flat piece of rock : his head was bent down; he did not see his father approach, nor did he hear his footstep for the rush of blood to his head in the stooping effort of lifting the stone; the Squire had grappled with him before he rose up again, before he fully knew whose hands detained him, now, when his liberty of person and action seemed secure. He made a vigorous struggle to free himself; he wrestled with his father for a moment—he pushed him hard, and drove him on to the great displaced stone, all unsteady in its balance.

Down went the Squire, down into the deep waters below—down after him went Owen, half consciously, half unconsciously, partly compelled by the sudden cessation of any opposing body, partly from a vehement irrepressible impulse to rescue his father. But he had instinctively chosen a safer place in the deep sea-water pool than that into which his push had sent his father. The Squire had hit his head with much violence against the side of the boat, in his fall; it is, indeed, doubtful whether he was not killed before ever he sank into the sea. But Owen knew nothing save that the awful doom seemed even now present. He plunged down, he dived below the water in search of the body which had none of the elasticity of life to buoy it up; he saw his father in those depths, he clutched at him, he brought him up and cast him, a dead weight, into the boat, and, exhausted by the effort, he had begun himself to sink again before he instinctively strove to rise and climb into the rocking boat. There lay his father, with a deep dent in the side of his head where the skull had been fractured by his fall; his face blackened by the arrested course of the blood. Owen felt his pulse, his heart—all was still. He called him by his name.

" Father, father !" he cried, " come back! come back ! You never knew how I loved you! how I could love you still—if—oh God!"

And the thought of his little child rose before him. " Yes, father," he cried afresh, " you never knew how he fell—how he died ! Oh, if I had but had patience to tell you ! If you would but have borne with me and listened! And now it is over! Oh father! father !"

Whether she had heard this wild wailing voice, or whether it was only that she missed her husband and wanted him for some little every-day question, or, as was perhaps more likely, she had discovered Owen's escape, and come to inform her husband of it, I do not know, but on the rock, right above his head, as it seemed, Owen heard his stepmother calling her husband.

He was silent, and softly pushed the boat right under the rock till the sides grated against the stones, and the overhanging branches concealed him and it from all not on a level with the water. Wet as he was, he lay down by his dead father the better to conceal himself; and, somehow, the action recalled those early days of childhood—the first in the Squire's widowhood—when Owen had shared his father's bed, and used to waken him in the morniug to hear one of the old Welsh legends. How long he lay thus—body chilled, and brain hard-working through the heavy pressure of a reality as terrible as a nightmare—he never knew; but at length he roused himself up to think of Nest.

Drawing out a great sail, he covered up the body of his father with it where he lay in the bottom of the boat. Then with his numbed hands he took the oars, and pulled out into the more open sea toward Criccaeth. He skirted along the coast till he found a shadowed cleft in the dark rocks ; to that point he rowed, and anchored his boat close in land. Then he mounted, staggering, half longing to fall into the dark waters and he at rest —half instinctively finding out the surest foot-rests on that precipitous face of rock, till he was high up, safe landed on the turfy summit. He ran off, as if pursued, toward Penmorfa; he ran with maddened energy. Suddenly he paused, turned, ran again with the same speed, and threw himself prone on the summit, looking down into his boat with straining eyes to see if there had been any movement of life—any displacement of a fold of sail-cloth. It was all quiet deep down below, but as he gazed the shifting light gave the appearance of a slight movement. Owen ran to a lower part of the rock, stripped, plunged into the water, and swam to the boat. When there, all was still—awfully still! For a minute or two, he dared not lift up the cloth. Then reflecting that the same terror might beset him again—of leaving his father unaided while yet a spark of life lingered—he removed the shrouding cover. The eyes looked into his with a dead stare ! He closed the lids and bound up the jaw. Again he looked. This time he raised himself out of the water and kissed the brow.

" It was my doom, father! It would have been better if I had died at my birth !"

Daylight was fading away. Precious daylight! He swam back, dressed, and set off afresh for Penmorfa. When he opened the door of Ty Glas, Ellis Pritchard looked at him reproachfully, from his seat in the darkly-shadowed chimney corner.

" You're come at last," said he. " One of our kind (i. e.y station) would not have left his wife to mourn by herself over her dead child; nor would one of our kind have let his father kill his own true son. I've a good mind to take her from you for ever."

" I did not tell him," cried Nest, looking piteously at her husband; " he made me tell him part, and guessed the rest."

She was nursing her babe on her knee as if it was alive. Owen stood before Ellis Pritchard.

" Be silent," said he, quietly. " Neither words nor deeds but what are decreed can come to pass. I was set to do my work, this hundred years and more. The time waited for me, and the man waited for me. I have done what was foretold of me for generations!"

Ellis Pritchard knew the old tale of the prophecy, and believed in it in a dull, dead kind of way, but somehow never thought it would come to pass in his time. Now, however, he understood it all in a moment,

though he mistook Owen's nature so much as to believe that the deed was intentionally done, out of revenge for the death of his boy; and viewing it in this light, Ellis thought it little more than a just punishment for the cause of all the wild despairing sorrow he had seen his only child suffer during the hours of this long afternoon. But he knew the law would not so regard it. Even the lax Welsh law of those days could not fail to examine into the death of a man of Squire Griffiths' standing. So the acute Ellis thought how he could conceal the culprit for a time.

" Come," said he; " don't look so scared ! It was your doom, not your fault;" and he laid a hand on Owen's shoulder.

" You're wet," said he, suddenly. " Where have you been? Nest, your husband is dripping, drookit wet. That's what makes him look so blue and wan/'

Nest softly laid her baby in its cradle; she was half stupified with crying, and had not understood to what Owen alluded, when he spoke of his doom being fulfilled, if indeed she had heard the words.

Her touch thawed Owen's miserable heart.

" Oh, Nest!" said he, clasping her in his arms; "do you love me still—can you love me, my own darling?"

" Why not ?" asked she, her eyes filling with tears.

" I only love you more than ever, for you were my poor baby's father!"

" But, Nest— Oh, tell her, Ellis! yw know."

"No need, no need!" said Ellis. "She's had enough to think on. Bustle, my girl, and get out my Sunday clothes."

" I don't understand," said Nest, putting her hand up to her head. " What is to tell ? and why are you so wet ? God help me for a poor crazed thing, for I cannot guess at the meaning of your words and your strange looks ! I only know my baby is dead 1" and she burst into tears.

" Come, Nest! go and fetch him a change, quick !" and as she meekly obeyed, too languid to strive further to understand, Ellis said rapidly to Owen, in a low, hurried voice,

" Are you meaning that the Squire is dead ? Speak low, lest she hear! Well, well, no need to talk about how he died. It was sudden, I see; and we must all of us die; and he'll have to be buried. It's well the night is near. And I should not wonder now if you'd like to travel for a bit; it would do Nest a power of good ; and then—there's many a one goes out of his own house and never comes back again ; and—I trust he's not lying in his own house—and there's a stir for a bit, and a search, and a wonder—and, by-and-by, the heir just steps in, as quiet as can be. And that's what you'll do, and bring Nest to Bodowen after all. Nay, child, better stockings nor those ; find the blue woollens I bought at Llanrwst fair. Only don't lose heart It's done now and can't be helped. It was the piece of work set you to do from the days of the Tudors, they say. And he deserved it. Look in yon cradle. So tell us where he is, and I'll take heart of grace and see what can be done for him."

But Owen sat wet and haggard, looking into the peat fire as if for visions of the past, and never heeding a word Ellis said. Nor did he move when Nest brought the armful of dry clothes.

" Come, rouse up, man!" said Ellis, growing impatient.

But he neither spoke nor moved.

"What is the matter, father?" asked Nest, bewildered.

Ellis kept on watching Owen for a minute or two, till, on his daughter's repetition of the question, he said,

" Ask him yourself, Nest."

" Oh, husband, what is it ?" said she, kneeling down and bringing her face to a level with his.

" Don't you know ?" said he, heavily. " You won't love me when you do know. And yet it was not my doing. It was my doom."

" What does he mean, father ?" asked Nest, looking up; but she caught a gesture from Ellis urging her to go on questioning her husband.

" I will love you, husband, whatever has happened. Only let me know the worst."

A pause, during which Nest and Ellis hung breath-

" My father is dead, Nest."

Nest caught her breath with a sharp gasp.

" God forgive him !" said she, thinking on her babe.

" God forgive me " said Owen.

" You did not" Nest stopped.

" Yes, I did. Now you know it. It was my doom. How could I help it? The devil helped me—he placed the stone so that my father fell. I jumped into the water to save him. I did, indeed, Nest. I was nearly drowned myself. But he was dead—dead— killed by the fall!"

" Then he is safe at the bottom of the sea?" said Ellis, with hungry eagerness.

" No, he is not; he lies in my boat," said Owen, shivering a little, more at the thought of his last glimpse at his father's face than from cold.

" Oh, husband, change your wet clothes!" pleaded Nest, to whom the death of the old man was simply a

horror with which she had nothing to do, while her husband's discomfort was a present trouble.

While she helped him to take off the wet garments which he would never have had energy enough to remove of himself, Ellis was busy preparing food, and mixing a great tumbler of spirits and hot water. He stood over the unfortunate young man and compelled him to eat and drink, and made Nest too taste some mouthfuls—all the while planning in his own mind how best to conceal what had been done, and who had done it; not altogether without a certain feeling of vulgar triumph in the reflection that Nest, as she stood there, carelessly dressed, dishevelled in her grief, was in reality the mistress of Bodowen, than which Ellis Pritchard had never seen a grander house, though he believed such might exist.

By dint of a few dexterous questions he found out all he wanted to know from Owen, as he ate and drank. In fact, it was almost a relief to Owen to dilute the horror by talking about it. Before the meal was done, if meal it could be called, Ellis knew all he cared to know.

"Now, Nest, on with your cloak and haps. Pack up what needs to go with you, for you and your husband must be half way to Liverpool by to-morrow's morn. I'll take you past Rhyl Sands in my fishing-boat, with yours in tow; and, once over the dangerous part, I'll return with my cargo of fish, and learn how much stir there is at Bodowen. Once safe hidden in Liverpool, no one will know where you are, and you may stay quiet till your time comes for returning."

" I will never come home again," said Owen, doggedly. " The place is accursed!"

" Hoot! be guided by me, man. Why, it was but an accident, after all! And we'll land at the Holy Island, at the Point of Llyn ; there is an old cousin of mine, the parson, there—for the Pritchards have known better days, Squire—and we'll bury him there. It was but an accident, man. Hold up your head ! You and Nest will come home yet and fill Bodowen with children, and I'll live to see it."

" Never !" said Owen. " I am the last male of my race, and the son has murdered his father!"

Nest came in laden and cloaked. Ellis was for hurrying them off. The fire was extinguished, the door was locked.

" Here, Nest, my darling, let me take your bundle while I guide you down the steps." But her husband bent his head, and spoke never a word. Nest gave her father the bundle (already loaded with such things as he himself had seen fit to take), but clasped another softly and tightly.

"No one shall help me with this," said she, in a low voice.

Her father did not understand her; her husband did, and placed his strong helping arm round her waist, and blessed her.

" We will all go together, Nest," said he. " But where ?" and he looked up at the storm-tossed clouds coming up from windward.

" It is a dirty night," said Ellis, turning his head round to speak to his companions at last. " But never fear, we'll weather it!" And he made for the place where his vessel was moored. Then he stopped and thought a moment.

" Stay here!" said he, addressing his companions. " I may meet folk, and I shall, maybe, have to hear and to speak. You wait here till I come back for you." So they sat down close together in a corner of the path.

" Let me look at him, Nest!" said Owen.

She took her little dead son out from under her shawl; they looked at his waxen face long and tenderly; kissed it, and covered it up reverently and softly,

" Nest," said Owen, at last, " I feel as though my father's spirit had been near us, and as if it had bent over our poor little one. A strange chilly air met me as I stooped over him. I could fancy the spirit of our pure, blameless child guiding my father's safe over the paths of the sky to the gates of heaven, and escaping those accursed dogs of hell that were darting up from the north in pursuit of souls not five minutes since."

" Don't talk so, Owen," said Nest, curling up to him in the darkness of the copse. " Who knows what may be listening ?"

The pair were silent, in a kind of nameless terror, till they heard Ellis Pritchard's loud whisper. " Where are ye ? Come along, soft and steady. There were folk about even now, and the Squire is missed, and madam in a fright."

They went swiftly down to the little harbour, and embarked on board Ellis's boat. The sea heaved and rocked even there ; the torn clouds went hurrying overhead in a wild tumultuous manner.

They put out into the bay; still in silence, except when some word of command was spoken by Ellis, who took the management of the vessel. They made for the rocky shore, where Owen's boat had been moored. It was not there. It had broken loose and disappeared.

Owen sat down and covered his face. This last event, so simple and natural in itself, struck on his excited and superstitious mind in an extraordinary manner. He had hoped for a certain reconciliation, so to say, by laying his father and his child both in one grave. But now it appeared to him as if there was to be no forgiveness; as if his father revolted even in death against any such peaceful union. Ellis took a practical view of the case. If the Squire's body was found drifting about in a boat known to belong to his son, it would create terrible suspicion as to the manner of his death. At one time in the evening, Ellis had thought of persuading Owen to let him bury the Squire in a sailor's grave; or, in other words, to sew him up in a spare sail, and weighting it well, sink it for ever. He had not broached the subject, from a certain fear of Owen's passionate repugnance to the plan; otherwise, if he had consented, they might have returned to Pen-morfa, and passively awaited the course of events, secure of Owen's succession to Bodowen, sooner or later; or if Owen was too much overwhelmed by what had happened, Ellis would have advised him to go away for a short time, and return when the buzz and the talk was over.

Now it was different. It was absolutely necessary that they should leave the country for a time. Through those stormy waters they must plough their way that very night. Ellis had no fear—would have had no fear, at any rate, with Owen as he had been a week, a day ago j but with Owen wild, despairing, helpless, fate-pursued, what could he do?

They sailed into the tossing darkness, and were never more seen of men.

The house of Bodowen has sunk into damp, dark ruins; and a Saxon stranger holds the lands of the Griffiths.

You cannot think how kindly Mrs. Dawson thanked Miss Duncan for writing and reading this story. She shook ray poor, pale governess so tenderly by the hand that the tears came into her eyes, and the colour into t her cheeks.

" I thought you had been so kind; I liked hearing about Lady Ludlow; I fancied perhaps I could do something to give a little pleasure," were the half-finished sentences Miss Duncan stammered out. I am sure it was the wish to earn similar kind words from Mrs. Dawson, that made Mrs. Preston try and rummage through her memory to see if she could not recollect some fact, or event, or history, which might interest Mrs. Dawson and the little party that gathered round her sofa. Mrs. Preston it was who told us the following tale:

" HALF A LIFE-TIME AGO."

HALF A LIFE-TdME AGO.

CHAPTER I.

HALF a life-time ago, there lived in one of the Westmoreland dales a single woman, of the name of Susan Dixon. She was owner of the small farm-house where she resided, and of some thirty or forty acres of land by which it was surrounded. She had also an hereditary right to a sheep-walk, extending to the wild fells that overhang Blea Tarn. In the language of the country, she was a Stateswoman. Her house is yet to be seen on the Oxenfell road, between Skelwith and Coniston. You go along a moorland track, made by the carts that occasionally came for turf from the Oxenfell. A brook babbles and brattles by the wayside, giving you a sense of companionship, which relieves the deep solitude in which this way is usually traversed. Some miles on this side of Coniston there is a farmstead—a gray stone house, and a square of farm-buildings surrounding a green space of rough turf, in the midst of which stands a mighty, funereal umbrageous yew, making a solemn shadow, as of death, in the very heart and centre of the light and heat of the brightest summer day. On the side away from the house, this yard slopes down to a dark-brown pool, which is supplied with fresh water from the overflowings of a stone cistern, into which some rivulet of the brook before mentioned continually and melodiously falls bubbling. The cattle drink out of this cistern. The household bring their pitchers and fill them with drinking-water by a dilatory, yet pretty, process. The water-carrier brings with her a leaf of the hound's-tongue fern, and, inserting it in the crevice of the gray rock, makes a cool, green spout for the sparkling stream. The house is no specimen, at the present day, of what it was in the lifetime of Susan Dixon. Then, every small diamond-pane in the windows glittered with cleanliness. You might have eaten off the floor; you could see yourself in the pewter plates and the polished oaken awmry, or dresser, of the state kitchen into which you entered. Few strangers penetrated further than this room. Once or twice, wandering tourists, attracted by the lonely picturesqueness of the situation, and the exquisite cleanliness of the house itself, made their way into this house-place, and offered money

enough (as they thought) 'to tempt the hostess to receive them as lodgers. They would give no trouble, they said; they would be out rambling or sketching all day long; would be perfectly content with a share of the food which she provided for herself; or would procure what they required from the Waterhead Inn at Coniston. But no liberal sum—no fair words— moved her from her stony manner, or her monotonous tone of indifferent refusal. No persuasion could induce her to show any more of the house than that first room; no appearance of fatigue procured for the weary an invitation to sit down and rest; and if one more bold and less delicate did so without being asked, Susan stood by, cold and apparently deaf, or only replying by the briefest monosyllables, till the unwelcome visitor had departed. Yet those with whom she had dealings, in the way of selling her cattle or her farm produce, spoke of her as keen after a bargain—a hard one to have to do with; and she never spared herself exertion or fatigue, at market or in the field, to make the most of her produce. She led the haymakers with her swift, steady rake, and her noiseless evenness of motion. She was about among the earliest in the market, examining samples of oats, pricing them, and then turning with grim satisfaction to her own cleaner corn.

She was served faithfully and long by those who were rather her fellow-labourers than her servants. She was even and just in her dealings with them. If she was peculiar and silent, they knew her, and knew that she might be relied on. Some of them had known her from her childhood; and deep in their hearts was an unspoken—almost unconscious—pity for her; for they knew her story, though they never spoke of it.

Yes; the time had been when that tall, gaunt, hard-featured, angular woman—who never smiled, and hardly ever spoke an unnecessary word—had been a fine-looking girl, bright-spirited and rosy; and when the hearth at the Yew Nook had been as bright as she, with family love and youthful hope and mirth. Fifty or fifty-one years ago, William Dixon and his wife Margaret were alive; and Susan, their daughter, was about eighteen years old—ten years older than the only other child, a boy named after his father. William and Margaret Dixon were rather superior people, of a character belonging—as far as I have seen —exclusively to the class of Westmoreland and Cumberland statesmen—just, independent, upright; not given to much speaking; kind-hearted, but not demonstrative ; disliking change, and new ways, and new people; sensible and shrewd; each household

self-contained, and its members having little curiosity as to their neighbours, with whom they rarely met for any social intercourse, save at the stated times of sheep-shearing and Christmas; having a certain kind of sober pleasure in amassing money, which occasionally made them miserable (as they call miserly people up in the north) in their old age; reading no light or ephemeral literature; but the grave, solid books brought round by the pedlars (such as the "

Paradise Lost" and "Regained," "The Death of Abel," "The Spiritual Quixote," and " The Pilgrim's Progress ") were to be found in nearly every house : the men occasionally going off laking, i.e. playing, i.e. drinking for days together, and having to be hunted up by anxious wives, who dared not leave their husbands to the chances of the wild precipitous roads, but walked miles and miles, lantern in hand, in the dead of night, to discover and guide the solemnly-drunken husband home; who had a dreadful headache the next day, and the day after that came forth as grave, and sober, and virtuous-looking as if there were no such things as malt arid spirituous liquors in the world; and who were seldom reminded of their misdoings by their wives, to whom such occasional outbreaks were as things of course, when once the immediate anxiety produced by them was over. Such were—such are—the characteristics

of a class now passing away from the face of the land, as their compeers, the yeomen, have done before them. Of such was William Dixon. He was a shrewd, clever farmer, in his day and generation, when shrewdness was rather shown in the breeding and rearing of sheep and cattle than in the cultivation of land. Owing to this character of his, statesmen from a distance, from beyond Kendal, or from Borrowdale, of greater wealth than he, would send their sons to be farm-servants for a year or two with him, in order to learn some of his methods before setting up on land of their own. When Susan, his daughter, was about seventeen, one Michael Hurst was farm-servant at Yew Nook. He worked with the master, and lived with the family, and was in all respects treated as an equal, except in the field. His father was a wealthy statesman at Wythburne, up beyond Grasmere; and through Michael's servitude the families had become acquainted, and the Dixons went over to the High Beck sheep-shearing, and the Hursts came down by Red Bank and Loughrig Tarn and across the Oxenfell when there was the Christmas-tide feasting at Yew Nook. The fathers strolled round the fields together, examined cattle and sheep, and looked knowing over each other's horses. The mothers inspected the dairies and household arrangements, each openly admiring

the plans of the other, but secretly preferring their own. Both fathers and mothers cast a glance from time to time at Michael and Susan, who were thinking of nothing less than farm or dairy, but whose unspoken attachment was, in all ways, so suitable and natural a thing that each parent rejoiced over it, although with characteristic reserve it was never spoken about—not even between husband and wife.

Susan had been a strong, independent, healthy girl; a clever help to her mother, and a spirited companion to her father; more of a man in her (as he often said) than her delicate little brother ever would have. He was his mother's darling, although she loved Susan well. There was no positive engagement between Michael and Susan—I doubt whether even plain words of love had been spoken ; when one winter-time Margaret Dixon was seized with inflammation consequent upon a neglected cold. She had always been strong and notable, and had been too busy to attend to the earliest symptoms of illness. It would go off, she said to the woman who helped in the kitchen ; or if she did not feel better when they had got the hams and bacon out of hand, she would take some herb-tea and nurse up a bit. But Death could not wait till the hams and bacon were cured: he came on with rapid strides, and , shooting arrows of portentous agony. Susan had never

seen illness—never knew how much she loved her mother till now, when she felt a dreadful, instinctive certainty that she was losing her. Her mind was thronged with recollections of the many times she had slighted her mother's wishes; her heart was full of the echoes of careless and angry replies that she had spoken. What would she not now give to have opportunities of service and obedience, and trials of her patience and love, for that dear mother who lay gasping in torture! And yet Susan had been a good girl and an affectionate daughter.

The sharp pain went off, and delicious ease came on; yet still her mother sunk. In the midst of this languid peace she was dying. She motioned Susan to her bedside, for she could only whisper; and then, while the father was out of the room, she spoke as much to the eager, hungering eyes of her daughter by the motion of her lips, as by the slow, feeble sounds of her voice.

" Susan, lass, thou must not fret. It is God's will, and thou wilt have a deal to do. Keep father straight if thou canst; and if he goes out Ulverstone ways, see that thou meet him before he gets to the Old Quarry. It's a dree bit for a man who has had a drop. As for lile Will"—here the poor woman's face began to work and her fingers to move nervously as they lay on the bed-quilt—"lile Will will miss me most of all. Father's often vexed with him because he's not a quick, strong lad; he is not, my poor lile chap. And father thinks he's saucy, because he cannot always stomach oat-cake and porridge. There's better than three pound in th' old black teapot on the top shelf of the cupboard. Just keep a piece of loaf-bread by you, Susan dear, for Will to corne to when he's not taken his breakfast. I have, may be, spoilt him; but there'll be no one to spoil him now."

She began to cry a low, feeble cry, and covered up her face that Susan might not see her. That dear face! those precious moments while yet the eyes could look out with love and intelligence. Susan laid her head down close by her mother's ear.

"Mother, I'll take tent of Will. Mother, do you hear ? He shall not want ought I can give or get for him, least of all the kind words which you had ever ready for us both. Bless you! bless you! my own mother."

" Thou'lt promise me that, Susan, wilt thou ? I can die easy if thou'lt take charge of him. But he's hardly like other folk; he tries father at times, though I think father'll be tender of him when I'm gone, for my sake. And, Susan, there's one thing more. I never spoke on it for fear of the bairn being called a tell-tale, but I just comforted him up. He vexes Michael at times, and Michael has struck him before now. I did not want to make a stir; but he's not strong, and a word from thee, Susan, will go a long way with Michael."

Susan was as red now as she had been pale before; it was the first time that her influence over Michael had. been openly acknowledged by a third person, and a flash of joy came athwart the solemn sadness of the moment. Her mother had spoken too much, and now came on the miserable faintness. She never spoke again coherently ; but when her children and her husband stood by her bedside, she took lile Will's hand and put it into Susan's, and looked at her with imploring eyes. Susan clasped her arms round Will, and leaned her head upon his curly little one, and vowed within herself to be as a mother to him.

Henceforward she was all in all to her brother. She was a more spirited and amusing companion to him than his mother had been, from her greater activity, and perhaps, also, from her originality of character, which often prompted her to perform her habitual actions in some new and racy manner. She was tender to lile Will when she was prompt and sharp with everybody else—with Michael most of all; for somehow the girl felt that, unprotected by her mother, she must keep up her own dignity, and not allow her lover to see how strong a hold he had upon her heart. He called her hard and cruel, and left her so ; and she smiled softly to herself, when his back was turned, to think how little he guessed how deeply he was loved. For Susan was merely comely and fine-looking ; Michael was strikingly handsome, admired by all the girls for miles round, and quite enough of a country coxcomb to know it and plume himself accordingly. He was the second son of his father ; the eldest would have High Beck farm, of course, but there was a good penny in the Kendal bank in store for Michael. When harvest was over, he went to Chapel Langdale to learn to dance; and at night, in his merry moods, he would do his steps on the flag-floor of the Yew Nook kitchen, to the secret admiration of Susan, who had never learned dancing, but who flouted him perpetually, even while she admired, in accordance with the rule she seemed to have made for herself about keeping him at a distance so long as he lived under the same roof with her. One evening he sulked at some saucy remark of hers; he sitting in the chimney-corner with his arms on his knees, and his head bent forwards, lazily gazing into the wood-fire on the hearth, and luxuriating in rest after a hard day's labour; she sitting among the geraniums on the long, low window-seat, trying to catch the last slanting rays of the autumnal light to enable her to finish stitching a shirt-collar for Will, who lounged fall length on the flags at the other side of the hearth to Michael, poking the burning wood from time to time with a long hazel-stick to bring out the leap of glittering sparks.

" And if you can dance a threesome reel, what good does it do ye?" asked Susan, looking askance at Michael, who had just been vaunting his proficiency. " Does it help you plough, or reap, or even climb the rocks to take a raven's nest? If I were a man, I'd be ashamed to give in to such softness."

" If you were a man, you'd be glad to do anything which made the pretty girls stand round and admire."

" As they do to you, eh ! Ho, Michael, that would not be my way o' being a man!"

" What would then ?" asked he, after a pause, during which he had expected in vain that she would go on with her sentence. No answer.

" I should not like you as a man, Susy; you'd be too hard and headstrong."

" Am I hard and headstrong?" asked she, with as indifferent a tone as she could assume, but which yet had a touch of pique in it. His quick ear detected the inflexion.

" No, Susy! You're wilful at times, and that's right enough. I don't like a girl without spirit.

There's a mighty pretty girl comes to the dancing-class ; but she is all milk and water. Her eyes never flash like yours when you're put out; why, I can see them flame across the kitchen like a cat's in the dark. Now, if you were a man, I should feel queer before those looks of yours ; as it is, I rather like them, because—"

" Because what ?" asked she, looking up and perceiving that he had stolen close up to her.

" Because I can make all right in this way," said he, kissing her suddenly.

" Can you ?" said she, wrenching herself out of his grasp and panting, half with rage. "Take that, by way of proof that making right is none so easy." And she boxed his ears pretty sharply. He went back to his seat discomfited and out of temper. She could no longer see to look, even if her face had not burnt and her eyes dazzled, but she did not choose to move her seat, so she still preserved her stooping attitude and pretended to go on sewing.

"Eleanor Hebthwaite may be milk-and-water," muttered he, "but— Confound thee, lad! what art doing ?" exclaimed Michael, as a great piece of burning wood was cast into his face by an unlucky poke of Will's. "Thou great lounging, clumsy chap, I'll teach thee better!" and with one or two good, round kicks he sent the lad whimpering away into the back-kitchen. When he had a little recovered himself from his passion, he saw Susan standing before him, her face looking strange and almost ghastly by the reversed position of the shadows, arising from the firelight shining upwards right under it.

" I tell thee what, Michael," said she, " that lad's motherless, but not friendless."

"His own father leathers him, and why should not I, when he's given me such a burn on my face ?" said Michael, putting up his hand to his cheek as if in pain.

" His father's his father, and there is nought more to be said. But if he did burn thee, it was by accident, and not o' purpose, as thou kicked him; it's a mercy if his ribs are not broken."

" He howls loud enough, I'm sure. I might ha' kicked many a lad twice as hard and they'd ne'er ha' said ought but ' damn ye ;' but yon lad must needs cry out like a stuck pig if one touches him," replied Michael, sullenly.

Susan went back to the window-seat, and looked absently out of the window at the drifting clouds for a minute or two, while her eyes filled with tears. Then she got up and made for the outer door which led into the back-kitchen. Before she reached it, however, she heard a low voice, whose music made her thrill, say—

" Susan, Susan !*

Her heart melted within her, but it seemed like treachery to her poor boy, like faithlessness to her dead mother, to turn to her lover while the tears which he had caused to flow were yet unwiped on Will's cheeks. So she seemed to take no heed, but passed into the darkness, and, guided by the sobs, she found her way to where Willie sat crouched among disused tubs and churns.

" Come out wi' me, lad;" and they went into the orchard, where the fruit-trees were bare of leaves, but ghastly in their tattered covering of gray moss: and the soughing November wind came with long sweeps over the fells till it rattled among the crackling boughs, underneath which the brother and sister sat in the dark ; he in her lap, and she hushing his head against her shoulder.

" Thou should'st na' play wi' fire. It's a naughty trick. Thoul't suffer for it in worse ways nor this before thou'st done, I'm afeared. I should ha' hit thee twice as lungeous kicks as Mike, if I'd been in his place. He did na' hurt thee, I am sure," she assumed, half as a question.

" Yes! but he did. He turned me quite sick."

And he let his head fall languidly down on his sister's breast

" Come lad! come lad!" said she, anxiously. " Be a man. It was not much that I saw. Why, when first the red cow came, she kicked me far harder for offering to milk her before her legs were tied. See thee! here's a peppermint-drop, and I'll make thee a pasty to-night; only don't give way so, for it hurts me sore to think that Michael has done thee any harm, my pretty."

Willie roused himself up, and put back the wet and ruffled hair from his heated face; and he and Susan rose up, and hand-in-hand went towards the house, walking slowly and quietly except for a kind of sob which Willie could not repress. Susan took him to the pump and washed his tear-stained face, till she thought she had obliterated all traces of the recent disturbance, arranging his curls for him, and then she kissed him tenderly, and led him in, hoping to find Michael in the kitchen, and make all straight between them. But the blaze had dropped down into darkness; the wood was a heap of gray ashes in which the sparks ran hither and thither; but, even in the groping darkness, Susan knew by the sinking at her heart that Michael was not there. She threw another brand on the hearth and lighted the candle, and sat down to her work in silence. Willie cowered on his stool by the side of the fire, eyeing his sister from time to time, and sorry and oppressed, he knew not why, by the sight of her grave, almost stern face. No one came. They two were in the house alone. The old woman who helped Susan with the household work had gone out for the night to some friend's dwelling. William Dixon, the father, was up on the fells seeing after his sheep. Susan had no heart to prepare the evening meal.

" Susy, darling, are you angry with me ?" said Willie, in his little piping, gentle voice. He had stolen up to his sister's side. " I won't never play with fire again ; and I'll not cry if Michael does kick me. Only don't look so like dead mother—don't—don't—please don't!" he exclaimed, hiding his face on her shoulder.

"I'm not angry, Willie," said she. "Don't be feared on me. You want your supper, and you shall have it; and don't you be feared on Michael. He shall give reason for every hair of your head that he touches—he shall."

When William Dixon came home, he found Susan and Willie sitting together, hand-in-hand, and apparently pretty cheerful. He bade them go to bed, for that he would sit up for Michael; and the next morning, when Susan came down, she found that Michael had started an hour before with the cart for lime. It was

a long day's work; Susan knew it would be late, perhaps later than on the preceding night, before he returned—at any rate, past her usual bed-time : and on no account would she stop up a minute beyond that hour in the kitchen, whatever she might do in her bedroom. Here she sat and watched till past midnight; and when she saw him coining up the brow with the carts, she knew full well, even in that faint moonlight, that his gait was the gait of-a man in liquor. But though she was annoyed and mortified to find in what way he had chosen to forget her, the fact did not disgust or shock her as it would have done many a girl, even at that day, who had not been brought up as Susan had, among a class who considered it no crime, but rather a mark of spirit, in a man to get drunk occasionally. Nevertheless, she chose to hold herself very high all the next day when Michael was, perforce, obliged to give up any attempt to do heavy work, and hung about the out-buildings and farm in a very disconsolate and sickly state. Willie had far more pity on him than Susan. Before evening, Willie and he were fast, and on his side, ostentatious friends. Willie rode the horses down to water; Willie helped him to chop wood. Susan sat gloomily at her work, hearing an indistinct but cheerful conversation going on in the shippon, while the cows were being milked. She almost felt irritated

with her little brother, as if he were a traitor, and had gone over to the enemy in the very battle that she was fighting in his cause. She was alone with no one to speak to, while they prattled on, regardless if she were glad or sorry.

Soon Willie burst in. " Susan ! Susan ! come with me ; I've something so pretty to show you. Round the corner of the barn—run! run!" (He was dragging her along, half reluctant, half desirous of some change in that weary day.) Round the corner of the barn ; and caught hold of by Michael, who stood there awaiting her.

" O Willie !" cried she, " you naughty boy. There is nothing pretty—what have you brought me here for ? Let me go ; I won't be held."

" Only one word. Nay, if you wish it so much, you may go," said Michael, suddenly loosing his hold as she struggled. But now she was free, she only drew off a step or two, murmuring something about Willie.

" You are going, then ?" said Michael, with seeming sadness. " You won't hear me say a word of what is in my heart."

" How can I tell whether it is what I should like to hear ?" replied she, still drawing back.

" That is just what I want you to tell me; I want you to hear it, and then to tell me whether you like it or not."

" Well, you may speak," replied she, turning her back, and beginning to plait the hem of her apron.

He came close to her ear.

" I'm sorry I hurt Willie the other night. He has forgiven me. Can you ?"

"You hurt him very badly," she replied. "But you are right to be sorry. I forgive you."

"Stop, stop!" said he, laying his hand upon her arm. "There is something more I've got to say. I want you to be my what is it they call it, Susan?"

"I don't know," said she, half-laughing, but trying to get away with all her might now; and she was a strong girl, but she could not manage it.

"You do. My what is it I want you to be?"

"I tell you I don't know, and you had best be quiet, and just let me go in, or I shall think you're as bad now as you were last night."

"And how did you know what I was last night? It was past twelve when I came home. Were you watching? Ah, Susan! be my wife, and you shall never have to watch for a drunken husband. If I were your husband, I would come straight home, and count every minute an hour till I saw your bonny face. Now you know what I want you to be. I ask you to be my wife. Will you, my own dear Susan?"

She did not speak for some time. Then she only said, "Ask father." And now she was really off like a lapwing round the corner of the barn, and up in her own little room, crying with all her might, before the triumphant smile had left Michael's face where he stood.

The "Ask father" was a mere form to be gone through. Old Daniel Hurst and William Dixon had talked over what they could respectively give their children long before this; and that was the parental way of arranging such matters. When the probable amount of worldly gear that he could give his child had been named by each father, the young folk, as they said, might take their own time in coming to the point which the old men, with the prescience of experience, saw that they were drifting to; no need to hurry them, for they were both young, and Michael, though active enough, was too thoughtless, old Daniel said, to be trusted with the entire management of a farm. Meanwhile, his father would look about him, and see after all the farms that were to be let.

Michael had a shrewd notion of this preliminary understanding between the fathers, and so felt less daunted than he might otherwise have done at making the application for Susan's hand. It was all right, there was not an obstacle; only a deal of good advice, which the lover thought might have as well been spared, and which it must be confessed he did not much attend to, although he assented to every part of it. Then Susan was called down stairs, and slowly came dropping "into view down the steps which led from the two family apartments into the house-place. She tried to look composed and quiet, but it could not be done. She stood side by side with her lover, with her head drooping, her cheeks burning, not daring to look up or move, while her father made the newly-betrothed a somewhat formal address in which he gave his consent, and many a piece of worldly wisdom beside. Susan listened as well as she could for the beating of her heart; but when her father solemnly and sadly referred to his own lost wife, she could keep from sobbing no longer; but throwing her apron over her face, she sat down on the bench by the dresser, and fairly gave way to pent-up tears. Oh, how strangely sweet to be comforted as she was comforted, by tender caress, and many a low-whispered promise of love! Her father sat by the fire, thinking of the days that were gone; Willie was still out of doors; but Susan and Michael felt no one's presence or absence — they only knew they were together as betrothed husband and wife.

In a week, or two, they were formally told of the arrangements to be made in their favour. A small farm in the neighbourhood happened to fall vacant; and Michael's father offered to take it foK him, and be responsible for the rent for the first year, while William Dixon was ]to contribute a certain amount of stock, and both fathers were to help towards the furnishing of the house. Susan received all this information in a quiet, indifferent way; she did not care much for any of these preparations, which were to hurry her through the happy hours ; she cared least of all for the money amount of dowry and of substance. It jarred on her to be made the confidant of occasional slight repinings of Michael's, as one by one his future father-in-law set aside a beast or a pig for Susan's portion, which were not always the best animals of their kind upon the farm. But he also complained of his own father's stinginess, which somewhat, though not much, alleviated Susan's dislike to being awakened out of her pure dream of love to the consideration of worldly wealth.

But in the midst of all this bustle, Willie moped and pined. He had the same chord of delicacy running through his mind that made his body feeble and weak. He kept out of the way, and was apparently occupied in whittling and carving uncouth heads on hazel-sticks in an out-house. But he positively avoided Michael, and shrunk away even from Susan. She was too much occupied to notice this at first. Michael pointed it out to her, saying, with a laugh,—

" Look at Wille ! he might be a cast-off lover and

jealous of me, he looks so dark and downcast at me." Michael spoke this jest out loud, and Willie burst into tears, and ran out of the house.

" Let me go. Let me go!" said Susan (for her lover's arm was round her waist). " I must go to him if he's fretting. I promised mother I would !" She pulled herself away, and went in search of the boy. She sought in byre and barn, through the orchard, where indeed in this leafless winter-time there was no great concealment, up into the room where the wool was usually stored in the later summer, and'at last she found him, sitting at bay, like some hunted creature, up behind the wood-stack.

" What are ye gone for, lad, and me seeking you everywhere ?" asked she, breathless.

" I did not know you would seek me. I've been away many a time, and no one has cared to seek me," said he, crying afresh.

" Nonsense," replied Susan, " don't be so foolish, ye little good-for-nought." But she crept up to him in the hole he had made underneath the great, brown sheafs of wood, and squeezed herself down by him. "What for should folk seek after you, when you get away from them whenever you can ?" asked she.

" They don't want me to stay. Nobody wants me. If I go with father, he says I hinder more than I help.

You used to like to have me with you. But now, you've taken up with Michael, and you'd rather I was away ; and I can just bide away; but I cannot stand Michael jeering at me. He's got you to love him and that might s-erve him."

" But I love you, too, dearly, lad !" said she, putting her arm round his neck.

" Which on us do you like best ?" said he, wistfully, after a little pause, putting her arm away, so that he might look in her face, and see if she spoke truth.

She went very red.

" You should not ask such questions. They are not fit for you to ask, nor for me to answer."

" But mother bade you love me !" said he, plaintively.

"And so I do. And so I ever will do. Lover nor husband shall come betwixt thee and me, lad— ne'er a one of them. That I promise thee (as I promised mother before), in the sight of God and with her hearkening now, if ever she can hearken to earthly word again. Only I cannot abide to have thee fretting, just because my heart is large enough for two."

" And thou'lt love me always ?"

"Always, and ever. And the more—the more thou'lt love Michael," said she, dropping her voice.

" I'll try," said the boy, sighing, for he remembered many a harsh word and blow of which his sister knew nothing. She would have risen up to go away, but he held her tight, for here and now she was all his own, and he did not know when such a time might come again. So the two sat crouched up and silent, till they heard the horn blowing at the field-gate, which was the summons home to any wanderers belonging to the farm, and at this hour of the evening, signified that supper was ready. Then the two went in.

## CHAPTER II.

SUSAN and Michael were to be married in April. He had already gone to take possession of his new farm, three or four miles away from Yew Nook—but that is neighbouring, according to the acceptation of the word in that thinly-populated district,—when William Dixon fell ill. He came home one evening, complaining of head-ache and pains in his limbs, but seemed to loathe the posset which Susan prepared for him ; the treacle-posset which was the homely country remedy against an incipient cold. He took to his bed with a sensation of exceeding weariness, and an odd, unusual looking-back to the days of his youth, when he was a lad living with his parents, in this very house.

The next morning he had forgotten all his life since then, and did not know his own children; crying, like a newly-weaned baby, for his mother to come and soothe away his terrible pain. The doctor from Conis-ton. said it was the typhus-fever, and warned Susan of its infectious character, and shook his head over his patient. There were no friends near to come and share her anxiety ; only good, kind old Peggy, who was faithfulness itself, and one or two labourers' wives, who would fain have helped her, had not their hands been tied by their responsibility to their own families. But, somehow, Susan neither feared nor flagged. As for fear, indeed, she had no time to give way to it, for every energy of both body and mind was required. Besides, the young have had too little experience of the danger of infection to dread it much. She did indeed wish, from time to time, that Michael had been at home to have taken Willie over to his father's at High Beck; but then, again, the lad was docile and useful to her, and his fecklessness in many things might make him be harshly treated by strangers ; so, perhaps, it was as well that Michael was away at Appleby fair, or even beyond that—gone into Yorkshire after horses.

Her father grew worse ; and the doctor insisted on sending over a nurse from Coniston. Not a professed nurse—Coniston could not have supported such a one ; but a widow who was ready to go where the doctor sent her for the sake of the payment When she came, Susan suddenly gave way; she was felled by the fever herself, and lay unconscious for long weeks. Her consciousness returned to her one spring afternoon ;

early spring ; April, -her wedding-month. There Was a little fire burning in the small corner-grate, and the flickering of the blaze was enough for her to notice in her weak state. She felt that there was some one sitting on the window-side of her bed, behind the curtain, but she did not care to know who it was; it was even too great a trouble for her languid mind to consider who it was likely to be. She would rather shut her eyes, and melt off again into the gentle luxury of sleep. The next time she wakened, the Coniston nurse perceived her movement, and made her a cup of tea, which she drank with eager relish; but still they did not speak, and once more Susan lay motionless— not asleep, but strangely, pleasantly conscious of all the small chamber and household sounds; the fall of a cinder on the hearth, the fitful singing of the half-empty kettle, the cattle tramping out to field again after they had been milked, the aged step on the creaking stair— old Peggy's, as she knew. It came to her door; it stopped; the person outside listened for a moment, and then lifted the wooden latch, and looked in. The watcher by the bedside arose, and went to her. Susan would have been glad to see Peggy's face once more, but was far too weak to turn, so she lay and listened.

" How is she ?" whispered one trembling, aged voice.

"Better," replied the other. "She's been awake, and had a cup of tea. She'll do now."

"Has she asked after him ?"

" Hush! No; she has not spoken a word."

" Poor lass! poor lass I"

The door was shut. A weak feeling of sorrow and self-pity came over Susan. What was wrong ? Whom had she loved? And dawning, dawning, slowly rose the sun of her former life, and all particulars were made distinct to her. She felt that some sorrow was coming to her, and cried over it before she knew what it was, or had strength enough to ask. In the dead of night,—and she had never slept again,—she softly called to the watcher, and asked,

"Who?"

"Who what?" replied the woman, with a conscious affright, ill-veiled by a poor assumption of ease. " Lie still, there's a darling, and go to sleep. Sleep's better for you than all the doctor's stuff."

"Who?" repeated Susan. " Something is wrong. Who?"

" Oh, dear!" said, the woman. " There's nothing wrong. Willie has taken the turn, and is doing nicely."

"Father?"

" Well! he's all right now," she answered, looking another way, as if seeking for something.

" Then it's Michael! Oh, me ! oh, me !" She set up a succession of weak, plaintive, hysterical cries before the nurse could pacify her, by declaring that Michael had been at the house not three hours before to ask after her, and looked as well and as hearty as ever man did.

" And you heard of no harm to him since ?" inquired Susan.

" Bless the lass, no, for sure! I've ne'er heard his name named since I saw him go out of the yard as stout a man as ever trod shoe-leather."

" It was well, as the nurse said afterwards to Peggy, that Susan had been so easily pacified by the equivocating answer in respect to her father. If she had pressed the questions home in his case as she did in Michael's, she would have learnt that he was dead and buried more than a month before. It was well, too, that in her weak state of convalescence (which lasted long after this first day of consciousness) her perceptions were not sharp enough to observe the sad change that had taken place in Willie. His bodily strength returned, his appetite was something enormous, but his eyes wandered continually; his regard could not be arrested; his speech became slow, impeded, and incoherent. People began to say, that the fever had taken away the little wit Willie Dixon had ever possessed,

and that they feared that he would end in being a " natural," as they call an idiot in the Dales.

The habitual affection and obedience to Susan lasted longer than any other feeling that the boy had had previous to his illness; and, perhaps, this made her be the last to perceive what every one else had long anticipated. She felt the awakening rude when it did come. It was in this wise :—

One June evening, she sat out of doors under the yew-tree, knitting. She was pale still from her recent illness ; and her languor, joined to the fact of her black dress, made her look more than usually interesting. She was no longer the buoyant self-sufficient Susan, equal to every occasion. The men were bringing in the cows to be milked, and Michael was about in the yard giving orders and directions with somewhat the air of a master, for the farm belonged of right to Willie, and Susan had succeeded to the guardianship of her brother. Michael and she were to be married as soon as she was strong enough—so, perhaps, his authoritative manner was justified ; but the labourers did not like it, although they said little. They remembered him a stripling on the farm, knowing far less than they did, and often glad to shelter his ignorance of all agricultural matters behind their superior knowledge. They would have taken orders from Susan with far more willingness; nay! Willie himself might have commanded them ; and from the old hereditary feeling toward the owners of land, they would have obeyed him with far greater cordiality then they now showed to Michael. But Susan was tired with even three rounds of knitting, and seemed not to notice, or to care, how things went on around her ; and Willie—poor Willie ! —there he stood lounging against the door-sill, enormously grown and developed, to be sure, but with restless eyes and ever-open mouth, and every now and then setting up a strange kind of howling cry, and then smiling vacantly to himself at the sound he had made. As the two old labourers passed him, they looked at each other ominously, and shook their heads.

"Willie, darling," said Susan, "don't make that noise—it makes my head ache."

She spoke feebly, and Willie did not seem to hear ; at any rate, he continued his howl from time to time.

" Hold thy noise, wilt 'a ?" said Michael, roughly, as he passed near him, and threatening him with his fist. Susan's back was turned to the pair. The expression of Willie's face changed from vacancy to fear, and he came shambling up to Susan, and put her arm round him, and, as if protected by that shelter, he began making faces at Michael. Susan saw what was going on, and, as if now first struck by the strangeness of her brother's manner, she looked anxiously at Michael for an explanation. Michael was irritated at Willie's defiance of him, and did not mince the matter.

" It's just that the fever has left him silly—he never was as wise as other folk, and now I doubt if he will ever get right."

Susan did not speak, but she went very pale, and her lip quivered. She looked long and wistfully at Willie's face, as he watched the motion of the ducks in the great stable-pool. He laughed softly to himself every now and then.

" Willie likes to see the ducks go overhead," said Susan, instinctively adopting the form of speech she would have used to a young child.

" Willie, boo ! Willie, boo!" he replied, clapping his hands, and avoiding her eye.

" Speak properly, Willie," said Susan, making a strong effort at self-control, and trying to arrest his attention.

" You know who I am—tell me my name!" She grasped his arm almost painfully tight to make him attend. Now he looked at her, and, for an instant, a gleam of recognition quivered over his face; but the exertion was evidently painful, and he began to cry at the vainness of the effort to recall her name. He hid his face upon her shoulder with the old affectionate trick of manner. She put him gently away, and went into the house into her own little bedroom. She locked the door, and did not reply at all to Michael's calls for her, hardly spoke to old Peggy, who tried to tempt her out to receive some homely sympathy, and through the open casement there still came the idiotic sound of "Willie, boo! Willie, boo!"

CHAPTER IIL

AFTER the stun of the blow came the realisation of the consequences. Susan would sit for hours trying patiently to recall and piece together fragments of recollection and consciousness in her brother's mind. She would let him go and pursue some senseless bit of play, and wait until she could catch his eye or his attention again, when she would resume her self-imposed task. Michael complained that she never had a word for him, or a minute of time to spend with him now; but she only said she must try, while there was yet a chance, to bring back her brother's lost wits. As for marriage in this state of uncertainty, she had no heart to think of it. Then Michael stormed, and absented himself for two or three days; but it was of no use. When he came back, he saw that she had been crying till her eyes were all swollen up, and he gathered from Peggy's scoldings (which she did not spare him) that Susan had eaten nothing since he went away. But she was as inflexible as ever.

"Not just yet. Only not just yet. And don't say again that I do not love you," said she, suddenly hiding herself in his arms.

And so matters went on through August. The crop of oats was gathered in; the wheat-field was not ready as yet, when one fine day Michael drove up in a borrowed shandry, and offered to take Willie a ride. His manner, when Susan asked him where he was going to, was rather confused; but the answer was straight and clear enough.

"He had business in Ambleside. He would never lose sight of the lad, and have him back safe and sound before dark." So Susan let him go.

Before night they were at home again: Willie in high delight at a little rattling, paper windmill that Michael had bought for him in the street, and striving to imitate this new sound with perpetual buzzings. Michael, too, looked pleased. Susan knew the look, although afterwards she remembered that he had tried to veil it from her, and had assumed a grave appearance of sorrow whenever he caught her eye. He put up his horse; for, although he had three miles further to go, the moon was up—the bonny harvest-moon—and he did not care how late he had to drive on such a road by such a light. After the supper which Susan had prepared for the travellers was over, Peggy went

up-stairs to see Willie safe in bed; for he had to have the same care taken of him that a little child of four years old requires.

Michael drew near to Susan.

"Susan," said he, "I took Will to see Dr. Preston, at Kendal. He's the first doctor in the county. I thought it were better for us—for you—to know at once what chance there were for him."

"Well!" said Susan, looking eagerly up. She saw the same strange glance of satisfaction, the same instant change to apparent regret and pain. "What did he say?" said she. "Speak! can't you?"

"He said he would never get better of his weakness."

"Never!"

"No; never. It's a long word, and hard to bear. And there's worse to come, dearest. The doctor thinks he will get badder from year to year. And he said, if he was us—you—he would send him off in time to Lancaster Asylum. They've ways there both of keeping such people in order and making them happy. I only tell you what he said," continued he, seeing the gathering storm in her face.

"There was no harm in his saying it," she replied, with great self-constraint, forcing herself to speak coldly instead of angrily. "Folk is welcome to their opinions."

They sat silent for a minute or two, her breast heaving with suppressed feeling.

"He's counted a very clever man," said Michael, at length.

"He may be. He's none of my clever men, nor am I going to be guided by him, whatever he may think. And I don't thank them that went and took my poor lad to have such harsh notions formed about him. If I'd been there, I could have called out the sense that is in him."

"Well! I'll not say more to-night, Susan. You're not taking it rightly, and I'd best be gone, and leave you to think it over. I'll not deny they are hard words to hear, but there's sense in them, as I take it; and I reckon you'll have to come to 'em. Anyhow, it's a bad way of thanking me for my pains, and I don't take it well in you, Susan," said he, getting up, as if offended.

"Michael, I'm beside myself with sorrow. Don't blame me, if I speak sharp. He and me is the only ones, you see. And mother did so charge me to have a care of him! And this is what he's come to, poor lile chap !" She began to cry, and Michael to comfort her with caresses.

"Don't," said she. "It's no use trying to make me forget poor Willie is a natural. I could hate myself for being happy with you, even for just a little minute. Go away, and leave me to face it out."

"And you'll think it over, Susan, and remember what the doctor says ?"

"I can't forget it," said she. She meant she could not forget what the doctor had said about the hopelessness of her brother's case; Michael had referred to the plan of sending Willie away to an asylum, or madhouse, as they were called in that day and place. The idea had been gathering force in Michael's mind for some time ; he had talked it over with his father, and secretly rejoiced over the possession of the farm and land which would then be his in fact, if not in law, by right of his wife. He had always considered the good penny her father could give her in his catalogue of Susan's charms and attractions. But of late he had grown to esteem her as the heiress of Yew Nook. He, too, should have land like his brother—land to possess, to cultivate, to make profit from, to bequeath. For some time he had wondered that Susan had been so much absorbed in Willie's present, that she had never seemed to look forward to his future, state. Michael had long felt the boy to be a trouble ; but of late he had absolutely loathed him. His gibbering, his uncouth gestures, his loose, shambling gait, all irritated Michael inexpressibly. He did not come near the Yew Nook for a couple of days. He thought that he would leave her time to become anxious to see him and reconciled to his plan. They were strange, lonely days to Susan. They were the first she had spent face to face with the sorrows that had turned her from a girl into a woman; for hitherto Michael had never let twenty-four hours pass by without coming to see her since she had had the fever. Now that he was absent, it seemed as though some cause of irritation was removed from Will, who was much more gentle and tractable than he had been for many weeks. Susan thought that she observed him making efforts at her bidding, and there was something piteous in the way in which he crept up to her, and looked wistfully in her face, as if asking her to restore him the faculties that he felt to be wanting.

"I never will let thee go, lad. Never! There's no knowing where they would take thee to, or what they would do with thee. As it says in the Bible, « Nought but death shall part thee and me !' "

The country-side was full, in those days, of stories of the brutal treatment offered to the insane; stories that were, in fact, but too well founded, and the truth of one of which only would have been a sufficient reason for the strong prejudice existing against all such places. Each succeeding hour that Susan passed, alone, or with the poor affectionate lad for her sole companion, served to deepen her solemn resolution never to part with him. So, when Michael came, he was annoyed and surprised by the calm way in which she spoke, as if following Dr. Preston's advice was utterly and entirely out of the question. He had expected nothing less than a consent, reluctant it might he, but still a consent; and he was extremely irritated. He could have repressed his anger, but he chose rather to give way to it; thinking that he could thus best work upon Susan's affection, so as to gain his point. But, somehow, he over-reached himself; and now he was astonished in his turn at the passion of indignation that she burst into.

" Thou wilt not bide in the same house with him, say'st thou? There's no need for thy biding, as far as I can tell. There's solemn reason why I should bide with my own flesh and blood, and keep to the word I pledged my mother on her death-bed; but, as for thee, there's no tie that I know on to keep thee fro' going to America or Botany Bay this very night, if that were thy inclination. I will have no more of your threats to make me send my bairn away. If thou marry me, thou'lt help me to take charge of Willie. If thou doesn't choose to marry me on those terms—why! I can snap my fingers at thee, never fear. I'm

not so far gone in love as that. But I will not have thee, if thou say'st in such a hectoring way that Willie must go out of the house—and the house his own too —before thou'lt set foot in it. Willie bides here, and I bide with him."

" Thou hast may-be spoken a word too much," said Michael, pale with rage. " If I am free, as thou say'st, to go to Canada or Botany Bay, I reckon I'm free to live where I like, and that will not be with a natural who may turn into a madman some day, for aught I know. Choose between him and me, Susy, for I swear to thee, thou shan't have both."

" I have chosen," said Susan, now perfectly composed and still. " Whatever comes of it, I bide with Willie."

" Very well," replied Michael, trying to assume an equal composure of manner. " Then I'll wish you a very good night." He went out of the house-door, half-expecting to be called back again; but, instead, he heard a hasty step inside, and a bolt drawn.

" Whew!" said he to himself, " I think I must leave my lady alone for a week or two, and give her time to come to her senses. She'll not find it so easy as she thinks to let me go."

So he went past the kitchen-window in nonchalant style, and was not seen again at Yew Nook for some

weeks. How did he pass the time? For the first day or two, he was unusually cross with all things and people that came athwart him. Then wheat-harvest began, and he was busy, and exultant about his heavy crop. Then a man came from a distance to bid for the lease of his farm, which, by his father's advice, had been offered for sale, as he himself was so soon likely to remove to the Yew Nook. He had so little idea that Susan really would remain firm to her determination, that he at once began to haggle with the man who came after his farm, showed him the crop just got in, and managed skilfully enough to make a good bargain for himself. Of course, the bargain had to be sealed at the public-house ; and the companions he met with there soon became friends enough to tempt him into Langdale, where again he met with Eleanor Hebthwaite.

How did Susan pass the time ? For the first day or so, she was too angry and offended to cry. She went about her household duties in a quick, sharp, jerking, yet absent way; shrinking one moment from Will, overwhelming him with remorseful caresses the next. The third day of Michael's absence, she had the relief of a good fit of crying; and after that, she grew softer and more tender; she felt how harshly she had spoken to him, and remembered how angry she had been.

She made excuses for him. " It was no wonder/' she said to herself, " that he had heen vexed with her; and no wonder he would not give in, when she had never tried to speak gently or to reason with him. She was to blame, and she would tell him so, and tell him once again all that her mother had bade her be to Willie, and all the horrible stories she had heard about madhouses, and he would be on her side at once."

And so she watched for his coming, intending to apologise as soon as ever she saw him. She hurried over her household work, in order to sit quietly at her sewing, and hear the first distant sound of his well-known step or whistle. But even the sound of her flying needle seemed too loud perhaps she was losing an exquisite instant of anticipation; so she stopped sewing, and looked longingly out through the geranium leaves, in order that her eye might catch the first stir of the branches in the wood-path by which he generally came. Now and then a bird might spring out of the covert; otherwise the leaves were heavily still in the sultry weather of early autumn. Then she would take up her sewing, and, with a spasm of resolution, she would determine that a certain task should be fulfilled before she would again allow herself the poignant luxury of expectation. Sick at heart was she when

the evening closed in, and the chances of that day diminished. Yet she stayed up longer than usual, thinking that if he were coming—if he were only passing along the distant road—the sight of a light in the window might encourage him to make his appearance even at that late hour, while seeing the house all darkened and shut up might quench any such intention.

Very sick and weary at heart, she went to bed; too desolate and despairing to cry, or make any moan. But in the morning hope came afresh. Another day —another chance! And so it went on for weeks. Peggy understood her young mistress's sorrow full well, and respected it by her silence on the subject. Willie seemed happier now that the irritation of Michael's presence was removed; for the poor idiot had a sort of antipathy to Michael, which was a kind of heart's echo to the repugnance in which the latter held him. Altogether, just at this time, Willie was the happiest of the three.

As Susan went into Coniston, to sell her butter, one Saturday, some inconsiderate person told her that she had seen Michael Hurst the night before. I said inconsiderate, but I might rather have said unobservant ; for any one who had spent half-an-hour in Susan Dixon's company might have seen that she

disliked having any reference made to the subjects nearest her heart, were they joyous or grievous. Now she went a little paler than usual (and she had never recovered her colour since she had had the fever), and tried to keep silence. But an irrepressible pang forced out the question—

" Where ?"

"At Thomas Applethwaite's, in Langdale. They had a kind of harvest-home, and he were there among the young folk, and very thick wi' Nelly Hebthwaite, old Thomas's niece. Thou'lt have to look after him a bit, Susan!"

She neither smiled nor sighed. The neighbour who had been speaking to her was struck with the gray stillness of her face. Susan herself felt how well her self-command was obeyed by every little muscle, and said to herself in her Spartan manner, " I can bear it without either wincing or blenching." She went home early, at a tearing, passionate pace, trampling and breaking through all obstacles of briar or bush. Willie was moping in her absence—hanging listlessly on the farm-yard gate to watch for her. When he saw her, he set up one of his strange, inarticulate cries, of which she was now learning the meaning, and came towards her with his loose, galloping run, head and limbs all shaking and wagging with pleasant excite-

ment. Suddenly she turned from him, and burst into tears. She sat down on a stone by the wayside, not a hundred yards from home, and buried her face in her hands, and gave way to a passion of pent-up sorrow; so terrible and full of agony were her low cries, that the idiot stood by her, aghast and silent. All his joy gone for the time, but not, like her joy, turned into ashes. Some thought struck him. Yes! the sight of her woe made him think, great as the exertion was. He ran, and stumbled, and shambled home, buzzing with his lips all the time. She never missed him. He came back in a trice, bringing with him his cherished paper windmill, bought on that fatal day when Michael had taken him into Kendal to have his doom of perpetual idiotcy pronounced. He thrust it into Susan's face, her hands, her lap, regardless of the injury his frail plaything thereby received. He leapt before her to think how he had cured all heart-sorrow, buzzing louder than ever. Susan looked up at him, and that glance of her sad eyes sobered him. He began to whimper, he knew not why: and she now, comforter in her turn, tried to soothe him by twirling his windmill. But it was broken ; it made no noise; it would not go round. This seemed to afflict Susan more than him. She tried to make it right, although she saw the task was hopeless ; and while she did so, the tears rained down unheeded from her bent head on the paper toy.

" It won't do," said she, at last. " It will never do again." And, somehow, she took the accident and her words as omens of the love that was broken, and that she feared could never be pieced together more. She rose up and took Willie's hand, and the two went slowly in to the house.

To her surprise, Michael Hurst sat in the house-place. House-place is a sort of better kitchen, where no cookery is done, but which is reserved for state occasions. Michael had gone in there because he was accompanied by his only sister, a woman older than himself, who was well married beyond Keswick, and who now came for the first time to make acquaintance with Susan. Michael had primed his sister with his wishes regarding Will, and the position in which he stood with Susan ; and arriving at Yew Nook in the absence of the latter, he had not scrupled to conduct his sister into the guest-room, as he held Mrs. Gale's worldly position in respect and admiration, and therefore wished her to be favourably impressed with all the signs of property which he was beginning to consider as Susan's greatest charms. He had secretly said to himself, that if Eleanor Hebthwaite and Susan Dixon were equal in point of riches, he would sooner have Eleanor by far. He had begun to consider Susan as a termagant; and when he thought of his intercourse with her, recollections of her somewhat warm and hasty temper came far more readily to his mind than any remembrance of her generous, loving nature.

And now she stood face to face with him; her eyes tear-swollen, her garments dusty, and here and there torn in consequence of her rapid progress through the bushy by-paths. She did not make a favourable impression on the well-clad Mrs. Gale, dressed in her best silk gown, and therefore unusually susceptible to the appearance of another. Nor were Susan's manners gracious or cordial. How could they be, when she remembered what had passed between Michael and herself the last time they met ? For her penitence had faded away under the daily disappointment of these last weary weeks.

But she was hospitable in substance. She bade Peggy hurry on the kettle, and busied herself among the tea-cups, thankful that the presence of Mrs. Gale, as a stranger, would prevent the immediate recurrence to the one subject which she felt must be present in Michael's mind as well as in her own. But Mrs. Gale was withheld by no such feelings of delicacy. She had come ready-primed with the case, and had undertaken to bring the girl to reason. There was no time to be lost. It had been prearranged between the brother and sister that he was to stroll out into the farm-yard before his sister introduced the subject; but she was so confident in the success of her arguments, that she must needs have the triumph of a victory as soon as possible ; and, accordingly, she brought a hail-storm of good reasons to bear upon Susan. Susan did not reply for a long time; she was so indignant at this intermeddling of a stranger in the deep family sorrow and shame. Mrs. Gale thought she was gaining the day, and urged her arguments more pitilessly. Even Michael winced for Susan, and wondered at her silence. He shrunk out of sight, and into the shadow, hoping that his sister might prevail, but annoyed at the hard way in which she kept putting the case.

Suddenly Susan turned round from the occupation she had pretended to be engaged in, and said to him in a low voice, which yet not only vibrated itself, but made its hearers thrill through all their obtuseness:

"Michael Hurst! does your sister speak truth, think you?"

Both women looked at him for his answer; Mrs. Gale without anxiety, for had she not said the very words they had spoken together before; had she not used the very arguments that he himself had suggested? Susan, on the contrary, looked to his answer as settling her doom for life ; and in the gloom of her eyes you might have read more despair than hope.

He shuffled his position. He shuffled in his words.

" What is it you ask ? My sister has said many things."

"I ask you," said Susan, trying to give a crystal clearness both to her expressions and her pronunciation, " if, knowing as you do how Will is afflicted, you will help me to take that charge of him which I promised my mother on her death-bed that I would do; and which means, that I shall keep him always with me, and do all in my power to make his life happy. If you will do this, I will be your wife; if not, I remain unwed."

" But he may get dangerous; he can be but a trouble; his being here is a pain to you, Susan, not a pleasure."

" I ask you for either yes or no," said she, a little contempt at his evading her question mingling with her tone. He perceived it, and it nettled him.

" And I have told you. I answered your question the last time I was here. I said I would ne'er keep house with an idiot; no more I will. So now you've gotten your answer."

" I have," said Susan. And she sighed deeply.

" Come, now," said Mrs. Gale, encouraged by the

sigh ; " one would think you don't love Michael, Susan, to be so stubborn in yielding to what I'm sure would be best for the lad."

" Oh! she does not care for me," said Michael. " I don't believe she ever did."

" Don't I ? Haven't I ?" asked Susan, her eyes blazing out fire. She left the room directly, and sent Peggy in to make the tea ; and catching at Will, who was lounging about in the kitchen, she went up-stairs with him and bolted herself in, straining the boy to her heart, and keeping almost breathless, lest any noise she made might cause him to break out into the howls and sounds which she could not bear that those below should hear.

A knock at the door. It was Peggy.

" He wants for to see you, to wish you good-bye."

" I cannot come. Oh, Peggy, send them away."

It was her only cry for sympathy ; and the old servant understood it. She sent them away, somehow; not politely, as I have been given to understand.

" Good go with them," said Peggy, as she grimly watched their retreating 6gures. " We're rid of bad rubbish, anyhow." And she turned into the house, with the intention of making ready some refreshment for Susan, after her hard day at the market, and her harder evening. But in the kitchen, to which she

passed through the empty house-place, making a face of contemptuous dislike at the used tea-cups and fragments of a meal yet standing there, she found Susan, with her sleeves tucked up and her working apron on, busied in preparing to make clap-bread, one of the hardest and hottest domestic tasks of a Daleswoman. She looked up, and first met and then avoided Peggy's eye; it was too full of sympathy. Her own cheeks were flushed, and her own eyes were dry and burning.

" Where's the board, Peggy ? We need clap-bread ; and, I reckon, I've time to get through with it to-night." Her voice had a sharp, dry tone in it, and her motions a jerking angularity about them.

Peggy said nothing, but fetched her all that she needed. Susan beat her cakes thin with vehement force. As she stooped over them, regardless even of the task in which she seemed so much occupied, she was surprised by a touch on her mouth of something— what she did not see at first. It was a cup of tea, delicately sweetened and cooled, and held to her lips, when exactly ready, by the faithful old woman. Susan held it off a hand's breath, and looked into Peggy's eyes, while her own filled with the strange relief of tears.

" Lass!" said Peggy, solemnly, " thou hast done

well. It is not long to bide, and then the end will come."

" But you are very old, Peggy," said Susan, quivering.

" It is but a day sin' I were young," replied Peggy; but she stopped the conversation by again pushing the cup with gentle force to Susan's dry and thirsty lips. When she had drunken she fell again to her labour, Peggy heating the hearth, and doing all that she knew would be required, but never speaking another word. Willie basked close to the fire, enjoying the animal luxury of warmth, for the autumn evenings were beginning to be chilly. It was 1 one o'clock before they thought of going to bed on that memorable night.

CHAPTER IV.

THE vehemence with which Susan Dixon threw herself into occupation could not last for ever. Times of languor and remembrance would come—times when she recurred with a passionate yearning to bygone days, the recollection of which was so vivid and delicious, that it seemed as though it were the reality, and the present bleak bareness the dream. She smiled anew at the magical sweetness of some touch or tone which in memory she felt and heard, and drank the delicious cup of poison, although at the very time she knew what the consequences of racking pain would be.

"This time, last year," thought she, "we went nutting together—this very day last year ; just such a day as to-day. Purple and gold were the lights on the hills; the leaves were just turning brown ; here and there on the sunny slopes the stubble-fields looked tawny; down in a cleft of yon purple slate-rock the beck fell like a silver glancing thread ; all just as it is

to-day. And he climbed the slender, swaying nut-trees, and bent the branches forme to gather ; or made a passage through the hazel copses, from time to time claiming a toll. Who could have thought he loved me so little ?—who ?—who ?"

Or, as the evening closed in, she would allow herself to imagine that she heard his coming step, just that she might recall the feeling of exquisite delight which had passed by without the due and passionate relish at the time. Then she would wonder how she could have had strength, the cruel, self-piercing strength, to say what she had done ; to stab herself with that stern resolution, of which the scar would remain till her dying day. It might have been right; but, as she sickened, she wished she had not instinctively chosen the right. How luxurious a life haunted by no stern sense of duty must be ! And many led this kind of life ; why could not she ? O, for one hour again of his sweet company ! If he came now, she would agree to whatever he proposed.

It was a fever of the mind. She passed through it, and came out healthy, if weak. She was capable once more of taking pleasure in following an unseen guide through briar and brake. She returned with tenfold affection to her protecting care of Willie. She acknowledged to herself that he was to be her all-in-all in life.

She made him her constant companion. For his sake, as the real owner of Yew Nook, and she as his steward and guardian, she began that course of careful saving, and that love of acquisition, which afterwards gained for her the reputation of being miserly. She still thought that he might regain a scanty portion of sense —enough to require some simple pleasures and excitement, which would cost money. And money should not be wanting. Peggy rather assisted her in the formation of her parsimonious habits than otherwise; economy was the order of the district, and a certain degree of respectable avarice the characteristic of her age. Only Willie was never stinted nor hindered of anything that the two women thought could give him pleasure, for want of money.

There was one gratification which Susan felt was needed for the restoration of her mind to its more healthy state, after she had passed through the whirling fever, when duty was as nothing, and anarchy reigned; a gratification—that, somehow, was to be her last burst of unreasonableness; of which she knew and recognised pain as the sure consequence. She must see him once more,—herself unseen.

The week before the Christmas of this memorable year, she went out in the dusk of the early winter evening, wrapped close in shawl and cloak. She wore her dark shawl under her cloak, putting it over her head in lieu of a bonnet; for she knew that she might have to wait long in concealment Then she tramped over the wet fell-path, shut in by misty rain for miles and miles, till she came to the place where he was lodging; a farm-house in Langdale, with a steep, stony lane leading up to it: this lane was entered by a gate out of the main road, and by the gate were a few bushes—thorns ; but of them the leaves had fallen, and they offered no concealment: an old wreck of a yew-tree grew among them, however, and underneath that Susan cowered down, shrouding her face, of which the colour might betray her, with a corner of her shawl. Long did she wait; cold and cramped she became, too damp and stiff to change her posture readily. And after all, he might never come! But, she would wait till daylight, if need were; and she pulled out a crust, with which she had providently supplied herself. The rain had ceased,—a dull, still, brooding weather had succeeded ; it was a night to hear distant sounds. She heard horses' hoofs striking and plashing in the stones, and in the pools of the road at her back. Two horses; not well-ridden, or evenly guided, as she could tell.

Michael Hurst and a companion drew near; not tipsy, but not sober. They stopped at the gate to bid each other a maudlin farewell. Michael stooped forward to catch the latch with the hook of the stick which he carried ; he dropped the stick, and it fell with one end close to Susan,—indeed, with the slightest change of posture she could have opened the gate for him. He swore a great oath, and struck his horse with his closed fist, as if that animal had been to blame ; then he dismounted, opened the gate, and fumbled about for his stick. When he had found it (Susan had touched the other end) his first use of it was to flog his horse well, and she had much ado to avoid its kicks and plunges. Then, still swearing, he staggered up the lane, for it was evident he was not sober enough to remount.

By daylight Susan was back and at her daily labours at Yew Nook. When the spring came, Michael Hurst was married to Eleanor Hebthwaite. Others, too, were married, and christenings made their firesides merry and glad; or they travelled, and came back after long years with many wondrous tales. More rarely, perhaps, a Dalesman changed his dwelling. But to all households more change came than to Yew Nook. There the seasons came round with monotonous sameness ; or, if they brought mutation, it was of a slow, and decaying, and depressing kind. Old Peggy died. Her silent sympathy, concealed under much roughness, was a loss to Susan Dixon. Susan was not yet thirty when this happened, but she looked a middle-aged, not to say an elderly woman. People affirmed that she had never recovered her complexion since that fever, a dozen years ago, which killed her father, and left Will Dixon an idiot. But besides her gray sallowness, the lines in her face were strong, and deep, and hard. The movements of her eyeballs were slow and heavy; the wrinkles at the corners of her mouth and eyes were planted firm and sure ; not an ounce of unnecessary flesh was there on her bones—every muscle started strong and ready for use. She needed all this bodily strength, to a degree that no human creature, now Peggy was dead, knew of: for Willie had grown up large and strong in body, and, in general, docile enough in mind; but, every now and then, he became first moody, and then violent. These paroxysms lasted but a day or two; and it was Susan's anxious care to keep their very existence hidden and unknown. It is true, that occasional passers-by on that lonely road heard sounds at night of knocking about of furniture, blows, and cries, as of some tearing demon within the solitary farm-house ; but these fits of violence usually occurred in the night; and whatever had been their consequence, Susan had tidied and redded up all signs of aught unusual before the morning. For, above all, she dreaded lest some one might find out in what danger and peril she occasionally was, and might assume a right to take

away her brother from her care. The one idea of taking charge of him had deepened and deepened with years. It was graven into her mind as the object for which she lived. The sacrifice she had made for this object only made it more precious to her. Besides, she separated the idea of the docile, affectionate, loutish, indolent Will, and kept it distinct from the terror which the demon that occasionally possessed him inspired her with. The one was her flesh and her blood,—the child of her dead mother; the other was some fiend who came to torture and convulse the creature she so loved. She believed that she fought her brother's battle in holding down those tearing hands, in binding whenever she could those uplifted restless arms prompt and prone to do mischief. All the time she subdued him with her cunning or her strength, she spoke to him in pitying murmurs, or abused the third person, the fiendish enemy, in no unmeasured tones. Towards morning the paroxysm was exhausted, and he would fall asleep, perhaps only to waken with evil and renewed vigour. But when he was laid down, she would sally out to taste the fresh air, and to work off her wild sorrow in cries and mutterings to herself. The early labourers saw her gestures at a distance, and thought her as crazed as the idiot-brother who made the neighbourhood a haunted place. But did any chance person

call at Yew Nook later on in the day, he would find Susan Dixon cold, calm, collected; her manner curt, her wits keen.

Once this fit of violence lasted longer than usual. Susan's strength both of mind and body was nearly worn out; she wrestled in prayer that somehow it might end before she, too, was driven mad; or, worse, might be obliged to give up life's aim, and consign Willie to a madhouse. From that moment of prayer (as she afterwards superstitiously thought) Willie calmed—and then he drooped—and then he sank—and, last of all, he died in reality from physical exhaustion.

But he was so gentle and tender as he lay on his dying bed; such strange, child-like gleams of returning intelligence came over his face, long after the power to make his dull, inarticulate sounds had departed, that Susan was attracted to him by a stronger tie than she had ever felt before. It was something to have even an idiot loving her with dumb, wistful, animal affection; something to have any creature looking at her with such beseeching eyes, imploring protection from the insidious enemy stealing on. And yet she knew that to him death was no enemy, but a true friend, restoring light and health to his poor clouded mind. It was to her that death was an enemy; to her, the survivor, when Willie died; there was no one to love

her. Worse doom still, there was no one left on earth for her to love.

You now know why no wandering tourist could persuade her to receive him as a lodger ; why no tired traveller could melt her heart to afford him rest and refreshment; why long habits of seclusion had given her a moroseness of manner, and how care for the interests of another had rendered her keen and miserly.

But there was a third act in the drama of her life.

## CHAPTER V.

IN spite of Peggy's prophecy that Susan's life should not seem long, it did seem wearisome and endless, as the years slowly uncoiled their monotonous circles. To be sure, she might have made change for herself, but she did not care to do it. It was, indeed, more than " not caring," which merely implies a certain degree of vis inertice to be subdued before an object can be attained, and that the object itself does not seem to be of sufficient importance to call out the requisite energy. On the contrary, Susan exerted herself to avoid change and variety. She had a morbid dread of new faces, which originated in her desire to keep poor dead Willie's state a profound secret. She had a contempt for new customs; and, indeed, her old ways prospered so well under her active hand and vigilant eye, that it was difficult to know how they could be improved upon. She was regularly present in Coniston market with the best butter and the earliest chickens of the season. Those were the common farm produce that every farmer's wife about had to sell; but Susan, after she had disposed of the more feminine articles, turned to on the man's side. A better judge of a horse or cow there was not in all the country round. Yorkshire itself might have attempted to jockey her, and would have failed. Her corn was sound and clean; her potatoes well preserved to the latest spring. People began to talk of the hoards of money Susan Dixon must have laid up somewhere; and one young ne'er-do-weel of a farmer's son undertook to make love to the woman of forty, who looked fifty-five, if a day. He made up to her by opening a gate on the road-path home, as she was riding on a bare-backed horse, her purchase not an hour ago. She was off before him, refusing his civility ; but the remounting was not so easy, and rather than fail she did not choose to attempt it. She walked, and he , walked alongside, improving his opportunity, which, as he vainly thought, had been consciously granted to him. As they drew near Yew Nook, he ventured on some expression of a wish to keep company with her. His words were vague and clumsily arranged. Susan turned round and coolly asked him to explain himself. He took courage, as he thought of her reputed wealth, and expressed his wishes this second time pretty plainly. To his surprise, the reply she made was in a series of smart strokes across his shoulders, administered through the medium of a supple hazel-switch.

" Take that I" said she, almost breathless, " to teach thee how thou darest make a fool of an honest woman old enough to be thy mother. If thou com'st a step nearer the house, there's a good horse-pool, and there's two stout fellows who'll like no better fun than ducking thee. Be off wi' thee."

And she strode into her own premises, never looking round to see whether he obeyed her injunction or not.

Sometimes three or four years would pass over without her hearing Michael Hurst's name mentioned. She used to wonder at such times whether he weie dead or alive. She would sit for hours by the dying embers of her fire on a winter's evening, trying to recall the scenes of her youth; trying to bring up living pictures of the faces she had then known— Michael's most especially. She thought it was possible, so long had been the lapse of years, that she might now pass by him in the street unknowing and unknown. His outward form she might not recognise, but himself she should feel in the thrill of her whole being. He could not pass her unawares. ;

What little she did hear about him, all testified a downward tendency. He drank—not at stated times when there was no other work to be done, but continually, whether it was seed-time or harvest. His children were all ill at the same time ; then one died, while the others recovered, but were poor sickly things. No one dared to give Susan any direct intelligence of her former lover; many avoided all mention of his name in her presence ; but a few spoke out either in indifference to, or ignorance of, those bygone days.

Susan heard every word, every whisper, every sound that related to him. But her eye never changed, nor did a muscle of her face move.

Late one November night she sat over her fire; not a human being besides herself in the house; none hut she had ever slept there since Willie's death. The farm-labourers had foddered the cattle and gone home hours before. There were crickets chirping all round the warm hearth-stones; there was the clock ticking with the peculiar beat Susan had known from her childhood, and which then and ever since she had oddly associated with the idea of a mother and child talking together, one loud tick, and quick—a feeble, sharp one following.

The day had been keen, and piercingly cold. The whole lift of heaven seemed a dome of iron. Black and frost-bound was the earth under the cruel east

wind. Now the wind had dropped, and as the darkness had gathered in, the weather-wise old labourers prophesied snow. The sounds in the air arose again, as Susan sat still and silent. They were of a different character to what they had been during the prevalence of the east wind. Then they had been shrill and piping; now they were like low distant growling; not unmusical, but strangely threatening. Susan went to the window, and drew aside the little curtain. The whole world was white—the air was blinded with the swift and heavy fall of snow. At present it came down straight, but Susan knew those distant sounds in the hollows and gulleys of the hills portended a driving wind and a more cruel storm. She thought of her sheep; were they all folded ? the new-born calf, was it bedded well ? Before the drifts were formed too deep for her to pass in and out—and by the morning she judged that they would be six or seven feet deep—she would go out and see after the comfort of her beasts. She took a lantern, and tied a shawl over her head, and went out into the open air. She had tenderly provided for all her animals, and was returning, when, borne on the blast as if some spirit-cry—for it seemed to come rather down from the skies than from any creature standing on earth's level —she heard a voice of agony; she could not distinguish

words; it seemed rather as if some bird of prey was being caught in the whirl of the icy wind, and torn and tortured by its violence. Again! up high above ! Susan put down her lantern, and shouted loud in return; it was an instinct, for if the creature were not human, which she had doubted but a moment before? what good could her responding cry do ? And her cry was seized on by the tyrannous wind, and borne farther away in the opposite direction to that from which the call of agony had proceeded. Again she listened ; no sound: then again it rang through space; and this time she was sure it was human. She turned into the house, and heaped turf and wood on the fire, which, careless of her own sensations, she had allowed to fade and almost die out. She put a new candle in her lantern; she changed her shawl for a maud, and leaving the door on latch, she sallied out. Just at the moment when her ear first encountered the weird noises of the storm, on issuing forth into the open air, she thought she heard the words, " O God! O help!" They were a guide to her, if words they were, for they came straight from a rock not a quarter of a mile from Yew Nook, but only to be reached, on account of its precipitous character, by a round-about path. Thither she steered, defying wind and snow; guided by here a thorn-tree, there an old, doddered oak, which had

not quite lost their identity under the whelming mask of snow. Now and then she stopped to listen; but never a word or sound heard she, till right from where the copse-wood grew thick and tangled at the base of the rock, round which she was winding, she heard a moan. Into the brake—all snow in appearance— almost a plain of snow looked on from the little eminence where she stood—she plunged, breaking down the bush, stumbling, bruising herself, fighting her way; her lantern held between her teeth, and she herself using head as well as hands to butt away a passage, at whatever cost of bodily injury. As she climbed or staggered, owing to the unevenness of the snow-covered ground, where the briars and weeds of years were tangled and matted together, her foot felt something strangely soft and yielding. She lowered her lantern; there lay a man, prone on his face, nearly covered by the fast-falling flakes; he must have fallen from the rock above, as, not knowing of the circuitous path, he had tried to descend its steep, slippery face. Who could tell ? it was no time for thinking. Susan lifted him up with her wiry strength ; he gave no help —no sign of life; but for all that he might be alive: he was still warm ; she tied her maud round him; she fastened the lantern to her apron-string; she held him tight: half-carrying, half-dragging—what did a few

bruises signify to him, compared to dear life, to precious life! She got him through the brake, and down the path. There, for an instant, she stopped to take breath ; but, as if stung by the Furies, she pushed on again with almost superhuman strength. Clasping him round the waist, and leaning his dead weight against the lintel of the door, she tried to undo the latch; but now, just at this moment, a trembling faintness came over her, and a fearful dread took possession of her— that here, on the very threshold of her home, she might be found dead, and buried under the snow, when the farm-servants came in the morning. This terror stirred her up to one more effort. Then she and her companion were in the warmth of the quiet haven of that kitchen; she laid him on the settle, and sank on the floor by his side. How long she remained in this swoon she could not tell; not very long she judged by the fire, which was still red and sullenly glowing when she came to herself. She lighted the candle, and bent over her late burden to ascertain if indeed he were dead. She stood long gazing. The man lay dead. There could be no doubt about it. His filmy eyes glared at her, unshut But Susan was not one tt) be affrighted by the stony aspect of death. It was not that; it was the bitter, woeful recognition of Michael Hurst!

She was convinced he was dead; but after a while she refused to believe in her conviction. She stripped off his wet outer-garments with trembling, hurried hands. She brought a blanket down from her own bed; she made up the fire. She swathed him in fresh, warm wrappings, and laid him on the flags before the fire, sitting herself at his head, and holding it in her lap, while she tenderly wiped his loose, wet hair, curly still, although its colour had changed from nut-brown to iron-gray since she had seen it last. From time to time she bent over the face afresh, sick, and fain to believe that the flicker of the fire-light was some slight convulsive motion. But the dim, staring eyes struck chill to her heart. At last she ceased her delicate, busy cares ; but she still held the head softly, as if caressing it. She thought over all the possibilities and chances in the mingled yarn of their lives that might, by so slight a turn, have ended far otherwise. If her mother's cold had been early tended, so that the responsibility as to her brother's weal or woe had not fallen upon her; if the fever had not taken such rough, cruel hold on Will; nay, if Mrs. Gale, that hard, worldly sister, had not accompanied him on his last visit to Yew Nook—his very last before this fatal, stormy night; if she had heard his cry,—cry uttered by those pale, dead lips with such wild, de-

spairing agony, not yet three hours ago!—O! if she had but heard it sooner, he might have been saved before that blind, false step had precipitated him down the rock! In going over this weary chain of unrealised possibilities, Susan learnt the force of Peggy's words. Life was short, looking back upon it. It seemed but yesterday since all the love of her being had been poured out, and run to waste. The intervening years—the long monotonous years that had turned her into an old woman before her time—were but a dream.

The labourers coming in the dawn of the winter's day were surprised to see the fire-light through the low kitchen-window. They knocked, and hearing a moaning answer, they entered, fearing that something had befallen their mistress. For all explanation they got these words:

"It is Michael Hurst. He was belated, and fell down the Raven's Crag. Where does

Eleanor, his wife, live?"

How Michael Hurst got to Yew Nook no one but Susan ever knew. They thought he had dragged himself there, with some sore, internal bruise sapping away his minuted life. They could not have believed the superhuman exertion which had first sought him out, and then dragged him hither. Only Susan knew of that.

She gave him into the charge of her servants, and went out and saddled her horse. Where the wind had drifted the snow on one side, and the road was clear and bare, she rode, and rode fast; where the soft, deceitful heaps were massed up, she dismounted and led her steed, plunging in deep, with fierce energy, the pain at her heart urging her onwards with a sharp, digging spur.

The gray, solemn, winter's noon was more night-like than the depth of summer's night; dim-purple brooded the low skies over the white earth, as Susan rode up to what had been Michael Hurst's abode while living. It was a small farm-house, carelessly kept outside, slatternly tended within. The pretty Nelly Hebthwaite was pretty still; her delicate face had never suffered from any long-enduring feeling. If anything, its expression was that of plaintive sorrow; but the soft, light hair had scarcely a tinge of gray; the wood-rose tint of complexion yet remained, if not so brilliant as in youth; the straight nose, the small mouth were untouched by time. Susan felt the contrast even at that moment. She knew that her own skin was weather-beaten, furrowed, brown,that her teeth were gone, and her hair gray and ragged. And yet she was not two years older than Nelly,she had not been, in youth, when she took account of these things.Nelly stood wondering at the strange-enough horsewoman, who stopped and panted at the door, holding her horse's bridle, and refusing to enter.

" Where is Michael Hurst ?" asked Susan, at last.

" Well, I can't rightly say. He should have been at home last night, but he was off, seeing after a public-house to be let at Ulverstone, for our farm does not answer, and we were thinking "

" He did not come home last night ?" said Susan, cutting short the story, and half-affirming, half-questioning, by way of letting in a ray of the awful light before she let it full in, in its consuming wrath.

" No! he'U be stopping somewhere out Ulverstone ways. I'm sure we've need of him at home, for I've no one but lile Tommy to help me tend the beasts. Things have not gone well with us, and we don't keep a servant now. But you're trembling all over, ma'am. You'd better come in, and take something warm, while your horse rests. That's the stable-door, to your left."

Susan took her horse there ; loosened his girths, and rubbed him down with a wisp of straw. Then she looked about her for hay; but the place was bare of food, and smelt damp and unused. She went to the house, thankful for the respite, and got some clap-bread, which she mashed up in a pailful of luke-warm water. Every moment was a respite, and yet every moment made her dread the more the task that lay before her. It would be longer than she thought at first. She took the saddle off, and hung about her horse, which seemed, somehow, more like a friend than anything else in the world. She laid her cheek against its neck, and rested there, before returning to the house for the last time.

Eleanor had brought down one of her own gowns, which hung on a chair against the fire, and had made her unknown visitor a cup of hot tea. Susan could hardly bear all these little attentions: they choked her, and yet she was so wet, so weak with fatigue and excitement, that she could neither resist by voice or by action. Two children stood awkwardly about, puzzled at the scene, and even Eleanor began to wish for some explanation of who her strange visitor was.

" You've, may-be, heard him speaking of me ? I'm called Susan Dixon.

Nelly coloured, and avoided meeting Susan's eye.

"I've heard other folk speak of you. He never named your name."

This respect of silence came like balm to Susan: balm not felt or heeded at the time it was applied, but very grateful in its effects for all that.

"He is at my house," continued Susan, determined not to stop or quaver in the operation—the pain which must be inflicted.

"At your house? Yew Nook?" questioned Eleanor, surprised. "How came he there?"—half jealously. "Did he take shelter from the coming storm? Tell me,—there is something—tell me, woman!"

"He took no shelter. Would to God he had!"

"O! would to God! would to God!" shrieked out Eleanor, learning all from the woful import of those dreary eyes. Her cries thrilled through the house; the children's piping wailings and passionate cries on "Daddy! Daddy!" pierced into Susan's very marrow. But she remained as still and tearless as the great round face upon the clock.

At last, in a lull of crying, she said,—not exactly questioning—but as if partly to herself—"You loved him, then?"

"Loved him! he was my husband! He was the father of three bonny bairns that lie dead in Grasmere Churchyard. I wish you'd go, Susan Dixon, and let me weep without your watching me! I wish you'd never come near the place."

"Alas! alas! it would not have brought him to life. I would have laid down my own to save his. My life has been so very sad! No one would have cared if I had died. Alas! alas!"

The tone in which she said this was so utterly mournful and despairing that it awed Nelly into quiet for a time. But by-and-by she said, "I would not turn a dog out to do it harm; but the night is clear, and Tommy shall guide you to the Red Cow. But, O! I want to be alone. If you'll come back tomorrow, I'll be better, and I'll hear all, and thank you for every kindness you have shown him,—and I do believe you've showed him kindness,—though I don't know why."

Susan moved heavily and strangely.

She said something—her words came thick and unintelligible. She had had a paralytic stroke since she had last spokea She could not go, even if she would. Nor did Eleanor, when she became aware of the state of the case, wish her to leave. She had her laid on her own bed, and weeping silently all the while for her lost husband, she nursed Susan like a sister. She did not know what her guest's worldly position might be; and she might never be repaid. But she sold many a little trifle to purchase such small comforts as Susan needed. Susan, lying still and motionless, learnt much. It was not a severe stroke; it might be the forerunner of others yet to come, but at some distance of time. But for the present she recovered, and regained much of her former health.

On her sick-bed she matured her plans. When she returned to Yew Nook, she took Michael Hurst's widow and children with her to live there, and fill up the haunted hearth with living forms that should banish the ghosts.

And so it fell out that the latter days of Susan Dixon's life were better than the former.

WHEN this narrative was finished, Mrs. Dawson called on our two gentlemen, Signer Sperano and Mr. Preston, and told them that they had hitherto been amused or interested, but that it was now their turn to amuse or interest. They looked at each other as if this application of hers took them by surprise, and seemed altogether as much abashed as well-grown men can ever be. Signer Sperano was the first to recover himself: after thinking a little, he said :—

"Your will, dear Lady, is law. Next Monday evening, I will bring you an old, old story, which I found among the papers of the good old Priest who first welcomed me to England. It was but a poor return for his generous kindness; but I had the opportunity of nursing him through the cholera, of which he died. He left me all that he had—no money—but his scanty furniture, his book of prayers, his crucifix and rosary, and his papers. How some of those papers came into his hands I know not. They had evidently been written many years before the venerable man was born; and I doubt whether he had ever examined the bundles, which had come down

to him from some old ancestor, or in some strange bequest. His life was too busy to leave any time for the gratification of mere curiosity; I, alas! have only had too much leisure."

Next Monday, Signer Sperano read to us the story which I will call

"THE POOR CLARE."

THE POOR CLARE.

CHAPTER I.

DECEMBEB 12th, 1747.—My life has been strangely bound up with extraordinary incidents, some of which occurred before I had any connection with the principal actors in them, or, indeed, before I even knew of their existence. I suppose, most old men are, like me, more given to looking back upon their own career with a kind of fond interest and affectionate remembrance, than to watching the events—though these may have far more interest for the multitude — immediately passing before their eyes. If this should be the case with the generality of old people, how much more so with me! . . . . If I am to enter upon that strange story connected with poor Lucy, I must begin a long way back. I myself only came to the knowledge of her family history after I knew her; but, to make

the tale clear to any one else, I must arrange events in the order in which they occurred—not that in which I became acquainted with them.

There is a great old hall in the north-east of Lancashire, in a part they call the Trough of Bolland, adjoining that other district named Craven. Starkey Manor-House is rather like a number of rooms clustered round a gray, massive, old keep than a regularly-built hall. Indeed, I suppose that the house only consisted of the great tower in the centre, in the days when the Scots made their raids terrible as far south as this; and that after the Stuarts came in, and there was a little more security of property in those parts, the Starkeys of that time added the lower building, which runs, two stories high, all round the base of the keep. There has been a grand garden laid out in my days, on the southern slope near the house; but when I first knew the place, the kitchen-garden at the farm was the only piece of cultivated ground belonging to it. The deer used to come within sight of the drawing-room windows, and might have browsed quite close up to the house if they had not been too wild and shy. Starkey Manor-House itself stood on a projection or peninsula of high land, jutting out from the abrupt hills that form the sides of the Trough of Bolland. These hills were rocky and

bleak enough towards their summit; lower down they were clothed with tangled copse wood and green depths of fern, out of which a gray giant of an ancient forest-tree would tower here and there, throwing up its ghastly white branches, as if in imprecation, to the sky. These trees, they told me, were the remnants of that forest which existed in the days of the Heptarchy, and were even then noted as landmarks. No wonder that their upper and more exposed branches were leafless, and that the dead bark had peeled away, from sapless old age.

Not far from the house there were a few cottages, apparently of the same date as the keep; probably built for some retainers of the family, who sought shelter—they and their families and their small flocks and herds—at the hands of their feudal lord. Some of them had pretty much fallen to decay. They were built in a strange fashion. Strong beams had been sunk firm in the ground at the requisite distance, and their other ends had been fastened together, two and two, so as to form the shape of one of those rounded waggon-headed gipsy-tents, only very much larger. The spaces between were filled with mud, stones, osiers, rubbish, mortar—anything to keep out the weather. The fires were made in the centre of these rude dwellings, a hole in the roof forming the only chimney. No Highland hut or Irish cabin could be of rougher construction.

The owner of this property, at the beginning of the present century, was a Mr. Patrick Byrne Starkey. His family had kept to the old faith, and were staunch Roman Catholics, esteeming it even a sin to marry any one of Protestant descent, however willing he or she might have been to embrace 11 the Romish religion. Mr. Patrick Starkey's father had been a follower of James the Second; and, during the disastrous Irish campaign of that monarch, he had fallen in love with an Irish beauty, a Miss Byrne, as zealous for her religion and for the Stuarts as himself. He had returned to Ireland after his escape to France, and married her, bearing her back to the court at St. Ger-mains. But some licence on the part of the disorderly gentlemen who surrounded King James in his exile, had insulted his beautiful wife, and disgusted him ; so he removed from St. Germains to Antwerp, whence, in a few years' time, he quietly returned to Starkey Manor-House — some of his Lancashire neighbours having lent their good offices to reconcile him to the powers that were. He was as firm a Roman Catholic as ever, and as staunch an advocate for the Stuarts and the divine right of kings; but his religion almost amounted to asceticism, and the conduct of those with whom he had been brought-in such close contact at St. Germains would little bear the inspection of a stern moralist. So he gave his allegiance where he could not give his esteem, and learned to respect sincerely the upright and moral character of one whom he yet regarded as an usurper. King William's government had little need to fear such a one. So he returned, as I have said, with a sobered heart and impoverished fortunes, to his ancestral house, which had fallen sadly to ruin while the owner had been a courtier, a soldier, and an exile. The roads into the Trough of Bolland were little more than cart-ruts; indeed, the way up to the house lay along a ploughed field before you came to the deer-park. Madam, as the country-folk used to call Mrs. Starkey, rode on a pillion behind her husband, holding on to him with a light hand by his leather riding-belt. Little master (he that was afterwards Squire Patrick Byrne Starkey) was held on to his pony by a serving-man. A woman past middle age walked, with a firm and strong step, by the cart that held much of the baggage; and, high up on the mails and boxes, sat a girl of dazzling beauty, perched lightly on the topmost trunk, and swaying herself fearlessly to and fro, as the cart rocked and shook in the heavy roads of late autumn. The girl wore the Antwerp faille, or black Spanish mantle over her head, and altogether her appearance was such that the old cottager, who described the procession to me many years after, said that all the country-folk took her for a foreigner. Some dogs, and the boy who held them in charge, made up the company. They rode silently along, looking with grave, serious eyes at the people, who came out of the scattered cottages to bow or curtsy to the real Squire, " come back at last," and gazed after the little procession with gaping wonder, not deadened by the sound of the foreign language in which the few necessary words that passed among them were spoken. One lad, called from his staring by the Squire to come and help about the cart, accompanied them to the Manor-House. He said that when the lady had descended from her pillion, the middle-aged woman whom I have described as walking while the others rode, stepped quickly forward, and taking Madam Starkey (who was of a slight and delicate figure) in her arms, she lifted her over the threshold, and set her down in her husband's house, at the same time uttering a passionate and outlandish blessing. The Squire stood by, smiling gravely at first; but when the words of blessing were pronounced, he took off his fine feathered hat, and bent his head. The girl with the black mantle stepped onward into the shadow of the dark hall, and kissed the lady's hand; and that was all the lad could tell to the group that gathered round him on his return, eager to hear everything, and to know how much the Squire had given him for his services.

From all I could gather, the Manor-House, at the time of the Squire's return, was in the most dilapidated state. The stout gray walls remained firm and entire; but the inner chambers had been used for all kinds of purposes. The great withdrawing-room had been a barn; the state tapestry-chamber had held wool, and so on. But, by-and-by, they were cleared out; and if the Squire had no money to spend on new furniture, he and his wife had the knack of making the best of the old. He was no despicable joiner; she had a kind of grace in whatever she did, and imparted an air of elegant picturesqueness to whatever she touched. Besides, they had brought many rare things from the Continent; perhaps I should rather say, things that were rare in that part of England— carvings, and crosses, and beautiful pictures. And then, again, wood was plentiful in the Trough of Bolland, and great log-fires danced and glittered in all the dark, old rooms, and gave a look of home and comfort to everything.

Why do I tell you all this ? I have little to do with the Squire and Madam Starkey; and yet I dwell upon them, as if I were unwilling to come to the real people with whom my life was so strangely mixed up. Madam had been nursed in Ireland by the very woman who lifted her in her arms, and welcomed her to her husband's home in Lancashire. Excepting for the short period of her own married life, Bridget Fitzgerald had never left her nursling. Her marriage—to one above her in rank—had been unhappy. Her husband had died, and left her in even greater poverty than that in which she was when he had first met with her. She had one child, the beautiful daughter who came riding on the waggon-load of furniture that was brought to the Manor-House. Madam Starkey had taken her again into her service when she became a widow. She and her daughter had followed " the mistress " in all her fortunes; they had lived at St. Germains and at Antwerp, and were now come to her home in Lancashire. As soon as Bridget had arrived there, the Squire gave her a cottage of her own, and took more pains in furnishing it for her than he did in anything else out of his own house. It was only nominally her residence. She was constantly up at the great house; indeed, it was but a short cut across the woods from her own home to the home of her nursling. Her daughter Mary, in like manner, moved from one house to the other at her own will. Madam loved both mother and child dearly. They had great influence over her, and, through her, over her husband. Whatever Bridget or Mary willed was sure to come to pass. They were not disliked; for, though wild and passionate, they were also generous by nature. But the other servants were afraid of them, as being in secret the ruling spirits of the household. The Squire had lost his interest in all secular things; Madam was gentle, affectionate, and yielding. Both husband and wife were tenderly attached to each other and to their boy; but they grew more and more to shun the trouble of decision on any point; and hence it was that Bridget could exert such despotic power. But if every one else yielded to her " magic of a superior mind," her daughter not unfrequently rebelled. She and her mother were too much alike to agree. There were wild quarrels between them, and wilder reconciliations. There were times when, in the heat of passion, they could have stabbed each other. At all other times they both—Bridget especially— would have willingly laid down their lives for one another. Bridget's love for her child lay very deep— deeper than that daughter ever knew; or I should think she would never have wearied of home as she did, and prayed her mistress to obtain for her some situation—as waiting-maid—beyond the seas, in that more cheerful continental life, among the scenes of which so many of her happiest years had been spent. She thought, as youth thinks, that life would last for ever, and that two or three years were but a small portion of it to pass away from her mother, whose only child she was. Bridget thought differently, but was too proud ever to show what she felt If her child wished to leave her, why—she should go. But people said Bridget became ten years older in the course of two months at this time. She took it that Mary wanted to leave her. The truth was, that Mary wanted for a time to leave the place, and to seek some change, and would thankfully have taken her mother with her. Indeed, when Madam Starkey had gotten her a situation with some grand lady abroad, and the time drew near for her to go, it was Mary who clung to her mother with passionate embrace, and, with floods of tears, declared that she would never leave her; and it was Bridget, who at last loosened her arms, and, grave and tearless herself, bade her keep her word, and go forth into the wide world. Sobbing aloud, and looking back continually, Mary went away. Bridget was still as death, scarcely drawing her breath, or closing her stony eyes; till at last she turned back into her cottage, and heaved a ponderous old settle against the door. There she sat, motionless, over the

gray ashes of her extinguished fire, deaf to Madam's sweet voice, as she begged leave to enter and comfort her nurse. Deaf, stony, and motionless, she sat for more than twenty hours; till, for the third time, Madam came across the snowy path from the great house, carrying with her a young spaniel, which had been Mary's pet up at the hall, and which had not ceased all night long to seek for its absent mistress, and to whine and moan after her. With tears Madam told this story, through the closed door—tears excited by the terrible look of anguish, so steady, so immovable—so the same to-day as it was yesterday—on her nurse's face. The little creature in her arms began to utter its piteous cry, as it shivered with the cold. Bridget stirred; she moved—she listened. Again that long whine ; she thought it was for her daughter; and what she had denied to her nursling and mistress she granted to the dumb creature that Mary had cherished. She opened the door, and took the dog from Madam's arms. Then Madam came in, and kissed and comforted the old woman, who took but little notice of her or anything. And sending up Master Patrick to the hall for fire and food, the sweet young lady never left her nurse all that night. Next-day, the Squire himself came down, carrying a beautiful foreign picture: Our Lady of the Holy

Heart, the Papists call it. It is a picture of the Virgin, her heart pierced with arrows, each arrow representing one of her great woes. That picture hung in Bridget's cottage when I first saw her; I have that picture now.

Years went on. Mary was still abroad. Bridget was still and stern, instead of active and passionate. The little dog, Mignon, was indeed her darling. I have heard that she talked to it continually; although, to most people, she was so silent. The Squire and Madam treated her with the greatest consideration, and well they might; for to them she was as devoted and faithful as ever. Mary wrote pretty often, and seemed satisfied with her life. But at length the letters ceased—I hardly know whether before or after a great and terrible sorrow came upon the house of the Starkeys. The Squire sickened of a putrid fever ; and Madam caught it in nursing him, and died. You may be sure, Bridget let no other woman tend her but herself; and in the very arms that had received her at her birth, that sweet young woman laid her head down, and gave up her breath. The Squire recovered, in a fashion. He was never strong—he had never the heart to smile again. He fasted and prayed more than ever; and people did say that he tried to cut off the entail, and leave all the property

away to found a monastery abroad, of which he prayed that some day little Squire Patrick might be the reverend father. But he could not do this, for the strictness of the entail and the laws against the Papists. So he could only appoint gentlemen of his own faith as guardians to his son, with many charges about the lad's soul, and a few about the land, and the way it was to be held while he was a minor. Of course, Bridget was not forgotten. He sent for her as he lay on his death-bed, and asked her if she would rather have a sum down, or have a small annuity settled upon her. She said at once she would have a sum down; for she thought of her daughter, and how she could bequeath the money to her, whereas an annuity would have died with her. So the Squire left her her cottage for life, and a fair sum of money. And then he died, with as ready and willing a heart as, I suppose, ever any gentleman took out of this world with him. The young Squire was carried off by his guardians, and Bridget was left alone.

I have said that she had not heard] from Mary for some time. In her last letter, she had told of travelling about with her mistress, who was the English wife of some great foreign officer, and had spoken of her chances of making a good marriage, without naming the gentleman's name, keeping it rather back as a

pleasant surprise to her mother; his station and fortune being, as I had afterwards reason to know, far superior to anything she had a right to expect. Then came a long silence; and Madam was dead, and the Squire was dead ; and Bridget's heart was gnawed by anxiety, and she knew not whom to ask for news of her child. She could not write, and the Squire had managed her communication with her daughter. She walked off to Hurst; and got a good priest there— one whom she had known at Antwerp—to write for her. But no answer came. It was like crying into the awful stillness of night.

One day, Bridget was missed by those neighbours who had been accustomed to mark her goings-out and comings-in. She had never been sociable with any of them; but the sight of her had become a part of their daily lives, and slow wonder arose in their minds, as morning after morning came, and her house-door remained closed, her window dead from any glitter, or light of fire within. At length, some one tried the door; it was locked. Two or three laid their heads together, before daring to look in through the blank, unshuttered window. But, at last, they summoned up courage ; and then saw that Bridget's absence from their little world was not the result of accident or death, but of premeditation. Such small articles of furniture as could be secured from the effects of time and damp by being packed up, were stowed away in boxes. The picture of the Madonna was taken down, and gone. In a word, Bridget had stolen away from her home, and left no trace whither she was departed. I knew afterwards, that she and her little dog had wandered off on the long search for her lost daughter. She was too illiterate to have faith in letters, even had she had the means of writing and sending many. But she had faith in her own strong love, and believed that her passionate instinct would guide her to her child. Besides, foreign travel was no new thing to her, and she could speak enough of French to explain the object of her journey, and had, moreover, the advantage of being, from her faith, a welcome object of charitable hospitality at many a distant convent. But the country people round Starkey Manor-House knew nothing of all this. They wondered what had become of her, in a torpid, lazy fashion, and then left off thinking of her altogether. Several years passed. Both Manor-House and cottage were deserted. The young Squire lived far away under the direction of his guardians. There were inroads of wool and corn into the sitting-rooms of the Hall; and there was some low talk, from time to time, among the hinds and country people, whether it would not be as well to break into

old Bridget's cottage, and save such of her goods as were left from the moth and rust which must be making sad havoc. But this idea was always quenched by the recollection of her strong character and passionate anger; and tales of her masterful spirit, and vehement force of will, were whispered about, till the very thought of offending her, by touching any article of hers, became invested with a kind of horror : it was believed that, dead or alive, she would not fail to avenge it.

Suddenly she came home; with as little noise or note of preparation as she had departed. One day, some one noticed a thin, blue curl of smoke, ascending from her chimney. Her door stood open to the noonday sun; and, ere many hours had elapsed, some one had seen an old travel-and-sorrow-stained woman dipping her pitcher in the well; and said, that the dark, solemn eyes that looked up at him were more like Bridget Fitzgerald's than any one else's in this world; and yet, if it were she, she looked as if she had been scorched in the flames of hell, so brown, and scared, and fierce a creature did she seem. By-and-by many saw her; and those who met her eye once cared not to be caught looking at her again. She had got into the habit of perpetually talking to herself; nay, more, answering herself, and varying her tones according to the side she took at the moment. It was no wonder that those who dared to listen outside her door at night, believed that she held converse with some spirit; in short, she was unconsciously earning for herself the dreadful reputation of a witch.

Her little dog, which had wandered half over the Continent with her, was her only companion; a dumb remembrancer of happier days. Once he was ill; and she carried him more than three miles, to ask about his management from one who had been groom to the last Squire, and had then been noted for his skill in all diseases of animals. Whatever this man did, the dog recovered; and they who heard her thanks, intermingled with blessings (that were rather promises of good fortune than prayers), looked grave at his good luck when, next year, his ewes twinned, and his meadow-grass was heavy and thick.

Now it so happened that, about the year seventeen hundred and eleven, one of the guardians of the young Squire, a certain Sir Philip Tempest, bethought him of the good shooting there must be on his ward's property; and, in consequence, he brought down four or five gentlemen, of his friends, to stay for a w r eek or two at the Hall. From all accounts, they roystered and spent pretty freely. I never heard any of their names but one, and that was Squire Gisborne's. He was hardly a middle-aged man then; he had been much abroad, and there, I believe, he had known Sir Philip Tempest, and done him some service. He was a daring and dissolute fellow in those days: careless and fearless, and one who would rather be in a quarrel than out of it. He had his fits of ill-temper beside, when he would spare neither man nor beast. Otherwise, those who knew him well, used to say he had a good heart, when he was neither drunk, nor angry, nor in any way vexed. He had altered much when I came to know him.

One day. the gentlemen had all been out shooting, and with but little success, I believe; anyhow, Mr. Gisborne had had none, and was in a black humour accordingly. He was coming home, having his gun loaded, sportsman-like, when little Mignon crossed his path, just as he turned out of the wood by Bridget's cottage. Partly for wantonness, partly to vent his spleen upon some living creature, Mr. Gisborne took his gun, and fired—he had better have never fired gun again, than aimed that unlucky shot. He hit Mignon; and at the creature's sudden cry, Bridget came out, and saw at a glance what had been done. She took Mignon up in her arms, and looked hard at the ound; the poor dog looked at her with his glazing eyes, and tried to wag his tail and lick her hand, all covered with blood. Mr. Gisborne spoke in a kind of sullen penitence:

" You should have kept the dog out of my way—a little poaching varmint."

At this very moment, Mignon stretched out his legs, and stiffened in her arms—her lost Mary's dog, who had wandered and sorrowed with her for years. She walked right into Mr. Gisborne's path, and fixed his unwilling, sullen look with her dark and terrible eye.

" Those never throve that did me harm," said she. " I'm alone in the world, and helpless; the more do the Saints in Heaven hear my prayers. Hear me, ye blessed ones! hear me while I ask for sorrow on this bad, cruel man. He has killed the only creature that loved me—the dumb beast that I loved. Bring down heavy sorrow on his head for it, O ye Saints! He thought that I was helpless, because he saw me lonely and poor; but are not the armies of Heaven for the like of me?"

"Come, come," said he, half-remorseful, but not one whit afraid. "Here's a crown to buy thee another dog. Take it, and leave off cursing! I care none for thy threats."

"Don't you?" said she, coming a step closer, and changing her imprecatory cry for a whisper which made the gamekeeper's lad, following Mr. Gisborne, creep all over. "You shall live to see the creature you love best, and who alone loves you—ay, a human creature, but as innocent and fond as my poor, dead darling—you shall see this creature, for whom death would be too happy, become a terror and a loathing to all, for this blood's sake. Hear me, O holy Saints, who never fail them that have no other help!"

She threw up her right hand, filled with poor Mignon's life-drops; they spirted, one or two of them, on his shooting-dress,—an ominous sight to the follower. But the master only laughed a little, forced, scornful laugh, and went on to the Hall. Before he got there, however, he took out a gold piece, and bade the boy carry it to the old woman on his return to the village. The lad was "afeared," as he told me in after years; he came to the cottage, and hovered about, not daring to enter. He peeped through the window at last; and by the flickering wood-flame, he saw Bridget kneeling before the picture of our Lady of the Holy Heart, with dead Mignon lying between her and the Madonna. She was praying wildly, as her outstretched arms betokened. The lad shrank away in redoubled terror; and contented himself with slipping the gold-piece under the ill-fitting door. The next day it was thrown out upon the midden; and there it lay, no one daring to touch it.

Meanwhile Mr. Gisborne, half curious, half uneasy, thought to lessen his uncomfortable feelings by asking Sir Philip who Bridget was? He could only describe her—he did not know her name. Sir Philip was equally at a loss. But an old servant of the Starkeys, who had resumed his livery at the Hall on this occasion—a scoundrel whom Bridget had saved from dismissal more than once during her palmy days— said:—

"It will be the old witch, that his worship means. She needs a ducking, if ever woman did, does that Bridget Fitzgerald."

"Fitzgerald!" said both the gentlemen at once. But Sir Philip was the first to continue :—

"I must have no talk of ducking her, Dickon. Why, she must be the very woman poor Starkey bade me have a care of; but when I came here last she was gone, no one knew where. I'll go and see her tomorrow. But mind you, sirrah, if any harm comes to her, or any more talk of her being a witch—I've a pack of hounds at home, who can follow the scent of a lying knave as well as ever they followed a dogfox; so take care how you talk about ducking a faithful old servant of your dead master's."

"Had she ever a daughter?" asked Mr. Gisborne, after a while.

"I don't know—yes! I've a notion she had; a kind of waiting-woman to Madam Starkey."

"Please your worship," said humbled Dickon, "Mistress Bridget had a daughter—one Mistress Mary—who went abroad, and has never been heard on since; and folk do say that has 'crazed her mother."

Mr. Gisborne shaded his eyes with his hand.

"I could wish she had not cursed me," he muttered. "She may have power—no one else could." After a while, he said aloud, no one understanding rightly what he meant, "Tush! it's impossible!"—and called for claret; and he and the other gentlemen set-to to a drinking-bout.

CHAPTER IL

I NOW come to the time in which I myself was mixed up with the people that I have been writing about And to make you understand how I became connected with them, I must give you some little account of myself. My father was the younger son of a Devonshire gentleman of moderate property; my eldest uncle succeeded to the estate of his forefathers, my second became an eminent attorney in London, and my father took orders. Like most poor clergymen, he had a large family; and I have no doubt was glad enough when my London uncle, who was a bachelor, offered to take charge of me, and bring me up to be his successor in business.

In this way I came to live in London, in my uncle's house, not far from Gray's Inn, and to be treated and esteemed as his son, and to labour with him in his office. I was very fond of the old gentleman. He was the confidential agent of many country squires, and had attained to his present position as much by

knowledge of human nature as by knowledge of law; though he was learned enough in the latter. He used to say his business was law, his pleasure heraldry. From his intimate acquaintance with family history, and all the tragic courses of life therein involved, to hear him talk, at leisure times, about any coat of arms that came across his path was as good as a play or a romance. Many cases of disputed property, dependent on a love of genealogy, were brought to him, as to a great authority on such points. If the lawyer who came to consult him was young, he would take no fee, only give him a long lecture on the importance of attending to heraldry; if the lawyer was of mature age and good standing, he would mulct him pretty well, and abuse him to me afterwards as negligent of one great branch of the profession. His house was in a stately new street called Ormond Street, and in it he had a handsome library; but all the books treated of things that were past; none of them planned or looked forward into the future. I worked away—partly for the sake of my family at home, partly because my uncle had really taught me to enjoy the kind of practice in which he himself took such delight. I suspect I worked too hard ; at any rate, in seventeen hundred and eighteen I was far from well, and my good uncle was disturbed by my ill looks.

One day, he rang the bell twice into the clerk's room at the dingy office in Gray's Inn Lane. It was the summons for me, and I went into his private room just as a gentleman—whom I knew well enough by sight as an Irish lawyer of more reputation than he deserved—was leaving.

My uncle was slowly rubbing his hands together and considering. I was there two or three minutes before he spoke. Then he told me that I must pack up my portmanteau that very afternoon, and start that night by post-horse for West Chester. I should get there, if all went well, at the end of five days' time, and must then wait for a packet to cross over to Dublin; from thence I must proceed to a certain town named Kildoon, and in that neighbourhood I was to remain, making certain inquiries as to the existence of any descendants of the younger branch of a family to whom some valuable estates had descended in the female line. The Irish lawyer whom I had seen was weary of the case, and would willingly have given Up the property, without further ado, to a man who appeared to claim them; but on laying his tables and trees before my uncle, the latter had foreseen so many possible prior claimants, that the lawyer had begged him to undertake the management of the whole business. In his youth, my uncle would have liked

nothing better than going over to Ireland himself, and ferreting out every scrap of paper or parchment, and every word of tradition respecting the family. As it was, old and gouty, he deputed me.

Accordingly, I went to Kildoon. I suspect I had something of my uncle's delight in following up a genealogical scent, for I very soon found out, when on the spot, that Mr. Rooney, the Irish lawyer, would have got both himself and the first claimant into a terrible scrape, if he had pronounced his opinion that the estates ought to be given up to him. There were three poor

Irish fellows, each nearer of kin to the last possessor; but, a generation before, there was a still nearer relation, who had never been accounted for, nor his existence ever discovered by the lawyers, I venture to think, till I routed him out from the memory of some of the old dependants of the family. What had become of him ? I travelled backwards and forwards ; I crossed over to France, and came back again with a slight clue, which ended in my discovering that, wild and dissipated himself, he had left one child, a son, of yet worse character than his father; that this same Hugh Fitzgerald had married a very beautiful serving-woman of the Byrnes— a person below him in hereditary rank, but above him in character; that he had died soon after his marriage, leaving one child,

whether a boy or a girl I could not learn, and that the mother had returned to live in the family of the Byrnes. Now, the chief of this latter family was serving in the Duke of Berwick's regiment, and it was long before I could hear from him; it was more than a year before I got a short, haughty letter—I fancy he had a soldier's contempt for a civilian, an Irishman's hatred for an Englishman, an exiled Jacobite's jealousy of one who prospered and lived tranquilly under the government he looked upon as an usurpation. " Bridget Fitzgerald," he said, " had been faithful to the fortunes of his sister—had followed her abroad, and to England when Mrs. Starkey had thought fit to return. Both her sister and her husband were dead; he knew nothing of Bridget Fitzgerald at the present time: probably Sir Philip Tempest, his nephew's guardian, might be able to give me some information." I have not given the little contemptuous terms; the way in which faithful service was meant to imply more than it said—all that has nothing to do with my story. Sir Philip, when applied to, told me that he paid an annuity regularly to an old woman named Fitzgerald, living at Coldholme (the village near Starkey Manor-House). Whether she had any descendants he could not say.

One bleak March evening, I came in sight of the

places described at the beginning of my story. I could hardly understand the rude dialect in which the direction to old Bridget's house was given.

" Yo' see yon furleets," all run together, gave me no idea that I was to guide myself by the distant lights that shone in the windows of the Hall, occupied for the time by a farmer who held the post of steward, while the Squire, now four or five and twenty, was making the grand tour. However, at last, I reached Bridget's cottage—a low, moss-grown place; the palings that had once surrounded it were broken and gone; and the underwood of the forest came up to the walls, and must have darkened the windows. It was about seven o'clock—not late to my London notions—but, after knocking for some time at the door and receiving no reply, I was driven to conjecture that the occupant of the house was gone to bed. So I betook myself to the nearest church I had seen, three miles back on the road I had come, sure that close to that I should find an inn of some kind; and early the next morning I set off back to Coldholme, by a field-path which my host assured me I should find a shorter cut than the road I had taken the night before. It was a cold, sharp morning; my feet left prints in the sprinkling of hoar-frost that covered the ground; nevertheless, I saw an old woman, whom I instinctively

suspected to be the object of my search, in a sheltered covert on one side of my path. I lingered and watched her. She must have been considerably above the middle size in her prime, for when she raised herself from the stooping position in which I first saw her, there was something fine and commanding in the erectness of her figure. She drooped again in a minute or two, and seemed looking for something on the ground, as, with bent head, she turned off from the spot where I gazed upon her, and was lost to my sight. I fancy I missed my way, and made a round in spite of the landlord's directions; for by the time I had reached Bridget's cottage she was there, with no semblance of hurried walk or discomposure of any kind. The door was slightly ajar. I knocked, and the majestic figure stood before me, silently awaiting the explanation of my errand. Her teeth were all gone, so the nose and chin were brought near together; the gray eyebrows were straight, and almost hung over her deep, cavernous eyes, and the thick white hair lay in silvery masses over the low, wide, wrinkled forehead. For a moment, I stood uncertain how to shape my answer to the solemn questioning of her silence.

" Your name is Bridget Fitzgerald, I believe ?"

She bowed her head in assent.

" I have something to say to you. May I come in ? I am unwilling to keep you standing."

" You cannot tire me," she said, and at first she seemed inclined to deny me the shelter of her roof. But the next moment—she had searched the very soul in me with her eyes during that instant—she led me in, and dropped the shadowing hood of her gray, draping cloak, which had previously hid part of the character of her countenance. The cottage was rude and bare enough. But before that picture of the Virgin, of which I have made mention, there stood a little cup filled with fresh primroses. While she paid her reverence to the Madonna, I understood why she had been out seeking through the clumps of green in the sheltered copse. Then she turned round, and bade me be seated. The expression of her face, which all this time I was studying, was not bad, as the stories of my last night's landlord had led me to expect; it was a wild, stern, fierce, indomitable countenance, seamed and scarred by agonies of solitary weeping; but it was neither cunning nor malignant.

" My name is Bridget Fitzgerald," said she, by way of opening our conversation.

" And your husband was Hugh Fitzgerald, of Knock-Mahon, near Kildoon, in Ireland ?"

A faint light came into the dark gloom of her eyes.

"He was."

" May I ask if you had any children by him ?"

The light in her eyes grew quick and red. She tried to speak, I could see; but something rose in her throat, and choked her, and until she could speak calmly, she would fain not speak at all before a stranger. In a minute or so she said :

"I had a daughter—one Mary Fitzgerald,"—then her strong nature mastered her strong will, and she cried out, with a trembling, wailing cry : " Oh, man! what of her ?—what of her ?"

She rose from her seat, and came and clutched at my arm, and looked in my eyes. There she read, as I suppose, my utter ignorance of what had become of her child; for she went blindly back to her chair, and sat rocking herself and softly moaning, as if I were not there; I not daring to speak to the lone and awful woman. After a little pause, she knelt down before the picture of our Lady of the Holy Heart, and spoke to her by all the fanciful and poetic names of the Litany.

" O Rose of Sharon! O Tower of David! O Star of the Sea! have you no comfort for my sore heart ? Am I for ever to hope ? Grant me at least despair!"

—and so on she went, heedless of my presence. Her prayers grew wilder and wilder, till they seemed to me to touch on the borders of madness and blasphemy. Almost involuntarily, I spoke as if to stop her.

" Have you any reason to think that your daughter is dead?"

She rose from her knees, and came and stood before me.

"Mary Fitzgerald is dead," said she. "I shall never see her again in the flesh. No tongue ever told me. But I know she is dead. I have yearned so to see her, and my heart's will is fearful and strong: it would j have drawn her to me before now, if she had been a wanderer on the other side of the world. I wonder often it has not drawn her out of the grave to come and stand before me, and hear me tell her how I loved her. For, sir, we parted unfriends."

1 knew nothing but the dry particulars needed for my lawyer's quest, but I could not help

feeling for the desolate woman; and she must have read the unusual sympathy with her wistful eyes.

"Yes, sir, we did. She never knew how I loved her; and we parted unfriends; and I fear me that I wished her voyage might not turn out well, only meaning,—O, blessed Virgin! you know I only meant that she should come home to her mother's arms as to the happiest place on earth; but my wishes are terrible—their power goes beyond my thought—and there is no hope for me, if my words brought Mary harm."

"But," I said, "you do not know that she is dead. Even now, you hoped she might be alive. Listen to me," and I told her the tale I have already told you, giving it all in the driest manner, for I wanted to recall the clear sense that I felt almost sure she had possessed in her younger days, and by keeping up her attention to details, restrain the vague wildness of her grief.

She listened with deep attention, putting from time to time such questions as convinced me I had to do with no common intelligence, however dimmed and shorn by solitude and mysterious sorrow. Then she took up her tale; and in few brief words, told me of her wanderings abroad in vain search after her daughter; sometimes in the wake of armies, sometimes in camp, sometimes in city. The lady, whose waiting-woman Mary had gone to be, had died soon after the date of her last letter home; her husband, the foreign officer, had been serving in Hungary, whither Bridget had followed him, but too late to find him. Vague rumours reached her that Mary had made a great marriage; and this sting of doubt was added,— whether the mother might not be close to her child under her new name, and even hearing of her every day, and yet never recognising the lost one under the appellation she then bore. At length the thought took possession of her, that it was possible that all this time Mary might be at home at Coldholme, in the Trough of Bolland, in Lancashire, in England; and home came Bridget, in that vain hope, to her desolate hearth, and empty cottage. Here she had thought it safest to remain; if Mary was in life, it was here she would seek for her mother.

I noted down one or two particulars out of Bridget's narrative that I thought might be of use to me; for I was stimulated to further search in a strange and extraordinary manner. It seemed as if it were impressed upon me, that I must take up the quest where Bridget had laid it down; and this for no reason that had previously influenced me (such as my uncle's anxiety on the subject, my own reputation as a lawyer, and so on), but from some strange power which had taken possession of my will only that very morning, and which forced it in the direction it chose.

"I will go," said I. "I will spare nothing in the search. Trust to me. I will learn all that can be learnt You shall know all that money, or pains, or wit can discover. It is true she may be long dead: but she may have left a child."

"A child!" she cried, as if for the first time this idea had struck her mind. "Hear him, Blessed Virgin! he says she may have left a child. And you have never told me, though I have prayed so for a sign, waking or sleeping!"

"Nay," said I, "I know nothing but what you tell me. You say you heard of her marriage."

But she caught nothing of what I said. She was praying to the Virgin in a kind of ecstacy, which seemed to render her unconscious of my very presence.

From Coldholme I went to Sir Philip Tempest's. The wife of the foreign officer had been a cousin of his father's, and from him I thought I might gain some particulars as to the existence of the Count de la Pour d'Auvergne, and where I could find him; for I mew questions de vive voix aid the flagging recollec-;ion, and I was determined to lose no chance for want if trouble.

But Sir Philip had gone abroad, and it would be some time before I could receive an answer. So I followed my uncle's advice, to whom I had mentioned how wearied I felt, both in body and mind, by my will-o'-the-wisp search. He immediately told me to go to Harrogate, there to await Sir Philip's reply. I should be near to one of the places connected with

my search, Coldholme; not far from Sir Philip Tempest, in case he returned, and I wished to ask him any further questions; and, in conclusion, my uncle bade me try to forget all about my business for a time.

This was far easier said than done. I have seen a child on a common blown along by a high wind, without power of standing still and resisting the tempestuous force. I was somewhat in the same predicament as regarded my mental state. Something resistless seemed to urge my thoughts on, through every possible course by which there was a chance of attaining to my object. I did not see the sweeping moors when I walked out: when I held a book in my hand, and read the words, their sense did not penetrate to my brain. If I slept, I went on with the same ideas, always flowing in the same direction. This could not last long without having a bad effect on the body. I had an illness, which, although I was racked with pain, was a positive relief to me, as it compelled me to live in the present suffering, and not in the visionary researches I had been continually making before. My kind uncle came to nurse me; and after the immediate danger was over, my life seemed to slip away in delicious languor for two or three months. I did not ask—so much did I dread falling into the old

channel of thought—whether any reply had been received to my letter to Sir Philip. I turned my whole imagination right away from all that subject. My uncle remained with me until nigh summer, and then returned to his business in London; leaving me perfectly well, although not completely strong. I was to follow him in a fortnight; when, as he said, " we would look over letters, and talk about several things." I knew what this little speech alluded to, and shrank from the train of thought it suggested, which was so intimately connected with my first feelings of illness. However, I had a fortnight more to roam on those invigorating Yorkshire moors.

In those days, there was one large, rambling inn at Harrogate, close to the Medicinal Spring; but it was already becoming too small for the accommodation of the influx of visitors, and many lodged round about, in the farm-houses of the district. It was so early in the season, that I had the inn pretty much to myself; and, indeed, felt rather like a visitor in a private house, so intimate had the landlord and landlady become with me during my long illness. She would chide me for being out so late on the moors, or for having been too long without food, quite in a motherly way; while he consulted me about vintages and wines, and taught me many a Yorkshire wrinkle about horses. In my walks

I met other strangers from time to time. Even before my uncle had left me, I had noticed, with half-torpid curiosity, a young lady of very striking appearance, who went about always accompanied by an elderly companion,—hardly a gentlewoman, but with something in her look that prepossessed me in her favour. The younger lady always put her veil down when any one approached; so it had been only once or twice, when I had come upon her at a sudden turn in the path, that I had even had a glimpse of her face. I am not sure if it was beautiful, though in after-life I grew to think it so. But it was at this time overshadowed by a sadness that never varied: a pale, quiet, resigned look of intense suffering, that irresistibly attracted me,—not with love, but with a sense of infinite compassion for one so young yet so hopelessly unhappy. The companion wore something of the same look: quiet, melancholy, hopeless, yet resigned. I asked my landlord who they were. He said they were called Clarke, and wished to be considered as mother and daughter; but that, for his part, he did not believe that to be their right name, or that there was any such relationship between them. They had been in the neighbourhood of Harrogate for some time, lodging in a remote farm-house. The people there would tell nothing about them ; saying that they paid handsomely, and never did any harm; so why should they be speaking of any strange things that might happen? That, as the landlord shrewdly observed, showed there was something out of the common way: he had heard that the elderly woman was a cousin of the farmer's where they lodged, and so the regard existing between relations might help to keep them quiet.

" What did he think, then, was the reason for their extreme seclusion ?" asked I.

" Nay, he could not tell, not he. He had heard that the young lady, for all as quiet as she seemed, played strange pranks at times." He shook his head when I asked him for more particulars, and refused to give them, which made me doubt if he knew any, for he was in general a talkative and communicative man. In default of other interests, after my uncle left, I set myself to watch these two people. I hovered about their walks, drawn towards them with a strange fascination, which was not diminished by their evident annoyance at so frequently meeting me. One day, I had the sudden good fortune to be at hand when they were alarmed by the attack of a bull, which, in those unenclosed grazing districts, was a particularly dangerous occurrence. I have other and more important things to relate, than to tell of the accident which gave me an opportunity of rescuing them ; it is enough to say, that this event was the beginning of an acquaintance, reluctantly acquiesced in by them, but eagerly prosecuted by me. I can hardly tell when intense curiosity became merged in love, but in less than ten days after my uncle's departure I was passionately enamoured of Mrs. Lucy, as her attendant called her; carefully—for this I noted well—avoiding any address which appeared as if there was an equality of station between them. I noticed also that Mrs. Clarke, the elderly woman, after her first reluctance to allow me to pay them any attentions had been overcome, was cheered by my evident attachment to the young girl; it seemed to lighten her heavy burden of care, and she evidently favoured my visits to the farm-house where they lodged. It was not so with Lucy. A more attractive person I never saw, in spite of her depression of manner, and shrinking avoidance of me. I felt sure at once, that whatever was the source of her grief, it rose from no fault of her own. It was difficult to draw her into conversation ; but when at times, for a moment or two, I beguiled her into talk, I could see a rare intelligence in her face, and a grave, trusting look in the soft, gray eyes that were raised for a minute to mine. I made every excuse I possibly could for going there. I sought wild flowers for Lucy's sake; I planned walks

for Lucy's sake; I watched the heavens by night, in hopes that some unusual beauty of sky would justify me in tempting Mrs. Clarke and Lucy forth upon the moors, to gaze at the great purple dome above.

It seemed to me that Lucy was aware of my love; but that, for some motive which I could not guess, she would fain have repelled me ; but then again I saw, or fancied I saw, that her heart spoke in my favour, and that there was a struggle going on in her mind, which at times (I loved so dearly) I could have begged her to spare herself, even though the happiness of my whole life should have been the sacrifice; for her complexion grew paler, her aspect of sorrow more hopeless, her delicate frame yet slighter. During this period I had written, I should say, to my uncle, to beg to be allowed to prolong my stay at Harrogate, not giving any reason; but such was his tenderness towards me, that in a few days I heard from him, giving me a willing permission, and only charging me to take care of myself, and not' use too much exertion during the hot weather.

One sultry evening I drew near the farm. The windows of their parlour were open, and I heard voices when I turned the corner of the house, as I passed the first window (there were two windows in their little ground-floor room). I saw Lucy distinctly; but when I had knocked at their door—the house-door stood always ajar—she was gone, and I saw only Mrs. Clarke, turning over the work-things lying on the table, in a nervous and purposeless manner. I felt by instinct that a conversation of some importance was coming on, in which I should be expected to say what was my object in paying these frequent visits. I was glad of the opportunity. My uncle had several times alluded to the pleasant possibility of my bringing home a young wife, to cheer and adorn the old house in Ormond Street. He was rich, and I was to succeed him, and had, as I knew, a fair reputation for so young a lawyer. So on my side I saw no obstacle. It was true that Lucy was shrouded in mystery; her name (I was convinced it was not Clarke), birth, parentage, and previous life were unknown to me. But I was sure of her goodness and sweet innocence, and although I knew that there must be something painful to be told, to account for her mournful sadness, yet I was willing to bear my share in her grief, whatever it might be.

Mrs. Clarke began, as if it was a relief to her to plunge into the subject.

" We have thought, sir—at least I have thought— that you know very little of us, nor we of you, indeed ; not enough to warrant the intimate acquaintance we

have fallen into. I beg your pardon, sir," she went on, nervously ; " I am but a plain kind of woman, and I mean to use no rudeness ; but I must say straight out that I—we—think it would be better for you not to come so often to see us. She is very unprotected, and "

" Why should I not come to see you, dear madam ?" asked I, eagerly, glad of the opportunity of explaining myself. " I come, I own, because I have learnt to love Mistress Lucy, and wish to teach her to love me."

Mistress Clarke shook her head, and sighed.

" Don't, sir—neither love her, nor, for the sake of all you hold sacred, teach her to love you! If I am too late, and you love her already, forget her,—forget these last few weeks. O! I should never have allowed you to come!" she went on, passionately ; " but what am I to do ? We are forsaken by all, except the great God, and even He permits a strange and evil power to afflict us—what am I to do ? Where is it to end?" She wrung her hands in her distress; then she turned to me: "Go away, sir; go away, before you learn to care any more for her. I ask it for your own sake—I implore. You have been good and kind to us, and we shall always recollect you with gratitude ; but go away now, and never come back to cross our fatal path !"

" Indeed, madam," said I, " I shall do no such thing.

You urge it for my own sake. I have no fear, so urged —nor wish, except to hear more— all. I cannot have seen Mistress Lucy in all the intimacy of this last fortnight, without acknowledging her goodness and innocence ; and without seeing,pardon me, madam—that for some reason you are two very lonely women, in some mysterious sorrow and distress. Now, though I am not powerful myself, yet I have friends who are so wise and kind, that they may be said to possess power. Tell me some particulars. Why are you in grief— what is your secret— why are you here? I declare solemnly that nothing you have said has daunted me in my wish to become Lucy's husband; nor will I shrink from any difficulty that, as such an aspirant, I may have to encounter. You say you are friendless why cast away an honest friend? I will tell you of people to whom you may write, and who will answer any questions as to my character and prospects. I do not shun inquiry."

She shook her head again. "You had better go away, sir. You know nothing about us."

"I know your names," said I, "and I have heard you allude to the part of the country from which you came, which I happen to know as a wild and lonely place. There are so few people living in it that, if I chose to go there, I could easily ascertain all about you ;

but I would rather hear it from yourself." You see I wanted to pique her into telling me something definite.

" You do not know our true names, sir," said she, hastily.

" Well, I may have conjectured as much. But tell me, then, I conjure you. Give me your reasons for distrusting my willingness to stand by what I have said with regard to Mistress Lucy."

" Oh, what can I do ?" exclaimed she. " If I am turning away a true friend as he says? —Stay!" coming to a sudden decision" I will tell you something—I cannot tell you all—you would not believe it. But, perhaps, I can tell you enough to prevent your going on in your hopeless attachment. I am not Lucy's mother."

" So I conjectured," I said. " Go on."

" I do not even know whether she is the legitimate or illegitimate child of her father. But he is cruelly turned against her; and her mother is long dead; and, for a terrible reason, she has no other creature to keep constant to her but me. She—only two years ago—such a darling and such a pride in her father's house ! Why, sir, there is a mystery that might happen in connection with her any moment; and then you would go away like all the rest; and, when you next heard her name, you would loathe her. Others, who have loved her longer, have done so before now. My poor child, whom neither God nor man has mercy upon or, surely, she would die!"

The good woman was stopped by her crying. I confess, I was a little stunned by her last words; but only for a moment. At any rate, till I knew definitely what was this mysterious stain upon one so simple and pure, as Lucy seemed, I would not desert her, and so I said; and she made answer:

" If you are daring in your heart to think harm of my child, sir, after knowing her as you have done, you are no good man yourself; but I am so foolish and helpless in my great sorrow, that I would fain hope to find a friend in you. I cannot help trusting that, although you may no longer feel towards her as a lover, you will have pity upon us; and perhaps, by your learning, you can tell us where to go for aid."

I implore you to tell me what this mystery is," I cried, almost maddened by this suspense.

"I cannot," said she, solemnly. "I am under a deep vow of secrecy. If you are to be told, it must be by her." She left the room, and I remained to ponder over this strange interview. I mechanically turned over the few books, and with eyes that saw nothing at the time, examined the tokens of Lucy's frequent presence in that room.

When I got home at night, I remembered how all these trifles spoke of a pure and tender heart and innocent life. Mistress Clarke returned; she had been crying sadly.

" Yes," said she, " it is as I feared: she loves you so much that she is willing to run the fearful risk of telling you all herself—she acknowledges it is but a poor chance; but your sympathy will be a balm, if you give it. To-morrow, come here at ten in the morning; and, as you hope for pity in your hour of agony, repress all show of fear or repugnance you may feel towards one so grievously afflicted."

I half smiled. "Have no fear," I said. It seemed too absurd to imagine my feeling dislike to Lucy.

" Her father loved her well," said she, gravely, " yet he drove her out like some monstrous thing."

Just at this moment came a peal of ringing laughter from the garden. It was Lucy's voice; it sounded as if she were standing just on one side of the open casement and as though she were suddenly stirred to merriment merriment verging on boisterousness, by the doings or sayings of some other person. I can scarcely say why, but the sound jarred on me inexpressibly. She knew the subject of our conversation, and must have been at least aware of the state of agitation her friend was in: she herself usually so gentle and quiet. I half rose to go to the window, and satisfy my instinctive curiosity as to what had provoked this burst of ill-timed laughter; but Mrs. Clarke threw her whole weight and power upon the hand with which she pressed and kept me down.

"For God's sake!" she said, white and trembling all over, " sit still; be quiet. Oh! be patient. Tomorrow you will know all. Leave us, for we are all sorely afflicted. Do not seek to know more about us."

Again that laugh so musical in sound, yet so discordant to my heart. She held me tight—tighter; without positive violence I could not have risen. I was sitting with my back to the window, but I felt a shadow pass between the sun's warmth and me, and a strange shudder ran through my frame. In a minute or two she released me.

" Go," repeated she. " Be warned, I ask you once more. I do not think you can stand this knowledge that you seek. If I had had my own way, Lucy should never have yielded, and promised to tell you all. Who knows what may come of it?"

" I am firm in my wish to know all. I return at ten to-morrow morning, and then expect to see Mistress Lucy herself."

I turned away; having my own suspicions, I confess, as to Mistress Clarke's sanity.

Conjectures as to the meaning of her hints, and uncomfortable thoughts connected with that strange laughter, filled my mind. I could hardly sleep. I rose early ; and long before the hour I had appointed, I was on the path over the common that led to the old farm-house where they lodged. I suppose that Lucy had passed no better a night than I; for there she was also, slowly pacing with her even step, her eyes bent down, her whole look most saintly and pure. She started when I came close to her, and grew paler as I reminded her of my appointment, and spoke with something of the impatience of obstacles that, seeing her once more, had called up afresh in my mind. All strange and terrible hints, and giddy merriment were forgotten. My heart gave forth words of fire, and my tongue uttered them. Her colour went and came, as she listened; but, when I had ended my passionate speeches, she lifted her soft eyes to me, and said—

" But you know that you have something to learn about me yet. I only want to say this: I shall not think less of you less well of you, I mean if you, too, fall away from me when you know all Stop!" said she, as if fearing another burst of mad words. " Listen to me. My father is a man of great wealth. I never knew my mother ; she must have died when I was very young. When first I remember anything, I

was living in a great, lonely house, with my dear and faithful Mistress Clarke. My father, even, was not there ; he was he is a soldier, and his duties lie abroad. But he came, from time to time, and every time I think he loved me more and more. He brought me rarities from foreign lands, which prove to me now how much he must have thought of me during his absences. I can sit down and measure the depth of his lost love now, by such standards as these. I never thought whether he loved me or not, then; it was so natural, that it was like the air I breathed. Yet he was an angry man at times, even then; but never with me. He was very reckless, too ; and, once or twice, I heard a whisper among the servants that a doom was over him, and that he knew it, and tried to drown his knowledge in wild activity, and even sometimes, sir, in wine. So I grew up in this grand mansion, in that lonely place. Everything around me seemed at my disposal, and I think every one loved me ; I am sure I loved them. Till about two years ago—I remember it well—my father had come to England, to us; and he seemed so proud and so pleased with me and all I had done. And one day his tongue seemed loosened with wine, and he told me much that I had not known till then,— how dearly he had loved my mother, yet how his wilful usage had caused her death ; and then he went on to say how he loved me better than any creature on earth, and how, some day, he hoped to take me to foreign places, for that he could hardly bear these long ab-scences from his only child. Then he seemed to change suddenly, and said, in a strange, wild way, that I was not to believe what he said; that there was many a thing he loved better his horse his dog I know not what.

" And 'twas only the next morning that, when I came into his room to ask his blessing as was my wont, he received me with fierce and angry words. ' Why had I,' so he asked, been delighting myself in such wanton mischief—dancing over the tender plants in the flower-beds, all set with the famous Dutch bulbs he had brought from Holland?' I had never been out of doors that morning, sir, and I could not conceive what he meant, and so I said; and then he swore at me for a liar, and said I was of no true blood, for he had seen me doing all that mischief himself with his own eyes. What could I say? He would not listen to me, and even my tears seemed only to irritate him. That day was the beginning of my great sorrows. Not long after, he reproached me for my undue familiarity all unbecoming a gentlewoman— with his grooms. I had been in the stable-yard, laughing and talking, he said. Now, sir> I am some-

thing of a coward by nature, and I had always dreaded horses; besides that, my father's servants—those whom he brought with him from foreign parts—were wild fellows, whom I had always avoided, and to whom I had never spoken, except as a lady must needs from time to time speak to her father's people. Yet my father called me by names of which I hardly know the meaning, but my heart told me they were such as shame any modest woman; and from that day he turned quite against me;—nay, sir, not many weeks after that, he came in with a riding-whip in his hand; and, accusing me harshly of evil doings, of which I knew no more than you, sir, he was about to strike me, and I, all in bewildering tears, was ready to take his stripes as great kindness compared to his harder words, when suddenly he stopped his arm mid-way, gasped and staggered, crying out, ' The curse—the curse!' I looked up in terror. In the great mirror opposite I saw myself, and, right behind, another wicked, fearful self, so like me that my soul seemed to quiver within me, as though not knowing to which similitude of body it belonged. My father saw my double at the same moment, either in its dreadful reality, whatever that might be, or in the scarcely less terrible reflection in the mirror; but what came of it at that moment I cannot say, for I suddenly swooned away; and when I came to myself I was lying in my bed, and my faithful Clarke sitting by me. I was in my bed for days; and even while I lay there my double was seen by all, flitting about the house and gardens, always about some mischievous or detestable work. What wonder that every one shrank from me in dread—that my father drove me forth at length, when the disgrace of which I was the cause was past his patience to bear. Mistress Clarke came with me; and here we try to live such a life of piety and prayer as may in time set me free from the curse."

All the time she had been speaking, I had been weighing her story in my mind. I had hitherto put cases of witchcraft on one side, as mere superstitions; and my uncle and I had had many an argument, he supporting himself by the opinion of his good friend Sir Matthew Hale. Yet this sounded like the tale of one bewitched; or was it merely the effect of a life of extreme seclusion telling on the nerves of a sensitive girl ? My scepticism inclined me to the latter belief, and when she paused I said:

" I fancy that some physician could have disabused your father of his belief in visions "

Just at that instant, standing as I was opposite to her in the full and perfect morning light, I saw behind her another figure—a ghastly resemblance, complete in

likeness, so far as form and feature and minutest touch of dress could go, but with a loathsome demon soul looking out of the gray eyes, that were in turns mocking and voluptuous. My heart stood still within me; every hair rose up erect; my flesh crept with horror. I could not see the grave and tender Lucy— my eyes were fascinated by the creature beyond. I know not why, but I put out my hand to clutch it; I grasped nothing but empty air, and my whole blood curdled to ice. For a moment I could not see; then my sight came back, and I saw Lucy standing before me, alone, deathly pale, and, I could have fancied, almost, shrunk in size.

" IT has been near me ?" she said, as if asking a question.

The sound seemed taken out of her voice; it was husky as the notes on an old harpsichord when the strings have ceased to vibrate. She read her answer in my face, I suppose, for I could not speak. Her look was one of intense fear, but that died away into an aspect of most humble patience. At length she seemed to force herself to face behind and around her: she saw the purple moors, the blue distant hills, quivering in the sunlight, but nothing else.

" Will you take me home ?" she said, meekly.

I took her by the hand, and led her silently through

the budding heather—we dared not speak; for we could not tell but that the dread creature was listening, although unseen, but that IT might appear and push us asunder. I never loved her more fondly than now when—and that was the unspeakable misery—the idea of her was becoming so inextricably blended with the shuddering thought of IT. She seemed to understand what I must be feeling. She let go my hand, which she had kept clasped until then, when we reached the garden gate, and went forwards to meet her anxious friend, who was standing by the window looking for her. I could not enter the house: I needed silence, society, leisure, change—I knew not what—to shake off the sensation of that creature's presence. Yet I lingered about the garden—I hardly know why; I partly suppose, because I feared to encounter the resemblance again on the solitary common, where it had vanished, and partly from a feeling of inexpressible compassion for Lucy. In a few minutes Mistress Clarke came forth and joined me. We walked some paces in silence.

" You know all now," said she, solemnly.

" I saw IT," said I, below my breath.

" And you shrink from us, now," she said, with a hopelessness which stirred up all that was brave or good in me.

" Not a whit," said I. " Human flesh shrinks from encounter with the powers of darkness: and, for some reason unknown to me, the pure and holy Lucy is their victim."

" The sins of the fathers shall be visited upon the children," she said.

"Who is her father?" asked I. "Knowing as much as I do, I may surely know more—know all. Tell me, I entreat you, madam, all that you can conjecture respecting this demoniac persecution of one so good."

" I will; but not now. I must go to Lucy now. Come this afternoon, I will see you alone ; and oh, sir! I will trust that you may yet find some way to help us in our sore trouble !"

I was miserably exhausted by the swooning affright which had taken possession of me. When I reached the inn, I staggered in like one overcome by wine. I went to my own private room. It was some time before I saw that the weekly post had come in, and brought me my letters. There was one from my uncle, one from my home in Devonshire, and one, re-directed over the first address, sealed with a great coat of arms. It was from Sir Philip Tempest: my letter of inquiry respecting Mary Fitzgerald had reached him at Liege, where it so happened that the Count de la Tour d'Auvergne was quartered at the very time. He remembered his wife's beautiful attendant; she had had high words with the deceased countess, respecting her intercourse with an English gentleman of good standing, who was also in the foreign service. The countess augured evil of his intentions; while Mary, proud and vehement, asserted that he would soon marry her, and resented her mistress's warnings as an insult. The consequence was, that she had left Madame de la Tour d'Auvergne's service, and, as the Count believed, had gone to live with the Englishman ; whether he had married her, or not, he could not say. " But," added Sir Philip Tempest, " you may easily hear what particulars you wish to know respecting Mary Fitzgerald from the Englishman himself, if, as .1 suspect, he is no other than my neighbour and former acquaintance, Mr. Gisborne, of Skipford Hall, in the West Riding. I am led to the belief that he is no other by several small particulars, none of which are in themselves conclusive, but which, taken together, make a mass of presumptive evidence. As far as I could make out from the Count's foreign pronunciation, Gisborne was the name of the Englishman : I know that Gisborne of Skipford was abroad and in the foreign service at that time—he was a likely fellow enough for such an exploit, and, above all, certain expressions recur to my mind which he used in reference to old Bridget Fitzgerald, of Coldholme, whom he once encountered while staying with me at Starkey Manor-House. I remember that the meeting seemed to have produced some extraordinary effect upon his mind, as though he had suddenly discovered some connection which she might have had with his previous life. I beg you to let me know if I can be of any further service to you. Your uncle once rendered me a good turn, and I will gladly repay it, so far as in me lies, to his nephew."

I was now apparently close on the discovery which I had striven so many months to attain. But success had lost its zest. I put my letters down, and seemed to forget them all in thinking of the morning I had passed that very day. Nothing was real but the unreal presence, which had come like an evil blast across my bodily eyes, and burnt itself down upon my brain. Dinner came, and went away untouched. Early in the afternoon I walked to the farm-house. I found Mistress Clarke alone, and I was glad and relieved. She was evidently prepared to tell me all I might wish to hear.

" You asked me for Mistress Lucy's true name; it is Gisborne," she began.

" Not Gisborne of Skipford ?" I exclaimed, breathless with anticipation.

" The same," said she, quietly, not regarding my manner. " Her father is a man of note; although, being a Roman Catholic, he cannot take that rank in this country to which his station entitles him. The consequence is that he lives much abroad—has been a soldier, I am told."

" And Lucy's mother ?" I asked

She shook her head. " I never knew her," said she. " Lucy was about three years old when I was engaged to take charge of her. Her mother was dead."

" But you know her name ?—you can tell if it was Mary Fitzgerald ?"

She looked astonished. " That was her name. But, sir, how came you to be so well acquainted with it ? It was a mystery to the whole household at Skipford Court. She was some beautiful young woman whom he lured away from her protectors while he was abroad. I have heard said he practised some terrible deceit upon her, and when she came to know it, she was neither to have nor to hold, but rushed off from his very arms, and threw herself into a rapid stream and was drowned. It stung him deep with remorse, but I used to think the remembrance of the mother's cruel death made him love the child yet dearer."

I told her, as briefly as might be, of my researches after the descendant and heir of the Fitzgeralds of

Kildoon, and added—something of ray old lawyer spirit returning into me for the moment—that I had no doubt but that we should prove Lucy to be by right possessed of large estates in Ireland.

No flush came over her gray face; no light into her eyes. " And what is all the wealth in the whole world to that poor girl ?" she said. " It will not free her from the ghastly bewitchment which persecutes her. As for money, what a pitiful thing it is; it cannot touch her."

" No more can the Evil Creature harm her," I said. " Her holy nature dwells apart, and cannot be defiled or stained by all the devilish arts in the whole world."

" True ! but it is a cruel fate to know that all shrink from her, sooner or later, as from one possessed— accursed."

" How came it to pass ?" I asked.

" Nay, I know not. Old rumours there are, that were bruited through the household at Skipford."

" Tell me," I demanded.

" They came from servants, who would fain account for everything. They say that, many years ago, Mr. Gisborne killed a dog belonging to an old witch at Coldholme ; that she cursed, with a dreadful and mysterious curse, the creature, whatever it might be, that he should love best; and that it struck so deeply

into his heart that for years he kept himself aloof from any temptation to love aught. But who could help loving Lucy ?"

" You never heard the witch's name ?" I gasped.

"Yes—they called her Bridget; they said he would never go near the spot again for terror of her. Yet he was a brave man!"

"Listen," said I, taking hold of her arm, the better to arrest her full attention; "if what I suspect holds true, that man stole Bridget's only child—the very Mary Fitzgerald who was Lucy's mother; if so, Bridget cursed him in ignorance of the deeper wrong he had done her. To this hour she yearns after her lost child, and questions the saints whether she be living or not. The roots of that curse lie deeper than she knows: she unwittingly banned him for a deeper guilt than that of killing a dumb beast. The sins of the fathers are indeed visited upon the children."

"But," said Mistress Clarke, eagerly, "she would never let evil rest on her own grandchild? Surely, sir, if what you say be true, there are hopes for Lucy. Let us go—go at once, and tell this fearful woman all that you suspect, and beseech her to take off the spell she has put upon her innocent grandchild."

It seemed to me, indeed, that something like this was the best course we could pursue. But first it was necessary to ascertain more than what mere rumour or careless hearsay could tell. My thoughts turned to my uncle—he could advise me wisely—he ought to know all. I resolved to go to him without delay; but I did not choose to tell Mistress Clarke of all the visionary plans that flitted through my mind. I simply declared my intention of proceeding straight to London on Lucy's affairs. I bade her believe that my interest on the young lady's behalf was greater than ever, and that my whole time should be given up to her cause. I saw that Mistress Clarke distrusted me, because my mind was too full of thoughts for my words to flow freely. She sighed and shook her head, and said, "Well, it is all right!" in such a tone that it was an implied reproach. But I was firm and constant in my heart, and I took confidence from that.

I rode to London. I rode long days drawn out into the lovely summer nights: I could not rest. I reached London. I told my uncle all, though in the stir of the great city the horror had faded away, and I could hardly imagine that he would believe the account I gave him of the fearful double of Lucy which I had seen on the lonely moor-side. But my uncle had lived many years, and learnt many things; and, in the deep secrets of family history that had been confided to him, he had heard of cases of innocent people bewitched and taken possession of by evil spirits yet more fearful than Lucy's. For, as he said, to judge from all I told him, that resemblance had no power over her—she was too pure and good to be tainted by its evil, haunting presence. It had, in all probability, so my uncle conceived, tried to suggest wicked thoughts and to tempt to wicked actions; but she, in her saintly maidenhood, had passed on undefiled by evil thought or deed. It could not touch her soul: but true, it set her apart from all sweet love or common human intercourse. My uncle threw himself with an energy more like six-and-twenty than sixty into the consideration of the whole case. He undertook the proving Lucy's descent, and volunteered to go and find out Mr. Gisborne, and obtain, firstly, the legal proofs of her descent from the Fifczgeralds of Kildoon, and, secondly, to try and hear all that he could respecting the working of the curse, and whether any and what means had been taken to exorcise that terrible appearance. For he told me of instances where, by prayers and long fasting, the evil possessor had been driven forth with howling and many cries from the body which it had come to inhabit; he spoke of those strange New England cases which had happened not so long before; of Mr. Defoe, who had written a book, wherein he had named many modes of subduing apparitions, and sending them back whence they came; and, lastly, he spoke low of dreadful ways of compelling witches to undo their witchcraft. But I could not endure to hear of those tortures and burnings. I said that Bridget was rather a wild and savage woman than a malignant witch; and, above all, that

Lucy was of her kith and kin; and that, in putting her to the trial, by water or by fire, we should be torturing—it might be to the death—the ancestress of her we sought to redeem.

My uncle thought awhile, and then said, that in this last matter I was right—at any rate, it should not be tried, with his consent, till all other modes of remedy had failed ; and he assented to my proposal that I should go myself and see Bridget, and tell her all.

In accordance with this, I went down once more to the wayside inn near Coldholme. It was late at night when I arrived there; and, while I supped, I inquired of the landlord more particulars as to Bridget's ways. Solitary and savage had been her life for many years. Wild and despotic were her words and manner to those few people who came across her path. The country-folk did her imperious bidding, because they feared to disobey. If they pleased her, they prospered ; if, on the contrary, they neglected or traversed her behests, misfortune, small or great, fell on them and theirs. It was not detestation so much as an indefinable terror that she excited.

In the morning I went to see her. She was standing on the green outside her cottage, and received me with the sullen grandeur of a throneless queen. I read in her face that she recognised me, and that I was not unwelcome; but she stood silent till I had opened my errand.

"I have news of your daughter," said I, resolved to speak straight to all that I knew she felt of love, and not to spare her. " She is dead!"

The stern figure scarcely trembled, but her hand sought the support of the door-post.

" I knew that she was dead," said she, deep and low, and then was silent for an instant. "My fears that should have flowed for her were burnt up long years ago. Young man, tell me about her."

" Not yet," said I, having a strange power given me of confronting one, whom, nevertheless, in my secret soul I dreaded.

"You had once a little dog," I continued. The words called out in her more show of emotion than the intelligence of her daughter's death. She broke in upon my speech :

" I had ! It was hers—the last thing I had of hers —and it was shot for wantonness! It died in my arms. The man who killed that dog rues it to this day. For that dumb beast's blood, his best-beloved stands accursed."

Her eyes distended, as if she were in a trance and saw the working of her curse. Again I spoke :

" O, woman !" I said, " that best-beloved, standing accursed before men, is your dead daughter's child."

The life, the energy, the passion came back to the eyes with which she pierced through me, to see if I spoke truth; then, without another question or word, she threw herself on the ground with fearful vehemence, and clutched at the innocent daisies with convulsed hands.

" Bone of my bone! flesh of my flesh! have I cursed thee—and art thou accursed ?"

So she moaned, as she lay prostrate in her great agony. I stood aghast at my own work. She did not hear my broken sentences; she asked no more, but the dumb confirmation which my sad looks had given that one fact, that her curse rested on her own daughter's child. The fear grew on me lest she should die in her strife of body and soul; and then might not Lucy remain under the spell as long as she lived ?

Even at this moment, I saw Lucy coming through the woodland path that led to Bridget's cottage; Mistress Clarke was with her: I felt at my heart that it was she, by the balmy peace which the look of her sent over me, as she slowly advanced, a glad surprise shining out of her soft quiet eyes. That was as her gaze met mine. As her looks fell on the woman lying stiff, convulsed on the earth, they became full of tender pity; and she came forward to try and lift her up. Seating herself on the turf, she took Bridget's head into her lap; and, with gentle touches, she arranged the dishevelled gray hair streaming thick and wild from beneath her mutch.

"God help her!" murmured Lucy. "How she suffers!"

At her desire we ^sought for water; but when we returned, Bridget had recovered her wandering senses, and was kneeling with clasped hands before Lucy, gazing at that sweet sad face as though her troubled nature drank in health and peace from every moment's contemplation. A faint tinge on Lucy's pale cheeks showed me that she was aware of our return; otherwise it appeared as if she was conscious of her influence for good over the passionate and troubled woman kneeling before her, and would not willingly avert her grave and loving eyes from that wrinkled and careworn countenance.

Suddenly—in the twinkling of an eye—the creature appeared, there, behind Lucy; fearfully the same as to outward semblance, but kneeling exactly as Bridget knelt, and clasping her hands in jesting mimicry as Bridget clasped hers in her ecstasy that was deepening into a prayer. Mistress Clarke cried out—Bridget arose slowly, her gaze fixed on the creature beyond: drawing her breath with a hissing sound, never moving her terrible eyes, that were steady as stone, she made a dart at the phantom, and caught, as I had done, a mere handful of empty air. We saw no more of the creature—it vanished as suddenly as it came, but Bridget looked slowly on, as if watching some receding form. Lucy sat still, white, trembling, drooping — I think she would have swooned if I had not been there to uphold her. While I was attending to her, Bridget passed us, without a word to any one, and, entering her cottage, she barred herself in, and left us without

All our endeavours were now directed to get Lucy back to the house where she had tarried the night before. Mistress Clarke told me that, not hearing from me (some letter must have miscarried), she had grown impatient and despairing, and had urged Lucy to the enterprise of coming to seek her grandmother; not telling her, indeed, of the dread reputation she possessed, or how we suspected her of having so fearfully blighted that innocent girl; but, at the same time, hoping much from the mysterious stirring of blood, which Mistress Clarke trusted in for the removal of the curse. They had come, by a different route from that which I had taken, to a village inn not far from Coldholme, only the night before. This was the first interview between ancestress and descendant.

All through the sultry noon I wandered along the tangled wood-paths of the old neglected forest, thinking where to turn for remedy in a matter so complicated and mysterious. Meeting a countryman, I asked my way to the nearest clergyman, and went, hoping to obtain some counsel from him. But he proved to be a coarse and common-minded man, giving no time or attention to the intricacies of a case, but dashing out a strong opinion involving immediate action. For instance, as soon as I named Bridget Fitzgerald, he exclaimed:—

"The Coldholme witch! the Irish papist! I'd have had her ducked long since but for that other papist, Sir Philip Tempest. He has had to threaten honest folk about here over and over again, or they'd have had her up before the justices for her black doings. And it's the law of the land that witches should be burnt! Ay, and of Scripture, too, sir!

Yet you see a papist, if he's a rich squire, can overrule both law and Scripture. I'd carry a faggot myself to rid the country of her!"

Such a one could give me no help. I rather drew back what I had already said; and tried to make the parson forget it, by treating him to several pots of beer, in the village inn, to which we had adjourned for our conference at his suggestion. I left him as soon as I could, and returned to

Coldholme, shaping my way past deserted Starkey Manor-House, and coming upon it by the back. At that side were the oblong remains of the old moat, the waters of which lay placid and motionless under the crimson rays of the setting sun; with the forest-trees lying straight along each side, and their deep-green foliage mirrored to blackness in the burnished surface of the moat below—and the broken sun-dial at the end nearest the hall—and the heron, standing on one leg at the water's edge, lazily looking down for fish—the lonely and desolate house scarce needed the broken windows, the weeds on the door-sill, the broken shutter softly flapping to and fro in the twilight breeze, to fill up the picture of desertion and decay. I lingered about the place until the growing darkness warned me on. And then I passed along the path, cut by the orders of the last lady of Starkey Manor-House, that led me to Bridget's

cottage. I resolved at once to see her ; and, in spite of closed doors—it might be of resolved will—she should see me. So I knocked at her door, gently, loudly, fiercely. I shook it so vehemently that at length the old hinges gave way, and with a crash it fell inwards, leaving rne suddenly face to face with Bridget—I, red, heated, agitated with my so long-baffled efforts—she, stiff as any stone, standing right facing me, her eyes dilated with terror, her ashen lips trembling, but her body motionless. In her hands she held her crucifix, as if by that holy symbol she sought to oppose my entrance. At sight of me, her whole frame relaxed, and she sank back upon a chair. Some mighty tension had given way. Still her eyes looked fearfully into the gloom of the outer air, made more opaque by the glimmer of the lamp inside, which she had placed before the picture of the Virgin. " Is she there ?" asked Bridget, hoarsely. " No ! Who ? I am alone. You remember me." " Yes," replied she, still terror-stricken. " But she that creature—has been looking in upon me through that window all day long. I closed it up with my shawl; and then I saw her feet below the door, as long as it was light, and I knew she heard my very breathing nay, worse, my very prayers; and I could not pray, for her listening choked the words

ere they rose to my lips. Tell me, who is she ?—what means that double girl I saw this morning ? One had a look of my dead Mary; but the other curdled my blood, and yet it was the same !"

She had taken hold of my arm, as if to secure herself some human companionship. She shook all over with the slight, never-ceasing tremor of intense terror. I told her my tale, as I have told it you, sparing none of the details.

How Mistress Clarke had informed me that the resemblance had driven Lucy forth from her father's house —how I had disbelieved, until, with mine own eyes, I had seen another Lucy standing behind my Lucy, the same in form and feature, but with the demon-soul looking out of the eyes. I told her all, I say, believing that she—whose curse was working so upon the life of her innocent grandchild—was the only person who could find the remedy and the redemption. When I had done, she sat silent for many minutes.

" You love Mary's child?" she asked.

" I do, in spite of the fearful working of the curse— I love her. Yet I shrink from her ever since that day on the moor-side. And men must shrink from one so accompanied; friends and lovers must stand afar off. Oh, Bridget Fitzgerald! loosen the curse! Set her free!"

" Where is she ?"

I eagerly caught at the idea that her presence was needed, in order that, by some strange prayer or exorcism, the spell might be reversed.

" I will go and bring her to you," I exclaimed. But Bridget tightened her hold upon my arm.

" Not so," said she, in a low, hoarse voice. " It would kill me to see her again as I saw her this morning. And I must live till I have worked my work. Leave me!" said she, suddenly, and again taking up the cross. " I defy the demon I have called up. Leave me to wrestle with it!"

She stood up, as if in an ecstasy of inspiration, from which all fear was banished. I lingered—why, I can hardly tell—until once more she bade me begone. As I went along the forest way, I looked back, and saw her planting the cross in the empty threshold, where the door had been.

The next morning Lucy and I went to seek her, to bid her join her prayers with ours. The cottage stood open and wide to our gaze. No human being was there : the cross remained on the threshold, but Bridget was gone.

CHAPTER III.

WHAT was to be done next ? was the question that I asked myself. As for Lucy, she would fain have submitted to the doom that lay upon her. Her gentleness and piety, under the pressure of so horrible a life, seemed over-passive to me. She never complained. Mrs. Clarke complained more than ever. As for me, I was more in love with the real Lucy than ever ; but I shrunk from the false similitude with an intensity proportioned to my love. I found out by instinct that Mrs. Clarke had occasional temptations to leave Lucy. The good lady's nerves were shaken, and, from what she said, I could almost have concluded that the object of the Double was to drive away from Lucy this last and almost earliest friend. At times, I could scarcely bear to own it, but I myself felt inclined to turn recreant; and I would accuse Lucy of being too patient —too resigned. One after another, she won the little children of Coldholme. (Mrs. Clarke and she had resolved to stay there, for was it not a,s good a place

as any other to such as they ? and did not all our faint hopes rest on Bridget—never seen or heard of now, but still we trusted to come back, or give some token ?) So, as I say, one after another, the little children came about my Lucy, won by her soft tones, and her gentle smiles, and kind actions. Alas! one after another they fell away, and shrunk from her path with blanching terror; and we too surely guessed the reason why. It was the last drop. I could bear it no longer. I resolved no more to linger around the spot, but to go back to my uncle, and among the learned divines of the city of London, seek for some power whereby to annul the curse.

My uncle, meanwhile, had obtained all the requisite testimonials relating to Lucy's descent and birth, from the Irish lawyers, and from Mr. Gisborne. The latter gentleman had written from abroad (he was again serving in the Austrian army), a letter alternately passionately self-reproachful and stoically repellent. It was evident that when he thought of Mary—her short life—how he had wronged her, and of her violent death, he could hardly find words severe enough for his own conduct; and from this point of view, the curse that Bridget had laid upon him and his was regarded by him as a prophetic doom, to the utterance of which she was moved by a Higher Power, working for the

fulfilment of a deeper vengeance than for the death of the poor dog. But then, again, when he came to speak of his daughter, the repugnance which the conduct of the demoniac creature had produced in his mind, was but ill disguised under a show of profound indifference as to Lucy's fate. One almost felt as if he would have been as content to put her out of existence, as he would have been to destroy some disgusting reptile that had invaded his chamber or his couch.

The great Fitzgerald property was Lucy's ; and that was all—was nothing.

My uncle and I sat in the gloom of a London November evening, in our house in Ormond Street. I was out of health, and felt as if I were in an inextricable coil of misery. Lucy and I wrote to each other, but that was little ; and we dared not see each other for dread of the fearful Third, who had more than once taken her place at our meetings. My uncle had, on the day I speak of, bidden prayers to be put up, on the ensuing Sabbath, in many a church and meeting-house in London, for one grievously tormented by an evil spirit. He had faith in prayers —I had none; I was fast losing faith in all things. So we sat —he trying to interest me in the old talk of other days, I oppressed by one thought—when our old servant, Anthony, opened the door, and, without speaking, showed in a very gentlemanly and prepossessing man, who had something remarkable about his dress, betraying his profession to be that of the Roman Catholic priesthood. He glanced at my uncle first, then at me. It was to me he bowed.

" I did not give my name," said he, " because you would hardly have recognised it ; unless, sir, when in the north, you heard of Father Bernard, the chaplain at Stoney Hurst ?"

I remembered afterwards that I had heard of him, but at the time I had utterly forgotten it ; so I professed myself a complete stranger to him ; while my ever-hospitable uncle, although hating a papist as much as it was in his nature to hate anything, placed a chair for the visitor, and bade Anthony bring glasses and a fresh jug of claret.

Father Bernard received this courtesy with the graceful ease and pleasant acknowledgment which belongs to the man of the world. Then he turned to scan me with his keen glance. After some slight conversation, entered into on his part, I am certain, with an intention of discovering on what terms of confidence I stood with my uncle, he paused, and said gravely—

" I am sent here with a message to you, sir, from a woman to whom you have shown kindness, and who

is one of my penitents, in Antwerp—one Bridget Fitzgerald."

" Bridget Fitzgerald I" exclaimed I. " In Antwerp? Tell me, sir, all that you can about her."

" There is much to be said," he replied. " But may I inquire if this gentleman—if your uncle is acquainted with the particulars of which you and I stand informed?"

" All that I know, he knows," said I, eagerly laying my hand on my uncle's arm, as he made a motion as if to quit the room.

" Then I have to speak before two gentlemen who, however they may differ from me in faith, are yet fully impressed with the fact, that there are evil powers going about continually to take cognizance of our evil thoughts; and, if their Master gives them power, to bring them int& overt action. Such is my theory of the nature of that sin, of which I dare not disbelieve— as some sceptics would have us do—the sin of witchcraft. Of this deadly sin, you and I are aware Bridget Fitzgerald has been guilty. Since you saw her last, many prayers have been offered in our churches, many masses sung, many penances undergone, in order that, if God and the Holy Saints so willed it, her sin might be blotted out. But it has not been so willed."

" Explain to me," said I, " who you are, and how

you come connected with Bridget. Why is she at Antwerp ? I pray you, sir, tell me more. If I am impatient, excuse me; I am ill and feverish, and in consequence bewildered."

There was something to me inexpressibly soothing in the tone of voice with which he began to narrate, as it were from the beginning, his acquaintance with Bridget

" I had known Mr. and Mrs. Starkey during their residence abroad, and so it fell out naturally that, when I came as chaplain to the Sherburnes at Stoney Hurst, our acquaintance was renewed; and thus I became the confessor of the whole family, isolated as they were from the offices of the Church, Sherburne being their nearest neighbour who professed the true faith. Of course, you are aware that facts revealed in confession are sealed as in the grave; but I learnt enough of Bridget's character to be convinced that I had to do with no common woman; one powerful for good as for evil. I believe that I was able to give her spiritual assistance from time to time, and that she looked upon me as a servant of that Holy Church, which has such wonderful power of moving men's hearts, and relieving them of the burden of their sins. I have known her cross the moors on the wildest nights of storm, to confess and be absolved; and then she would return, calmed and subdued, to her daily work about her mistress, no one witting where she had been during the hours that most passed in sleep upon their beds. After her daughter's departure—after Mary's mysterious disappearance—I had to impose many a long penance, in order to wash away the sin of impatient repining that was fast leading her into the deeper guilt of blasphemy. She set out on that long journey of which you have possibly heard—that fruitless journey in search of Mary—and during her absence, my superiors ordered my return to my former duties at Antwerp, and for many years I heard no more of Bridget.

" Not many months ago, as I was passing homewards in the evening, along one of the streets near St. Jacques, leading into the Meer Straet, I saw a woman sitting crouched up under the shrine of the Holy Mother of Sorrows. Her hood was drawn over her head, so that the shadow caused by the light of the lamp above fell deep over her face; her hands were clasped round her knees. It was evident that she was some one in hopeless trouble, and as such it was my duty to stop and speak. I naturally addressed her first in Flemish, believing her to be one of the lower class of inhabitants. She shook her head, but did not look up. Then I tried French, and she replied in that language, but speaking it so indifferently, that I was sure she was either English or Irish, and consequently spoke to her in my own native tongue. She recognised my voice; and, starting up, caught at my robes, dragging me before the blessed shrine, and throwing herself down, and forcing me, as much by her evident desire as by her action, to kneel beside her, she exclaimed:

" ' O Holy Virgin ! you will never hearken to me again, but hear him ; for you know him of old, that he does your bidding, and strives to heal broken hearts. Hear him !'

" She turned to me.

" ' She will hear you, if you will only pray. She never hears me: she and all the saints in Heaven cannot hear my prayers, for the Evil One carries them off, as he carried that first away. O, Father Bernard, pray for me I"

" I prayed for one in sore distress, of what nature I could not say; but the Holy Virgin would know. Bridget held me fast, gasping with eagerness at the sound of my words. When I had ended, I rose, and, making the sign of the Cross over her, I was going to bless her in the name of the Holy Church, when she shrank away like some terrified creature, and said:

" ' I am guilty of deadly sin, and am not shriven.'

" ' Arise, my daughter,' said I, * and come with me.' And I led the way into one of the confessionals of St. Jacques.

" She knelt; I listened. No words came. The evil powers had stricken her dumb, as I heard afterwards they had many a time before, when she approached confession.

" She was too poor to pay for the necessary forms of exorcism; and hitherto those priests to whom she had addressed herself were either so ignorant of the meaning of her broken French, or her Irish-English, or else esteemed her to be one crazed—as, indeed, her wild and excited manner might easily have led any one to think—that they had neglected the sole means of loosening her tongue, so that she might confess her deadly sin, and after due penance, obtain absolution. But I knew Bridget of old, and felt that she was a penitent sent to me. I went through those holy offices appointed by our church for the relief of such a case. I was the more bound to do this, as I found that she had come to Antwerp for the sole purpose of discovering me, and making confession to me. Of the nature of that fearful confession I am forbidden to speak. Much of it you know; possibly all.

" It now remains for her to free herself from mortal guilt, and to set others free from the consequences thereof. No prayers, no masses, will ever do it, although they may strengthen her with that strength by which alone acts of deepest love and purest self-

devotion may be performed. Her words of passion, and cries for revenge— her unholy prayers could never reach the ears of the Holy Saints! Other powers intercepted them, and wrought so that the curses thrown up to Heaven have fallen on her own flesh and blood; and so, through her very strength of love, have bruised and crushed her heart. Henceforward her former self must be buried,—yea, buried quick, if need be,—but never more to make sign, or utter cry on earth! She has become a Poor Clare, in order that, by perpetual penance and constant service of others, she may at length so act as to obtain final absolution and rest for her soul. Until then, the innocent must suffer. It is to plead for the innocent that I come to you ; not in the name of the witch, Bridget Fitzgerald, but of the penitent and servant of all men, the Poor Clare, Sister Magdalen."

" Sir," said I, " I listen to your request with respect ; only I may tell you it is not needed to urge me to do all that I can on behalf of one, love for whom is part of my very life. If for a time I have absented myself from her, it is to think and work for her redemption. I, a member of the English Church— my uncle, a Puritan—pray morning and night for her by name: the congregations of London, on the next Sabbath, will pray for one unknown, that she may be

set free from the Powers of Darkness. Moreover, I must tell you, sir, that those evil ones touch not the great calm of her soul. She lives her own pure and loving life, unharmed and untainted, though all men fall off from her. I would I could have her faith !"

My uncle now spoke.

" Nephew," said he, " it seems to me that this gentleman, although professing what I consider an erroneous creed, has touched upon the right point in exhorting Bridget to acts of love and mercy, whereby to wipe out her sin of hate and vengeance. Let us strive after our fashion, by almsgiving and visiting of the needy and fatherless, to make our prayers acceptable. Meanwhile, I myself will go down into the north, and take charge of the maiden. I am too old to be daunted by man or demon. I will bring her to this house as to a home; and let the Double come if it will! A company of godly divines shall give it the meeting, and we will try issue."

The kindly, brave old man ! But Father Bernard sat on musing.

" All hate," said he, " cannot be quenched in her heart ; all Christian forgiveness cannot have entered into her soul, or the demon would have lost its power. You said, I think, that her grandchild was still tormented ?"

" Still tormented!" I replied, sadly, thinking of Mistress Clarke's last letter.

He rose to go. We afterwards heard that the occasion of his coming to London was a secret political mission on behalf of the Jacobites. Nevertheless, he was a good and a wise man.

Months and months passed away without any change. Lucy entreated my uncle to leave her where she was,—dreading, as I learnt, lest if she came, with her fearful companion, to dwell in the same house with me, that my love could not stand the repeated shocks to which I should be doomed. And this she thought from no distrust of the strength of my affection, but from a kind of pitying sympathy for the terror to the nerves which she observed that the demoniac visitation caused in all.

I was restless and miserable. I devoted myself to good works; but I performed them from no spirit of love, but solely from the hope of reward and payment, and so the reward was never granted. At length, I asked my uncle's leave to travel; and I went forth, a wanderer, with no distincter end than that of many another wanderer — to get away from myself. A strange impulse led me to Antwerp, in spite of the wars and commotions then raging in the Low Countries—or rather, perhaps, the very craving to become interested in something external, led me into the thick of the struggle then going on with the Austrians. The cities of Flanders were all full at that time of civil disturbances and rebellions, only kept down by force, and the presence of an Austrian garrison in every place.

I arrived in Antwerp, and made inquiry for Father Bernard. He was away in the country for a day or two. Then I asked my way to the Convent of Poor Clares; but, being healthy and prosperous, I could only see the dim, pent-up, gray walls, shut closely in by narrow streets, in the lowest part of the town. My landlord told me, that had I been stricken by some loathsome disease, or in desperate case of any kind, the Poor Clares would have taken me, and tended me. He spoke of them as an order of mercy of the strictest kind, dressing scantily in the coarsest materials, going barefoot, living on what the inhabitants of Antwerp chose to bestow, and sharing even those fragments and crumbs with the poor and helpless that swarmed all around; receiving no letters or communication with the outer world; utterly dead to everything but the alleviation of suffering. He smiled at my inquiring whether I could get speech of one of them; and told me that they were even forbidden to speak for the purposes of begging their daily food; while yet they lived, and fed others upon what was given in charity.

" But," exclaimed I, " supposing all men forgot them! Would they quietly lie down and die, without making sign of their extremity ?"

" If such were their rule, the Poor Clares would willingly do it; hut their founder appointed a remedy for such extreme case as you suggest. They have a bell—'tis but a small one, as I have heard, and has yet never been rung in the memory of man: when the Poor Clares have been without food for twenty-four hours, they may ring this bell, and then trust to our good people of Antwerp for rushing to the rescue of the Poor Clares, who have taken such blessed care of us in all our straits."

It seemed to me that such rescue would be late in the day; but I did not say what I thought. I rather turned the conversation, by asking my landlord if he knew, or had ever heard, anything of a certain Sister Magdalen."

" Yes," said he, rather under his breath; " news will creep out, even from a convent of Poor Clares. Sister Magdalen is either a great sinner or a great saint. She does more, as I have heard, than all the other nuns put together; yet, when last month they would fain have made her mother-superior, she begged rather that they would place her below all the rest, and make her the meanest servant of all."

" You never saw her?" asked I.

" Never," he replied.

I was weary of waiting for Father Bernard, and yet I lingered in Antwerp. The political state of things became worse than ever, increased to its height by the scarcity of food consequent on many deficient harvests. I saw groups of fierce, squalid men, at every corner of the street, glaring out with wolfish eyes at my sleek skin and handsome clothes.

At last Father Bernard returned. We had a long-conversation, in which he told me that, curiously enough, Mr. Gisborne, Lucy's father, was serving in one of the Austrian regiments, then in garrison at Antwerp. I asked Father Bernard if he would make us acquainted; which he consented to do. But, a day or two afterwards, he told me that, on hearing my name, Mr. Gisborne had declined responding to any advances on my part, saying he had abjured his country, and hated his countrymen.

Probably he recollected my name in connection with that of his daughter Lucy. Anyhow, it was clear enough that I had no chance of making his acquaintance. Father Bernard confirmed me in my suspicions of the hidden fermentation, for some coming evil, working among the "blouses" of Antwerp, and he would fain have had me depart from out the city;

but I rather craved the excitement of danger, and stubbornly refused to leave.

One day, when I was walking with him in the Place Verte, he bowed to an Austrian officer, who was crossing towards the cathedral.

"That is Mr. Gisborne," said he, as soon as the gentleman was past.

I turned to look at the tall, slight figure of the officer. He carried himself in a stately manner, although he was past middle age, and from his years, might have had some excuse for a slight stoop. As I looked at the man, he turned round, his eyes met mine, and I saw his face. Deeply lined, sallow, and scathed was that countenance; scarred by passion as well as by the fortunes of war. 'Twas but a moment our eyes met. We each turned round, and went on our separate way.

But his whole appearance was not one to be easily forgotten; the thorough appointment of the dress, and evident thought bestowed on it, made but an incongruous whole with the dark, gloomy expression of his countenance. Because he was Lucy's father, I sought instinctively to meet him everywhere. At last he must have become aware of my pertinacity, for he gave me a haughty scowl whenever I passed him. In one of these encounters, however, I chanced to be of some service to him. He was turning the corner of a street, and came suddenly on one of the groups of discontented Flemings of whom I have spoken. Some words were exchanged, when my gentleman out with his sword, and with a slight but skilful cut drew blood from one of those who had insulted him, as he fancied, though I was too far off to hear the words. They would all have fallen upon him had I not rushed forwards and raised the cry, then well known in Antwerp, of rally, to the Austrian soldiers who were perpetually patrolling the streets, and who came in numbers to the rescue. I think that neither Mr. Gisborne nor the mutinous group of plebeians owed me much gratitude for my interference. He had planted himself against a wall, in a skilful attitude of fence, ready with his bright glancing rapier to do battle with all the heavy, fierce, unarmed men, some six or seven in number. But when his own soldiers came up, he sheathed His sword; and, giving some careless word of command, sent them away again, and continued his saunter all alone down the street, the workmen snarling in his rear, and more than half-inclined to fall on me for my cry for rescue. I cared not if they did, my life seemed so dreary a burden just then; and, perhaps, it was this daring loitering among them that prevented their attacking me.

Instead, they suffered me to fall into conversation with them; and I heard some of their grievances. Sore and heavy to be borne were they, and no wonder the sufferers were savage and desperate.

The man whom Gisborne had wounded across his face would fain have got out of me the name of his aggressor, but I refused to tell it. Another of the group heard his inquiry, and made answer:

"I know the man. He is one Gisborne, aide-decamp to the General-Commandant. I know him well."

He began to tell some story in connection with Gisborne in a low and muttering voice; and while he was relating a tale, which I saw excited their evil blood, and which they evidently wished me not to hear, I sauntered away and back to my lodgings.

That night Antwerp was in open revolt. The inhabitants rose in rebellion against their Austrian masters. The Austrians, holding the gates of the city, remained at first pretty quiet in the citadel; only, from time to time, the boom of a great cannon swept sullenly over the town. But, if they expected the disturbance to die away, and spend itself in a few hours' fury, they were mistaken. In a day or two, the rioters held possession of the principal municipal buildings. Then the Austrians poured forth in bright

flaming array, calm and smiling, as they marched to the posts assigned, as if the fierce mob were no more to them than the swarms of buzzing summer flies. Their practised manoeuvres, their well-aimed shot, told with terrible effect; but in the place of one slain rioter, three sprang up of his blood to avenge his loss. But a deadly foe, a ghastly ally of the Austrians, was at work. Food, scarce and dear for months, was now hardly to be obtained at any price. Desperate efforts were being made to bring provisions into the city, for the rioters had friends without. Close to the city port nearest to the Scheldt, a great struggle took place. I was there, helping the rioters, whose cause I had adopted. We had a savage encounter with the Austrians. Numbers fell on both sides; I saw them lie bleeding for a moment; then a volley of smoke obscured them; and when it cleared away, they were dead—trampled upon or smothered, pressed down and hidden by the freshly-wounded whom those last guns had brought low. And then a gray-robed and gray-veiled figure came right across the flashing guns, and stooped over some one, whose life-blood was ebbing away; sometimes it was to give him drink from cans which they carried slung at their sides, sometimes I saw the cross held above a dying man, and rapid prayers were being uttered, unheard by men in that

hellish din and clangour, but listened to by One above. I saw all this as in a dream: the reality of that stern time was battle and carnage. But I knew that these gray figures, their bare feet all wet with blood, and their faces hidden by their veils, were the Poor Clares — sent forth now because dire agony was abroad and imminent danger at hand. Therefore, they left their cloistered shelter, and came into that thick and evil melee.

Close to me—driven past me by the struggle of many fighters—came the Antwerp burgess with the scarce-healed scar upon his face ; and in an instant more, he was thrown by the press upon the Austrian officer Gisborne, and ere either had recovered the shock, the burgess had recognised his opponent.

" Ha! the Englishman Gisborne !" he cried, and threw himself upon him with redoubled fury. He had struck him hard—the Englishman was down; when out of the smoke came a dark-gray figure, and threw herself right under the uplifted flashing sword. The burgess's arm stood arrested. Neither Austrians nor Anversois willingly harmed the Poor Clares.

"Leave him to me !" said a low stern voice. " He is mine enemy—mine for many years."

Those words were the last I heard. I myself was struck down by a bullet. I remember nothing more

for days. When I came to myself, I was at the extremity of weakness, and was craving for food to recruit my strength. My landlord sat watching me. He, too, looked pinched and shrunken; he had heard of my wounded state, and sought me out. Yes! the struggle still continued, but the famine was sore; and some, he had heard, had died for lack of food. The tears stood in his eyes as he spoke. But soon he shook off his weakness, and his natural cheerfulness returned. Father Bernard had been to see me—no one else. (Who should, indeed?) Father Bernard would come back that afternoon—he had promised. But Father Bernard never came, although I was up and dressed, and looking eagerly for him.

My landlord brought me a meal which he had cooked himself: of what it was composed he would not say, but it was most excellent, and with every mouthful I seemed to gain strength. The good man sat looking at my evident enjoyment with a happy smile of sympathy; but, as my appetite became satisfied, I began to detect a certain wistfulness in his eyes, as if craving for the food I had so nearly devoured—for, indeed, at that time I was hardly aware of the extent of the famine. Suddenly, there was a sound of many rushing feet past our window. My landlord opened one of the sides of it, the better to

learn what was going on. Then we heard a faint, cracked, tinkling bell, coming shrill upon the air, clear and distinct from all other sounds. " Holy Mother!" exclaimed my landlord, " the

Poor Clares!"

He snatched up the fragments of my meal, and crammed them into my hands, bidding me follow. Down-stairs he ran, clutching at more food, as the women of his house eagerly held it out to him; and in a moment we were in the street, moving along with the great current, all tending towards the Convent of the Poor Clares. And still, as if piercing our ears with its inarticulate cry, came the shrill tinkle of the bell. In that strange crowd were old men trembling and sobbing, as they carried their little pittance of food; women with the tears running down their cheeks, who had snatched up what provisions they had in the vessels in which they stood, so that the burden of these was in many cases much greater than that which they contained; children, with flushed faces, grasping tight the morsel of bitten cake or bread, in their eagerness to carry it safe to the help of the Poor Clares; strong men yea, both Anversois and Aus-trians—pressing onwards with set teeth, and no word spoken; and over all, and through all, came that sharp tinkle—that cry for help in extremity.

We met the first torrent of people returning with blanched and piteous faces: they were issuing out of the convent to make way for the offerings of others. " Haste, haste!" said they. " A Poor Clare is dying! A Poor Clare is dead for hunger! God forgive us, and our city!"

We pressed on. The stream bore us along where it would. We were carried through refectories, bare and crumbless; into cells over whose doors the conventual name of the occupant was written. Thus it was that I, with others, was forced into Sister Magdalen's cell. On her couch lay Gisborne, pale unto death, but not dead. By his side was a cup of water, and a small morsel of mouldy bread, which he had pushed out of his reach, and could not move to obtain. Over against his bed were these words, copied in the English version: " Therefore, if thine enemy hunger, feed him ; if he thirst, give him drink."

Some of us gave him of our food, and left him eating greedily, like some famished wild animal. For now it was no longer the sharp tinkle, but that one solemn toll, which in all Christian countries tells of the passing of the spirit out of earthly life into eternity; and again a murmur gathered and grew, as of many people speaking with awed breath, " A Poor Clare is dying ! a Poor Clare is dead!"

Borne along once more by the motion of the crowd,

we were carried into the chapel belonging to the Poor Clares. On a bier before the high altar, lay a woman —lay sister Magdalen—lay Bridget Fitzgerald. By her side stood Father Bernard, in his robes of office, and holding the crucifix on high while he pronounced the solemn absolution of the Church, as to one who had newly confessed herself of deadly sin. I pushed on with passionate force, till I stood close to the dying woman, as she received extreme unction amid the breathless and awed hush of the multitude around. Her eyes were glazing, her limbs were stiffening ; but when the rite was over and finished, she raised her gaunt figure slowly up, and her eyes brightened to a strange intensity of joy, as, with the gesture of her finger and the trance-like gleam of her eye, she seemed like one who watched the disappearance of some loathed and fearful creature.

" She is freed from the curse!" said she, as she fell back dead.

Now, of all our party who had first listened to my Lady Ludlow, Mr. Preston was the only one who had not told us something, either of information, tradition, history, or legend. We naturally turned to him ; but we did not like asking him directly for his contribution, for he was a grave, reserved, and silent man.

He understood us, however, and, rousing himself as it were, he said :

"I know you wish me to tell you, in my turn, of something which I have learnt or heard during my life. I could tell you something of my own life, and of a life dearer still to my memory;

but I have shrunk from narrating anything so purely personal. Yet, shrink as I will, no other but those sad recollections will present themselves to my mind. I call them sad when I think of the end of it all. However, I am not going to moralize. If my dear brother's life and death does not speak for itself, no words of mine will teach you what may be learnt from it."

THE HALF-BROTHERS.

MY mother was twice married. She never spoke of her first husband, and it is only from other people that I have learnt what little I know about him, I believe, she was scarcely seventeen when she was married to him: and he was barely one-and-twenty. He rented a small farm up in Cumberland, somewhere towards the sea-coast; but he was perhaps too young and inexperienced to have the charge of land and cattle : anyhow, his affairs did not prosper, and he fell into ill health, and died of consumption before they had been three years man and wife, leaving my mother a young widow of twenty, with a little child only just able to walk, and the farm on her hands for four years more by the lease, with half the stock on it dead, or sold off one by one to pay the more pressing debts, and with no money to purchase more, or even to buy the pro-

THE HALF-BROTHERS.

visions needed for the small consumption of every day. There was another child coming, too; and sad and sorry, I believe, she was to think of it. A dreary winter she must have had in her lonesome dwelling, with never another near it for miles around ; her sister came to bear her company, and they two planned and plotted how to make every penny they could raise go as far as possible. I can't tell you how it happened that my little sister, whom I never saw, came to sicken and die; but, as if my poor mother's cup was not full enough, only a fortnight before Gregory was born the little girl took ill of scarlet fever, and in a week she lay dead. My mother was, I believe, just stunned with this last blow. My aunt has told me that she did not cry ; aunt Fanny would have been thankful if she had ; but she sat holding the poor wee lassie's hand, and looking in her pretty, pale, dead face, without so much as shedding a tear. And it was all the same, when they had to take her away to be buried. She just kissed the child, and sat her down in the window-seat to watch the little black train of people (neighbours—my aunt, and one far-off cousin, who were all the friends they could muster) go winding away amongst the snow, which had fallen thinly over the country the night before. When my aunt came back from the funeral, she found my mother in

the same place, and as dry-eyed as ever. So she continued until after Gregory was born ; and, somehow, his coming seemed to loosen the tears, and she cried day and night, day and night, till my aunt and the other watcher looked at each other in dismay, and would fain have stopped her if they had but known how. But she bade them let her alone, and not be over-anxious, for every drop she shed eased her brain, which had been in a terrible state before for want of the power to cry. She seemed after that to think of nothing but her new little baby ; she hardly appeared to remember either her husband or her little daughter that lay dead in Brigham churchyard—at least so aunt Fanny said; but she was a great talker, and my mother was very silent by nature, and I think aunt Fanny may have been mistaken in believing that my mother never thought of her husband and child just because she never spoke about them. Aunt Fanny was older than my mother, and had a way of treating her like a child ; but, for all that, she was a kind, warm-hearted creature, who thought more of her sister's welfare than she did of her own; and it was on her bit of money that they principally lived, and on what the two could earn by working for the great Glasgow sewing-merchants. But by-and-by my mother's eye-sight began to fail. It was not that she

was exactly blind, for she could see well enough to guide herself about the house, and to do a good deal of domestic work; but she could no longer do fine sewing and earn money. It must have been with the heavy crying she had had in her day, for she was but a young creature at this time, and as pretty a young woman, I have heard people say, as any on the country side. She took it sadly to heart that she could no longer gain anything towards the keep of herself and her child. My aunt Fanny would fain have persuaded her that she had enough to do in managing their cottage and minding Gregory; but my mother knew that they were pinched, and that aunt Fanny herself had not as much to eat, even of the commonest kind of food, as she could have done with; and as for Gregory, he was not a strong lad, and needed, not more food—for he always had enough, whoever went short—but better nourishment, and more flesh-meat. One day—it was aunt Fanny who told me all this about my poor mother, long after her death—as the sisters were sitting together, aunt Fanny working, and my mother hushing Gregory to sleep, William Preston, who was afterwards my father, came in. He was reckoned an old bachelor; I suppose he was long past forty, and he was one of the wealthiest farmers thereabouts, and had known my grandfather well, and my mother and my aunt in their more prosperous days. He sat down, and began to twirl his hat by way of being agreeable; my aunt Fanny talked, and he listened and looked at my mother. But he said very little, either on that visit, or on many another that he paid before he spoke out what had been the real purpose of his calling so often all along, and from the very first time he came to their house. One Sunday, however, my aunt Fanny stayed away from church, and took care of the child, and my mother went alone. When she came back, she ran straight up-stairs, without going into the kitchen to look at Gregory or speak any word to her sister, and aunt Fanny heard her cry as if her heart was breaking; so she went up and scolded her right well through the bolted door, till at last she got her to open it. And then she threw herself on my aunt's neck, and told her that William Preston had asked her to marry him, and had promised to take good charge of her boy, and to let him want for nothing, neither in the way of keep nor of education, and that she had consented. Aunt Fanny was a good deal shocked at this; for, as I have said, she had often thought that my mother had forgotten her first husband very quickly, and now here was proof positive of it, if she could so soon think of marrying again. Besides, as aunt Fanny used to say, she herself would

    have been a far more suitable match for a man of William Preston's age than Helen, who, though she was a widow, had not seen her four-and-twentieth summer. However, as aunt Fanny said, they had not asked her advice; and there was much to be said on the other side of the question. Helen's eyesight would never be good for much again, and as William Preston's wife she would never need to do anything, if she chose to sit with her hands before her ; and a boy was a great charge to a widowed mother; and now there would be a decent, steady man to see after him. So, by-and-by, aunt Fanny seemed to take a brighter view of the marriage than did my mother herself, who hardly ever looked up, and never smiled after the day when she promised William Preston to be his wife. But much as she had loved Gregory before, she seemed to love him more now. She was continually talking to him when they were alone, though he was far too young to understand her moaning words, or give her any comfort, except by his caresses.

    At last William Preston and she were wed; and she went to be mistress of a well-stocked house, not above half-an-hour's walk from where aunt Fanny lived. I believe she did all that she could to please my father; and a more dutiful wife, I have heard him himself say, could never have been. But she did not

    love him, and he soon found it out. She loved Gregory, and she did not love him. Perhaps, love would have come in time, if he had been patient enough to wait; but it just turned him sour to see how her eye brightened and her colour came at the sight of that little child, while for him who had given her so much, she had only gentle words as cold as ice. He got to taunt her with the difference in her manner, as if that would bring love : and he took a positive dislike to Gregory, he was so jealous of the ready love that always gushed out like a spring of fresh water when he came near. He wanted her to love him more, and perhaps that was all well and good; but he wanted her to love her child less, and that was an evil wish. One day, he gave way to his temper, and cursed and swore at Gregory, who had got into some mischief, as children will; my mother made some excuse for him; my father said it was hard enough to have to keep another man's child, without having it perpetually held up in its naughtiness by his wife, who ought to be always in the same mind that he was; and so from little they got to more; and the end of it was, that my mother took to her bed before her time, and I was born that very day. My father was glad, and proud, and sorry, all in a breath; glad and proud that a son was born to him; and sorry for his poor wife's state,

and to think how his angry words had brought it on. But he was a man who liked better to be angry than sorry, so he soon found out that it was all Gregory's fault, and owed him an additional grudge for having hastened my birth. He had another grudge against him before long. My mother began to sink the day after I was born. My father sent to Carlisle for doctors, and would have coined his heart's blood into gold to save her, if that could have been ; but it could not. My aunt Fanny used to say sometimes, that she thought that Helen did not wish to live, and so just let herself die away without trying to take hold on life; but when I questioned her, she owned that my mother did all the doctors bade her do, with the same sort of uncomplaining patience with which she had acted through life. One of her last requests was to have Gregory laid in her bed by my side, and then she made him take hold of my little hand. Her husband came in while she was looking at us so, and when he bent tenderly over her to ask her how she felt now, and seemed to gaze on us two little half-brothers, with a grave sort of kindliness, she looked up in his face and smiled, almost her first smile at him; and such a sweet smile! as more besides aunt Fanny have said. In an hour she was dead. Aunt Fanny came to live with us. It was the best thing

that could be done. My father would have been glad to return to his old mode of bachelor life, but what could he do with two little children ? He needed a woman to take care of him, and who so fitting as his wife's elder sister ? So she had the charge of me from my birth; and for a time I was weakly, as was but natural, and she was always beside me, night and day watching over me, and my father nearly as anxious as she. For his land had come down from father to son for more than three hundred years, and he would have cared for me merely as his flesh and blood that was to inherit the land after him. But he needed something to love, for all that, to most people, he was a stern, hard man, and he took to me as, I fancy, he had taken to no human being before—as he might have taken to my mother, if she had had no former life for him to be jealous of. I loved him back again right heartily. I loved all around me, I believe, for everybody was kind to me. After a time, I overcame my original weakliness of constitution, and was just a bonny, strong-looking lad whom every passer-by noticed, when my father took me with him to the nearest town.

At home I was the darling of my aunt, the tenderly-beloved of my father, the pet and plaything of the old domestic, the " young master " of the farm-labourers,

before whom I played many a lordly antic, assuming a sort of authority which sat oddly enough, I doubt not, on such a baby as I was.

Gregory was three years older than I. Aunt Fanny was always kind to him in deed and in action, but she did not often think about him, she had fallen so completely into the habit of being engrossed by me, from the fact of my having come into her charge as a delicate baby. My father never got over his grudging dislike to his stepson, who had so innocently wrestled with him for the possession of my mother's heart I mistrust me, too, that my father always considered him as the cause of my mother's death and my early delicacy ; and utterly unreasonable as this may seem, I believe my father rather cherished his feeling of alienation to my brother as a duty, than strove to repress it. Yet not for the world would my father have grudged him anything that money could purchase. That was, as it were, in the bond when he had wedded my mother. Gregory was lumpish and loutish, awkward and ungainly, marring whatever he meddled in, and many a hard word and sharp scolding did he get from the people about the farm, who hardly waited till my father's back was turned before they rated the stepson. I am ashamed—my heart is sore to think how I fell into the fashion of the family, and slighted

my poor orphan step-brother. I don't think I ever scouted him, or was wilfully ill-natured to him ; but the habit of being considered in all things, and being treated as something uncommon and superior, made me insolent in my prosperity, and I exacted more than Gregory was always willing to grant, and then, irritated, I sometimes repeated the disparaging words 1 had heard others use with regard to him, without fully understanding their meaning. Whether he did or not I cannot tell. I am afraid he did. He used to turn silent and quiet—sullen and sulky my father thought it; stupid, aunt Fanny used to call it. But every one said he was stupid and dull, and this stupidity and dullness grew upon him. He would sit without speaking a word, sometimes, for hours; then my father would bid him rise and do some piece of work, maybe, about the farm. And he would take three or four tellings before he would go. When we were sent to school, it was all the same. He could never be made to remember his lessons; the schoolmaster grew weary of scolding and flogging, and at last advised my father just to take him away, and set him to some farm-work that might not be above his comprehension. I think he was more gloomy and stupid than ever after this, yet he was not a cross lad ; he was patient and good-natured, and

would try to do a kind turn for any one, even if they had been scolding or cuffing him not a minute before. But very often his attempts at kindness ended in some mischief to the very people he was trying to serve, owing to his awkward, ungainly ways. I suppose I was a clever lad ; at any rate, I always got plenty of praise ; and was, as we called it, the cock of the school. The schoolmaster said I could learn anything I chose, but my father, who had no great learning himself, saw little use in much for me, and took me away betimes, and kept me with him about the farm. Gregory was made into a kind of shepherd, receiving his training under old Adam, who was nearly past his work. I think old Adam .was almost the first person who had a good opinion of Gregory. He stood to it that my brother had good parts, though he did not rightly know how to bring them out ; and, for knowing the bearings of the Fells, he said he had never seen a lad like him. My father would try to bring Adam round to speak of Gregory's faults and shortcomings; but, instead of that, he would praise him twice as much as «soon as he found out what my father's object was.

One winter-time, when I was about sixteen, and Gregory nineteen, I was sent by my father on an errand to a place about seven miles distant by the road, but only about four by the Fells. He bade me return

by the road, whichever way I took in going, for the evenings closed in early, and were often thick and misty; besides which, old Adam, now paralytic and bedridden, foretold a downfall of snow before long. I soon got to my journey's end, and soon had done my business ; earlier by an hour, I thought, than my father -had expected, so I took the decision of the way by which I would return into my own hands, and set off back again over the Fells, just as the first shades of evening began to fall. It looked dark and gloomy enough; but everything was so still that I thought I should have plenty of time to get home before . the snow came down. Off I set at a pretty quick pace. But night came on quicker. The right path was clear enough in the day-time, although at several points two or three exactly similar diverged from the same place ; but when there was a good light, the traveller was guided by the sight of distant objects, a piece of rock, a fall in the 'ground—which were quite invisible to me now. I plucked up a brave heart, however, and took what seemed to me the right road. It was wrong, however, and led me whither I knew not, but to some wild boggy moor where the solitude seemed painful, intense, as if never footfall of man had come thither to break the silence. I tried to shout, with the dimmest possible hope of being heard rather to reassure my-self by the sound of my own voice; but my voice came husky and short, and yet it dismayed me ; it seemed so % weird and strange in that noiseless expanse of black darkness. Suddenly the air was filled thick with dusky flakes, my face and hands were wet with snow. It cut me off from the slightest knowledge of where I was, for I lost every idea of the direction from which I had come, so that I could not even retrace my steps; it hemmed me in, thicker, thicker, with a darkness that might be felt. The boggy soil on which I stood quaked under me if I remained long in one place, and yet I dared not move far. All my youthful hardiness seemed to leave me at once. I was on the point of crying, and only very shame seemed to keep it down, To save myself from shedding tears, I shouted terrible, wild shouts for bare life they were. I turned sick as I paused to listen; no answering sound came but the unfeeling echoes. Only the noiseless, pitiless snow kept falling thicker, thicker faster, faster ! I was growing numb and sleepy. I tried to move about, but I dared not go far, for fear of the precipices which, I knew, abounded in certain places on the Fells. Now and then, I stood still and shouted again ; but my voice was getting choked with tears, as I thought of the desolate, helpless death I was to die, and how little they at home, sitting round the warm, red, bright fire,

  wotted what was become of me, and how my poor father would grieve for me—it would surely kill him— it would break his heart, poor old man ! Aunt Fanny too—was this to be the end of all her cares for me ? I began to review my life in a strange kind of vivid dream, in which the various scenes of my few boyish years passed before me like visions. In a pang of agony, caused by such remembrance of my short life, I gathered up my strength and called out once more, a long, despairing, wailing cry, to which I had no hope of obtaining any answer, save from the echoes around, dulled as the sound might be by the thickened air. To my surprise, I heard a cry—almost as long, as wild as mine so wild that it seemed unearthly, and I almost thought it must be the voice of some of the mocking spirits of the Fells, about whom I had heard so many tales. My heart suddenly began to beat fast and loud. I could not reply for a minute or two. I nearly fancied I had lost the power of utterance. Just at this moment a dog barked. Was it Lassie's bark—my brother's collie?an ugly enough brute, with a white, ill-looking face, that my father always kicked whenever he saw it, partly for its own demerits, partly because it belonged to my brother. On such occasions, Gregory would whistle Lassie away, and go off and sit with her in some outhouse. My father had

  once or twice been ashamed of himself, when the poor collie had yowled out with the suddenness of the pain, and had relieved himself of his self-reproach by blaming my brother, who, he said, had no notion of training a dog, and was enough to ruin any collie in Christendom with his stupid way of allowing them to lie by the kitchen fire. To all which Gregory would answer nothing, nor even seem to hear, but go on looking absent and moody.

  Yes ! there again ! It was Lassie's bark ! Now or never! I lifted up my voice and shouted " Lassie ! Lassie ! For God's sake, Lassie!" Another moment, and the great white-faced Lassie was curving and gambolling with delight round my feet and legs, looking, however, up in my face with her intelligent, apprehensive eyes, as if fearing lest I might greet her with a blow, as I had done oftentimes before. But I cried with gladness, as I stooped down and patted her. My mind was sharing in my body's weakness, and I could not reason, but I knew that help was at hand. A gray figure came more and more distinctly out of the thick, close-pressing darkness. It was

Gregory wrapped in his maud.

" Oh, Gregory!" said I, and I fell upon his neck, unable to speak another word. He never spoke much, and made me no answer for some little time.

Then he told me we must move, we must walk for the dear life—we must find our road home, if possible; but we must move or we should be frozen to death.

" Don't you know the way home ?" asked I.

" I thought I did when I set out, but I am doubtful now. The snow blinds me, and I am feared that in moving about just now, I have lost the right gait homewards."

He had his shepherd's staff with him, and by dint of plunging it before us at every step we took—clinging close to each other, we went on safely enough, as far as not falling down any of the steep rocks, but it was slow, dreary work. My brother, I saw, was more guided by Lassie and the way she took than anything else, trusting to her instinct. It was too dark to see far before us; but he called her back continually, and noted from what quarter she returned, and shaped our slow steps accordingly. But the tedious motion scarcely kept my very blood from freezing. Every bone, every fibre in my body seemed first to ache, and then to swell, and then to turn numb with the intense cold. My brother bore it better than I, from having been more out upon the hills. He did not speak, except to call Lassie. I strove to be brave, and not complain; but now I felt the deadly fatal sleep stealing over me.

" I can go no farther," I said, in a drowsy tone. I

remember, I suddenly became dogged and resolved. Sleep I would, were it only for five minutes. If death were to be the consequence, sleep I would. Gregory stood still. I suppose, he recognised the peculiar phase of suffering to which I had been brought by the cold.

" It is of no use," said he, as if to himself. " We are no nearer home than we were when^we started, as far as I can tell. Our only chance is in Lassie. Here! roll thee in my maud, lad, and lay thee down on this sheltered side of this bit of rock. Creep close under it, lad, and I'll lie by thee, and strive to keep the warmth in us. Stay! hast gotten aught about thee they'll know at home ?"

I felt him unkind thus to keep me from slumber, but on his repeating the question, I pulled out my pocket-handkerchief, of some showy pattern, which Aunt Fanny had hemmed for me Gregory took it, and tied it round Lassie's neck.

" Hie thee, Lassie, hie thee home!" And the white-faced, ill-favoured brute was off like a shot in the darkness. Now I might lie down—now I might sleep. In my drowsy stupor I felt that I was being tenderly covered up by my brother; but what with I neither knew nor cared I was too dull, too selfish, too numb to think and reason, or I might have known that

in that bleak bare place there was nought to wrap me in, save what was taken off another. I was glad enough when he ceased his cares and lay down by me. I took his hand.

" Thou canst not remember, lad, how we lay together thus by our dying mother. She put thy small, wee hand in mine I reckon, she sees us now; and belike we shall soon be with her. Anyhow, God's will be done."

"Dear Gregory," I muttered, and crept nearer to him for warmth. He was talking still, and again about our mother, when I fell asleep. In an instant or so it seemed there were many voices about me— many faces hovering round me the sweet luxury of warmth was stealing into every part of me. I was in my own little bed at home. I am thankful to say, my first word was " Gregory ?"

A look passed from one to another my father's stern old face strove in vain to keep its sternness; his mouth quivered, his eyes filled slowly with unwonted tears.

"I would have given him half my land I would have blessed him as my son,—oh God! I would have knelt at his feet, and asked him to forgive my hardness of heart."

I heard no more. A whirl came through my brain, catching me back to death.

I came slowly to my consciousness, weeks afterwards. My father's hair was white when I recovered, and his hands shook as he looked into my face.

We spoke no more of Gregory. We could not speak of him; but he was strangely in our thoughts. Lassie came and went with never a word of blame; nay, my father would try to stroke her, but she shrank away; and he, as if reproved by the poor dumb beast, would sigh, and be silent and abstracted for a time.

Aunt Fanny—always a talker—told me all. How, on that fatal night, my father, irritated by my prolonged absence, and probably more anxious than he cared to show, had been fierce and imperious, even beyond his wont, to Gregory : had upbraided him with his father's poverty, his own stupidity which made his services good for nothing—for so, in spite of the old shepherd, my father always chose to consider them. At last, Gregory had risen up, and whistled Lassie out with him poor Lassie, crouching underneath his chair for fear of a kick or a blow. Some time before, there had been some talk between my father and my aunt respecting my return; and when Aunt Fanny told me all this, she said she fancied that Gregory might have noticed the coming storm, and gone out silently to meet .me. Three hours afterwards, when all were running about in wild alarm, not knowing whither to go in

search of me not even missing Gregory, or heeding his absence, poor fellow poor, poor fellow! Lassie came home, with my handkerchief tied round her neck. They knew and understood, and the whole strength of the farm was turned out to follow her, with wraps, and blankets, and brandy, and everything that could be thought of. I lay in chilly sleep, but still alive, beneath the rock that Lassie guided them to. I was covered over with my brother's plaid, and his thick shepherd's coat was carefully wrapped round my feet. He was in his shirt-sleeves his arm thrown over me  a quiet smile (he had hardly ever smiled in life) upon his still, cold face.

My father's last words were, "God forgive me my hardness of heart towards the fatherless child!"

And what marked the depth of his feeling of repentance, perhaps more than all, considering the passionate love he bore my mother, was this: we found a paper of directions after his death, in which he desired that he might lie at the foot of the grave, in which, by his desire, poor Gregory had been laid with OUR MOTHER.


THE END.
VOL. II.

CPSIA information can be obtained
at www.ICGtesting.com
Printed in the USA
LVOW09s1108140517
534483LV00001B/9/P

9 781533 387370